Sins of the Fathers

KRISTEN HOUGHTON

SINS OF THE FATHERS
by Kristen Houghton

© Copyright 2017 by Kristen Houghton
ISBN: 978-0-692-05876-3
Library of Congress Cataloguing-in-Publication Data Houghton, Kristen
Sins of the Fathers: A Cate Harlow Private Investigation crime/ thriller
novel/KristenHoughton-2nd. ed.

1.Cate Harlow (Fictitious character)-Fiction 2. private investigator
3. Crime/thriller 4. female sleuth 5. cozy mystery 6. detective mystery
7. New York City

Published by **Criminal Element** an imprint of
Skylight-NYC Publishers, LLC
175 Fifth Avenue
New York, NY, 10010
Skylight-NYCPublishers.com
skylight-nyc@outlook.com

Cover by 2Hopper Production & Design Studio
in association with KH Koehler Design

Sins of the Fathers

A Cate Harlow Private Investigation

Kristen Houghton

Skylight-NYC Publishers, LLC

Books by Kristen Houghton

CRIME AND MYSTERY

CATE HARLOW PRIVATE INVESTIGATION SERIES

Do Unto Others
Grave Misgivings
Unrepentant: Pray for Us Sinners

FANTASY

THE TEDDY JAMESON CHRONICLES

Welcome to Hell, Teddy Jameson
Leaving Hell with the Angel of Redemption

HISTORICAL ROMANCE

The Anchoress: A Romantic Tale of Terror

ANTHOLOGY

No Woman Diets Alone-There's Always a Man Behind Her
Eating a Doughnut

And Then I'll Be Happy! Stop Sabotaging Your Happiness and
Put Your Own Life First

YOUNG ADULT NOVELLA

Remember, Hetty?

COMING IN 2018

Lilith Angel, a YA fantasy series

FOR ALAN WILLIAM HOPPER, my husband and friend and the inspiration for my stories, and to New York City for providing a perfect setting for my book.

CONTENTS

AUGUST 1995

THE CONFESSIONAL SMELLED OF mouse droppings and old wood. The young boy's knees were uncomfortable on the old worn leather kneeler that was rough and cracked. He nervously waited in the hot, stuffy confines for Father Moore to finish with the person on the other side of the confessional. He recognized the raised voice of old Mrs. Carletti, who was eighty-six years old and nearly deaf. She said everything loudly and twice. *Just keep the hell talking, Mrs. Carletti. Save me. Please God, let me get through this and I'll try real hard to be a better kid*, he prayed. *Please. I'm sorry God. Don't let my penance be the "bad-boy" penance. Please, please!*

He listened as Father Moore gave Mrs. Carletti absolution and told her she could go now; her sins were forgiven. The boy guessed that the fact that he'd thought the word *hell* added to his sins and sighed a deep, ragged sigh. The window slid back and he saw the shadowy presence of Father Moore. He knew that the priest could see him too and knew exactly who was kneeling there.

"Bless me, Father, for I have sinned. It has been two weeks since my last confession. These are my sins."

He hadn't really sinned too much but, sometimes, a sin can happen even when you don't expect it or can't control it. A small lie about homework, a rude answer to his mother, being late to Mass—these were small sins compared to the unexpected sin, the sin that would get him the "bad-boy" penance. He rattled off the smaller sins and stopped. He hoped Father Moore would be too busy to ask about other sins. Sometimes the priest *was* too busy and issued a mild penance, just some prayers to say at the altar railing. Today was not going to be one of those times. Father Moore didn't say anything for a few minutes, which seemed like hours to the boy. When he did speak, the boy knew he was in for it.

"*And?* And Joey? What else? What other sins did you commit?"

The boy's mouth felt like it was full of cotton.

"*Joey?* Did you have impure thoughts again? Did you commit the worst sin a young boy can commit? *Again?*"

"I ... I ... I, yes, I'm sorry, I'm sorry, Father!" he whispered. His throat was closing up and he felt as if he couldn't breathe.

"Say what you did Joey, say it to me and to Jesus. It is your sin. Say it."

Father Moore's words were said low and almost sweetly. "Say what you did so Jesus can hear you."

"I ... I t-t-touched myself. Down there, I t-t-touched myself. I'm sorry!"

"Did it feel good, Joey? Did you like it?"

"I was asleep though, Father, I was asleep, I ... I ... I think I was anyway."

"That doesn't matter, Joey. You had the impure thought in your mind before you fell asleep so it is still sinful. You thought about doing it. You thought about how it felt. A person can still commit a sin in their sleep, Joey, if the impure thoughts are there." Pause. "Joey? I asked you if it felt good. Did it feel good, Joey? Did it? Jesus wants to hear you say the truth."

"Y-yes."

"And did you like the way it felt, Joey? It felt good, didn't it, Joey, like always, right?"

"I, y-yes, Father."

"What else happened, Joey? Was there the sticky stuff again?"

The boy began to cry. All he could think of was *I'm-sorry, I'm-sorry, I'm-sorry, please-God-forgive-me—I'm scared to answer.*

"I can tell by your silence that the sticky stuff was there on your nice clean pajamas. Your poor mother has to wash them. How awful for her. She knows that you have committed a great sin, the greatest sin a boy can commit. She is disgusted by what you did."

"I'm sorry, I'm so sorry, Father!"

"I hope your dad doesn't find out, but I guess your mother would be too ashamed to tell him. It's a good thing too because I believe your father might send you away to juvenile hall, that terrible place for bad boys who do very bad things. That would be awful, don't you think?"

"Yes, Father." He was crying now and hiccupping.

"It's okay, Joey. You and I, we know how to deal with this behavior."

Silence.

"Joey, you have to come to me after confessions. You know where."

"Yes." The school basement—that horrible, dark, scary place where Father Moore punished bad boys like Joey. *Oh God. Please, I'm afraid, I'm afraid.*

"I can't absolve your sin until you've done your special, *bad-boy* penance. You understand?" The priest's voice was soft and loving.

"Please, Father Moore. Please! Don't give me that penance. I promise, I promise with my whole heart I won't commit that sin again. I won't, I won't! Please don't hurt me ... that penance ... please ..."

"Joey, Joey, think of what our Lord felt, think of His pain, how He suffered so much more pain just for *your* sins. Do you think I like doing that to you, Joey? Do you really believe I like giving you that penance? It breaks my heart to do it but I have to do it, Joey. Your sin is great and if you want to become a decent man like your father, you must take the punishment. It is my duty as a holy priest of God to give you that penance."

Joey sobbed quietly.

"What you have to endure for your sins is nothing compared to what Jesus suffered. This sin that you committed hurts Jesus all over again. He went through so much pain just to save your soul from Hell, Joey. You don't want to hurt Jesus, do you?"

"No, Father, but ... I don't, I ... I ... I don't want to go there, to the basement. Please, Father."

"Do *you* want to suffer the pains of *Hell*, Joey?" Father Moore's voice was still low but it had changed. The tone was one that Joey knew well. Stern and commanding.

"N-n-no."

"Then you must do the bad-boy penance. I will see you in our special place at three o'clock. Your mother doesn't need to know where we will be. She's embarrassed enough, Joey. Just tell her that you need to ... do something with me. That is not a lie either, is it, Joey? We know, you and I, what has to be done."

"Y-y-yes, Father Moore."

～

The priest gently helped the sobbing boy put his shirt back on. "Don't cry, Joey. Your sin has been forgiven. The bad-boy penance took it away and your soul is clean. Now you can kiss your mother because you are a good boy again. Be at peace, Joey. I'll always be here to help you because I love you."

CHAPTER 1

THE PHONE RINGS AND wakes me out of the soundest sleep I've had in four nights. I answer it and hear the charming voice of my ex-husband Will—that bastard.

"Hey, Cate, wakey, wakey. You alert?"

"What the hell do *you* want?" I am such a bitch to him. The lighted numbers from my smartphone say 4:37 a.m.

"Jennifer Aniston naked on my bed for starters." He is *so* funny!

"Anything, or should I say, *anyone* else?" I say, dripping with venom.

"Maybe, hmmmm, maybe *you* naked? Been a while, Cate. Think about it."

I do not want to answer him and am on the verge of hanging up when he says, "Found a mutilated body wearing a priest's collar. You interested? I need your expertise, since you were on that case ten months ago. Body's at the morgue."

I sigh. The last thing I want to do is to go down to the morgue at four in the morning and before I have even had my coffee. But I am intrigued. This is the second body wearing the collar of a Catholic priest found dead and mutilated in the tri-state area in less than a year. The last one had been my case, a private investigation, and it had turned out to be a mess—and unsolved. It still haunts me. I don't like unfinished business.

I'm the Catherine in *Catherine Harlow, Private Investiga-tions*. PI license number 420731-6632. I was named Catherine Sophie-Victoria Christina Marie Harlow; my parents got carried away naming their only child. They were in their forties when I was born, so finally having a child was a miracle to them. The only places you'll find this name, however, are on my birth and marriage certificates—and my divorce decree. While I like the name Catherine, I prefer Cate. But I'm easy; either name is fine with me.

A year ago, a nursing home director had contacted my office for help finding a patient who, as he put it, "simply wandered away." The male patient had slight dementia but was basical-ly healthy and had never gone missing before. The staff at the home had searched for two days to no avail. The director was adamant to keep it discreet—no police, no publicity. I was to work the case alone. A news story about a patient who had been allowed to disappear from this upscale, expensive nursing home would spell disaster for the place and its highly paid director. That was fine with me. Working alone and being discreet is part of being a good private investigator. Besides, I tend to get a lot done on my own. For my discreetness I was paid three times what I usually get.

I had taken the case, which I thought was going to be a sim-ple one concerning a missing elderly man. 95 percent of these cases end well; the person is found, albeit confused and a little scared. I had every confidence that this was going to be one of those cases. As it turned out, this was not one with a happy end-ing. Two months later I found the nude, horribly mutilated and sodomized body of the missing man dumped in a drainage ditch in the New York State countryside. Around his neck was the un-mistakable collar worn by Roman Catholic priests. The funny thing was that the nursing home had no idea that one of their patients was a cleric. His admittance paperwork stated that he had been a retired professor of theology. It took me a while to find out that he had been a priest for more than fifty years before he admitted himself to an assisted-care facility. From there he transferred to the adjacent nursing home.

No one was ever charged in the priest's murder and there were no solid leads. The police and I were able to keep the details about the crime out of the news. Still being discreet, I tried for months to find any leads into the murder—anything, no matter how small, that might point the way to a suspect, but I came up as empty-handed as the cops had. To this day, it baffles me that we found nothing at all to connect anyone to the murder. All we had was a body.

"Cate? I can hear you breathing and if you're breathing you're thinking. Are you up to it? Your *boy*friend is there. That should make it easier on you."

The emphasis he puts on the word *boy* is meant as a slight to the other man in my life. Even though Will and I are divorced, he has a certain proprietary air that annoys me. He dislikes anyone I date or anyone with whom I might have a semi-serious relationship.

As far as relationships go, I've got two men in my life; Giles, the city's top-notch medical examiner; and my ex-husband, Will, who is kind of a lawyer. I say *kind of* because at the age of forty he has yet to sit for the bar exam, something he's been avoiding for a number of years now. At the moment, he is a homicide detective and a good one. He is a bastard in many ways but fair is fair: he is excellent and relentless at what he does.

Will and Giles are great lovers in different ways. Giles is smooth, sweet, romantic, and tender, all wine 'em, dine 'em, with an all-day foreplay agenda that is incredibly hot and makes me shiver and cross my legs just thinking about it. Will, on the other hand, makes sex a bit dangerous, but wildly exciting, and likes to do it in the most unexpected places. You remember that scene in the movie *Unfaithful* where Olivier Martinez is giving it hard and fast to Diane Lane in the ladies room of a restaurant while her totally oblivious girlfriends are waiting for her back at the table? Been there, done that, enjoyed it immensely. That, and doing it with Will in a MINI Cooper in a parking garage, has been duly catalogued in the erotica library of my mind.

"Cate?"

"Same type of killing?" I ask, yawning and trying to stretch.

"Preliminary findings at the scene say yes."

"Same dump site?"

"Nope, this one's off of Interstate 95, an hour ago, smack on the side of the road. Some driver called in and said he thought he saw an injured *albino deer*."

Oh God! I debate getting out of my warm bed. "And you need me because ... ?"

"You worked the last case and there's a message with this one. A hand-printed note in Latin on the inside of the clerical collar."

I pause. Since the last murder was never solved, it is still open. There are no suspects and there is no real evidence. If this one has a note with it that can possibly provide clues to the first murder ... Suddenly I'm alert.

"Okay," I say into the phone. "Give me thirty minutes. I'll be there."

"Anything I can do to make getting up this early easier for you?"

"Yes, a large cup of hazelnut coffee from Timothy's and re-member—"

"To put some half-and-half in first, pour the coffee up to an inch from the top, and add more half-and-half. Absolutely no sugar. I know, I remember how you like your coffee . . . and a lot of *other things* you like. See you at the morgue, and thanks."

I lay back in bed for a couple of minutes, but know that I will fall asleep if I stay prone for too long. Quick shower, no time to wash my hair, just brush my teeth, and I am good to go as soon as I get dressed in my *uniform* of jeans, sneakers, and a hoodie. I pull my hair into a ponytail and put on a Yankees baseball cap and sunglasses.

Will's right about me; if I'm breathing, I'm thinking, and as I walk to my car I am musing about what I'll find at the morgue, why I'm even *going* to the morgue, and then I think about my latest case. My mind is a convoluted trail of what's happening in my life.

On the whole, my latest case seems to be one that is simple and easy to close. A woman, Marie McElroy, wants me to find her brother who disappeared ten years ago at the age of fifteen. I feel as if I'm taking her money—ten years missing and not much to go on.

But for some reason this woman got to me. She had the saddest, sweetest eyes I have ever seen, and she looked at me with a directness and honesty that hit my emotions hard. I wanted to find her brother just to make the sadness go away.

"Ms. Harlow?" she said as she stood up to leave my office late last week. "One thing. I have to know, no matter how bad the information is that you may find out, I have to know everything. Promise me you won't hold anything back. If he isn't ... alive, I need to know, I *have* to know."

I promised her that I would tell her the truth about anything I found out and she walked slowly out the door as if she barely had the strength to move her body forward.

At some time in their lives, most people think that they need the services of a private investigator and they're pretty much willing to pay whatever is charged. Usually they're looking to nail a cheating spouse, find a long-lost relative, or uncover some secret about their family's past. And while I certainly don't want to put myself out of business, in my experience they'd be better off saving their money. The truth is that if you suspect a spouse is cheating, he, or she, usually is. That long-lost relative you feel that you just have to find? In nine out of ten cases, that person doesn't want to be found. And that crucial info, that secret, you're so eager to find out about your family's past? Forget it. Unless you're prepared to face some horrible, frightening fact about your ancestors that may haunt you forever, leave it alone. When you open a locked door, you never know what slime will ooze through.

That's my advice. But then, who would really listen to realistic, professional advice? Not many people, so I learned to keep my mouth shut. Rent's got to be paid, car payments come monthly, credit card bills, groceries—that's my reality.

In my business I've learned to give the clients what they want. I've stopped trying to convince them that they're wasting their money on something their hearts tell them is what they need to know. If they want proof of a spouse cheating I'll give them that proof. If they want to find someone or learn about a skeleton in a family closet, I can provide that too.

People pay PIs well because they think that we have some natural psychic ability about situations, but that's just wishful thinking. A good PI is simply a damn good observer. Going into a case I don't know any more than what I've been told by my clients. But the thing that separates me from them is that what their eyes and ears didn't catch, mine will. I watch people all the time and I can tell them things about themselves their own mothers probably don't know. Being a successful PI has less to do with anything psychic and a whole lot more to do with observation and rational thought.

To say I'm good at my job is an understatement. It's not vanity; it's a fact. I can get into a lot of places that other PIs can't. Maybe it's my looks. I don't look threatening. I'm five five, fairly athletic, and blonde. Not a *dumb blonde*, either. I speak softly and listen carefully. People tell me things they wouldn't mention to someone who looks tough and street-smart. Let's say that they do underestimate me and I *am* very good at what I do.

My former profession lacked excitement. I was a forensic law linguist who got tired of simply translating the law into lay terms and decided to change my daily routine from sitting at a desk or in a courtroom to actually going out and trying to help people who have need of a good legal investigator.

As I said, looks can be deceiving. I usually wear my hair pulled back into a ponytail and my green eyes are always hidden by sunglasses—even when it's dark. I'm a bit near-sighted but that's my secret. When people can't see your eyes they don't know what you're thinking and that's good.

I've got a decent enough body from playing a mean game of

tennis, which means that if I feel outnumbered by "the bad guys" I have a better than average chance of running away on legs used to chasing a ball up and down a court. And while I can dress the part that best suits my needs for a particular job, for everyday work I prefer jeans, a velour hoodie, and top-of-the-line sneakers. My one weakness in clothes is that silky, girly lingerie goes on under the jeans and hoodie. I spend a lot of money on panties and bras.

It makes me smile when I see an actress playing a detective on TV wearing heels and chasing down criminals. Seriously, if you've got to run you better be wearing shoes that won't trip you up or have you end up with a broken ankle.

I'm pretty low maintenance most days, but I've been known to dress up for a case; three-inch heels, short skirts, and smoky-eyed makeup make me a totally different lady in upscale areas. Or a hooker, depending on what part I'm playing for a case. Lady of disguises—that's me.

I'm kind to animals, have two cats and we all live in a nice, neat, old brownstone that is sparsely, but I think nicely, furnished. Again, low maintenance is key here. I'm also lucky to have a parking space right in front of the brownstone, which is carefully guarded by my neighbor who only charges me fifteen bucks a week for her services. I'm not all that sociable but I do have a few really good friends who know me and accept me for who, and what, I am. My closest friend is New Orleans transplant Melissa who doesn't seem to have a job, is perpetually taking classes in whatever interests her, and has some well-heeled male *clients*. Melissa's a solid source of much-needed girl-power for me.

༺

So as I'm driving, I'm thinking about my client and her lost brother. He left his house on a warm spring day to go to the library and vanished. No one at the library that day had any recollection of seeing him. Someone would have noticed him because, according to his sister, he spent a lot of time there, especially on school breaks.

Ten years is a long time, and my initial thought, one that I gently voiced to her, was that he's dead. I don't like having to bring bad news to my clients, something that I've had to do way too often. I had to be honest with her, though. All she said to that statement was that she knew that he was alive, at least as short a time as a week ago.

A letter had been left in her mailbox telling her to pray for him. No date, no time, no envelope, she tells me—just plain white paper with a few lines scribbled on it. She handed it to me.

"Do you see the underlined question and the answer following it?" Marie asked eagerly, willing me to understand their significance. "It's a line from *Peter Pan*; it's something Peter says to Wendy about birds. That's how I know this is really from my brother! We used it all the time and it was our secret code."

I didn't say anything as she continued talking.

"It's not the first time I've gotten one of these. Since my parents died, at least twice a year, I'll find one in my mailbox. It's his handwriting; no mistake. Usually he just says not to forget him. He's never asked me to pray for him before though. That scares me. Josh doesn't believe in God."

"Was there ever a letter from Joshua when your parents were alive? Because if there wasn't, maybe someone is playing a cruel joke on you."

"No, no letters, no contact but ..."

"Yes?"

"You might think I'm crazy but, well, there were times when I sensed that Joshua was nearby, as if he were watching me, protecting me somehow. I don't know, maybe some people might say it was wishful thinking or say that I wanted him back so badly that I was imagining I felt him, but I really *did* feel that he was somehow nearby. And I know the letters are from my brother. I know it. It's not just that I know his handwriting. In the letters, he always mentions that quote from *Peter Pan*, a code that only he and I know and used. No one, not even my parents knew what it was." She looked at me with those sad eyes.

"Can you help me?"

"If you don't mind my suggesting this, you might be better off bringing the letter to the police. Do you want to do that? You might be wasting your money on a private investigator when the police are more than ready to help. I can call a friend down at headquarters if you like."

"Ms. Harlow, I know what you charge and I have the money to pay you, believe me. I don't see it as wasting my money. I'd rather hire *you* to try to find my brother than go to the police again. I have been to the police many times. They take my statement, they listen to me, and then they inevitably, very kindly, tell me to try to go on with my life. *Go on with my life, as if that were a possibility!* I was fourteen when my brother disappeared. We're what you call Irish twins, only ten months apart. We were so close. His disappearance destroyed my family. Not knowing what has happened to someone you love takes a terrible toll on those left behind. My mother had a debilitating stroke a year after Josh went missing and she died when I was eighteen. My father simply stopped living when Mom died; he lost two people he loved so very much and it broke him, it just broke his spirit. Eleven months later I buried him next to Mom.

"Look, I'm not blaming the police. They were so good to us right after ... you know. And they worked so hard. But after a while what can they do? They say it's what's called a, a ..."

"Cold case file," I offered. "Did they tell you that the case remains open?"

"Yes, I know they *say* it remains open but it is not something that is currently on their minds. They have other cases, new cases. The old cases, well, there's just so much they can do with them. I'm asking for your help. I saw you on the *Morning News* show last month, a missing person case. You found that young woman. I thought if you could find someone who was kidnapped twenty-two years ago, then maybe you could help me."

I nodded and remembered. The Reynolds case. It had garnered some real media attention. I had been able to locate a twenty-two-year-old young woman who had been stolen from a hospital nursery when she was three days. The case had been referred to me by a paralegal for whom I had done some free surveillance work. It had taken me eight months of intense research and following obscure leads to find her. Reuniting the woman with her birth parents had made me a mini-celebrity.

"All right, Marie. I'll take the case. The first thing I'll do is search the shelters and addiction clinics around your area and here in the city as well. Then I'll get the police file from the main archives here in the city. We'll go on from there and see what can be found."

I asked Marie McElroy a few more questions and requested a picture of her brother. She wrote me a retainer check, asked only that I tell her the truth about what I found out, and left. *Catherine Harlow, Private Investigations* had a new client.

⋘⋙

I drive an SUV, a Ford Edge to be exact. It's just big enough for my needs and it makes me feel safer on the highways when I'm competing with eighteen-wheelers. Being in a small car next to a tractor-trailer makes me feel like an ant about to be squashed.

Pulling up to the morgue I see Will standing there with a bag from Timothy's. Yay! Coffee!

"Here it is, Cate, just the way you like it. Drink up before you go in, okay? It's a messy one." Will takes the lid off the cup carefully before handing it to me.

"Worse than the other one I told you about last year?" I say grabbing the cup and appreciatively inhaling the smell before I sip.

"Not worse, no, but still foul. He hasn't been cleaned up yet. My request."

We stand there leaning against the wall and drinking coffee while Will fills me in on where the body was found. To see us together you'd never know that the last year of our marriage we barely spoke to each other. That was after months of screaming at one another and detailing each other's shortcomings. It even included a rowdy fight which ended with him telling me I didn't know how to be a wife, and me punching him hard in the jaw.

Will wanted a real wife, and that meant a woman who wasn't, as he was so fond of telling me, *domestically challenged*. He liked and respected the fact that I had a career; I was still a forensic law linguist back then, thinking about going after my dream of becoming a private investigator.

But he also needed someone who was a gourmet cook and kept a spotless house. That was not on my life's agenda. In the throes of lust and love of that first year, I did try to be what I knew he wanted. But two months into our second year, even the hot sex wasn't enough to stop the resentment I felt at doing what I hated. I'm domestically challenged by choice. I wanted him to accept me as such.

The marriage took a fatal hit the night I came home early to the wonderful smell of chicken cacciatore cooking and Will and his patrol partner, Debbie, drinking wine in our living room. I watched her refill his empty wine glass from my Baccarat crystal decanter, the one my elderly, wealthy aunt had given me for a bridal shower gift. They were laughing over some private little exchange and they looked so intimate and cozy; so much more like a couple than Will and me.

They both got up when they saw me standing there, and Will explained that he had asked his partner to come over for dinner because there had been a transmitter break in her neighborhood earlier the night before and her apartment building was without electricity. A lame excuse. The kicker was that he then demanded to know why *I* was home so early, as if I was somehow to blame for walking into my own home and finding them drinking wine out of our wedding crystal. Even though I knew in my heart that nothing had happened *yet*, I also knew that it was only a matter of time until something *did* happen. I didn't want to be the injured spouse in a divorce hearing. That little scene ended a marriage that never should've happened.

"Catherine." Giles says my name like it's the beginning of a song, soft and low; he's one of the few people who sometimes call me *Catherine*. I've known Giles for a couple of years, but we've only been seriously dating for two months. He glances at Will and they nod at each other.

"Will."

"Giles."

They're professionals. I try not to think about the fact that both men have seen me nude. I wonder if they're thinking the same thing.

"Good, now that you're both here we can take a look. I haven't unloaded the body yet as per your request, Will. He's still bagged. Just did some preliminary checking. It's interesting. Let's go have a look and see what we can see."

I gulp my coffee and toss the empty cup in a trash bin then follow Giles and Will inside. Personally, I never get over seeing a corpse. You would think that after a while in my profession you'd become immune; not so with me. There's always the very brief startle factor. No matter how badly damaged the body, it still seems as if it will come back to life again, like some modern Frankenstein. Stupid, I know, but that's always my momentary reaction. After that I get down to business and hunt for evidence.

The morgue is cold and too white with harsh lighting that hurts my eyes. Giles unzips the body bag and he and his assistant move the body, naked except for a priest's black-and-white collar, over onto the slab. I step forward. The death-released smells of urine, defecation, and fear-sweat hit us. It is a brutal murder. There's lots of anger here and it looks very personal. The eyes are open with terror as if the victim knew that he was going to die in a horrible way. Ligature marks on his wrists, waist, and ankles tell me he was restrained before death, and a deep, stabbing slice to the carotid shows me how he died. The killer, I am sure, wanted him to know what was coming.

"Well? Post-mortem like before?" asks Will, gesturing to what is inside the dead man's mouth.

Giles looks down to where the male genitalia *should* be but *isn't* and then uses his gloved hand and a large tweezer-like instrument to remove the fleshy object, the man's penis, which was jammed into the mouth.

"Yes. The ME from Westchester County, where you found that body last year, Cate, sent over the report on the first victim and the details match what was done here too."

They roll the body over onto the stomach and Giles says, "Sodomizing was done several times while the victim was still alive and done with enough force to cause anal tearing and internal damage. It looks like it might be the same murderer or murderers since everything has been done in precisely the exact same manner. Looks like a sharp surgical tool was used for the mutilation."

I examine the body front and back, check the marks on the wrists and ankles, and note that everything, down to the last detail, is exactly the same as with the other murder. A naked man in his late sixties, early seventies, dressed only in a priest's collar, had been brutally sodomized with a large blunt instrument while he was alive. After having his throat slit, the same blade was used to remove his penis, which was then placed deep inside his mouth. This was an angry killing.

"Okay, Will." I say. "This looks the same as the other one last year. I gave you my thoughts on that one. Let's see what else we have here."

I stifle a yawn. The kick from the coffee is starting to wear off. Will looks at Giles and nods.

"Read the message and tell me what you think of it, Cate."

Reaching over, Giles turns the white priest collar inside out. Carefully and neatly printed across it in black marker are the words *Lasciate ogne speranza, voi ch'intrate.*

"It's from *The Divine Comedy* by Dante Alighieri," I say after reading it out loud. "*L'Inferno,* the first part of Dante's fourteenth-century poem."

"Yes," says Giles, eyes lighting up in recognition. "Right. The author, Dante, imagines himself going on a journey through Hell, Purgatory, and then Heaven. He's guided by the Roman poet Virgil. Great epic poem. A touch of heartfelt love there too. Virgil was sent by Béatrice, the love of Dante's life, to help guide him safely through it all."

He turns to me. "You read it in the original language, right, Catherine? I remember you telling me that."

I nod. He smiles at me over the body, which is kind of creepy but I smile back.

"And what *exactly* do the words *signify*?" Will is getting impatient and looks totally pissed at Giles. God forbid Giles and I should share a memory. "Want to clue me in on what it means or do you two want to continue going down the memory lane of epic poetry?"

"Oh, sure," I snap back to the fact that I'm standing in a morgue. I can't help feeling surprised and strangely happy that Giles remembered me telling him that little bit of trivia. I take a breath and become professional again.

"The words, okay. They're from the part of the story just before Dante passes through the gate of Hell. There's an inscription written on the gate for all sinners to read. The Devil, it seems, wants them to fully understand their plight:

"'*Lasciate ogne speranza, voi ch'intrate.*'"

"Uh-huh. Which *means*?"

"'Abandon hope, all ye who enter here.'"

CHAPTER 2

THE KILLER'S MESSAGE IS obvious to all three of us. Abandon all hope, there's no way out. "The person who did this is no dummy, Will. Those words were written by someone who knows classical Latin as well as ancient history. They have a meaning and it appears as if the meaning is sadistic."

Dante may have written the words in his poem, but the idea behind them was pretty common knowledge during his time. Anyone imprisoned and sentenced to any one of the numerous horrible deaths during the thirteenth and fourteenth centuries knew there was no hope.

Prisons were made up of dirt floor cells in dungeons below ground with only small windows high up out of reach. The prisoner was shackled to an iron oval hammered deep inside a stone wall. Torture and mutilation of prisoners were common during the Holy Roman Empire. The Catholic Church was notorious for the most awful tortures. The Hell that Dante wrote about was conceived from what he knew happened inside those prisons run by the Church.

"The *real* message of those insidious acts was to instill fear and terror into the minds of the people," I tell Will.

"So what you're saying is that we're dealing with someone who knows the history of torture and is sending a message from ancient poetry to terrify people? A scholarly killer?"

"In a sense. I mean, the note is telling us that the perpetrator let the victim know what was going to happen to him and made him realize he couldn't escape his fate. Like the sinners in Dante's version of Hell, he's letting his victim realize the awful truth; I've got you, you're going to suffer horribly, and you won't leave here alive."

"Great, a thinking man's sadist who hates priests, and quotes poetry."

I look at the body. The mutilation is methodical. I tell Will as much and ask what he thinks.

"I think we're looking for someone who may have known both victims. There's a connection here."

"Is it possible we're looking at a serial killer?" Giles asks.

"This is deeply personal and it seems directed at the clergy," I answer him gesturing toward the body. "If this guy turns out to have been a genuine Roman Catholic priest, I'd say we're looking for someone who is going after Catholic clergy. The possibility of a serial killer can't be ruled out, but this is too one-on-one. There's a lot of anger present and, except for the act of sodomy, which was done violently, it seems to be controlled anger. That can change though."

Giles and his assistant need to get evidence from the body and then ready it for the autopsy. Will walks out first. He can only be civil to Giles for so long and, anyway, he has to get to the station to write his report. I follow him out; it's only six-thirty and I want breakfast. I also want to go home to wash my hair before I go to my office; it smells like morgue. When we're almost to the door, Giles says that he'll call me later.

"Um, and you'll call *me* about the results, right Doc?" Will says in a demanding way.

"You're first on my list, detective," answers Giles smiling. He coughs and continues, "By the way, there's a bar exam coming up in two months. My cousin Jennifer is taking it, she's all excited. Thought maybe you two might want to study together. I can set up a study-date if you like. She's a brain."

Oh dagger to the heart! This is Giles's subtle way of hitting back at Will's sarcasm. His cousin Jenn met Will only once and declared him a prize ass to his face.

Will looks steadily at Giles for a long minute and mouths an obscenity at him as I steer him quickly out the door.

Once outside I grab Will's arm. I don't mince words. "I want in on this case."

He turns to face me.

"This isn't a private investigation, Cate. This isn't *your* case."

"Technically no, but I was the PI who found the first body last year. I did more legwork than the cops did during that investigation; they were getting evidence and reports from *me*. Come on, Will, except for the message, this is *identical* to the last body found."

He sighs deeply and fixes me with a level stare. "The best I can do, and I'm not saying I *will* do it, is to keep you informed of certain developments in the case. That's it."

"You can keep me informed as a private consultant. I won't even charge you."

"Damn right you won't charge me because I am not hiring you!"

"Will, I am totally serious here. Why the hell did you ask me to come down here if you didn't want me involved?"

"I asked you to come down because last year you found a body murdered and mutilated in the same way. I wanted your opinion on the message. You gave it and that's it. Professional courtesy is what I expected."

"*You* are the one who asked *me* to consult on this case."

"Jeez, don't you ever listen to what people say? You are *not* a consultant. If I do keep you informed it is only as a matter of my *own* professional courtesy. You mess too much with what the police are doing and I swear, it'll not only cost you your license but you could end up in jail for obstruction. Listen to me for once, for God's sake, Cate. Besides, you told me you have a new case; work on that and earn some money."

I stare straight back at him. "I *am* working it. As for this priest case, I'm smart enough not to get caught. Don't worry about me, Will, I know what I'm doing. Give me a break on this. You don't need to know *what* I'm doing, but if I find something, some info or lead, you'll be the first person I tell. How's that for a deal?"

"God, you are something else, you know that Cate? I'll think about it. I can't promise you anything. Just let me think about it."

I smile my thanks.

"Email me the words on the collar and the translation, along with your analysis of their meaning, when you get to your office," is all he says to me as he walks to his unmarked car. Bye Will. Thanks for getting me up at four a.m.

⸺

Nine blocks from my home I pass my friend Melissa's more upscale brownstone. She is just entering her front door, coming home from a *client* meeting no doubt, when I honk and pull up to the curb. In her area of the city, brownstone owners have parking spaces. Melissa has a spot that she never uses. Her BMW is in a private garage.

She waves a beautifully manicured hand in greeting, her matching yellow diamond bracelets and rings sparkling in the early morning sun.

"All night stake-out?" she asks as I get out of the car cradling another Timothy's bag that contains a large coffee and two bagels with Taylor ham and egg. I made a quick stop on my way home.

"Morgue," I say. She grimaces. "Victim was found early this morning and Detective Benigni wanted my opinion on something."

"Ah, yes," she smiles with perfect teeth, "The delicious Will Benigni." She pronounces his name in perfect phonics, *Bay-nee-nee*. "How is he?"

"He's fine, I guess. Will's, well you know how he is when he's got a case, all business."

Melissa laughs and gestures toward the bag. "Want to come upstairs and have your coffee? I'm not tired yet."

"Sure," I say grateful for a little girl talk. I've had enough testosterone for one morning.

Melissa's digs are as different from mine as they can get. Whereas I have the bare minimum in furniture and accessories, her place looks like it is ready for a photo shoot for *Architectural Digest*. Nothing ever seems out of place, even her refrigerator is neat and in order.

I sit on the comfortably wide chairs by her kitchen island and take out my food. I am starving and I certainly need another caffeine jolt. Melissa puts on a pot of tea and takes eggs out of the fridge to make herself an omelet.

For the good part of an hour she tells me about the class she took on ancient cults, which ended last week; the new class she's taking on Peruvian archeology; an outfit she bought to wear to some gala next week; and a new restaurant opening up in SoHo. I tell her about a pair of shoes I bought but can't really afford, and ask her why, after seven years of living together, my two cats still don't get along all that well.

I mention my missing person cold file case and she comments how horrible it must be to not know what happened to someone you love. We don't talk about my love life with Giles or lack thereof with Will, or her *clients*. Finally the small talk is exhausted and she asks about my early morning sojourn down at the morgue.

One of the many things that I really like about Melissa is she's discreet. I know I can tell her anything and she will never repeat what I say. That discreetness is probably a necessity in her line of work. Anyway, I tell her about the body with the priest's collar and the message in Latin.

"This is the second body wearing a religious collar?" she asks as she joins me at the banquette and settles back into her chair. I nod yes.

"Did you ever ID the first body? Was the victim a real priest?"

"The body found last year *was* an actual priest, a Father Martin Duquesne, seventy-six years old. Took a while to ID him. He was living in a nursing home community in upstate New York. No living relatives. He had left the priesthood years ago and was teaching at a small Catholic college for a short time. People at the college knew very little about him except that he mostly kept to himself.

"His old diocese didn't have a lot of info on him either. The church was in a transient community so there weren't any pa-rishioners who had actually known him for long. No motive was ever found for the crime. No suspects either. The police finally put it down to a violent, random killing. The case is still open, but no real leads have ever been found."

"Well, I hope they have more luck finding info about this one." She shivers. "God, what a horror. Sounds like Detective Benigni has a real psycho on his hands. Someone doesn't like priests."

⁓

The sign on my battered, old office door that reads *Catherine Harlow, Private Investigations* is in bold brass letters. I picked it out of a catalogue not realizing how much its shiny newness would contrast with the ancient wood of the door on which it is attached. Still, I think it's me; the past mixing with the present and getting along just fine.

My office is a mess; the domestically challenged part of my persona extends to where I work. There are semi-filled coffee containers, junk mail, papers all over my desk, and three empty cartons of Chinese take-out on the file cabinets. My windowsill is where plants come to die. I either over-water them or forget to water at all. Will once jokingly called me a plant murderer and threatened to report me to the New York Horticultural Society. I probably deserve the infamy.

Separated from my own work area by a pretty decorated screen is the desk of the woman who takes my calls and makes my appointments, Mrs. Myrtle Goldberg Tuttle, who has been on vacation with her husband Harry for two weeks. They have no children and see me as a daughter. That's fine with me; there are times when I need pampering.

Myrtle isn't in yet. She will have a fit when she sees this mess and give me an over-the-top-of-her-glasses frown. Myrtle was a schoolteacher in her previous life and a good friend of my late parents. I can't afford to pay Myrtle a whole lot but I think she comes in more to have something to do, and for the occasional excitement she gets courtesy of my profession.

I locate my phone, which is hidden under a few flyers and other junk mail, and check for messages. I used to have my calls automatically forwarded to my cell phone, but I stopped after having some prank calls wake me up during the early morning hours. Some idiots, I have found, have nothing better to do with their time. It's easier for me to check office calls from my cell or have Myrtle forward important business calls to me

Before I forget to do it, I turn on my laptop, which I left on a filing cabinet, and email Will the translation along with my observations of the body and what I think the message signifies.

The file on the McElroy boy is on my desk chair. Picking it up I sit down and read the small bit of information I've written there. I look at the picture, a snapshot of a fifteen-year-old boy with sweet eyes that remind me of his sister's, but with one major difference: his have a cat-like wariness about them. As the owner of two cats, I know that look. It's an instinctual caution. My cats have this look whenever they think some type of danger might be present. It's an alertness, an internal early warning system. Be aware, be cautious, stay safe. That's the feline motto, but it's also good for the human mammal. This kid has that look.

So, where to start for info on Josh McElroy? The day after I met with Marie, I did a search of the shelters in her area and in the city as I had promised her I would but came up empty. Now I need something more official. I call an acquaintance who works at the police archives office. A happy-go-lucky voice answers. When he hears my voice he says, "Hey, Cate, how the hell are you? What can I do for you, kid?"

He's two years away from retirement and is happy to be

settled into a job where the only real danger is getting a paper cut. He did his time on the beat, got shot once, and his reward, besides not getting killed, was a desk job. A full pension and benefits await him in twenty-four months. He's a happy guy.

"Hi Jimmy. I'm fine. You? Oh, good, good. Listen, I need a file. It's a cold case file, goes back ten years. A boy by the name of Joshua McElroy, that's J-o-s-h-u-a M-c-E-l-r-o-y, went missing at the age of fifteen." I don't tell him anything else. He doesn't want to know why I want it anyway. "If you've got it I can come by this afternoon."

I hear a chair creak as he swivels to check the data in the computer. Click, click, click; Jimmy is a slow typist and he asks me to spell McElroy again. Ten minutes go by and I listen to Jimmy talk about his fly-fishing, his wife's arthritis, his daughter-in-law's pregnancy, his son's new job, his daughter's promotion at work. Finally I hear, "Yeah kid, I have it here. Come by around two, okay?"

"Thanks, Jimmy. I owe you one."

"So when you see me at The Shannon Rose you'll buy me a beer."

"You're on." I laugh.

Myrtle comes in just as I'm hanging up. As predicted she gives me the look she so perfected during her thirty-five years teaching eighth grade. Sighing and shaking her head, she begins to tidy up. All's well with the world. She's surprised when I hug her on my way out the door and I see that stern facade of hers melt. Myrtle loves me.

It's only eight o'clock, but I want to see Marie McElroy before I go check out the file on her brother.

CHAPTER 3

THE MCELROY HOUSE, WHERE Marie has lived all her life, is on a shady tree-lined street in Bellerose, Queens. It's a small clapboard house not very different from the others tucked closely beside each other on the street. You can get lost in Queens if you don't know your way around. There's 92nd Road, 92nd Street, 92nd Avenue. My aunt lived here until recently, so I know Queens like my own brownstone. By 9:05 I am standing on the front doorstep and ringing the bell until I realize it isn't working, so I begin a rapid staccato on the door.

"Coming!" Marie McElroy opens the door, dressed in black pants, a grey T-shirt, and flats. She told me when she was at my office that she's a hairdresser for a small shop in Queens. "Ms. Harlow!" I know she has a brief moment of hope that I am bringing her information about her brother, I can see it in her eyes, but it quickly subsides. I'm good at what I do but not that good. She only hired me a few days ago. Besides, I need more info.

"Hi, Marie. Please call me Cate, okay? Do you have a minute? I'm going to go read the case file on your brother at the police archives this afternoon and before I do I wanted to ask you some more questions. I know it's early but your input to this is a vital part of my job. Got some time for me?"

"Oh, yes, of course, Ms., um ... Cate. Anything you need. I

don't have to be at work until around eleven really. We're kinda slow this week. I just go in early to set up because it keeps me busy. Come on in."

The furniture is old-fashioned and worn, but the house is immaculate. I see religious pictures hanging on the walls and one prominent picture of a sad-faced Jesus on the wall in the stairwell. She asks me if I want coffee or orange juice. Having had two more cups of coffee during my girl talk with Melissa earlier this morning, coupled with the super-large one from Timothy's, I'm all "coffeed" out so I opt for juice. I really don't want the juice but in my business I have found that people are much more receptive to giving out information if you make it seem as if you're being sociable. They're off their guard in that type of scene and will answer questions easily.

I watch her go down the hall to the kitchen. As I said, it's a small house. Marie comes back with a tray. She hands me the glass of orange juice and a paper napkin. I shake my head at the proffered cookies. My gut is still in the process of digesting those delicious Timothy's bagels.

"I would have come to your office. You didn't have to drive all the way out here," she says, sitting back and taking the mug of coffee.

"That's okay. I've been up since four and the drive helped me clear my head."

I politely sip my drink and look around the living room. Pictures of the McElroy family abound, especially ones of Marie and her brother, Joshua. I see baby pictures in which they're both smiling or mugging for the camera lens. Pictures of the two of them around three or four, laughing and hugging each other; they looked as if they had a happy family life as children. I see a couple of black-and-white photos in the sea of colored ones and it's a nice touch; the modern pictures take on a dated look. Somebody must have been an amateur photographer.

There's even a picture of them in communion outfits. Both are dressed all in white down to their shoes, Marie in a lace dress with that little veil hanging down to her shoulders, and Joshua in a little suit and tie. They're posed by a statue of some saint, both trying to look serious for the occasion but those dimpled smiles keep peeking through. There's one large picture with *Happy 8th Birthday Marie* written on a huge cake. The camera caught Joshua with a devilish grin sticking his finger in the icing. He had to be just nine years old.

For some reason, the smiling pictures of Joshua seem to stop a little while after the birthday picture. Marie is always smiling at the camera but Joshua doesn't even look at it; his eyes are gazing off in the distance, wary, a little scared. In another picture he looks angry. What happened after his ninth year that caused this change in his face? What made him stop smiling?

Marie sees me staring at the pictures and looks at me questioningly. I take a final sip of juice and put the glass back on the tray.

"Marie, some questions are hard to answer but I wouldn't be doing my job if I didn't ask them." She nods.

"Those family pictures of you and Joshua make me believe that you had a happy childhood." She smiles and begins to say something about how her childhood was almost perfect.

"Up to a point, that is," I say, forestalling her. "In the earlier ones, Joshua is always smiling. But after your eighth birthday picture, he looks sad and angry. Were there any family problems that suddenly occurred when you were around that age?"

She wrinkles her brow but immediately shakes her head no.

"Family problems such as a parent losing a job, parental fights, alcohol or drug abuse, even prescription drugs; anything you can remember," I prompt.

"If you mean my parents, God no. We were lucky; our parents really were good, decent people. One or two beers at a barbecue maybe, they hardly ever had a disagreement. My dad had a good job as a construction foreman and my mom worked part-time as a lunchroom lady. She liked being home for us when we got out of school. It *is* true when I tell you that we had a pleasant childhood.

"And Joshua did seem to change when he was nine or ten,

you're right. Our parents didn't know why Joshua was what my mom called moody. The few times when they tried to talk to him about why he seemed so down, he became upset, saying nothing was wrong, and for them to just leave him alone. That was so unlike Josh. He also told them once that they didn't know anything about life. Imagine that, he was not even a teen yet and here he was telling our parents that they knew nothing about life! Josh did have a couple of tough years though. My mother finally decided that maybe it was a hormonal thing. You know, like he was going through puberty early or something. Dad wasn't too concerned. He said that Josh was just having some quiet times and that a lot of kids go through that.

"One strange thing though, was that he stopped playing any sports, even swimming, which he was really good at and loved. He just up and quit the team. Dad didn't understand that at all. Josh had won junior swim competition medals. Mom said that he was shy about his body, almost as if he hated it, because he was always a skinny kid. I don't know. He read a lot the summer he turned eleven and until the day he disappeared. He was what my Dad called a bookworm. But, no, there was nothing that happened here at home to justify why he was suddenly moody."

I write that down. I love technology but find that a pen and a pad are sometimes quicker for my needs. Keying info into a tablet takes too much time. I'm old-fashioned that way.

"What about school? Any fighting, any bullying, or enemies?"

"No, nothing like that at all. Other kids liked him a lot. He never had any problems with them. In fact he was always the peacemaker if kids got into a fight or had problems with each other. They respected him. Our school was small and everyone knew each other."

"Did he have a lot of friends? A best friend or girlfriend?"

"You know, not really. He got *along* with everyone, boys and girls, but he liked being by himself. *We* were really best friends. No one knew him like I did."

"Was there anything you can remember about Joshua's behavior right before he disappeared? I know you must have answered a lot of questions from the police, but I need to ask you some, too. Memories are funny sometimes, Marie. From a distance of years you might remember something small but significant that you forgot to tell the cops. Can you think of any problems, anything that may have upset your brother? Whatever you can remember, no matter how small, will be a help, Marie. Think about the week before he went missing. Think about the last time you saw him."

She drained her coffee and cuddled the empty mug to her chest. Tears appeared in her eyes and one trailed its way down her cheek before she brushed it away. I waited.

"The thing is, Cate, I don't know. I wasn't here the week before he left. I was away at camp. That summer was going to be my first year as a junior counselor and I had to go for a week of training during spring break. I left really early the day after Easter Sunday while Josh was still sleeping. I should have said goodbye, but I didn't want to wake him. I know that he hadn't been sleeping well. I used to hear him at night walking around in his room.

"The last time I saw him was after dinner on Easter." She began really crying then and buried her face in one hand while the other held the mug as if it were a protective talisman. "I'm sorry."

"That's okay Marie, that's okay. This is hard, I know. Tell me about that Easter then. Did you notice anything different about him that day? Did he say anything that seemed strange or out of place to you?"

Marie was wiping her face with a napkin from the tray and trying to compose herself.

"I don't think so. My grandparents were here. We all had dinner together and after helping Mom clean up, Josh and I went outside. We were out on the back porch just sitting and watching the birds flying back to the tree in our yard. I guess they had built a nest. It was quiet. You know, it was that time of the year, April, just like now."

"Were you talking about anything special?"

"Nothing really. I mean we were kind of tired. I did mention how excited I was to be a junior counselor and what I was going to do. He just told me to enjoy what I was doing and to take care of myself at camp. That last part? That was nothing out of the ordinary. My brother always looked out for me and was forever telling me to be careful."

She stopped.

"Anyway, the last thing I told Joshua before we went into the house was that pretty soon we'd hear chirps from baby birds. See, my brother loves all animals. He wants—wanted to be an artist and draw pictures of animals in their natural habitats. And he said ..." She stops and her eyes well up again at the memory of the last time she ever saw her brother.

"What, Marie? Joshua said what?"

"He said, 'Baby birds need protection.' That's the last thing he said to me. 'Baby birds need protection.' The very last thing he said to me was about birds and the next morning I was gone."

CHAPTER 4

BEFORE I GO TO the police archives office, I stop at a local Italian trattoria near my office. Besides having tables both inside and out for customers, the trattoria does a brisk take-out business. The last time I ate was at Melissa's earlier this morning and it's now past one in the afternoon; I'm starving. A nice Italian sub is what I want. I inherited my green eyes and coloring from the Dutch ancestors on my dad's side but I got my healthy genes and love of food from my mother, whose ancestry is a nice combo of Italian with a sprinkling of French.

As I'm watching Enzo, the owner of the place, masterfully create my generously proportioned Genoa salami, capicola, provolone, hot peppers, and onion sub, my cell buzzes a text. It's from Will. "I'll be at your office late this afternoon."

I smile. Will refuses to use text lingo. To me, with my background in linguistics, text-speak is just another language. Usually, I don't use it much either. I prefer to call rather than text. But just to bust him I reply, "C u la8r." It'll drive him crazy.

"Here's your sandwich, Cate," says Enzo, handing me a neatly wrapped sub. "I put in a lot of the Genoa just the way you like it."

I grab an iced tea, smile my thanks, pay him, and head out

the door to savor it in my car.

~⚓~

The Vault, as the police archives department is known, is located on a dead-end street. There are two new personal storage warehouses and some old office buildings that have been there since the turn of the 19th century. I park my car a block from where I have to go, and, downing the last of my ice tea, walk down to the front door on the side of the building. I'm a little early, but Jimmy won't mind. On the way over I made a pit stop at his favorite deli to get him a nice corned beef on rye and a cream soda. It pays to feed those who help you. The beer will have to wait until he's off duty sitting on a bar stool at the Shannon Rose.

I walk in the door but don't see Jimmy at his desk; he must be off in the back. There's a bell-button on the wall by the door and I push it. A few minutes later Jimmy comes walking from the back of the Vault carrying a box.

"Hey, Cate! How's the girl?"

"Good, good, Jimmy. How about you? Everything good?"

"Yeah, can't complain, huh? Let me put this box on the desk. I got to go through it for some high up lazy-ass lieutenant who can't get his tired old butt down here to find what he wants. Asks me to do his work, can you beat that? Give me a break. I should say screw him but I won't. I know where my bread gets buttered."

I laugh. Jimmy's got a way with words and an opinion of everyone and everything. Fortunately he likes me and he thinks what I do for a living is great "for a girl" if a bit dangerous.

"C'mon, kid, I'll take you to the back and you can get your hands dirty on this, what's the name? Oh yeah, *Mc-El-roy* file."

The file room is a veritable warehouse of boxes of evidence. Stacked floor to ceiling are sealed boxes with old stories of crimes committed, police investigations, personal frustrations, and the sadness of people's lives. Jimmy locates the file box I need, which is way up on top of the ribbed steel compartments, climbs up a ladder, and carries it down for me. It's small and dusty.

I take the box over to a cart that's been set up as a desk and, perching myself on a cracked leather stool, open it. There isn't much. A few pictures of Josh McElroy, an old shirt, a backpack emblazoned with the name of his school, the original police report and notes of the investigation, and a police officer's list of what was found in the backpack. I look at the statements the cops took from the members of the McElroy family, neighbors, classmates, and teachers. As Marie said, no really close friends. Nothing out of place there, simple statements: good kid, above average student, no problems with classmates, wonderful son and brother. There are no clues as to why he disappeared.

I empty out the backpack carefully and find everything that was documented. There's the usual student stuff like pens, pencils, a couple of sticks of gum dried hard as plaster from age, a flyer advertising some local band, a key that the list describes as a locker key, and an old three-subject notebook. Some of the pages of the notebook are dog-eared as if he were bookmarking them. Opening them up, I see that they're filled with hand drawn pictures and that they are surprisingly good. One picture captures my attention; it's a picture of a female lion standing tall and alert. Between her massive front paws she is holding two cubs that look out at the world with calm eyes. A male lion sits to the right of the lioness, his shaggy head up and proud. To the left, as if it is a distance away, there seems to be some other animal drawn in a stalking position. I look closely and see that it is a hyena. Its yellow eyes are staring directly at the cubs. The detail is excellent.

There are various drawings of the hyena; some showing large pointed teeth and a snarl. Always the yellow eyes are prominent and staring. Drawn by a teenage boy, these pictures evoke evil and menace. Why this theme? There's got to be an answer and that answer may lead me to Josh himself. The cops might have bypassed the drawings as just something a kid might do, but I think that the drawings may hold a clue to Joshua's disappearance.

I read and re-read the statements from Josh's family. Sometimes fresh eyes see a word or phrase that might give a clue
someone else may have missed. I check carefully and concentrate, trying to imagine how they felt and how they looked when
they were giving their statements. God knows they were scared,
stressed beyond belief that this was happening at all. The statements are all accompanied by notes from the cop who took
them, notes that may prove to be crucial. Were the parents and
siblings believed to be telling the truth? Yes. Were the individual
statements, taken from the parents and from Marie, concerning
any family problems, consistent? It seemed so. Who was the last
person to have contact with the missing person and what happened? At the house, his mom waved goodbye as he walked to
the library. It's a cat-and-mouse game because the cops are going in cold and everyone is a potential suspect. The police *have*
to eliminate family members as persons of interest. This is un-
believably hard on the family because they're desperate to have
the cops find their loved ones. At the same time, they're imagining what horrible things may have happened to them.

Everything about the investigation the morning after Joshua
went missing seems to be upfront and by the book. The officer
who did the initial interviews at the McElroy home wrote that
the parents, Joseph and Denise McElroy, seemed to be genuinely upset about their son and he had no reason to suspect either one of them. The sister, Marie, who had to come home from
camp, was almost hysterical and a doctor had to be called to
sedate her.

A preliminary report written by an Officer Coronato reads:

*"The alibis of the people in the neighboring area check
out. Several people saw him leave the house around ten in the
morning with a couple of library books and a gym bag. The
head librarian, a Mrs. Brenda Rosehill, said it was common
for Joshua McElroy to be at the library from around ten until
near five during a school break. She said he usually read in the
main lounge area and then drew pictures from the books he*

read. Said in days leading up to the disappearance, he seemed the same as always to her. She doesn't remember seeing him the day he went missing so there's a hole in the timeline. Everyone's stories check out. There's no reason to suspect any one of them. Looks like a runaway kid but we're still checking everything out. No leads, no signs of violence or a struggle. Joshua McElroy left to go to the library between nine-thirty and ten. His mother went food shopping that afternoon and came home around 5:25. She just assumed her son had come home at his regular time. Right before the usual family dinner hour of six o'clock, she went to call him to help set the table but he couldn't be found. He seemed to just have vanished after leaving his house."

Another report about two weeks later confirms no leads found in the disappearance of Joshua McElroy. Known sex offenders in the area and beyond had been questioned with no results. Unmarked police cars had been watching the McElroy house but had found nothing out of the ordinary. Cadaver dogs brought to the McElroy property found nothing.

⚚

"Hello, Father. Do you remember me?

"Joey! It's so good to see you again, my son. Oh my Joey. It's been so long."

CHAPTER 5

CATHERINE HARLOW, PRIVATE INVESTIGATIONS has had a minor face-lift. I notice it as soon as I open the door. The pleasant, lemony smell of furniture polish hits me immediately. Armed with copies of the McElroy files I arrive back at my office around four-thirty to find that Myrtle has done a fantastic job of tidying up; as a nice touch, she has put fresh flowers in a vase on my desk as well as on her own smaller one. Even the plants have semi-revived due to her special maternal touch. It looks good; how long it will stay that way is something else entirely.

Myrtle greets me by coming out of the bathroom wearing rubber gloves and carrying a bucket and mop.

"Good, you're back."

"Wow, Myrtle, you are one hell of a lady." I smile, putting down my files on a shiny, neat desk.

"More like one hell of a *cleaning* lady, miss," she frowns. "I'm away for two weeks visiting my cousins and their grandbabies and this place looks as if a tornado hit it not once but twice. You should at least throw out the half-empty cartons of food. Haven't you heard of rats? This is New York City, you know."

Roaches would be the more likely culprits, but the owner of

the building is a good guy who checks for what he calls "those indoor pest things" every two weeks. He's from Italy and there isn't a rat or a roach that would dare cross him. He's that vigilant about his property.

"Yes ma'am," I say like a chastised middle-school-er. "Thank you for cleaning up."

That gets a smile from Mrs. Myrtle Goldberg Tuttle, and an announcement.

"That nice young Detective Benigni was here. He stepped out to get something but he'll be back in about twenty minutes." Then she coyly adds, "Do you want to freshen up, honey?"

I size up the situation and her intention. "Myrtle," I say, "if you are thinking that Detective Benigni is here for a romantic assignation of any kind, get it out of your head. I'm helping him on a case, that's why he came here. I don't need to freshen up. I've already had two showers today so I'm going to assume that I'm still fresh."

"But honey, you were married and ..."

"*Were* is the key word here, Myrtle, we *were* married and we *were* divorced over four years ago."

Myrtle looks at me and sighs. I know she has some Jewish mother idea of my getting back together with Will and living happily ever after. That's not going to happen. Occasional sex, yes. Friends, sure, most of the time anyway. Married? Never again.

"It's not an option, Myrtle, not an option at all," I say to end the conversation as I start to check my email. But Myrtle seems intent on having the last word.

"Well, *you're* not getting any younger and he *is* familiar territory if you know what I mean."

These are both statements I know all too well so I have no answer. Thanks Myrtle.

⟶

I'm re-reading the file on Joshua McElroy when Will steps through my office doorway. He's carrying a large bag of chips and a Pepsi, which are either his snack or a late lunch on the run. Truthfully he has some bad eating habits for a guy who expected a wife to be a gourmet cook. I wonder what happened to his chicken-cacciatore-cooking police partner, Debbie.

"Hi Myrtle," he says and she acknowledges him with a nod and a big, motherly smile. Like most women, she really adores him.

"Cate, have you got a few minutes?" He gets right to the point. If Myrtle had any hope of sparks flying between us, she's got to be disappointed. I'm a little bit disappointed too; no sarcastic banter, no ha-ha's with which to regale me about dumb stuff at the precinct or on the streets. He's just all business.

"Sure." Putting down the file and leaning back in my chair, I give Will my full professional attention and gesture him to the chair in front of my desk.

"An hour *before* the official ME's report was sent over to my office I received a special delivery letter with the seal of the Archbishop of New York *asking* about the body. That was a shock since I didn't have the report from Giles yet. Seems the bishop got some *very* detailed information about the dead man with the priest collar. His letter says that a sealed note was slipped under the door of his residence early this morning. Now that's interesting, but disturbing. Who had this type of info except the officers on the scene, you, me, Giles, and the people down at the morgue, right? I'm pretty sure the info didn't come from my people. It's always possible but I seriously doubt it."

"Interesting," I nod. Will is damned good at his job and has absolute trust in his team.

He continues.

"Now we can eliminate the poor guy who found the body. The man just said he saw what he thought was a deer and went to see if it was still alive. When it turned out to be a naked human body he called 911. He was totally freaked by the scene and he didn't stay near the body long enough to see any details. My officers found him throwing up outside his car. And, for want of a better phrase, there was no one else around that area to make any *intimate discoveries* such as noticing that the guy's penis had been sliced off and shoved into his mouth. Neither the man who found the body nor my officers saw anyone else. My people checked the area thoroughly and they found no other person or evidence of anyone else." He pauses. "It may have come from the ME's office."

"Giles? Are you saying Giles gave the information to the archbishop's office?"

I lean forward in surprise.

"No. Giles is a consummate professional and scrupulous in following the letter of the law. Whatever my own personal dislikes are about any relationship that may have existed between you and the ME have nothing to do with my respect for his integrity and his professionalism. I would never suspect him, understand?"

I do understand even though I dislike his positive assertion that I no longer *have* a relationship with Giles. Will Benigni is fair and a good judge of a person's integrity. I decide to let it pass.

"Well, then who?" I ask settling back in the chair again. "Who do you think supplied the detailed information about this body to the bishop?"

He looks out the double windows of my office. There are nesting turtledoves in an empty flowerpot on my fire escape. The female dove sits and warms two newly hatched chicks in the well-made nest while the male sits on a utility pole by the street keeping watch for any dangers. When I've been here in the mornings I can hear the cooing owl-like sounds they make. I always put seeds on the window ledge for them. They trust me and they know they're safe this high up. I like having them here.

"Will? Who do you think it could be?"

"I don't know, maybe some new jerk working there who finds this case sensational and ghoulish enough to talk about it; maybe some morgue employee who's an overzealous churchgoer and feels compelled to tell what's going on. But that seriously doesn't make a lot of sense because Giles picks his staff with special care. Most of them who come into contact with the bodies, and the reports on them, have been with his office for at least ten years."

"Are you going to ask Giles about it? There might be someone working there, someone we don't really know who's looking for some sort of attention, or maybe there's a temporary assistant clerk."

Even as I say this I know Giles would never have anyone in his office who he felt was untrustworthy. He is, as Will says, scrupulous and professional and personally chooses the people who work with him.

Will turns back to face me. "Yeah, I am going to give him a call. Who knows? I might get lucky. Then Giles can fire the ass who did it and I can charge the fired bastard with case-tampering." He gets up. "After that call I'll have to make another one to the archbishop's secretary and see if I can somehow twist the story and slur the details."

I smile at him. "You're good at slurring details. Use your God-given charm."

He just glances at me wondering if I'm being sarcastic or just wishing him luck. It's a little of both on my part.

Looking at Myrtle he says his usual goodbye.

"Myrtle, sweetheart, what's said here stays here."

She responds as she always does. "What was said? *I* didn't hear a word."

CHAPTER 6

I AM ALONE IN my office. Myrtle left about an hour after Will did. Even though I have been up since before four a.m. and it is now after six at night I can't stop looking at the pictures drawn by a teenage Joshua McElroy. These are worthy of being shown in a gallery.

Every picture has the same theme drawn in a variety of different ways. There's always some type of predator lurking in the background, watching innocent victims who are unaware of the danger. The hyena figures prominently in several large drawings, hungry yellow eyes, and saliva dripping from sharp teeth, but there are other predators as well. Some of the smaller sketches show hooded cobras with their venomous tongues out, looking at nests of birds, and large rats with dagger canines looking at newborn puppies. The eyes of the predators are always the focal point: evil, cold, and calculating. It's mesmerizing.

Giles calls me just as he promised he would, and surprises me by asking if I'd like dinner. I tell him I'm still at my office and truly do not feel like going out. I'd have to go home and change, put on makeup, all things you don't want to do when you're tired and have a lot going on in your mind.

"We don't have to go out Catherine. I can bring dinner to

your place. How about it?"

It sounds good. I'm a healthy girl with a healthy appetite and now that's he's mentioned food, I feel hungry.

"Well ..." I hesitate. The day is catching up to me and I'm starting to feel it. The *freshness* has worn off. The thought of someone bringing me food, however, seems comforting and an excellent end to a long day. My idea of dinner was going to be two breakfast bars washed down with a bottle of seltzer. I relent.

"Okay, but, listen, I'm not going to be back at the brownstone until around eight. And I have to tell you that you really saw me at my best early this morning at the morgue. Since then I've gone considerably downhill. Right now I look like hell but I just don't have the energy to make myself pretty."

He laughs and tells me he'll be over around eight-thirty. I hang up and go back to the report on Joshua McElroy.

Flipping through the notebook I find that, aside from the pictures, there's really nothing that can offer any clues to why Joshua disappeared. There's just school stuff the same as any other fifteen-year-old boy would have. Class notes, times written for afterschool activities, several passes to class signed by the nurse—nothing out of the ordinary. I decide to do a final read of the officer's report and the statements.

It may be because I'm tired and that my eyes can't seem to completely focus on the words but I don't read anything new that would give me a lead. Tomorrow I'll go back to them and maybe see something different. I put the files back in the folder on my desk and turn off the desk light. There's a small nightlight plugged into an outlet by the door and that's enough light for me to locate my bag and my keys. Walking to the windows I look out into the night. An ambulance is roaring off in the distance and there are the sounds of cars honking and trucks misfiring. Very few people are on the street below. I check on the doves settled down for the night in their nest, the tiny tail feather of one of the two chicks protruding from underneath a parent's wing. All's well in their little nook.

As I walk out the door and turn the keys in the double locks

I remember Josh McElroy's last words to his sister: *"Baby birds need protection."*

A large antipasto, pepperoni pizza, and two bottles of a good merlot put my overfilled day into perspective. I will deal with what's on my desk tomorrow. Nothing to do but sit back and let my mind clear.

The table is set with my good china and wine glasses. Giles knows how to make even pizza look elegant. Before he puts the food on the table, he makes one rule. We won't discuss anything about cases, bodies, runaways, or any other job-talk during dinner.

"Let's make it a night of nothing but good thoughts and good things."

"Okay. I agree. One question though."

"Just one, only one, Catherine. What do you want to ask?"

"Did Will call you today about the archbishop?"

"Yes, and we discussed how the info could have gotten out. It wasn't anyone in the ME's office. I would bet good money on that."

"So if you're sure it's none of your staff and Will's sure it's none of his officers, then who? I think it's possible it's the killer. He, or she, was never found in the first case. The evidence is the same. Maybe the killer is bragging. Maybe he wants to get caught?"

"Will said something like that too. The thing is, the information was typed in graphic detail but also very clinically written. Exactly the way a doctor or lab technician would write one. It really does look as if someone had access to the official report and wrote the details verbatim, the mutilation, the message; everything was exactly what I would, and did, put in *the official report.*"

I think about what he's saying. "Then the person who typed the note must either have had access to your evidence, which both you and Will don't think happened, or the killer is the one who sent the detailed report and has knowledge of medical terms and forensics."

"That's pretty much what we concluded. Whoever sent this is no dummy. There's a knowledge here of anatomy as well as forensic terminology."

"Yes, but why this time? Why involve anyone else this time? The last body, no one outside of the police or I knew any details. And the public only knew about the murder through an article on the second page in the area's small town press. Nothing big. The article didn't mention details: the police made sure that they were kept from the newsperson covering the story. There were no church authorities involved either. In fact, I was surprised that no one I contacted seemed to care at all about that dead priest."

Giles looks at me before he speaks. "Catherine, I know if we keep talking about this that will be *all* we do tonight. We'll end up eating soggy antipasto and cold pizza. Your adrenaline mixed with the wine will give you a hyper-buzz and the night will be completely shot. You've been up since before four and so have I. It's going on nine now. Let's put this on the back burner and talk about it tomorrow. If I know you, we damn well will talk about it tomorrow. But not tonight, all right? Let's eat and let the wine do its celebrated work. We both need to unwind."

I look at his face and suddenly have the need to be catered to—something Giles is very good at doing. Suddenly the prospect of food and wine is welcoming. The aroma of the pizza is delicious and I place my napkin on my lap while Giles heaps antipasto on to my salad plate.

I realize I'm starving.

❧

We're sitting on the couch enjoying the second bottle of wine. A combination of the mellow feeling the wine brings coupled with the carbs in the pizza has left me relaxed and kind of limp. I smile and then giggle.

"Pleasant thoughts?" asks Giles as he drains his wineglass

and places it on the small table next to the couch.

"I was just thinking about Myrtle and how proud she'd be of me that I helped clean up after dinner. Usually the pizza box would sit on my counter for two days." I laugh.

"Myrtle is a gem," he says, reaching for the elastic that holds my hair in a ponytail. He pulls it slowly and seductively down the length of my hair. I'm suddenly glad I washed it this morning. I like the feel of the silkiness of it on my shoulders. Thank you, Melissa, for giving me that expensive jar of conditioner. The logo on it says, *For women who want sexy hair*. My sexy hair makes me feel sexy! I giggle again.

"Please tell me *you're not* still thinking about Myrtle." Giles plays with my hair gently and kisses my neck, my cheek, my lips. His right hand is deftly unzipping my sweatshirt and sliding smoothly inside while his left hand finds its way between my legs. He smells good; his breath is warm and I can taste wine and pepperoni on his lips. Wine and seduction: very nice, Giles, very nice.

"Nope," I say, putting my own wineglass down and turning into the kiss. "Definitely not Myrtle."

CHAPTER 7

IWAKE A LITTLE after two a.m. and find a nude Giles wrapped around my body. He's warm and I snuggle deep into the hardness of his chest. My two cats, Mouse and Little Guy, are at the foot of the bed deep in cat sleep. I feel happy and relaxed. Amazing what a wonderful combination food, wine, and lovemaking can be. Potent stuff.

There's enough light coming through my window for me to see my clothes are not on the floor. They must be in the living room. Right, okay, I remember and smile. Before I close my eyes and drift back into sleep I think about the message on the dead body. Who would write that phrase? And on a dead body ... I yawn and close my eyes.

The dead body must have been in my subconscious because I dream of Nonna Rita, who has been gone for almost thirty years.

⤙

The first dead body I ever saw was that of my grandmother, my Nonna Rita. I was only eight years old. She had volunteered to pick me up from school every Thursday afternoon and bring me to my violin lessons. After my lesson, and before she drove me home, we'd go for a pistachio ice cream cone a few doors down from the music store where I had my lessons. We both loved pistachio and I looked forward to it. Thursday was the highlight of my week.

I waited impatiently on the front steps of my school until there were no other kids around. Everybody but me had been duly picked up. School let out at two forty-five; it was now going on four o'clock and still no Nonna Rita. The afterschool aide who was sitting on the steps with me told me to wait right there, and then she went inside the school to call Nonna Rita's house. I knew I wasn't supposed to leave the school but when the aide was in the building making the call, I fled down the front steps. I knew where Nonna Rita lived and I ran all the way, all seven long blocks, to my grandmother's house alone.

I found her sitting in the garden in one of her favorite chairs by her beloved petunias and I thought she was sleeping. That made me a little bit angry. Nonna Rita had fallen asleep and forgotten about me! Flushed and out of breath I called out to her, asking her with the selfish concern of a child, if we could still go for ice cream even though I missed my violin lesson. She didn't answer me.

"Nonna Rita?" I said, going over to where she sat sleeping so deeply, a little smile on her face. "Nonna Rita wake up! Can we *still* go for ice cream? *Please*?"

When I touched her shoulder to wake her, she fell over onto the ground right into her well-cared-for petunias. Something, some horrible animal fear told me she hadn't fainted or was sick. I knew she was dead and I ran like hell to her neighbor's house. The neighbor called the police and she made me stay in her kitchen, away from the living room windows, when the hearse came to take the body out. Later, while waiting for my parents to pick me up, the neighbor gave me a dish of pistachio ice cream. I ate it and then threw up all over her dining room table.

❧

Seven o'clock the sound of New Age music wakes me up. It's coming from my Bose system which is my musical alarm clock, another leftover from my married days. I hear Giles whistling as he takes a shower in my bathroom. Little Guy is sitting on my chest while Mouse gently paws my face. They're hungry. I swing my legs over the side of the bed and go into the kitchen. On the way I pick up Giles's discarded shirt and put it on.

I make coffee for us, feed the cats, and hope Giles understands that the only breakfast food I have on hand are raspberry breakfast bars and toast. At least, thank God, I have half-and-half. I refuse to drink coffee without that. Food I can always pick up on the way to my office but I need my caffeine fix with half-and-half as soon as I wake up. I make a mental note to get to the supermarket as soon as I can, knowing that with all I have on my mind that will be the least important item on my list.

Standing in the doorway waiting for the coffee to brew, I watch a nude Giles coming out of the bathroom and going into the bedroom. Great view. I wolf-whistle. He pauses, looks over his shoulder at me and winks.

A few minutes later he comes into the kitchen dressed in sweats, a T- shirt, and new running shoes, everything he had in his gym bag when he came over last night. We've talked about him leaving some of his things here for the overnight stays but I'm just not ready—yet. I still have some personal items left from Will, not to mention tons of emotional baggage.

Giles smiles appreciatively when he sees me wearing his shirt and grabs a mug for coffee.

"I'm just going to have coffee, Catherine, then I'm out for a run. I want to get to the morgue early. I have some tests to run."

I marvel at the way he says "the morgue" the same way other people say the office. And I have to wonder why it is that for me it sounds completely normal. Melissa once asked me if it bothered me to have sex with a man who handles and performs autopsies on dead bodies for a living. I told her that I never even think about it.

The truth is that I never think about it because I *know* that he showers and scrubs his hands before he comes to see me. I asked him.

With Giles out the door on his morning run, I go to the bath-room and take a long hot bath. I love this old bathtub. One of the great things about brownstones is the bathrooms which are pretty roomy and have large old claw-footed tubs. It's a luxury since so many newer rentals have these dinky little bathing ar-eas the size of a cat litter box. I got lucky with this place.

I lay back and soak for about fifteen minutes then get out to towel off. I like to get to my office by eight-thirty and start my day without anyone else around. Despite the dream about my grandmother, I feel better and more alert than I have in days.

It's hot for an April day so I vary my usual outfit by pair-ing a soft, lilac-colored Tory Burch T-shirt with my jeans and sneakers. The tee was a birthday gift from Melissa and I know this one present probably costs more than half of the clothes in my closet.

I put on lip gloss, some bronzer for color and, after pony-tailing my hair, I'm good to go. Grabbing my bag and sunglasses, I survey myself in the hall mirror. Not too bad, girl.

The magic hands of Giles Barrett, ME have done me a world of good.

On my way to Timothy's for coffee and a bagel, I allow myself to let my mind wander. That's a good thing because it helps me think. Sometimes by not concentrating too hard on the specific problem or issue in a case, a random thought about it gives me a clue as to how I should proceed. As I reach my office building, I think I know where to start on the McElroy case. Go back to the beginning and find the real problem, the one that is more than likely hiding in plain sight.

I enjoy being alone in my office, drinking coffee, eating a bagel, and going through files. As I said before, I tend to get a lot of work done when I'm by myself.

The first thing I did when I came in was to check on the turtledoves. The mama is still sitting on her nest taking care of the chicks. I hear a low coo-coo-coo and look up. The male dove is across the street on a phone wire. I raise my unopened coffee cup to the doves in a silent greeting; this is my little family group.

Reading the file on Joshua McElroy, I make a few executive decisions. I'm going to concentrate on the library where he spent his days and then interview some of the people there. That may be tough because in ten years, there can be a lot of changes. The head librarian, Mrs. Brenda Rosehill, may not even be employed there anymore. People retire, some may have moved away; life moves forward. Tragedies stay in the past.

Around nine o'clock I call the library to find out when it opens. I drum my fingers restlessly when an automated voice reading a menu answers and I put it on speakerphone.

"Press one if you want to continue in English, press two for Spanish, press three if you know your party's extension, press four if you want to reserve a book, press five if you want an extension on a book you have already borrowed. Please note the time limit for extended borrowing is two weeks. Press six for library hours."

Finally! I jam my finger on number six.

"Summer hours begin after the Memorial Day weekend. The library will be closed for the Memorial Day weekend. Summer hours are Monday to Thursday, 10 a.m. to 4:30 p.m. Evening hours are offered from 6:00 p.m. to 8:00 p.m. only on Wednesday."

I inhale and exhale deeply. I hate menus unless I am looking at a particularly nice one in a good restaurant. Phone menus drive me crazy.

"The current library hours are Monday to Thursday, 10:00 a.m. to 5:00 p.m. Friday's hours are from 10 a.m. to 3 p.m. To hear a repeat of this menu please press zero. Thank you and have a good day."

I reach the library a little after ten thirty to give the workers time to get settled and into what they need to do. A sign warns me *No food or drink allowed in the library* so I dump my second coffee into the gutter and throw the cup away in the garbage.

Libraries have always seemed like safe and magical places to me. I love the smells of old books, the dried glue on the bindings, and the varnished old wooden bookcases. If you have a good imagination, the stories in books can bring you anywhere you want to go. No wonder Joshua liked being here. It can almost be called a sanctuary.

The lady at the desk is on the computer as I walk up and she holds up a finger telling me to wait a second. When she looks up from her computer I show her my PI plastic-coated license. She looks at me, then down at my license, and back up at me again before speaking.

"Yes, Ms. Harlow? How can I help you?"

"I'm looking for someone who worked here ten years ago." I consult the pad I have in my pocket. "A Mrs. Brenda Rosehill. Is she still employed here as head librarian?"

"Brenda? Oh, yes, but she works in the upstairs wing now. She's in charge of the media center for young adults. You know," she says smiling, "everything's on the web now so we had to change with the times. A media center is a necessity."

I half smile back at her. I don't want her going off on what the library has done in the way of modernization. I'm here on business.

"I'd like to speak with her. Can you show me how to get to the media center?"

"Sure, but Brenda's not in yet. She had a special PowerPoint presentation for a fundraiser last night. When she stays late for those she comes in around eleven. You're welcome to wait here if you want. There're some new magazines over there by the window or feel free to just walk around."

I check my watch; it's a quarter to eleven. The magazine rack looks inviting so I saunter over and sit down to wait. A new *Architectural Digest* catches my eye and I leaf through it half expecting to see Melissa's brownstone featured inside. When I glance at my watch again, a half hour has passed and someone is standing in front of me.

"You asked to see me?" says a polite voice.

I look up into the face of a woman with softly waved white hair and kind blue eyes.

"Mrs. Rosehill?"

"Yes, I'm Brenda Rosehill and you are?"

"Cate Harlow." I hand her my card and pull out my license again. "I'm a private investigator and was wondering if I could speak with you about a missing person's case, actually a cold case. I'm looking for some information on someone who spent a lot of time in this library. A boy named Joshua McElroy. Can we go somewhere a little more private to talk?"

"Joshua McElroy?" She pauses thinking, looking at my card. "The teenager who went missing years ago?"

"Yes, ten years to be exact."

"Oh that was quite some time ago." She hands my card back to me. "I really don't know how I can help you. At the time of the disappearance I did speak with a police detective. Everyone here did. I don't think anything I said back then was very helpful at all."

"I'll only take a few minutes of your time," I say quickly and give her my serious face, no smile, all business.

"Well, all right, I guess if you really feel it's necessary. We can go to my office upstairs. It's quiet there."

We walk up the stairs located in the back of the library, Brenda Rosehill making small talk about the new improvements being made in the media center and the need for the fundraiser to be successful. I listen politely adding *ohs, uh-huhs*, and *reallys*, as needed.

At the top of the stairs, there's a large open area and off to one side is an office with a wall made of glass facing the media center. Brenda Rosehill brings me to that room.

"Please sit down." I sit. "Now, how is it that you think I can help you?"

I start right in. "Joshua McElroy was a kid who spent a great deal of time in this library, Mrs. Rosehill. I know it's been ten years since he went missing but his sister, Marie, has retained me to take the case and see if I can uncover anything that might lead to finding her brother."

Her eyes grow wide. "Finding him? You mean finding out what happened to him or actually *finding* him? Does she think it's possible that he's still alive?"

"Yes, she does."

"But why come to me, Ms. Harlow? I didn't really know Joshua. I told all that to the police. He was just a boy who came to the library, that's all. I don't know what else I can tell you."

"Tell me what you thought of him. Do you remember what he did here? Was he friendly, did he ever talk to you?" I look directly into her eyes.

"Well, he was a nice enough boy, very quiet. He liked to read in one of the window seats downstairs. I was librarian in that section until a few years ago. Yes, I do remember him coming in, choosing books, and sitting down in the window seat to read. The only times we ever spoke was when he asked me if a certain book was available."

"Did he do anything else besides read?"

She thinks for a few minutes then answers, "He did, actually. He liked to go through the old microfiche we had. You know those old files, well, now of course they're all on computer, but he did ask if he could go through them pretty often. Most of what he wanted he said was information about history. Oh, and old newspaper files, the ones you viewed on a high beam screen. He also spent time drawing pictures sometimes. I remember I told that to the investigating officer back then."

"Mrs. Rosehill, did he ever give any indication that anything was wrong or that something was bothering him? I know it's been ten years but think about his demeanor when he was here in the library."

Brenda Rosehill looks out the glass wall of her office. There are people coming in to use the computers. One woman waves at Brenda and holds up a flash drive.

"Seriously, he was just one of many children who came here to read or do research for book reports. We don't get many book readers today; everything you want is on the Internet now. Back then children still came to the library for real books.

"As for his demeanor, I never got the impression that anything was bothering him. The only thing I can say about the McElroy boy was that he was always polite and, as I said before, quiet. Always alone. Nothing else, I'm really sorry."

"That's okay. Mrs. Rosehill. It *has* been ten years and I guess you've seen a lot of kids pass through this building."

I stand and stretch and put my notebook back in my pocket. Not much here but what did I really expect? I give her my card again and tell her that if she does remember anything else to please call me. She says she will but I don't hold out much hope that will happen. Then again, you never know.

Leaving the library I decide to drive my Edge over to a nearby trattoria for an early lunch. On the way there I call my office answering machine and find that there have been no calls. Then I call Will's cell, get his voicemail, and leave a message asking if there're any new developments with the priest case and how his meeting with the archbishop went. Finally, I call Giles just because I need to talk and his assistant informs me that he's in the middle of an evidence examination and asks me if I can call back in a couple of hours. Within the span of fifteen minutes, I'm zero for three with my phone calls.

⤜⤛

"Catherine Harlow Private Investigations." I hear Myrtle's crisp, professional voice answer the phone. She sounds like a switchboard operator from an old black and white movie. "Yes, she is. May I ask who's calling? Thank you. Please hold and I'll put you through."

"Cate, there's a call from a Brenda Rosehill. Want to pick up?"

I pick up the phone on my desk. "Hello Mrs. Rosehill. This is Cate Harlow."

"Oh, Ms. Harlow, how are you? You said to call if I remembered anything about the McElroy boy and I did, well I sort of did, I guess you could say. It's just something small—I don't know if it will help you."

"It might, Mrs. Rosehill. I can't know what will help but it pays to cover all details. It can add more to what I've already got on the case, which isn't a whole lot at the moment. Tell me what you remembered."

"Well, this morning I was going through some DVDs for the young adult section that came in this week. That section is mostly for teens under the age of seventeen. We really should only have those DVDs which are rated G, you know, but some of them get a PG rating because the content shows some violence or mild sexual content. If a parent borrows it, it's okay. The kids can't get it on their own cards.

"Anyway, one of the movies was an R-rated one, *The Shawshank Redemption*. The subject matter is upsetting to say the least and I am thinking about placing it in the adult section. Strangely though, it sparked a small memory about Joshua McElroy."

"Joshua liked books on prisons?" I'm sitting forward, pen in hand.

"I don't know about that. But the movie made me remember what he *did* like to read. Most boys in their early teens back then liked easy-read books or books on action heroes, larger than life with super powers and all. Joshua wasn't like that. He read biographies, books with characters who wanted to escape something. You know, books where the character uses his wits to get away from an unpleasant situation or thwart an antagonist. Those were the types of books favored by Joshua. He was always borrowing them. Some of the storylines were filled with despair but the protagonist always seemed to win his freedom at the end."

My eyes go to the file on my desk: Josh's drawings of predators. What was he trying to escape? He didn't seem to have been bullied by anyone at school. His sister said that his home life was good and the police reports from the neighbors all stated the same thing basically. Nice, average family.

Of course Marie McElroy could be lying about there not being any family problems but I didn't think she was. Or maybe she didn't know what had happened. Sometimes one child is targeted by a parent and the siblings don't really know what's going on. It happens in cases of parental abuse. One kid is basically the whipping boy for a parent's rage while another one in the same home is never touched. But I didn't think that was the case either. You have to go with your gut instinct on certain things and I believed Marie when she said that their childhood had been wonderful.

"Mrs. Rosehill, if you remember a few titles of those books, can you email them to me? I'd appreciate that."

"I can do better than that. About twelve years ago we started using computer cataloguing for books. Just simple data entry but the book titles and the names of everyone who borrowed them, whether to take home or to read while in the library, were put in the data bank. You might not believe this but there were people who stole books back then. Anyway, I can check back to when Joshua McElroy came here to read in the library. I'll send the titles to you later today."

With a small twinge of guilt I think about my own small collection of stolen library books, thank her and say goodbye, feeling that I may possibly have a lead on why Josh disappeared.

❧

I've decided to work late tonight against Myrtle's strenuous objections. She feels that I leave myself open and vulnerable to all the dangers there are in a city when I work alone at night in my office.

"There could be people watching this building, someone who might be out for revenge because you worked on a case that sent them to prison."

"I'll be fine, Myrtle."

"Anyone can find out if you're the only one in the building after dark. There are all kinds of crazy people roaming the streets. You are simply a woman alone here."

"Actually I'm a woman alone who has a Smith & Wesson semi-automatic. Don't worry about me."

"Worry? Why should I worry! Oh, maybe because the fact is that you can be overpowered by a big man or a group of men out for who knows what?"

"The gun pretty much levels the playing field for me, Myrtle."

"What about walking to your car? You could get mugged. You'll be alone."

"Yup, just me and my gun all alone *together*. Don't worry. Please."

"I can stay here a little longer. We can order in or maybe go out for a late dinner. Harry won't mind. I'll buy. Better yet, I'll wait here until you're done and you can come home with me. Harry will enjoy seeing you." She looks expectantly at me. I don't budge. "Or I *could* call Detective Benigni to come babysit you."

I close my eyes.

"Myrtle, go home to Harry, let your dog out, make something to eat. Stop worrying needlessly because I will be fine. Okay?"

Big sigh and a lot of head shaking.

"All right, Catherine. But I'm going to call you around nine o'clock."

"Why nine o'clock?"

"Three reasons. One, to see if you're still *alive*, two, to tell you to be careful walking to your car, and three, to order you to get the hell home."

CHAPTER 8

THE LIST OF BOOK titles emailed to me by Brenda Rosehill is interesting, to say the least. Joshua was reading some very heavy stuff for a teen. All of the stories have to do with some form of abuse and the main character's plans for escape. True stories of people fleeing the Holocaust, *Papillon*, the biography of Henri Charriere's escape from Devil's Island, a book about convict Frank Morris who disappeared from Alcatraz and was never found; all of them detailing people in terrifying situations and how they managed to escape their captors.

Technically I could simply be looking at a book nerd's reading list. I personally devoured all the vampire and witch novels by Anne Rice. I liked the power exhibited by characters like *Lestat* and *Rowan*. What does that say about me? All it really says is that I like stories about vampires and witches.

But I have a very strong feeling that Joshua McElroy wasn't reading this genre for pleasure. The topics and the drawings of predators signal that something was happening to Josh, that he was being harmed in some way by someone who seemed to be invincible. A powerful force that he felt he had to escape. Who had such power over Joshua? Did this person murder Joshua and hide the body? All I seem to know right now is that there was someone Josh feared.

While pondering this question my cell phone rings. Without checking the caller ID, I answer. "Myrtle my darling, it's not nine o'clock yet. I'm fine; stop worrying about me. And for God's sake, don't call Benigni to babysit me."

"Why do you need a babysitter?" Will's unmistakable voice comes into my ear.

"Will? Sorry. I thought ..."

"Why is Myrtle checking up on you? Where are you?"

"I'm still at my office. She worries about me being here alone. Says there are crazy people roaming the streets."

"You're a big girl packing a gun. She doesn't have to worry about you."

"Yeah, well, I'm guessing she doesn't think my gun and I are tough enough. She and Harry are like overly protective surrogate parents."

"Right." He breathes out heavily. I know that sound.

"Listen I know I'm returning your call late but I didn't get a chance to call earlier. It's been a nuthouse here. Is there a full moon out or what? All the lunatics seem to be out today."

"It'll be full tomorrow. The loonies must have started a day early. What's new with your case?" I make sure that I say *your case* to let him feel he's in charge. "How goes it with the archbishop?"

"I think he'd like to have me excommunicated which doesn't mean a whole lot to me since I haven't stepped foot in church since I was twelve. That's another story, but on the whole I didn't take, or give, any bullshit. I was professional, polite, and made it clear that we're doing everything to solve the murder. He was pissed but I can't help that.

"By the way, there are no reports of missing priests, or ministers, or rabbis, or any clergy of *any* religion for that matter, in the Tri-State area. We're hitting the nursing homes tomorrow, but so far, nothing blips on the radar. No ID, no elderly missing persons, absolutely nothing."

"Someone has to know who this guy is, Will. The last body *did* turn out to have been a real priest so there's a good chance this one is too."

"I guess. We'll see. How's the cold case?"

"Still relatively cold."

"Sorry, but if I know you, Cate, you'll keep digging until you find something. You're tenacious."

I hear him blow out his breath. That sound plus the compliment he gave me means he's preoccupied. Something's on his mind that has nothing to do with his case or mine. On the job he's tough, relentless, and shows no emotion. If anything is bothering him it has to be something personal.

"What's the matter?" I cautiously ask.

"Nothing, why?"

"Come on now, Will, you're talking to *me*. I know something's bothering you."

"You really want to know?"

"I just asked you, didn't I?"

"You did. Okay." Another heavy expelled breath.

"What?" I ask impatiently.

"Francesca called. She's in town."

"So, that's good, right?" Francesca is his mother. "You enjoy seeing your mom."

"I do, but that's not the issue. She wants to go out to *dinner*."

His exhaled breath practically whistles in my ear over the phone.

"Sorry, but how is that an issue? Dinner's usually a pleasant thing for most people."

"She wants to go out to dinner with both of *us*."

"Shit!"

"My thought exactly."

You can talk all you want about how daughters-in-law, especially *ex*-daughters-in-law, have horrible relationships with their mothers-in-law but that is not the case with Will's mom and me. We actually *like* each other. Francesca Sutton Benigni is a woman of taste and intelligence who is beautiful, polite and has a dry sense of humor. She's a highly paid art historian who is active and on the board of the Metropolitan Museum of Art. She has residences in Naples, Florida and New York. Will got his share of good looks and charm from the maternal side of the family, believe me. She made me feel comfortable the minute I met her.

The problem isn't that I don't want to have dinner with her because Will and I are divorced. She was very gracious about it and didn't place blame on either one of us. In fact, she never spoke about it. How's that for a nice mother-in-law?

The problem is that, the two times I did see her after our divorce, she unintentionally made me feel *uncomfortable*. She will ever so subtly mention that *people she knows* have gotten back together after a divorce. Francesca will tell me about a distant cousin who reconciled with her ex-husband, or a friend's son who is back with his wife. I get the feeling that she thinks her son and I will eventually realize we made a horrible mistake, fall into each other's arms, and rush off to get remarried. *And that is not going to happen.*

"When?" I finally say into the phone after a long silence on both our parts.

"Saturday night. She's only here for a week. Look, I can say you're busy with something else. Give me an excuse, Cate. I know it's awkward."

It would be easy to give Will an excuse, to say that I'm working a case Saturday night, or to give that wonderfully ambiguous excuse called *I have other plans* but I suddenly feel sorry for him. He doesn't need to be alone with Francesca answering questions about his life and his dubious future as a lawyer. The hurt feelings I had for him after the divorce are fighting with the warm memories I have of us when we were first so hotly in love. One sweet memory in particular is of him making me French toast when I was horribly sick with the flu. After I ate he gently held me until I fell into a feverish sleep. Mentally I sigh. Okay.

"Tell her I'll be there. Just give me the time and the place."

Big pause and a very long relieved expulsion of breath.

"Francesca and I can pick you up at your place."

"Uh, no, that's okay. I've got a million things to do Saturday. I might be at my office during the day. When I get home I don't want to have to rush around getting ready while you two sit waiting for me in the brownstone. It's better if I meet you. Which restaurant and what time?"

The truth is that I have no desire to have Francesca sitting in my minimally decorated living room feeling sorry for me. She'll think that I can't afford furniture since the divorce. Meeting in a neutral zone is better.

"Regina Margherita, at eight o'clock."

"That's fine. No problem, I'll be there."

"Good. Francesca will be happy."

At least one of us will be, I think.

With the issue about Francesca resolved, we talk for a few more minutes about all the crazies who seem on the prowl tonight. Will sounds much more relaxed and even tries to turn Myrtle's comment about crazy people roaming the streets to his advantage. Suddenly he becomes pseudo-concerned with my safety.

"Cate, listen, maybe Myrtle is right about you being alone. There *are* nutcases around. I mean if you want, I can swing by your office to, uh, babysit you. I could follow you home, make sure you're all right, maybe come in for a while. I miss you, you know what I mean?"

I know exactly what he means.

"No, stop that, I'm fine," I say annoyed. "Damn! Do you never stop thinking with your male equipment? And besides, you're out of the picture. You know I'm involved with someone else now."

"That's not going to last." I hear him laugh. "Giles is your interim man, the guy you date until you get back together with the man you really want."

What an ego he has! It annoys me no end that he chooses to believe I'm not serious about Giles.

"How the hell do you know it's not serious between Giles and me?"

"I just know."

Omigod! He *is* relentless; I'll give him that

"And my male *equipment,* as you put it, is thinking of you

nude right now. *I* can't help what it does."

"Well tell it to think of someone else."

"You can't say that you didn't like what we had in the sex department, Cate. I know you did. You certainly *sounded* like you did. All that moaning and all the ..."

"I loved it, okay? God, *Will, please, stop already!"* I practically shout into the phone. "I'm leaving in about an hour. *And*, as you said, I'm a big girl packing a gun. I can take care of myself. Don't mess with me. May I remind you that I am one tough woman; *you* think about *that*."

"Uh-huh. Okay." He laughs again. "But let me give *you* a reminder from our past, Cate."

"What now?"

"You were never too tough for me to spank. *You* think about *that*."

⋙

An hour after our phone conversation I'm still in my office. I've got the McElroy cold case box on top of the filing cabinet. I decide to go through it once more before I go home. It's late and I'm hungry and, *damn it*, I wished Will hadn't annoyed me. He has to start all the sexual chemistry crap. It's never-ending.

The backpack reveals nothing new. I root around in the contents and my fingers brush the key. I thought that it could be a locker key but now I don't know. Different schools do things differently. My old high school used the combination locks, no keys needed. They were a pain to open between classes, but they worked. My cousin, who went to a different school, had locks that required a key, which he was always losing.

I pick up the key and look at it, rolling it around in my hand. Just because it was in his backpack doesn't mean that it is a locker key. The person detailing the contents may have just assumed it was. I decide that tomorrow I'll check with Marie and find out if their school had key locks. If the answer is no, I'll have to find out what this key opened and how it could have an impact on the cold case.

Before I leave I walk silently to the window and check on my doves. They are all nestled together sleeping securely in their nest on a fifth-floor fire escape. If Joshua McElroy said baby birds need protection, here's a perfect example. My doves certainly seem protected. I grab my bag, put my gun in the waistband of my jeans and walk out making sure the double locks on the old, battered oak door of *Catherine Harlow, Private Investigations* are securely in place.

Despite Myrtle's dire warnings, I make it to my car just fine. There are some rough-looking people walking on the street and a group of young toughs hanging around on the corner. I keep my right hand loose and close to my gun. I pass the homeless man who regularly washes my car windows whether they need it or not and take out the twenty I give him once a week. He is what my grandmother's generation would have called "slow," a nice person who got handed a hard life.

"Buy food, Bo," I say as I hand him the money. He smiles a toothless grin and nods his head. He'll probably buy a couple of sandwiches and some packaged Twinkies to go along with any beer, but at least it will be something. There's a story my grandmother once told me about how people in old ethnic neighborhoods took care of their own. No one went hungry or without basic life necessities if they were down on their luck. There was no need for public assistance. Helping each other was a way of life.

I know that Bo won't go to any shelters or any city places that might help him out. He's a man on the street for a reason and doesn't want to risk losing what he considers his freedom. I'd like to think that my small contribution keeps him from being hungry. I hope so anyway.

⚓

"I want to see you again. We were so close once, do you remember? How about dinner next week? It will be my treat, all right, Joey?"

"Sure, Father. That would be fine. I'll pick you up here, five o'clock."

CHAPTER 9

THWACK! THE BALL HITS the wall and comes racing back at me. Thwack! I backhand it with all my strength the way my dad taught me. Back and forth I make myself run as I deliberately hit the ball hard and to the opposite sides of the practice wall. Sweat runs down my face and the front of my sports bra. I've been doing this for an hour but still feel the tension from my conversation last night with Will. Thwack! I ram the ball with controlled precision at the wall and it flies back at me only to get backhanded again and again. Thwack! Thwack! Tennis makes me feel in charge, and I need that feeling to be strong in my business and in my personal life.

I try to play tennis twice a week, and if there's no one available to play against I go to the wall. Lately it's been me versus the wall, but that's fine; sometimes it's even better. Not many people use the wall and I don't have to wait for a court to be free.

After smashing the ball one last time, I bend forward exhaling, put my hands on my knees, and feel the pleasant rise of endorphins. My legs ache in a good way.

I check the old tower clock near the tennis courts and see that it's not even nine yet. I'm meeting Marie McElroy at the hair salon around noon to take her to lunch, so I've got plenty of time to go home, shower, dress, and stop by my office to pick up Josh's key. Also plenty of time to call Will and see if there's any progress on the priest's case. I grab my racquets, retrieve my balls, and head out of the park for the short walk to the brownstone.

A short distance from the courts my phone vibrates from the side pocket of my tennis bag. I fish it out and see that it's a text from Giles.

"FYI body w/priest collar ID'd."

⌇

I feel a little exposed in my tennis skirt and top as I'm speeding down to the morgue through early morning traffic. No time to change because I need to talk to Giles before info gets to Detective Will Benigni. I know Giles gave me a heads-up on this one because of the body I found last year. The thing is, he can only hold the information he has for so long. There's a strict protocol involved. If he ID'd the body through forensics then he is bound by law to give the presiding detective on the case all the information as soon as possible. He can't email, fax, or text anyone outside the official investigation any specifics until, and unless, it's cleared by Will or his captain. He's risking a lot by notifying me first.

There's no parking in the lot by the morgue so I drive around and find an empty space near a warehouse five blocks away. There's a sign in front of the space: *Delivery Zone No Parking Any Time*. But I can't worry about that now. I sprint easily down the street on my well-exercised legs, congratulating myself for having spent time at the tennis wall and arrive at the morgue to see Giles waiting outside for me.

He looks at my outfit, nods his approval, then motions me to the side of the building where we'll be out of direct sight of anyone coming out of, or going into, the front door. Giles wastes no time.

"His name is Francis Xavier Murphy, seventy-two, and he was a Roman Catholic priest out of New Jersey. We went through dental records. His last known address was in Washington Township in Morris County; he was living in a rented apartment in a building owned by the Diocese of Paterson. I have no other info except for the method of murder which you already know." He pauses and looks at me.

"I have to call Will and give him the information. Be careful Catherine."

As he walks away, I'm already bending to retrieve the crumpled scrap of paper he dropped by my feet. There's an address written on it. I palm it and begin making my way back to my car. Another priest who lived outside the confines of a rectory or religious community. Now that is another link to both murders.

⌇

Some whistles, *oh mamas*, and *hey babes* from construction workers along the road greet me as I walk back to my car. I casually wave a hand in acknowledgement. Better to make nice to them than to cop an attitude. They're harmless.

A block away from where I parked I see a delivery truck in the street in front of my car, which is being ticketed as I approach. A man is standing on the loading dock platform looking angry as hell. *Damn it!* I pull out my PI license and run over to the cop placing the ticket under my windshield wiper.

"Officer, I was on official business and really had nowhere to park. Can you give me a break on this one? Please?"

"You're kidding, right? Playing tennis ain't official business. Sorry, read the sign lady." He jerks his head in the direction of the loading platform. "Just count yourself lucky the owner over there didn't ask to have your ride towed. Yet."

I glance at the guy on the platform and he flips me the finger. I mutter Will's favorite obscenity at him then turn back to the officer. I hate myself for what I'm going to say next, but a ticket blocking access to a business can cost me a lot and my checking account is low.

"Would it make a difference if I told you I'm related to Detective Will Begnini of the Twelfth?"

"Related? To Begnini? How?" My ex's name got his interest.

Will's reputation is well known and other cops respect him. "You his sister?"

"Um, no," I say too quickly without thinking. Stupid! To make things easy for myself I should have just said yes. "His ..."

"Cousin?"

Damn!

"Girlfriend?"

"No, um ... I'm ... his ... ex-wife."

"Oh, yeah? Ex-wife, huh? Well, *that* alone should make me rip up the ticket right now, shouldn't it!" The cop lets out a snort of laughter. "Honey," he leans in closer to me, "No cop worth his badge has ever asked me to fix a ticket for an *ex-anyone*, most *especially* for an ex-*wife*. Cop divorces are seldom friendly deals, you should know that."

"Seriously we *are* still friends, sort of, anyway."

"Yeah, right, and I'm taking both my first and second ex-wives out for a steak dinner with my new twenty-year-old hot-ter-than-hell girlfriend. Sorry, miss, no deal." He tips his cap and pulls the ticket from my windshield. Handing it to me he says, "Have a nice day," gets in his vehicle and drives away.

The minute he's gone the man on the platform jumps down and starts walking over toward me.

"Hey! Bitch! Move your fuckin' car before I have it towed!"

With that ringing in my ears, and a ticket for 150 bucks, which I don't have, I get in my car and head back to my brown-stone.

And my day had started out with so much promise!

⌘

I feel a little better driving to meet Marie at her salon. A change out of my tennis clothes did wonders for my mood and I decided to deal with the ticket tomorrow. Maybe Will can help me get out of it, who knows?

Back at the brownstone I had changed into crème-colored linen pants, a sheer cobalt blue blouse with a crème camisole, and blue wedge sandals. I pulled my hair back with pearl combs.

I was taking Marie to The Curry Club, the best Indian restaurant on Long Island. Dressing nicely was a must. It was my decision to take her out for lunch and then ask her about the key. Her sadness brings out a protective instinct in me, and I want to do something that will maybe put a smile on her face. Good food can do that.

The key that was in Josh's backpack is in my handbag. I retrieved it from my office on the way to meet Marie. While I was there, and before Myrtle came in, I Googled "Washington Township" and found the address of the apartment of the victim/priest. I also did a search on the Diocese of Paterson, New Jersey. I sent all of it to my cell phone so I could check into it later. I also left a note on Myrtle's computer screen to forward any calls to my cell since I would be out for much of the day.

The salon where Marie works is pleasantly surprising. It is more upscale than I had anticipated. She's waiting near the door for me and tells me that she just has to do a blowout and asks me if I mind waiting. I tell her no and then say that I'm going outside to walk around a little bit.

Marie works a distance from her home. With the cute shops and several small stores, the area here may pretend to have a small town feel but make no mistake this is not a small town. Queens is the easternmost of the five boroughs of New York City, the largest in area, and the second-largest in population. It's a mix of Italian-Americans, Irish-Americans, Indians, West Indians, Greek, Chinese, and a few other ethnic groups. It has a unique flavor all its own

Marie and Josh lived in a small Irish-American neighborhood that was a town unto itself. It is bordered by familiarity; Madison Methodist Church to the west, St. Matthew's Catholic Church to the east, the library smack in-between them. Stores, the Presbyterian Church and day care, little boutiques, public and private schools, and homes make up the rest of the area. Just about everything is within walking distance.

"I'm sorry that you had to wait," says a flustered Marie meeting me as I am walking back to the salon. "This was a last minute appointment from a regular customer and I didn't want to say no." A brief smile passes over her face as she says, "The fact that she tips really well too is a plus."

That tiny smile touches a chord in me and I say, "I understand that, no problem, Marie. Let's go eat, okay?"

On the way to the restaurant I deliberately talk about things not related to her brother's case. Everything is inconsequential and safe: cars, the surprisingly warm weather, and even the price of gas. Finally I pull into the parking lot of The Curry Club and hand my keys to a waiting valet.

Inside the restaurant, we're ushered into a room with colorful décor and seated near a large fish tank containing brilliantly colored fish. We order two teas and settle in with the menus. I ask her if she'd like to split two appetizers and we decide on one order each of vegetable samosas, and chicken pakora plus two bowls of lentil soup. As her main course Marie asks for shrimp tikka masala and I get shrimp vindalu.

After we finish the soup and appetizers I bring out the key from my wallet and place it on the table. Marie doesn't react. The key doesn't seem to mean anything to her.

"Marie, this key was found in Josh's school backpack. Any idea what it's for?"

"That was in his backpack? I didn't know that."

"Do you know what it's for?" I press.

She picks it up to examine it and then shakes her head.

"No. I never saw it before. Are you sure it's Josh's?"

"Yes, it was in his backpack. The evidence officer thought it was a locker key. Did you have key locks at your high school?"

"We did, but that's not a locker key. It's too small. The keys for the lockers were thicker and longer, almost like a house key."

"So you have no idea what lock this would open then." I palm the key then place it on the table in front of Marie. I want to make sure the key doesn't jog some memory of her seeing Josh with it before I put it away. But she just looks at it and truly doesn't seem to recognize it.

Our conversation is interrupted by the arrival of the main

course and I put the key back in wallet. Eating, my mother would have said, shouldn't be disturbed by anything that isn't dinner-table conversation. The shrimp vindalu is excellent and I make a point of raving about it. Marie seems to enjoy her dish too and we spend an hour just eating and talking about food.

Over a shared dessert of fruit kheer and strongly brewed American coffee, Marie tells me about her and Josh's high school, Roosevelt High.

"You know, we went to a Catholic elementary school and our parents assumed we'd go to that school's brother school, St. Matthew High School, but Josh didn't want to go there."

"Oh? Why was that?"

"He loved art and science and Roosevelt High had just built a fantastic science wing with all the latest tech stuff. Actually for that time the equipment they had was pretty advanced. Their art center too—it was state-of-the-art. Josh was a real scholar. He convinced Mom and Dad that the advanced courses at Roosevelt High were what he needed if he wanted to get into a good college. So, they agreed to send both of us there as long as we promised that we'd attend CCD classes, you know, classes about Catholicism. I mean, we're a real Irish Catholic family; that was a big thing for our parents. We went every Wednesday night even though Joshua told me that he didn't believe in God anymore. I never told my parents; it would have hurt them. I thought it was just what the priests call a crisis of faith and he'd start believing again but ... he didn't. Still, no one could have been a better or kinder person than Joshua."

That little smile flickers across her face again. She looks pretty when she smiles and I find myself thinking that if the case concerning her brother can come to some type of closure, maybe she'll be able to find things in life that will make her smile again.

"What about your high school?" she asks me. "Where did you go?"

"Well, I went to a private all-girls school, but it wasn't a parochial one. My parents taught at The Brearley School in the city and the tuition was pretty much waived for teachers' kids.

Anyway, it was lowered significantly, so my parents were able to afford it."

"Was it a big school? Did you have a lot of friends there?"

"No, it wasn't big. I did have a couple of close friends. Some of the girls were snobby but on the whole it was a good experience. The best thing for me was that I was on the tennis team and I was very good. I won trophies for the school. That earned everybody's respect."

"What about college?" she asks me wistfully. "I always wanted to go to college, but after what happened and all, well, you know."

"NYU; major in linguistics, minor in Medieval history. I used to be what is called a linguistic forensics expert. Basically, I translated legalese into layman's terms. Being around lawyers and reading court cases got me interested in investigating. Eventually I got my license as a private investigator and opened my own business. I've never regretted it."

"You're brave. I could never do that."

"Either brave or crazy."

I motion the server over to refill our cups and to bring the check. When Marie begins to ruffle through her handbag, I stop her immediately.

"This is my treat. *I* invited you, Marie." Then, to make her not feel as if she couldn't afford it, I add, "Next time we go out, you can treat me."

She nods and puts her bag to the side.

As I'm placing my debit card on the little tray with the bill, I ask Marie about her high school experience.

"Did a lot of your friends go to Roosevelt High or did they go to St. Matthew?"

"Oh I'd say just about a small group of our friends went to Roosevelt. The tuition at St. Matt's was steeper than our elementary school had been, so some families just decided to send their kids to public high. We were blue-collar families and money was usually tight. I liked Roosevelt. It was small and I got to know so many of the kids there."

"And Josh?"

"He liked Roosevelt too. He said he was looking forward to starting fresh in a new place. Even though we had some of the same friends there, Josh said that going to a new school was like being given a chance to become a new person. That's when he began insisting that everyone call him Joshua. He wouldn't answer to any family pet names."

"No nicknames, huh? I know about that. My ex-mother-in-law, who is a very nice woman, will not allow anyone to call her Fran. Her name is Francesca and she politely, but firmly, insists on being called her full name."

Marie nods and gives me the ghost smile again.

While we're waiting for the server to return with my debit card and receipt, we talk about life after school, working, why people choose certain professions, and finally, men.

"Are you dating anyone special?" I ask her as I sign the receipt and put cash out for a tip. I hope she is because she seems as if she's alone too much and she needs distraction.

"No, not really. Sometimes I feel that I can't really do anything for me until I know for sure about Joshua. I feel, I don't know ..."

"Guilty?"

"Yes! I do. I feel guilty for being alive, even for being here enjoying a lunch when I don't know if Josh has food or if he's ..."

I grab her hand across the table.

"Listen to me Marie. It's normal to feel this way. You don't know where Joshua is or even if he's alive and it's eating you up inside. You want some answers for what's happened in your life and up until now you haven't gotten them. You *still* haven't gotten them but I'm working on it, believe me.

"I'm not going to tell you to go on with your life as the police did, even though their intentions were good. But I am going to tell you that if you enjoy yourself, if you smile or laugh, it doesn't mean that you've forgotten your brother or abandoned his memory.

"You're human and we humans are fragile. You need to get

out and live a little, just a little so you don't keep dying over and over again in your heart."

She thinks about what I'm saying for what seems a long time while the server politely waits to get his tip.

"I did meet someone," she says shyly, "Someone who just moved here a few months ago. He seems nice but I don't know. He asked for my phone number and I gave it to him. We talk pretty often on the phone and we've met a couple of times at the movies. I want to ask him over for dinner but I feel kind of scared. Like maybe he'll accept to be polite but then he'll make an excuse and not come. I'm not very good about dating."

I grab my handbag and get up. "Ask him," I tell her. "You won't lose anything by asking and you might be pleasantly surprised. Where men are concerned, Marie, it doesn't pay to be shy. This is the twenty-first century; women are just as much the pursuer as the pursued."

"What if he says no? Then what?"

"Then he says no and you look elsewhere. His saying no is not a big deal; don't make it one. There are a lot of guys out there, Marie."

"Do *you* have a ... a man in your life?" she asks shyly.

"More like two men," I smile and am pleased when my statement brings a giggle from her.

"Wow! I guess, well then ... I guess I should say ... have fun!" She blushes to the roots of her hair and we both laugh over her unexpected comment.

Back in the car I ask Marie if she'd mind if I came over to her house tomorrow morning around ten and looked through the house and property. There might be something, some box, something hidden somewhere that the key in my handbag would open.

"Oh, sure. But I won't be home. One of the other girls is having her car serviced and I promised her I'd pick her up. She lives a distance from me so I'm leaving really early. You can go over today while I'm at work if you'd like. I don't have a problem with you looking around the house when I'm not there. I trust you."

Trust. Such a simple word but one with one helluva powerful meaning. Who did Josh trust? I wonder.

"Thanks Marie but I have to do some other work this afternoon. Tomorrow will be much better for me. Is that okay with you? I'll come pick up the house key at the salon."

"Tomorrow is good and you don't have to come all the way out here for the house key. I'll leave it with Mr. O'Leary who lives next door, the house on the left side. But listen, when you go to get the key just make sure that you tell him you're really busy or he'll talk your ear off. He remembers *everything* from years ago and he's very sharp, even if he is ninety-four."

She thanks me for lunch and I watch her walk back to the door of the salon and disappear inside.

As I drive toward the city I'm thinking that, if I'm lucky tomorrow, maybe Mr. O'Leary will remember something important from ten years ago.

CHAPTER 10

THE PHONE NUMBER I got for the address in Washington Township rings and rings. Finally a generic, computerized voice says, "No one can answer your call right now. Please leave a message." So I do.

"This is Cate Harlow. My number is 212.555.2992. This is in reference to Francis Murphy. Please call me as soon as possible."

My next call is to the Paterson Diocese main office. If the diocese owned the apartment where Father Murphy lived that could mean that he was a priest in one of the many churches in the area. The fact that the info Giles gave me has Murphy living in an apartment and not a rectory isn't necessarily a problem, but it bears checking out. I'm going to say that I've lost touch with Father Murphy and want to contact him. It's possible that they don't know that he's dead yet.

Voicemail picks up and of course I get a menu. I listen to the extensions for various business or church needs until I come to the one for clergy, then press the digit and hear, "One moment please."

A man's voice answers "Rectory. This is Father Richard Boyd, how may I help you?"

He sounds so boyish. I have a hard time calling him *Father*.

"Good afternoon, Father. My name is Cate Harlow and I wonder if you can help me. I'm looking for a priest from your diocese, Father Francis Murphy."

"Who?"

"Father Murphy, Francis Xavier Murphy. Do you know how I can reach him? It's important."

"I'm afraid you've gotten the name wrong. You probably mean Father *Farrell* Xavier Murphy of St. Ann's. I know him. I can get his number if you can hang on for a couple of minutes."

"No, wait, Father. The first name *is* Francis. The person I'm looking for is named Father *Francis* Xavier Murphy. He's about seventy-two. I'd like to speak with him if you can tell me what church he's serving." There are probably more than a few Irish Catholic priests with the middle name Xavier and the last name Murphy.

I hear pages from a book being rapidly turned.

"You know, I don't see his name in the diocese listings. Murphy *is* a common name. I'm in the process of installing a new accounting program in the computer system so I might not have all the names and parishes. Also, I've only been here five years so it is possible that I wouldn't know of him.

"But, listen—if you give me a minute I'll get Father Bill, one of the other priests, to help you. He knows all the 'old men of the cloth,' as we affectionately call them. If this other Father Murphy is still on active service, he'll know, and if he's retired he may be at our retirement home in Ocean County. Hold on."

Elevator music plays statically as I hold. You'd think that in a church office they would have some type of religious music playing, but I'm being entertained by Fleetwood Mac on one of those easy listening stations favored by Myrtle.

Finally I hear, "This is Father Bill Mulcahy. May I help you?" Older, pleasant voice, maybe he knows Murphy. I hear laughter and talking in the background. It sounds busy.

"Yes, good afternoon, Father. I was told by the priest who answered that you might be able to help me find a clergyman I knew years ago, a man in his early seventies. I've lost contact with him over the years." Then, to enlist his help I charmingly add, "I heard that you know all the old men of the cloth."

He laughs and says jovially, "When you've been around as long as I have, you do tend to know just about everyone in the diocese. I'm pretty sure I can help you. Who are you looking to find?"

"Oh I hope so, Father. I'm looking for a Father Francis Xavier Murphy. Do you know where I might be able to contact him? I would so love to speak with him." I make myself sound as sweet and innocent as I can but there's dead silence on the other end. "Father Mulcahy? Hello?"

"Who is this?" The pleasant voice has suddenly gone cold and has a cutting, straight edge to it. Something's not right, I can feel it.

"My name is Cate Harlow and I'm trying to find Father *Francis* Xavier Murphy." Then I add a concerned, "Is he all right?"

More silence, then, "Are you with SNAP?"

SNAP? I have no idea what he means but I quickly jot down the acronym, s-n-a-p.

"No I'm not. I don't even know what that is," I say truthfully.

There's a long pause at the other end. I hear a whispered conversation but I can only make out the words, "no knowledge", "we can't", "don't say anything…"

"Look," I say, "I don't know about any *snap* but I do know that I need to contact Father Francis Xavier Murphy. Can you help me or not?"

"No, I can't help you. There's no Father Francis Murphy here and no one knows anything about this, this *Francis* Murphy. Don't call again. Good day."

"Wait. Just tell me …" A sharp click lets me know the call has ended.

Two seconds after the priest ends our brief conversation, Myrtle puts a call through from Will.

"Cate? Are you busy with that cold case or can you take a minute and grab a Timothy's macchiato coffee with me? I'm two minutes from your office."

"I've got time. I'll go right down and wait for you."

I hang up and tell Myrtle I'm going out for coffee with Will and ask her if she wants me to bring anything back for her.

"No, I've got my iced tea." She smiles at me approvingly. "You look very pretty today. You should dress up more often. It looks professional and attractive."

I smile back. "Yeah, well, maybe. I *do* feel pretty." I sigh and shake my head. "But I'd hate to go finding a dead body dressed like this and in these shoes!"

⚞

"What's up?" I say as I settle into the nice leather seat of Will's unmarked car. He looks at me. "You look great. I like your hair like that." He's got that look on his face that I know so well from the past.

"Thanks." I buckle my seat belt and look down so we don't make eye contact.

Timothy's Coffee Emporium is about ten minutes from my office, but with afternoon traffic it takes thirty. Will puts his police light on the roof of his car and parks by a *No Parking* sign. Of course, I think; he's allowed to park wherever he wants. We decide to sit outside and I grab an empty table while Will goes to get our coffees. He returns with two steaming large cups topped with whipped cream and drizzled with caramel, and we sit and inhale the aroma. Then he looks over at me and says, "I probably shouldn't be doing this but I said I'd think about letting you know what's going on with the murder case, that priest collar one you're so interested in. I've decided to give you the info from the ME's office."

Oh goody! I think. Tell me what I *already* know.

"Thanks, Will. What did you find out?"

"Well, he is—was a real priest. Father Francis X. Murphy. Lived in New Jersey. There's an address, so I'll be going out there tomorrow. I think he was somehow connected to the Paterson Diocese. Anyway, the diocese owned the place where he lived so there's some type of connection there."

"That's all?" I could tell you more darlin' Will, but hauling your charming butt out to New Jersey tomorrow just might be good for you. New Jersey makes you appreciate NYC all the more, yes it does.

"Yeah, but it's enough to go on for now. What about you and that missing kid case?"

"Oh you know, working the case. Might have a lead. I have a key from evidence that the sister doesn't recognize. It's not a locker key as the evidence people first surmised. Looks like it might be a key to some box or something. I'm going out to the McElroy property tomorrow to snoop around. With," I add, "the sister's full permission."

"All right. If I can help in any way, let me know."

"Fix my ticket."

"What ticket? What the hell are you talking about?"

"The one I got for illegally parking in front of a loading dock. I told the cop we were related."

"Related how?" he asks suspiciously.

"I told him the truth. I said I was your ex-wife but that we're still friends. He didn't buy the friends part though."

Will laughs. "Damn right he didn't buy it. You of all people should know that cop divorces are never friendly."

"That's what the officer said." I look at him and say teasingly, "You mean you're *not* my friend?"

"Oh I am," he says watching me spoon whipped cream into my mouth. "But I'd like to be more than just a friend, Cate."

I think about that statement.

"You just feel that way because Francesca's coming to town and you want to put on a good front for her."

"Maybe, but it's not only Francesca. Her coming here did get me thinking, but I do miss you. Don't *you* ever miss what we had?"

"Will, what we had was chaos, you know that. I will grant you that the sex was phenomenal, but that's only one part of what makes a marriage work. Face it; I'm not what you want in a partner. And truthfully, you're a good man but you're not good for *me*."

"It's possible we were too young to appreciate our differences, you ever think about that? We're older now. Maybe we could learn to see the true value of being different and work through it."

"Stop right there. I can't see us working through any differences. All I can see is that we'd be just fine in the sex department, but that we'd be at each other's throats the rest of the time. It wouldn't be good for either of us."

He sips his coffee and looks out at the streets. "Yeah, maybe you're right."

"I am right." I touch his hand and his fingers close hopefully over mine. "Besides, I'm with someone else now."

He flashes a sarcastic look and pulls his hand away. "Oh, right. I forgot. Doctor Death."

"Not fair, Will." I say gently but firmly. "So not fair."

"Sorry. It just pisses me off that's all. Whatever it is with him and you, I just can't see it. But who am I to say anything, huh?" He looks at me then out to the street again. "Anyway, it's your life such as it is."

I concentrate on finishing my coffee. It has to be a male thing, seriously; he knows I'm with Giles and he has this sudden urge to get me permanently back into his life? Until I started dating Giles a few months ago that wasn't the case at all. Oh, he always joked around about us getting together, and made numerous sexual innuendoes about our *fun* times. In fact I have been seduced into bed by his charm twice since our divorce, although technically we weren't in an actual *bed.* But he never said what he's said today: *We were too young to appreciate each other's differences ... maybe now that we're older we could learn to see the true value of our differences.* What crap! I feel as if my life has suddenly turned into a soap opera.

"How's Debbie?" I ask, remembering how she poured wine into my pricey crystal glasses.

"Married and pregnant with her second. It's been more than five years, Cate."

I have nothing to say. I guess she didn't wait around for our divorce to be finalized so she could have Will as her own.

"Oh, well good for her," I sniff. I know I sound bitchy, but I don't care.

We don't talk for a few minutes then Will's phone breaks the silence.

"Benigni. Yeah, I got it. I'll be there." He turns to me. "I've got to get back to the station. Finish your coffee then I'll drive you back to your office."

"Is it urgent?"

"No, just something about a call I made to the Diocese of Paterson. Someone there returned my call. The dispatcher says the guy sounded pretty pissed. He's saying they don't know this priest and then asked what organization was looking for him. Says we're the second call they got today about this so-called non-existent priest. He didn't elaborate, but it sounds weird. I have to go over a few things at my desk and then call them back."

I don't say anything about the word *SNAP,* but I make another mental note to Google it back at my office. There's something not quite kosher, for want of a better word, about no one having *any* knowledge of the murdered priest.

After I get out of his car in front of my office building, Will gets out of the driver's side, walks around to the sidewalk, and leans against the passenger's side door. He was not too talkative on the drive back and now just says, "I need to start going to the gym again. My legs feel cramped from sitting in the car. Tomorrow's going to be a real joy going to Paterson, New Jersey."

"I know," I answer him, "It will probably take almost your entire day."

"Hell, yeah, well, those are the perks of being in my business. Hope there's a good diner out there."

"In New Jersey? The state has more diners per capita than any other," I laugh. "You'll find one."

"If I get any more info today on the murdered priest, I'll call you, okay?"

"Sure. Me too. If I hear anything that is."

"Promise?"

I nod my head and turn to say goodbye. His arms go around me as he catches me in a full-mouth kiss. I'm surprised but don't resist. His mouth is sweet and warmly familiar and it feels really good to be in his arms. The kiss is passionate and long. I hear someone walking on the street whistle and call out, "'Attaboy! Go for it!"

When he pulls me against his chest, I rest there inhaling his delicious scent, listening to his heartbeat, and feeling the heat from his body. His *male equipment* is rising to the occasion and I feel a little dizzy. My body automatically presses into his and I remember that hot need I always have for him. Damn! He feels so good.

"I better go," I whisper into his shirt, but I don't move. After a long few minutes of pressing together, he pulls back and lets me go.

"Yeah, um, okay." I see him do a quick adjustment of his pants and I smile. "I'll call you if there's anything new tomorrow." His voice sounds husky and low.

"Great. Thanks. Bye, Will."

He doesn't say anything more, just gives me a half wave as he walks around to the driver's door and gets in his car. Then he's gone.

⁂

Upstairs in my office Myrtle is talking on the phone and she hands it to me as I walk in.

"Hello, this is Cate Harlow."

"Cate?" I hear a breathless Marie on the other end.

"Hi Marie. What's up?"

"I just called you to tell you that I did what you said I should do. That man I told you about? His name is David. Anyway, I asked him to come for dinner Saturday and guess what?"

"He said yes?"

"Oh, I'm sorry; you must think I'm an idiot to call about this. I mean this is your place of business, but well, you were so nice to give me advice at lunch and I wanted to let you know that I took it and it worked! He *did* say yes."

"I'm happy for you, Marie, really. And don't ever feel that you can't call here just to talk. It may be a place of business but I'm always available for more than that."

"Oh gosh, thank you. I ... I ... thanks again." I hear her sigh and then she says, "Oh and I *do* have a bit of business to tell you. I asked Mr. O'Leary to hold the key for you so just go over there tomorrow morning. It's the house to the left of mine, you know, as you're facing my front door, the one on your left side. He'll be there."

"Thanks Marie. I'll talk to you soon."

"Thank *you*, Cate," she says softly before hanging up.

∗

"It's so nice to just drive for awhile. Where are we going, Joey?"

CHAPTER 11

WE ARE SNAP, THE Survivors Network of those Abused by Priests. We are the largest, oldest, and most active support group for women and men wounded by religious authority figures (priests, bishops, deacons, nuns, and others). We are an independent and confidential organization, with no connections with the church or church officials. We are also a non-profit, certified 501 (c) (3) organization and we are here to help.

SNAP was founded by Chicago's Barbara Blaine in 1988. Since then, SNAP has helped thousands of survivors. We offer support in person (via monthly self-help group meetings in chapters across the country), over the phone, online, and twice a year at national meetings.

I'm sitting at the computer desk in my living room waiting for Will. After reading about this abuse survivors' organization, I left my office early and called him.

There's a lot more on the SNAP website including personal statements made by the survivors. Their stories are chilling. Childhood innocence is such a precious thing and these degenerates in the clergy stole it from their victims. I think back to my own sheltered childhood. There were times when I felt my Mom and Dad sheltered me too much but after reading these accounts, I suddenly feel intensely grateful that my parents were so protective of me. These adults writing their stories were not so lucky; they were victims of pedophiles.

Pedophilia is a curious word. It comes from the joining of two Greek words; paîs, meaning *child,* and philía meaning *friendly love* or *friendship.* Yet the one word they form is linked forever in modern infamy as an act so atrocious that simply saying it makes you want to vomit.

I look at my coffee table. After I called Will, I put out chips and dip and a pitcher of iced tea. I figured he might be a little hungry. I don't really cook but any port in a storm and *any food when you're hungry* are my mottos. My bell rings and Will's there. He walks in and pulls a chair up to my computer.

"Okay, what have you got?"

He doesn't say anything about how I got the information. He knows better than to question me on what I do. I jump right in telling him about my phone call.

"So the older priest I spoke to at the diocese office thought I was from SNAP after I mentioned Father Francis Xavier Murphy whom he claimed didn't exist. The organization I told you about on the phone?" Will nods. "That's a telling bit of suspicion right there. Piecing it together now, we can assume that Murphy was a child molester, a disgrace to the diocese. That's why he was living in an apartment away from any rectories and that's why I was suddenly cut off on the phone.

"The thing that bothers me is that this Francis Murphy had still been on the loose, so to speak, probably for years. The church did nothing to bring him to justice. In fact, they were allowing him to live rent-free in an apartment owned by the diocese and more than likely were giving him some type of financial support. They weren't concerned with him *continuing* his pedophilia, they were simply condoning it by hiding it."

"The connection to the other priest murder last year?"

"The other priest I found last year, no one knew a lot about him either or maybe they weren't talking. As I said in my report to the police, it's a transient community. He was more than likely moved from one parish to another and finally ended up teaching theology at a Catholic college. If he was a pedophile, too, then it can also be assumed that he was being protected by the church. *In* the church but at the same time *not*, if that makes any sense. The murders have to be connected."

"By what, groups of abuse survivors who have become vigilantes?"

"That's a strong possibility, Will."

"It is. Do you think it's this SNAP group?"

"No, no I don't. Read the personal stories. None of them sound like they themselves want to harm the priests who committed the crimes; they just want justice and they want it done legally."

"But there are other groups out there. This has to be investigated."

"I'm already on it."

I hear Will sigh with exasperation. "No."

"Why not? All I'm doing is finding out information about survivors' groups. It's easy enough to do, Will."

"Yes, it is. Tedious but easy and I've got an entire department of people who can research and get information. Let it go, Cate. I'm not even asking you how you found out about SNAP."

"I Googled it."

"I am telling you not to go any further on this. Let it go. We'll handle it."

"But this is personal."

"Exactly how is it personal? You don't know either one of the victims."

"The whole thing started on my case. I found the first body and the evidence."

"Which you rightly turned over to the police. Let me deal with this investigation."

"Sometimes I can get a lead on something you can't find right away. My methods may not always be legal, but they get results."

"Don't tell me anything else. I don't want to know about illegal."

"All I meant was that *you* have to identify yourself as a detective, I don't. I can play a game to find out what I need to know."

"What about your cold case? Doesn't the woman who is paying you deserve your full attention on it?"

"She has it. I'm going out to her house tomorrow, I already told you. Will, I'm only investigating survivors' groups online in my free time. I might ask some of my contacts on the street if they've heard about any of these groups but that's it. How can that hurt?"

"You know, I don't understand why you never became a *real* detective." He stresses the word real. "You're dogged enough."

"Why? Because I'd be hamstrung by bullshit bureaucracy. As a *private* detective I have more leeway. I'm going to do this, Will, make no mistake about that. What I find out I'll give to you."

Big exasperated sigh, then, "All right. I can't stop you, God knows, but don't get yourself into anything you can't easily get out of. If these murders are being done by vigilantes, you have to figure that they won't tolerate anyone interfering with what they're doing."

"No problem. I know how to take care of myself. I'm a girl with a gun, remember?"

"Right, and the bad guys and girls have no weapons of their own, I assume?"

"Don't worry about me. Concentrate on what you have to do out in the field tomorrow. Have fun in Jersey."

"Just watch out for yourself."

"I will," I say as I pour him some tea and proffer the chips. He digs in like a man who has missed dinner and I decide to microwave him some pizza rolls and chicken nuggets. I'm not the best cook in the world but I can microwave with the best of them. Will seems genuinely happy that I have snack food and we sit and talk about the case while he eats. Me, I have no appetite tonight. The lunch I had with Marie has kept me going all day. Not to mention the fact that the personal stories on the SNAP site have made me feel a little sick.

"Cate, this whole pedophile priest thing has been in the news a lot and it's not going away. It's even been proven that child-molesting priests were given money by the Catholic hierarchy to help them start new lives. I have to make sure that the media doesn't pick up on any information we may have about vigilantes. The last thing we want is for the murderer or murderers to get wind that we're on to something and go into hiding."

I nod my head and tell him I completely understand, that the less people who know he's investigating organizations like SNAP, the better.

"Be careful who you ask about vigilante groups, Cate. Keep it on the DL. Can you trust your contacts?"

"Yes. I've never had one who has let me down or given me away yet. Don't be concerned on that score."

Will gets up, stretches, and says, "Thanks for the snacks. I'm beat and I want to get up early tomorrow. Unless of course you *want* me to stay?" His eyes have that sexy look even though his whole body oozes fatigue. I look at him and think about his offer. Maybe I should let him stay and take a power nap. When we were together I remember his exhaustion would give way to incredibly hot sex after thirty minutes of eyes closed, feet up rest. Then I also remember Giles and that I should be a good girl, damn it.

"No, that's okay. You'd probably fall asleep on me, pun intended."

"You won't know for sure unless I stay."

I lead him to the door.

"Go home and get some real sleep. I'll see you Saturday at eight. And I will look ravishing, I promise you that."

He smiles. "I know you will," is all he says as he gives me a tired, chaste kiss on the forehead.

The McElroy house looks the same as the last time I was there except that the lilac bush is blooming and the scent is sweet and full. I park the Edge across the street, get out and walk over to the house on the left. An elderly man is on the side of the house weeding and I see a watering can next to the steps.

"Mr. O'Leary?" I call out, a little louder than I intended.

"That's me," he says straightening up. "I'm not deaf though, miss. A little arthritis and stronger glasses, but my hearin' is damn near perfect." He smiles at me, removes his gardening glove, and extends a hand. "Always remove the gloves to shake hands with a lady. You are a lady, I assume?"

"I like to think I am," I say grasping his hand. His handshake is firm and positive. "My name is Cate Harlow, sir. Nice to meet you. I'm here for the house key from Marie McElroy."

"Yup. Young Marie gave it to me." He fishes in his shirt pocket and retrieves an old-fashioned key, which he hands to me.

"Marie tells me you're a female private investigator. You don't look like what I imagined. "

"What did you think I'd look like?"

"Oh, kinda big, tough-looking. Brassy-blonde type. You're blonde but you're not big and brassy."

I grin. "Well, I am a private investigator and I can be tough when I have to be."

"That right? I guess girls do just about every job that men do nowadays."

"I guess. We girls like to be called women, though. Boys to men, girls to women, you know."

"You sound like my wife used to. Standin' up for women's rights and all. That's good; that does mean you're tough, young lady."

I thank him and, remembering what Marie said about how he can talk for hours, I tell him I have to get to work. Then I tell him that when I'm done I'll bring back the key and we can talk some more. I'm hoping he'll talk about Joshua and the spring he went missing ten years ago.

"Well I'd like that. I'll make you some of my special Irish coffee. Got some real whipped cream to go with too, Miss Cate. Let me warn you, the coffee's got quite a kick."

"I look forward to it. Thanks Mr. O'Leary."

When you enter a house that's not your own and the owner is not there, there's a vague feeling of being someplace that you shouldn't be. Everything in the house is personal to the owner, from the family photos on the mantle to the hand soap in the kitchen, and you're touching and examining it all. To do a thorough job, a private investigator has to go through drawers, cabinets, and closets—all places that are usually off-limits to strangers. And I am a stranger to Marie even though we have had some serious talks and shared a dessert together at The Curry Club.

From the front door I can see the stairwell with the faded wallpaper and the large painting of a sad-faced Jesus with a shepherd's crook, holding a baby lamb. I start with the living room, opening the drawers to the end tables, feeling under the drawers for false bottoms, and checking the backs of the framed photos and that of the mirror hanging over the fireplace. There's nothing really, certainly nothing that can be unlocked with the key from Joshua's backpack. There are no locks.

There's nothing underneath the furniture I upend, either. Nothing stuffed in an opening made in the bottom fabric of a couch or loveseat. The furniture is old and heavy and I pause before tackling the dining room.

These old houses were built for families, nothing like the houses or condos today, which all boast great rooms and open floor-planning. These homes had *real* rooms separated by walls. I admire the built-in breakfront and the open stained glass door that, when closed, can hide a messy kitchen. The breakfront yields nothing but the usual things like cutlery, chipped china, and assorted glassware including jelly jar glasses. In the linen drawer, wrapped in yellowing white cotton napkins, I find broken glass rosaries, religious prayer cards, and a couple of medals with pictures of saints. *We're a real Irish Catholic family,* Marie had said yesterday at the restaurant. It sure seems that way.

Then a memory strikes me; Marie had also told me something else when she had first approached me about taking on the cold case. In describing that last letter from her brother she told me, *It's his handwriting, no mistake. Usually he just says not to forget him. He's never asked me to pray for him before though. That scares me. Josh doesn't believe in God.*

A boy from a devout Irish Catholic family, broken rosaries carefully kept as religious icons too precious to throw away, a picture of Jesus in the stairwell; what had made him not believe in God? Was the clue to that in this house and, if it was, did it also lead to another clue that would tell me what happened to Joshua McElroy?

I finish with the dining room, even checking under the fake Oriental rug beneath the table, and move to the kitchen. Everything is in perfect order and the cabinets are filled with food. I empty them one at a time so that when I'm finished checking one I can replace the contents easily before going on to the next one. The kitchen drawers have nothing much except old menus for take-out, measuring spoons, ladles, and two pancake turners. Nothing there to try my key on.

The refrigerator and freezer are stocked for one person and I see a half-frozen crown roast defrosting in a bowl of water. That must be for Marie's dinner date on Saturday night. Looks good. I guess that she's a better cook than I am. In my hands it would turn to something resembling an old leather handbag.

I look under the stove, under the cabinets, inside the dishwasher and find nothing, not even a speck of dust.

On the stairwell, I check behind the picture of Jesus just to be sure there's no tiny box affixed to the back and I check the stairs for any movable wooden pieces where something can be hidden. Upstairs I go through Marie's room first, thoroughly turning out the closets and drawers before putting everything back. A religious picture hangs on one wall and a picture of Marie and Josh, pre-teen, is next to it. There's a white pearl rosary on the top of her dresser beside a ceramic statue of a guardian angel. I look under the bed, comb the tops of the closets; there's nothing out of order. It's the same when I carefully go over the small bathroom in the hall.

The room that must have belonged to her parents still has a

portable commode in a corner, possibly for use by her mother after the stroke. A heavy crucifix hangs over the center of their bed. Family pictures are prominently displayed on the dressers and a rosary is on a nightstand. The room holds sadness. I can imagine the couple talking in the stillness of the night, wondering where Josh was, and trying to comfort each other. Still, I have to do what I have to do. I methodically check everything and every inch of their room with no results.

Josh's room is last. Ten years after his disappearance, it still looks like a TV version of a teen boy's room. Robots, a poster of the 1983 movie *Star Wars: Return of the Jedi*, a bicycle wheel hanging on the closet door, and a radio, all silently waiting for their owner to come home.

It's not unusual for families to make a shrine out of a lost family member's room. Everything is made to stay exactly the way it was when the person was there. This is even true of families who have lost children in combat. Keep everything intact.

I worked on a case where the mother of a runaway girl left the girl's bed unmade for years because that was how her daughter had left it. Nothing gets changed even though the rooms are dusted and kept as pristine as a doll's house. The unspoken thought is that if anything in the room is disturbed, the missing or dead person is lost forever.

Josh's closet is neat and there are about five pairs of sneakers all perfectly lined up. In fact, everything is in perfect order. There's no mess. I turn over the hamper in his closet and check inside. The only thing that falls out is an air-freshener.

There's something not quite right here, though. Most teenage boys do not have pristine bedrooms. It looks as if instead of keeping Josh's room exactly the way it was on the day he left, either her parents or Marie straightened it up. That's a bit strange and out of the ordinary for families of those gone missing.

The two-shelf bookcase near his closet yields titles similar to the list Brenda Rosehill from the library had sent to me. I go through Josh's room inch-by-inch and even pull up a loose piece of carpet under his bed only to find a bag of old pennies marked *pirate treasure*. A typical kid's thing—finding make-believe treasure. I would bet that he "buried" it there as a little boy and forgot about it.

Checking his small desk I find artists' pencils and drawing pads. I leaf through them and see the same theme as the ones found in the notebook from his school backpack: innocent animal families with the evil predators looming in the background. The day is hot but the pictures make me shiver. It's the same as reading the graphic horror comics that are so popular today. They're drawn to scare you or give you a message about evil.

There's actually one drawing that is very graphic and different; a lion cub that seems as if it has wandered off by itself in the tall grass. It's all alone and has no idea of a hyena in a crouching position, with saliva-dripping fangs showing. This time, it is the animal's family in the distance seemingly unaware that the cub is in danger.

There are no fake drawers or locked boxes in his desk or on the small bookcase. I make a note that his is the only bedroom in the house without any religious articles.

I've spent over an hour and a half checking the first floor rooms and all three of the upstairs bedrooms. Now it's on to the attic and basement.

There are pull-down stairs to the attic and I take out the small flashlight I carry in my back jeans pocket. In the attic, the beam from my flashlight locates a light switch at the top of the stairs. Flipping it on and surveying the room in front of me, I find myself looking at probably over forty years of family storage. Sighing I begin methodically checking through holiday things, old rollerblades, sleds, and boxes with blankets, discarded toys, and old clothes. I still don't find anything that needs a key to open it. My arms ache from moving heavy boxes of mementos.

Before I tackle the basement I go into the bathroom to splash water on my face and to get a drink using a paper cup from the dispenser Marie has there. It's a frilly old-fashioned bathroom and I sit on the edge of the narrow tub to try to regroup. *Okay, now what?* I've searched two floors of rooms and the attic. Assuming there's a box that fits this key, where is it? The basement is a possibility.

The McElroy basement is gloomy and mostly empty, except for a washer/dryer combo and a ping-pong table. No hidden wall openings, no breaks in the cement floor where someone could hide personal items. These older homes don't have garages; when they were built very few people had cars, so the only place left for me to search is the grounds.

When I come out the back door I see Mr. O'Leary still doing the gardening. He waves at me and calls out, "Whenever you're ready for that coffee, I'll be here."

I smile and wave back then turn my attention to the yard. The lot is a narrow twenty-five-by-seventy-five-foot property. There's a big dogwood tree near the back of the lot and that's where I head. There's something about trees and kids. Maybe Josh had a hiding place in that tree, a squirrel hole or one he carved out himself.

The tree is a sturdy one and has some low-lying thick branches. I grab the bottom-most one, plant one foot on the trunk and haul myself up. I haven't climbed trees since I was a kid but I haven't lost the knack. Climbing higher I take in the view. Nice, peaceful, you can see a lot from this vantage point—the whole layout of the small community. There are some birds sitting on the roof of the McElroy house watching me.

I don't see any holes in the base of the tree. Looking closer I see little berries hidden by the foliage. A flurry of activity in the top branches of the tree and the sudden sharp bird calls from the roof of the house tell me that someone takes me as an intruder. I see two birds above me with the small berries in their beaks; they look panicked. Poor things!

Careful not to disturb them any more I climb downward one branch and jump to earth just as I did as a kid, remembering to bend my knees as I land. My dad used to tell me my landing was as graceful as that of a trapeze artist. This time however, even with the bent knees, I fall backward and land, ungracefully, on my ass. I'll have to practice my landing for next time … if there is a next time. I get up slowly and dust myself off.

I walk the perimeter of the property carefully looking for any signs of a depression in the earth that would signal something had been buried there. Crisscrossing the yard I do the same thing. But, the same as in the house, I come up empty. Maybe I'm reading too much into a simple key. Who knows? It's possible that it was a friend's key or something he found and kept for who knows what reason. Still, my instinct tells me differently. The more I learn about Josh the less inclined I am to think he did anything frivolously. He had a reason for everything. The key has to have been for some lock that he had. I just haven't found it yet.

Mr. O'Leary is sitting on his porch watching me.

"Mr. O'Leary? I could go for that coffee now."

"You're goin' to need it, miss. Got the wind knocked out of you there."

While he goes in the get the "coffee with some kick" I look over at the McElroy house trying to imagine Josh as a young boy and where he might have hidden what was important to him.

Mr. O'Leary comes back with two steaming tall mugs of coffee and I can smell the whiskey in them. He's also brought out four thick slices of raisin bread.

"I figured if you're goin' to drink my Irish coffee, you need something solid in your stomach. This bread's from the mom and pop store two blocks from here. I like to walk there to get milk and a few staples. The lady who owns the place makes the bread. Best damn bread around. Got raisins, pieces of macadamia nuts too. You'll like it."

He goes on talking about the neighborhood, the stores, and the people, and I let him. I'll know when it's time to ease in with a question about the time Josh went missing ten years ago.

After letting the coffee cool a bit, I take a sip, and practically choke. It's loaded! Mr. O'Leary laughs and says, "I *told* you it's got a kick. Got my own distillin' barrel and kit in the basement. Try dippin' the bread in it. That'll ease the whiskey down your throat."

A suburban moonshiner! I do as he suggests and he keeps on talking about mundane things until he surprises me by saying, "So, what's goin' on at the McElroy house? Marie told me you were lookin' for something that might've belonged to young Joshua."

I pause. Marie is a little too free with her words, I think, but I say that yes, that's what I was doing. Then I ask him how well he knew Joshua and the entire McElroy family.

"Oh the Macs were regular people. Shame what happened. Nice family. Marie was quite a tree-climber, kinda like you used to be I guess. Saw you fall, you seem okay though."

"I'm fine, just some injured dignity." I laugh. "What about Josh?"

"Young Joshua, he climbed the tree, the drain pipes; saw him climb in and out of the upstairs windows too. Nimble kid, nice boy. He once sent a baseball through my picture window. Came over to apologize and said he'd pay for it from his allowance. He did, too, no tryin' to get out of it like some kids would. I liked him for that."

"You and Josh ever talk about anything?" The detective in me is asking much-needed questions.

"Sure. He spent a good deal of time over here, especially after my wife passed. We played chess. Josh was damn good at the game, careful and in charge of his every move. He wasn't rowdy like some boys. Quiet most of the time. He'd sit here with me and I'd do most of the talkin'. He said he liked hearin' about old days. Liked talkin' to old people too. He was very polite and helpful when some of the folks from Madison Methodist came over the day I buried my wife."

I don't say anything and he makes an assumption about my silence.

"You surprised? You thought I was a Catholic. Well, lady detective, I'm not. Name like O'Leary, you think Catholic, but no. I'm what the old Catholic Church in Ireland used to call Black Irish; Protestant through and through goin' back to the fifteen hundreds. An Orangeman. You know anything about the religious problems in Ireland you'll know what that means. My family was all Anglicans but my wife was a Methodist so I kinda went her way. Been goin' to the Madison Methodist church for over sixty years." He stops and looks at me. "You a Catholic?"

"No. My parents weren't any religion. My dad once told me that he had gone to church too much as a boy and it had turned him off to formal religions. The only grandparent I remember was more spiritual than religious and she lit blue candles for peace. So no, I'm not a Catholic or really anything else."

"Believe in God?"

"I'd like to think I do. Got to be something out there." I smile. He nods.

"'Course I respect anybody's religious beliefs; don't have to agree with 'em, just respect 'em. The Macs were Catholics, you know. Marie goes to that Saint Matthew's over on the other side of town every Sunday. Parents went there too."

"And Joshua?"

"He went. He was an altar boy. Funny because he told me once that he didn't think there was a God. I always got the feelin' that he hated goin'; sometimes boys do, you know."

"Why is that?"

"You get to a certain age and you start questioning authority in *all* its forms, God included. You start thinkin' that all grown-ups don't know anything and you start to see the flaws and bad-ness in adults; you feel as if you want to bust out of the life they want for you and become your own person. I felt like that. You grow up and it passes. Would've passed with that boy too."

"Girls question authority too, Mr. O'Leary. God knows I did and still do."

"Yep, I guess that's true. Never thought of that," he says, taking a long sip of his coffee.

I decide to come to the real reason I'm sitting here with him.

"Mr. O'Leary, do you remember the weeks leading up to the day Joshua McElroy went missing?"

He takes his time before answering. "Yes, damned shame. Joshua was a good kid and for him to just disappear like that doesn't make much sense. But I'll tell you this, miss. Something was botherin' that boy, some deep, heavy thing weighin' on his mind. I knew it then and I know it now. Something was troublin' him."

"Do you know *what* was bothering him?"

Mr. O'Leary shakes his head. "I wish I did. Maybe I could have helped him, but the one time I told him that if anything was on his mind, we could always have a man-to-man talk and I'd help him the best I could, he just looked at me kinda sad. We were in the middle of a chess game and he was beatin' me. Well anyway, then he smiled, real bitter-like and asked me if I knew why he liked to play chess. I said I thought it was because he just liked the game. He said no, that wasn't it. Said that unlike his life, he was in control of that board game, and then he laughed. Never spoke about it again."

"What about the day he disappeared? Do you remember any details or what happened?"

"Lady detective, I remember it like it was this mornin'."

I wait for him to tell me about the day ten years ago when Joshua McElroy walked down the street toward the library and went missing.

"It was about ten or so in the mornin' and I was putting the trash on the curb. I had a real heavy load. Was cleanin' out the basement, you know all the shit you accumulate over the years. Sorry, miss, should watch my mouth."

I shake my head and say, "I've heard a lot worse."

"I bet you have in your line of work! Anyway, I see young Josh comin' out of his house with a couple of books. Kid was always readin', not like nowadays, nobody reads except old folks. Had a gym bag too, probably filled with sandwiches and snacks his mother made him. I called out to him to come help me and he looks at his watch and hesitates. Maybe had to meet a friend or somethin', I don't know.

"Take you only a few minutes, son," I yell over to him. I see him look at the backyard where his mother is hangin' laundry. She waves at me and blows a kiss to Josh. I swear I saw his shoulders slump when Mrs. Mac did that. But it passes and in the next minute he's walkin' over to me. Puts his books 'n' stuff down on my steps and helps me haul all the barrels to the curb. I ask if he's goin' to the library and he doesn't really answer, just asks—real polite as usual—if I need more of his help, and then says he's got to run."

"And after the library he never came home," I say.

Mr. O'Leary seems to be thinking about that, begins to say something, and stops.

"That's what the police report says, Mr. O'Leary. He left around ten o'clock on his way to the library and no one saw him after that." Then I add, "Right? He didn't come back home."

He looks at me for a few moments, gauging to see my reaction and says, "I'm not so sure about that, miss. I could swear ... well, I didn't say anything about it to the police."

"Mr. O'Leary, I'm here to help Marie find closure about her brother. If there's something you know, I'm asking you to please tell me. For Marie's sake at least."

"I didn't tell the police this 'cause I thought maybe I was wrong. I been wearin' glasses most of my life and my sight wasn't so hot ten years ago, I can tell you. But remember what I said about not bein' deaf? Little girl, my hearin' is damn good. Had a hearin' test a few months ago and the doctor said he was impressed by how acute my hearin' is. Told you this morning that my hearin' is damn near perfect."

"Yes, I remember ... Go on."

"The day that boy went missin' I was in the kitchen. Got a good view from my kitchen into my backyard. Now it had to be about four or so. I know because I was thinkin' about what I wanted for dinner that night and I looked at the kitchen clock to see if it was too late to go to that mom-and-pop store I told you about to get some ham. But I knew I wouldn't make it to the store before they closed at five. Well, I looked out my window and I thought I saw Joshua walkin' past my back gate goin' back toward town. Now that means he must've come home and went out again. I can't be sure, near-sighted as I am, could've been someone else walkin' by. So it isn't what I *saw,* miss."

"What is it then?"

"It's what I *heard.* Joshua McElroy said it clear and I know damn well that I heard his voice. He looks toward my house and he says, 'Goodbye, Mr. O'Leary, thank you.'"

Some people might be inclined to disregard what a man in his nineties tells you that he heard a decade ago, but I'm not one of those people. I believe Mr. O'Leary. Elderly people are old in years, but many of them like O'Leary can be credible witnesses, sometimes better than younger ones. They're more observant because they don't have all of the distractions younger people have. Not everyone feels the way I do. Even though I think he should have told the police back then, I can understand why he didn't. He was eighty-four years old, his eyesight wasn't good, and the police would have felt that someone else walking by had said something and O'Leary had imagined it was Josh.

Still, what he's told me gives me a new timeline. Josh didn't disappear around ten o'clock as everyone assumed. If he passed by Mr. O'Leary's back gate six hours later, then that means he was still in the vicinity. He had come home, but why? It wasn't to say goodbye. Marie was at camp, his father was working, and his mother, off from her job as a lunch matron during the Easter break, was food shopping. Did he come back for something? If he had something hidden then he would have ample time to get it without anyone being around to see him.

Then a thought hits me. What if he wasn't getting something *out* of a hidden place? What if he was hiding something, something he didn't want to take with him but something he hoped others, like his sister, might somehow find. The key had been found in his school backpack. Was that deliberate?

"Mr. O'Leary? Do you remember if Josh was carrying anything with him besides books and a gym bag when you last saw him that day"

He shakes his head and answers, "Nope, he didn't have anything that I could see. Why do you ask?"

I decide to be truthful. He might know what the key's for so

I dig it out of my jeans pocket and hand it to him.

"I found a key in Josh's school backpack. The police in evidence assumed it was for a locker at the high school, but Marie says it isn't. Any ideas on what this might open?"

Mr. O'Leary moves the key around in his hand, looking at it up close. "Nope, haven't ever seen this before. Looks to me like a treasure key, you know what that is?"

"Not really. I guess it would open a box that held things that had special meaning to someone."

"Yup, that it would. I got a key like this to my wife's jewelry box. 'Course, she never had anything much of value like women nowadays. Just her weddin' rings, you know. Small diamond engagement ring, she treasured it." He turns the key toward the sunlight. "Then again, a key like this could open one of them bigger strongboxes, you know like for important papers and such, birth and marriage certificates, mortgages."

I think about the empty safety deposit box that Myrtle insisted I get when she came to work for me. I never use it. All my important papers, as well as my passport and a costly bangle bracelet that had belonged to Nonna Rita, are kept in a shoebox in my bedroom closet. I know Myrtle would have a fit if she knew that, so I humor her and let her think that my things are safe and sound in a bank. Someday I'll get around to putting everything where it should be.

"Well," I say, "There was no box like that in the house or outside on the grounds. Whatever lock this key opens is either hidden really well or isn't here at all."

"Wish I could help you, miss, but I have never seen that key and Joshua never told me anything about hidden treasures. You might want to ask Marie. They were very close."

"I'll ask her about that again but when I showed her the key she didn't seem to know what it was for either."

I finish eating the raisin bread, which is good and solid, and take one last sip of the Irish coffee. Then I stretch slowly and tell Mr. O'Leary that I've got to go.

"Want a coffee kick for the road? My gift."

I wobble a bit getting up. My tailbone and back hurt and I know I'm going to feel sore later on tonight.

"No thanks, Mr. O'Leary. I do have to drive you know."

"Take some in a thermos. Not much left. Tastes even better after it sets for a while."

He gets up and goes into the house. Ten minutes later he comes out with a very old, very small thermos and walks with me down the steps to the sidewalk.

"Listen, miss, come back anytime," he says handing me his little gift. "You're welcome here. Been a while since I had a nice conversation with an intelligent lady."

I tell him he'll more than likely see me around by the McElroy house and I'll stop by when I come to see Marie and return his thermos.

"Hell, you can keep it! Don't have any need for it anymore." He laughs. "Take care. Good luck with what you're doin' for Marie. Life hasn't been fair to her."

"I know, Mr. O'Leary, I know it hasn't. She needs a break. Oh, and thanks for the coffee with a kick," I add waving the old thermos in the air.

"You haven't changed much at all, Joey. You still look like my shy little boy."

"I don't think you've changed either, Father."

CHAPTER 12

BY THE TIME I make it back to the city it's past six o'clock, so I decide to skip going to the office and head home. I am hurting more than I want to admit. Landing on my butt from five feet up has taken its toll and all I want to do is take some ibuprofen and soak in a tub of hot water. I take off my hoodie and hit the button for maximum air in my Edge. While I wait for the air to cool the car, I listen to my voice mail.

There are several messages on my phone that Myrtle has forwarded. One is from Marie asking how everything went, another is from Will, who for some reason feels it necessary to tell me he has found a fantastic chili dog place in New Jersey and wants to take me there for lunch sometime, and one is from a man who suspects his wife, a middle school principal, is cheating and wants me to nail her. The last one is from Giles—a sultry, foreplay-like message to let me know he's thinking about me. This is my life; chilidog dates, cheating spouses, and sweet Giles.

I put business before anything else and call the potential client from my Bluetooth Sync. I leave a message asking him to please make an appointment to see me within the next couple of days. Then I call Marie and tell her that all went well but that I didn't find any lock for the key.

"Mr. O'Leary is something else. He gave me Irish coffee and

raisin bread. Oh, and, before O'Leary tells you, I fell out of the tree in your yard, but I'm fine."

"Oh, Cate, I'm sorry! But what were you doing in the tree?"

"It's a long story, honey. Private investigators tend to do weird things to get information. Don't ask."

"Okay. I'm glad you're all right. I hope Mr. O'Leary didn't talk your ear off. My dad used to say he was a pip, whatever that is."

"No, he was very interesting." I don't tell her what he said about the day Josh went missing. I want to see her personally for that.

"I guess I'll hang up now. I have to clean up and close the shop soon."

"I'm heading home now so I'll talk to you another time, Marie. Call me whenever you want, whether it's business or not."

"Oh, thanks, I, I will! Bye."

I debate calling Will then decide that that can wait until tomorrow. Giles I'll call or text later. I'm beat.

Traffic is a bitch and I don't make it home until nearly eight. I'm achy and tired. As I'm putting the key into my door, I hear music coming from my living room. There's a note on the inner door from Giles.

There's a quiche in the oven and beer in the fridge. I'll try to come back later. Had to go back to work for an hour or two. Giles

Giles likes what he refers to as Zen music. He says it helps him to relax and I have to say that it does have a soothing effect after several hours spent listening to the city noise. I limp slowly to the bathroom discarding my clothes on a dining room chair. I definitely need that long soak in my big bathtub. I decide to drink the remaining contents of the thermos while I'm soaking.

In the bathroom I twist my neck to look at my rear in the mirror. I'm bruised but not too badly. The back of my left thigh has a hematoma and the flesh above my tailbone looks as if I had a small, lopsided dark blue tattoo placed there. I run a hot bath and throw in a couple of capfuls of lavender scented bath salts. Then I take two over-the-counter pain relievers and slurp cold water from the bathroom sink spigot to swallow them. I smile remembering the paper cup dispenser Marie had in her bathroom. I can never be that organized.

The Zen-inspired music combined with the hot water and soothing bath salts work their magic. I unscrew the cap of the thermos, sip slowly, and close my eyes. Once Mr. O'Leary's concoction kicks in I begin to feel better. Turning the water off, I let my thoughts wander and I think about the day, about Marie, and about old Mr. O'Leary, about the key and potential hiding places for locked-up treasures. Then I think about Saturday night and Will, seeing him dressed for dinner in a nice social setting. He is a bastard, but he's a hot bastard. Will ... me ... Will ....

I must have fallen asleep because the next thing I know, someone is kissing my hair and telling me to be careful when I stand up. I keep my eyes closed. He's wrapping me in a soft bath towel and gently rubbing me dry. It feels so good to be in his arms and I want to tell Will that he can stay with me tonight, that I want him to stay. I hear, "All right, now let me get you to bed."

And I open my eyes to see Giles smiling at me. "Hello, Catherine."

～

The sound of Giles's cell phone buzzing wakes me, I hear him in the kitchen and smell coffee brewing. I'm naked. The smartphone clock says it's going on nine. Oh boy, did I sleep!

"Giles, your phone is buzzing," I shout as I swing my legs over the side of the bed and wince when I stand up. "Ow! Damn!"

"You okay?" Giles comes in with a cup of hot coffee. "I checked your bruises and you'll be fine in a few days. The tailbone is a sensitive area, sort of the funny bone of the butt, and you must have slammed down on it pretty hard. You're just really sore right now. You said you fell out of a tree."

"Didn't I tell you the whole story?" I ask gratefully reaching for the cup.

"Nope, you were zonked out, my darling girl. You were too tired to even eat. Kind of like that time you played three sets of mixed doubles to raise money for that charity event of Myrtle's."

"Was I too tired for anything else?"

"I don't think that's possible for you. You were a great participant last night."

"Tell me that I shouldn't climb trees anymore and maybe I'll tell you why I was up a tree in the first place."

He grabs his phone and says, "Don't climb trees anymore," kisses me, and calls the morgue.

While he's on the phone I walk to the bathroom slowly to get my blood moving. I take two more pain pills, slurp from the spigot again, and sit down on the toilet seat. Sitting hurts.

A half hour later, fresh from a shower and shampoo and dressed in a large towel, I head for the kitchen and more coffee. Giles has heated up a nice wedge of quiche and I eat breakfast standing up, looking out of my window at the traffic. Little Guy and Mouse sit on the sill of the open window, tails flicking slowly, ears and eyes alert for any danger.

Giles is in the bedroom waiting for me with an after-breakfast treat and I am wide-awake.

⚜

"Let's walk over to my new car, Father. I want you to meet my friend. I've told him all about you."

"All right, Joey, I'd like that. Is that your car? It's very nice."

CHAPTER 13

"MYRTLE? WHERE'S THE MCELROY file? I put it on my desk the day before yesterday and now I can't find it."

"Try looking in the file cabinet under the letter *M*. That would make sense to me."

I do and there it is, right after the Marlinski file. "Thanks, Myrtle."

"You leave something on your desk, God knows if it will still be there two days later. That's why I put it in the filing cabinet."

"Gotcha," I say as I settle at my desk. I'm sitting on a throw pillow I brought from home. Myrtle looks at me with a bit of concern.

"That pillow help any? In my opinion you should go see a doctor. The tailbone is part of your spine, after all."

"I'm fine, seriously, Giles examined me and he *is* a medical doctor, Myrtle."

I hear her say, "Well ..." and stop. She knows enough not to mother me too much.

"By the way, that cheating wife client? He called yesterday to make an appointment."

"Good," I say absentmindedly.

"Not so good. He called earlier this morning to cancel it."

I look up. "Why?"

"It seems that he accidentally took care of it himself. He went to her school office unannounced late yesterday afternoon to talk and found his wife and the physics teacher naked and playful on her desk. He took a picture with his iPhone and says that's all he needs. Sorry, cookie."

I sigh out loud. Cheating-spouse money is easy money to make and my checking account is lower than I like at the moment. Still, maybe I have enough on my plate right now with the McElroy case and my interest in the priest murders. I'm mulling this over when the phone rings.

"Catherine Harlow, Private Investigations. Oh, good morning Detective Benigni. Yes, of course." I hear Myrtle giggle like a teenager at something Will says. The same as with any other woman who has ever met him, she's totally susceptible to the Benigni charm. Then her voice becomes professional again. "Certainly, I will. Cate? Detective Benigni on the line."

I pick up the phone on my desk. "Hi, Will, how was Jersey?"

"Great chili dogs, but no info from the Diocese. Very tight-lipped. How'd your search at that woman's house go?"

"Nada, absolutely nothing. I fell out of a tree; that was the most exciting part of my search."

"I'm going to assume that you're okay, otherwise I'm sure Myrtle would have told me what happened when she answered the phone." Pause. "Do I want to know *why* you fell out of a tree?"

"Not really, it's not that interesting."

"I'll take your word for it. Listen, Cate, I called to tell you there's been another body found. The victim is wearing a cleric's collar and there's another message."

"Where?"

"Would you believe Central Park? A woman out jogging with her German shepherd found it. Thank God she's a Marine home on leave and not freaked out by the discovery. She called 911, pretty much secured the area from gawkers, and calmly waited by the body until we came."

"Same as the others?"

"Oh yeah, nude, same mutilations as the two others plus a message on the inside of the collar, neatly printed like the last one."

"Has the body been taken to city morgue?"

"Actually, that's why I'm calling. You're in luck. The body's still at the scene and so am I. Can you make it down here within twenty minutes?"

"I'm on my way," I say as I hang up the phone.

⁓

The park is flooded with curiosity seekers being held back behind a yellow NYPD tape that has cordoned off the area. I show my license to a rookie cop who looks at me skeptically, but an older cop knows me and waves me through.

Giles and two assistants are crouched down by the body. Because of a brief but heavy downpour last night, the ground is soft and messy and my sneakers get mud-splattered immediately. I see Will talking to a shorthaired woman with military bearing who must be the person who found the body. There's a magnificent black and brown dog standing patiently beside her. I walk over to them, pet the dog, and look over and see the body partially covered by a morgue blanket.

"Want me to check the collar?" I ask Will.

"Yes. By the way, Cate, this is Master Sgt. Janet Bell who found the body. Sgt. Bell, this is Cate Harlow, a private investigator who's consulting on the case."

We nod at each other and shake hands.

Sgt. Bell tells Will that if the police need her for anything she can be reached at her parents' apartment for another two weeks before she returns to active duty. She gives him the address and phone number. Then she gives a short command to the dog and they jog away.

We walk over to the plastic-covered body and I squat down next to Giles who gives me a brief smile. He's working and we respect each other's jobs, so there's no idle talking.

"Can you let me see the collar?" I ask him. His assistant obliges.

Uncovering just the head, he turns the neck and exposes the words on the collar. The writing is clear, just as it was on the last one. In Latin I read, *Perdidit Innocentiae.*

"Lost innocence," I say to Will. "That's direct. So what do you think? I mean, lost innocence is clear. Those survivors of pedophile priests all confirm that they were robbed of their childhood innocence. Read the stories on SNAP."

"I have," he says looking at Giles and his crew working, carefully checking the body. When they're done they'll transport it over to the morgue. We move away from the dumpsite to talk.

"What are your thoughts on this, Will? Can we easily surmise from the messages that we have a person or persons who are killing and mutilating priests because they were sexually abused as children?"

"And he, she, or *they* are escalating," says Will. "The first murder was less than a year ago, the second was three weeks ago, and now this one. Identifying the body as an actual priest will pretty much give credence to the theory that they're all related murders. Any information on groups that might be going after priests?"

"No, the groups or organizations for sexual abuse survivors that I've been able to check out seem to be doing everything through lawyers and the legal system. They're being successful, too, it seems. The courts are taking this very seriously; they're taking on a powerful organization by suing the Catholic Church, but it needs to be done. What about the people you have working on it?"

"Found the same thing; everything is being done legally. But I still think there's a vigilante faction out there. Like you said, this is very personal and done with a lot of rage. This type of violence comes from personal pain and trauma. So, what about vigilantes? Your street sources know anything?"

"No, and that's strange. No one's heard a thing. If it is a group dedicated to offing priests it is certainly operating off the radar."

"They all get caught, Cate. It's just a matter of time and patience."

My cell phone vibrates but I let it go to voice mail. If it's a client I'll know about it soon enough. Giles walks over to Will and they talk about details and the ME's report. I walk back to near where the body was found, careful not to disturb evidence for the CSAs, the crime scene analysts. I stand a distance away and watch them minutely scour the ground for evidence. I feel my cell vibrate again. I let it go to voicemail a second time, but within a minute it vibrates once more. Sighing, I look at the number. It's from my office. Three calls, so it must be important.

"Hello Myrtle, I'll be back in about an hour or so. They're wrapping everything up now."

"You might want to try to get back here a little faster."

I'm trying to hear what Will is telling his officers and so I answer her flippantly.

"What's so important that would make me leave a crime scene? Did the cheater's husband change his mind about using my services?"

"No." She sounds too serious.

"What's the matter, Myrtle?"

"It's Marie McElroy. She's here with some information. Cate," I hear her voice drop to a whisper, "She's just sitting here crying and she says she'll wait for you. She won't tell me what happened."

"Put her on the phone, let me talk to her."

"I asked her if she wanted to speak to you over the phone but she says she has to show you something and wants to talk to you in person."

I glance over at Giles who gives me a quick wave goodbye as he gets into the ME's truck. The body has already been loaded. I lift my hand as he drives off and then I hear Will call my name.

"All right, Myrtle, I have to talk to Detective Benigni for a few minutes. Tell her I'll be on my way soon, but I have no control over traffic. I'll get there as fast as I can."

"She's not going anywhere. I've got some chamomile tea

brewing for her and I brought in some of Harry's nice apple crumb cake today. You be careful driving."

"Me? I'm always careful. Don't worry about me."

"Uh-huh, sure," Myrtle sighs and hangs up.

Will is impatiently motioning me over to his side. A young man I've never seen before is standing with him and looking very serious. I jam my phone back into my pocket and walk over to them. No one else is close to us but Will still speaks in a confidential tone.

"Cate, we have a development."

That's one of the things I respect the most about Will—on a professional level he never wastes time.

"This is Max Henders, our senior tech guy. He took a call thirty minutes ago that is disturbing and he also received an Internet photo." Now he nods to the man standing next to him and says, "Go ahead, Max. Tell her about the call and the picture."

"As Detective Benigni said, we received a call approximately thirty minutes ago. It was from the office of the archbishop. Someone sent a picture of the mutilated body we found here, with accompanying details, via the church email early this morning. It was marked personal and FYO, which means "for you only" to the archbishop."

"Worse than the last time then," I say. "There was no picture of that body, just a typed report."

"It's even more than that, Cate. Go on Max."

"The thing is that the picture and the details were received by the archdiocese office a short time *before* the body was even discovered. Then, right after the call came from the archbishop's secretary, a picture of the body showed up on our police computer."

"Can it be traced?" I ask.

"We're working on it, but whoever sent it is pretty savvy about covering their tracks. There's no online footprint that's easy to follow. Plus, their timing for sending the information before the body was discovered was impeccable."

"So it was well planned," I say.

"Oh yeah, and with precision."

"Anything else, Max?" Will asks.

"That's about it for now. I'm going back to tech to see if I can try to pinpoint where the e-mail and picture originated. This person may be really good at hiding his or her identity and location, but in my experience, there's always a way in, it just takes time."

He tells Will he'll see him later, and goes off toward his car.

Will looks at me. "I'm going back to the precinct and field the calls I know will come from the archbishop. You going back to your office?"

"Yes, I have a client waiting there. Call me later with an update, okay?"

"I will. If you hear anything from any of your sources, call me immediately."

"You know I will."

I half-jog back to my own car thinking about the latest murder, vigilantes, and Marie.

⟜

Back in my office I find an exhausted Marie McElroy, her face tear stained and haggard. Myrtle is sitting next to her, holding her hand, and talking in a gentle voice. In a crisis, Myrtle is your go-to person. That has to come from her years of comforting hormone-rattled pre-teenage girls through daily mini-crises when she was a teacher. She looks up when she sees me come in.

"Marie," she says, "Cate's here now. I'm going to get you more tea while you talk to her." She squeezes her hand and gets up.

I walk over to my desk, grab the swivel chair with my pillow and bring it over to where Marie is sitting. "What's happened, Marie? Tell me what has you so upset."

"My brother contacted me again. He's alive, I know it. Here. See?"

She looks at me as she pulls a folded paper out of her bag.

"I found this in my mailbox. It's from Joshua."

I take it from her and unfold it.

"Marie, I want you to know that I love you so much. Always re-member that.

Why do swallows build in the eaves of houses? You know. Stories. My story.

Don't forget me Marie. Pray for me, please pray for me. I want to be a good person.

Joshua"

I don't say anything. I'm examining the paper but there's nothing there besides the writing. It is plain white generic paper that you would use for a printer. Thousands of reams of these are sold all over the world. I re-read the short note. The few lines are written in a boyish scrawl. The paper is empty except for those eight lines.

"You see?" she says. "I know this is from Joshua."

"Pretty similar to the last letter you showed me. Tell me about the lines from *Peter Pan* again Marie. Is it a message? What do they mean?"

Marie closes her eyes and a tear forms in the corner of her right eye.

"Do you know what swallows are? They're those sweet little birds who have a habit of sometimes building their nests in the eaves of a house. When we were children, there was a family of swallows nesting in the eaves above my bedroom. I could hear them settling at night and during the day we would see them in that big tree in our backyard. Joshua and I loved seeing them. They were almost like family, you know?"

I do know; the doves that live in a nest outside my office window are pretty much like family to me, too.

"In the *Peter Pan* book, Peter asks Wendy this question: *Do you know why swallows build in the eaves of houses?* and the an-swer is, *It is to listen to the stories.* See, Wendy told her brothers bedtime stories so they'd get drowsy and eventually fall asleep. The stories were so good that the swallows and Peter Pan loved to listen, too. I did the same for Joshua; he'd come in my room and ask me if he could lie down on the floor because he was restless. I was good at making up little stories to help him relax so he could go to sleep. There were times that he fell asleep on the floor. Anyway, that's why those lines meant something special to us."

Myrtle discreetly leaves a fresh cup of tea on the desk near Marie and hands me a bottle of cold water. Marie takes a sip of tea and continues.

"We used that code since we were little kids—playing games, going to school, everywhere. It's not a message, it's just something we shared that made us feel connected. Silly I guess, but it was something that was just for us. No one else knew. But by writing those lines, Joshua is telling me the letter came from him, you see? He's letting me know that he's alive."

I feel a little skeptical. Perhaps Marie only thinks no one else knew.

"Is it at all possible that someone else, *anyone* at all, knew about this childhood code, Marie? Friends, maybe your parents?"

She shakes her head emphatically. "No. Believe me, no one else knew. I would bet my life on that."

I think back to my own childhood for a minute. A good friend and I had a code word, too. It was nothing as interesting as what Marie and Joshua had; ours was something totally ridiculous. Anything that was good or that we liked we called "beans-worthy." I have no idea who came up with it but it was our code. Chocolate was "beans-worthy," our art teacher was "beans-worthy"—an expression made up by two little girls who thought they'd created something cool and special. No one knew what we meant when we said the made-up word. "Beans-worthy." I have to smile at the memory.

I ask Marie when she found the letter and if she saw anyone around before or after.

"I didn't see anyone when I went to my mailbox this morning. I know it was before ten o'clock. After I found it, I was crying so much I don't remember if anyone else was around or not. I don't know, Cate, I just don't remember."

"That's all right. It doesn't matter."

I try to soothe her by downplaying the importance of another person having been there. If she had seen someone it would have been a lead that I could follow, but she's so distraught it isn't worth upsetting her more.

"But what if it was Joshua? Did I miss him if he was there? Did he want me to see him?"

"Marie, if Joshua wanted you to see him, then he would make his presence known. He would either be standing by your mailbox when you came out to get the mail or he would have come right to your door."

"You believe that this is from Joshua, don't you?" she asks hopefully.

I have to be honest. I don't want her thinking that I believe her brother is alive and has left a letter for her. It is certainly *possible* that he is alive and getting in touch with her, but it's also equally possible that someone with a cruel sense of humor is leaving the letters.

"I don't know if I do believe it," I say and watch her eyes fill with tears, "but I'm not saying it *isn't* from him. You say it's his handwriting and that only the two of you know about the lines from *Peter Pan*. It is a distinct possibility that this *is* from Joshua.

"I'm a private investigator and it's my job to be thorough about all details and question the veracity of everything involved with the case. But seriously? If this *is* from your brother then it means that he's close by and that's good."

"Do you think he's near our house?" Her eyes, the same sweet, sad eyes that made me take this cold case in the first place, look at me with hope.

"Marie, that's something I want to find out. I'm coming to your house later on today to check around, see if there are any clues that might tell me who left the letter. Now let me ask you something else about what he wrote. Why did he write the words 'my story'? Does that have any meaning for you? Is there something he wants you to know?"

"No, but then I don't understand why he asks me to pray for him, either. Joshua *is* a good person, he's never done anything bad or anything to be ashamed of. I don't understand why he would write that. It sounds like he's crazy or afraid that something will happen to him."

"We have to think about where he might be if he *is* nearby, Marie. Any ideas? Think about places where you may have played as kids or special hiding places."

She shakes her head and begins to cry again. Emotionally this girl is shot. I have to let it go for now. Standing up I pat her shoulder gently, tell her to drink the tea, and make eye contact with Myrtle who comes over and takes my place next to Marie. Myrtle will mother her and that's what she needs right now.

A private investigator has one good advantage over the police. Even though we know that getting involved emotionally with a client or a case is dangerous, we have a little more leeway. I can *allow* myself to feel empathy for Marie and have her sadness affect me for a while. That advantage lets me get inside her head and possibly find clues she may not even remember. But I can only do this for a short time; I can't become so emotionally connected that it affects my handling of the case or interferes with my instincts. As hard as it may be, I have to be professionally practical and be able to deliver whatever news I have gotten, good or bad, with honesty. After about an hour of crying off and on, Marie calms down to the point where she can talk rationally. She looks more like the young woman who first came to my office, sad-eyed and emotionally drained, than the one who held a spark of hope the day we had lunch.

Now that she seems calmer, I leave her in the capable hands of Myrtle and tell them I have to go out on business.

"You'll be okay here with Myrtle," I tell her. "I'll see you later."

The truth is that I need to get out of the building and walk around to think alone. Walking helps me make decisions. That's one of the great things about being in New York City: you can walk just about anywhere and, if you don't get mugged or groped, no one really bothers you. You're just one of the masses.

My walk takes me past Enzo's trattoria. The smells coming from there are good and comforting so I decide to stop and get an early lunch. While I'm standing by the small outside piazza, I see Bo, the Homeless Guy, walking with an old windshield cleaner and a dirty bottle of some type of cleaning spray. On an impulse I call him over.

"Hey! Hey, Bo! Come here for a second."

He walks over warily even though he knows me. He's seen Will's unmarked detective's car with the flasher on top when he parks outside my office building. My connection with the police makes me suspect in his eyes.

"I'm getting some lunch, Bo. Want to join me and have a couple of slices?"

I see him glance down at his clothes and then at the trattoria. He's probably been chased away from places like this many times. I stop his hesitation.

"Let's eat out here. Fresh air and all," I say to him just as a truck goes by belching fumes. He grins and I laugh. Then I settle him at one of the outside tables and go inside to order. I get him two large slices with mushrooms and sausage, and an Italian sub for me with extra Genoa salami. Two bottles of iced tea are added to my order.

Enzo eyes Bo perched outside on one of the wrought-iron chairs and asks, "He with you?"

"Yes, he is Enzo. No problem, right?"

"Oh, no, no problem, *signorina*, no problem. Wait outside, Cate, I bring to you."

He goes back to making food, glancing out the window at Bo and shaking his head. Italian compassion begins with food and Enzo is a compassionate guy. When he special-delivers my order I note with satisfaction that there's extra cheese, mushrooms, and sausage piled high on Bo's slices. He treats Bo the same as he treats all his customers, telling him to "*Mangia! Mangia!* Enjoy."

We eat in companionable silence. Bo hunches over his food

as if he's protecting it. Life on the streets. It can happen to anyone. No one is immune from being destitute no matter how
smug we might be about it never happening to us.

Enzo's attracts a diverse clientele. Women and men in tai-
lored suits from the upper echelons of business mingle freely
and easily with construction workers, traffic cops, and mothers
with kids in strollers. It's getting crowded; there are no tables
inside and people are scoping out the outdoor tables, grabbing
free ones quickly. A man, dressed in a polo shirt and faded jeans,
politely asks me if we need the extra chair at our table and I
shake my head no. Bo suddenly looks up from his hunched position and says to the man, "Hi, Father Pat."

"Bo! Hello, I'm sorry I didn't recognize you. How are you?
We miss seeing you at St. Mike's. Come and visit when you can."

He looks at me and extends a hand. "I'm Patrick Evans from
St. Michael and All Angels Church."

"Cate Harlow," I say shaking his hand. "You're a priest?"

"Yes." Then seeing me look at his shirt he smiles. "With the
work I do, I don't dress the part. People are more willing to accept me if I blend in."

"I have to agree with that. I'm a private investigator. Blend-
ing in is key in my business, too."

He doesn't look surprised, just says, "Then we both know
about putting people at ease. I try to provide a comfortable place
where people can come and have coffee, doughnuts, and just
talk. Kind of like going to a friend's house, no formalities involved. Sometimes, a place to go is all you need to get through
the hard parts of life."

Turning to Bo he says, "Let me know if you need anything,
okay? And don't be a stranger. I'm always there to talk with you
and your friends." Before he leaves to go sit at another table
where someone is waiting for him, he shakes my hand again.
"Nice to have met you, Cate."

Bo has finished his second slice and is eyeing half of my sub.
I hand it over to him. He takes a piece of newspaper from his
pants pocket, folds the half-sandwich in it, and stuffs it inside

his jacket. "For later," he says. I get up, throw away the trash from our lunch, and tell Bo I'm heading back to my office. He grabs his windshield cleaner and spray bottle and follows me. After a few minutes he asks me out of the blue, "Do you like priests?"

"I like good people, it doesn't matter who or what they are."

"My friend, he don't like priests."

"Oh? Why's that?" I ask.

"Yeah, he don't come to St. Mike's. Once, somebody cut him real bad on the arm with a box-cutter. I said, go see Father Pat at the church; he'll fix it up! But he wouldn't go. It got infected."

"Why wouldn't he go?"

"He don't like priests, he says he hates them. Maybe some priest hit him once when he was a kid. Just smashed him hard in the mouth, maybe."

I'm used to Bo's mixed thinking processes. I know he likes to talk to me since most people try to avoid him so I just ask questions or make comments to keep the conversational ball rolling along.

"What happened to your friend?"

"Maybe he died. No, no. Or maybe he went to Mexico. I don't see him much no more."

I don't ask when Bo last saw his friend; he gets confused with details and time sequence. Instead I ask, "Do you still go to St. Mike's?"

"Naw, they got some lady from the health place there. I don't want no blood test like she said I should get."

"I think you should go back. A blood test is no big deal."

He just shakes his head no, so I drop that part of our small conversation.

I think about his friend who doesn't like priests. It is possible that he was smacked by a priest as a kid. Will once told me that a priest hit him hard in the back of the head because he talked during Mass. His mother Francesca was incensed. Besides reaming the priest out in front of a Rosary Society luncheon, she had her prominent name and her generous donations removed from the rectory's lists and began attending an Episcopal church two blocks away. No one, Will said laughingly, messed with Francesca, the mother lion.

Maybe some priest did clock Bo's friend. But then again, I think it's equally possible that this friend has other reasons for hating priests. It might be a good idea to speak with him. I never discount anyone in an investigation.

"Bo, if you ever see your friend again, can you let me know? I'd like to talk to him."

"Okay, but I don't see him never."

"If you *do* see him, let me know." I give him a ten dollar bill and he nods.

"Can he get pizza too?" Bo asks me. "Me and him?"

"Sure."

"Yeah, I think he likes pizza. I hope he's not in Mexico or someplace."

We continue walking until we come to Bo's spot where he cleans windshields. This is where we part company. He takes up his position waiting for the light to change and cars to slow down so he can walk over to spray the windshields and hope for some money. Just before he rushes over to a stopped car he says to me, "Me, I like priests. I was an altar boy."

CHAPTER 14

MARIE ISN'T IN MY office when I return. Myrtle tells me that she wanted to go home *just in case.*

"She feels that maybe if she's at home her brother might miraculously come to the front door. Since I don't believe in miracles, I don't think that's a possibility." Myrtle looks at me and shakes her head. "You have to feel sorry for her, poor child. I sat with her until she was calm and we talked for a while. She's an intelligent girl who has seen her life come to an abrupt standstill ten years ago, through no fault of her own. I was glad that someone was coming to pick her up here so at least she's not alone."

"Someone picked her up here?"

"Yes. I'm assuming it's the same person who dropped her off."

"Did you meet the person who came for her?"

"No, she was looking out the window and when she saw the car pull up, she left. She must have texted him. I believe he had business elsewhere in the city."

"Him?"

"Yes, him, thank goodness. A man she met at a community center barbecue. I think she said his name was David. I hope he can take her mind off of her problems, at least for a while. Right now she needs a distraction."

"A distraction and a good private detective."

"You *are* a good private detective. You always tell your clients that you're very good at what you do, and you *are*. I believe in you. You'll be able to help her."

"Fingers crossed, Myrtle. I certainly hope so. This guy David must be the one for whom she was defrosting the roast."

"I don't follow you."

"She's got a date, Myrtle. Probably the first guy she's entertained in years. She's making him dinner tomorrow night."

"Yes, well, I hope he appreciates it."

"Me too. It looked like a good roast."

"I meant," says Myrtle, peering over the top of her glasses at me, "that I hope he appreciates the fact that she's making dinner for him."

"Right, that too." I sigh.

Thinking about Marie's date tomorrow night makes me remember my *own* dinner date with Will and his mother Francesca. I still have no idea what I'll be wearing. The double duty of my cold case and my unofficial involvement in Will's murder cases have left me little time to actually plan for Saturday night. I need to look really good and to be on guard for Francesca's little innuendoes and hints about reuniting with Will. I need to give Melissa a call later. Right now I'm on my way to Marie's house to check the area around her mailbox.

≈

Having found no evidence that was of any use at Marie's house, and frustrated by leads going nowhere and traffic jams, I decide to take a break and clear my head. I call Melissa from my car and ask if she is busy. It's just after three and I need some retail therapy. She immediately agrees, tells me we can have a late dinner back at her brownstone, and asks me to pick her up when I get back to the city. Just for a few hours, I need to be a woman with no thoughts other than finding the right outfit and getting some much needed girl-time.

On the drive to the boutique, without giving her any specifics, I mentioned the third murdered priest.

"I know all about it, and so does the whole tri-state area. Darling, it was all over the news! It's a hot topic. A Catholic priest not only murdered, but mutilated? How medieval can you get? This clergy murder is trending on the Internet. If Will doesn't have some answers soon he'll be on the slippery slope to Hell." Melissa's laugh is soft and tinkling.

"Great. Poor Will. The archbishop doesn't like him as it is. He'd send him to Hell in an instant if he had the power."

That prompted a discussion about a course she took on world religions.

"Ah, yes, the mental power of the clergy over the faithful hasn't really changed for all our modern society. The rules and laws of any religion were created by humanity, after all, and they were definitely used to keep the populace in line. Fear of God's wrath is a big motivator in being good, Cate. Obey the rules or you'll go to Hell. For many people, that was a terrifying thought and, to some extent, it still is. That's why I don't believe in organized religion. I don't want to believe in a punishing God. In my line of work I can't afford to believe in one."

Neither can I, I think. No punishing God for me. I don't always do things legally, I have no problem in lying to get what I need in a case, and I am not above breaking and entering to find something or someone. I'll break the law to get what I want; I have my own rules.

"When you get to Hell, look for me. I'll be sitting in the hot tub," I tell Melissa, making her laugh again.

I park in front of the expensive shop and once we're inside, my charming friend makes a final comment about the misguided power of religion.

"Seriously, religion is simply mind control, subtle brainwashing," says Melissa, looking through the racks of dresses in this upscale boutique. "It starts when you're a vulnerable child and continues for years. It's the ultimate guilt trip, too."

She holds up a beautiful indigo blue strapless dress in my size. A short, full skirt flows nicely from a tight bustier. Both the skirt and the bustier have just the slightest hint of sparkling lighter blue sequins. It's gorgeous but the price is outrageous. Melissa insists that I try it on anyway and she asks the clerk, who is standing discreetly nearby, to get a pair of blue rhinestone heels that are on display.

"The size, madame?" asks the clerk. Melissa turns to me questioningly. She has elegant size six feet; I can never borrow shoes from her.

"Eight and a half," I say firmly. My tennis feet are not tiny but they're strong and they look good in heels.

With the dress and the four-inch heels on, I am transformed. Even the exhaustion of the day doesn't diminish what I see in the mirror. The heels make my legs look long and sexy. The bustier top allows a perfect amount of cleavage and the indigo blue is a nice complement to my skin tone. Melissa makes for a wonderful personal shopper. She smiles and nods at me in satisfaction. She fusses with my hair, first holding it up then letting it cascade over my shoulders, trying to decide the best way to wear it.

"What time are you meeting Will and his mother on Saturday?"

"Dinner is set for eight."

"Good. I'll be at your place early to help you get ready. I don't have an engagement until ten."

"Wait a minute. I don't even know if I can afford this dress and I haven't even *looked* at the price of the *shoes*. Maybe I should try something else on, something less expensive."

But even as I say it, I can't stop looking at myself in the mirror. This entire outfit is perfect and I know it.

"I'll put it on my tab," says Melissa without blinking, "Seriously, it doesn't matter. I have an account here."

An account, I have to figure, which is paid for by one of her clients. I don't judge Melissa and God knows my own morals are definitely suspect, but somehow having one of her *clients* pay for my purchases feels a little bit weird.

I'm so tempted to put the dress back on the rack but I hesitate. Damn! Mostly I live in jeans and sneakers; I deserve to get dressed like this once in a while, I reason. Regina Margherita is a fashionable restaurant, after all. I'll tell her I'll pay her back. But before I can say anything to her, Melissa has walked over to the sales clerk. She is already telling the clerk to put the dress, shoes, and a gorgeous crystal evening bag she's selected from a glass case, on her tab.

"I'll pay you back next week. How much is everything?"

"Don't be silly, Cate. Think of these as an early birthday present."

"My birthday is two months away. Seriously, Melissa, I want to pay for all of them. It's a pride thing. Come on, a girl's got to have her pride, right?"

She sees that I mean it but insists that the shoes and the bag are her gift. I can pay her for the dress only, she says. And with that financial arrangement I have to be satisfied.

Truthfully, when I glance at the price of the shoes and the bag, which come to over $800, I'm glad she insisted. Pride, this one time, be damned.

CHAPTER 15

*A*S REPORTED EARLIER THIS *week, the body of a mutilated, nude male in his seventies, wearing a clerical collar was discovered by a jogger in Central Park early Wednesday morning ... there are no new leads or breaks in the homicide... police are investigating ... reports indicate that this murder is similar to another body discovered almost three weeks ago... no statements from police authorities have been given and no news conference has been scheduled ... we will keep you updated on this story ... and now on to breaking news. A four-alarm fire in...*

I've got the TV on as I'm waiting for Melissa to come over for brunch. She's spending the day with me and is going to help me get ready for my big night. Tonight's the night I'm meeting Will and his mother, Francesca, for dinner.

On the screen, there's a video of the crime scene that was taken by someone's iPhone, the same video that has been showing for three days. Though it's a bit choppy I can see Will walking over to the body where Giles is kneeling, then a pan around the crowd to where I'm being let through the yellow police tape, ending with a zoom in on the covered body. After that, nothing. I'm guessing that one of the cops either told the person to put the phone away, or confiscated it.

What a mess this is becoming now that the NYC media has gotten hold of it! It's been three days since the body was found and, like a dog chewing on a meaty bone, the news media won't let go of it. Unlike the small town in upstate New York where the first body was found last year, this one couldn't be hidden from the news. The discovery of the body found on I-95 three weeks ago had been kept quiet until the similar discovery in Central Park, and then that info had leaked out, too.

Central Park is an open area and, though the police did an excellent job of keeping curiosity-seekers away from the scene, news leaked out. This has been simplified with today's technology. Taking zoom pictures with an iPhone from a distance is easy. Sending information is fast. Nothing is kept under wraps for long.

Melissa was on target—this news has become a hot topic. As she said, it's even been on the top of the social media trending lists. Giles texted me yesterday evening to let me know that he had to walk past a cadre of news people and cameras when he left the morgue that afternoon.

Will called me and said pretty much the same thing. His abrupt, *No comment at this time. Let us do our job*, didn't go over well with the reporters in front of the station. He wasn't happy when I said that maybe all they wanted was one short statement that might keep them satisfied for the time being.

"I don't give a damn what they want. All they're doing is impeding the investigation. We don't give out detailed information for a reason and we don't let anyone know every damned step we're taking. It's bad enough that every idiot with a cell phone thinks he or she is a reporter; there are things that can't be released to the press during an investigation."

He's right. Too much public knowledge and you are tipping your hand to the perpetrators. People who commit crimes are avid news watchers. If you want to solve a crime you *can't* let them know exactly what you're doing. You need to psych them out and let them think you have no substantial clues. They need to feel comfortable enough to make mistakes that will get them caught.

While waiting for Melissa, I call Marie to see how she's doing. To my surprise a male voice answers.

"Hello, this is the McElroy residence."

I hide my surprise and say, "Good morning. I'd like to speak to Marie," making my voice sound professional and cool.

"She's outside talking with a neighbor. May I ask who's calling?" Polite male voice, sounds as if he's in his late twenties and not a native of any New York boroughs.

I don't give him any particulars, just tell him my name. But Marie must have told him who I was because he says, "Oh, yes, *you're* that private detective."

I'm silent for a moment then I ask, "Since you know who I am, may I ask who you are?"

"A real detective question. I'm flattered," he says smoothly. "My name is David; I'm a friend of Marie's." There's a pause and I hear the squeak of a screen door open, then he says, "Here's Marie now."

I hear the phone being handed to Marie and the words, "Cate Harlow for you."

"Hi, Cate," I hear Marie's voice. She sounds tired.

"Marie, how are you feeling? You sound as if you haven't had enough sleep. You okay?" I realize my statement about not enough sleep can be taken two ways but I want to hear her reaction.

"Well I am a little tired but I'm okay."

She's too innocent to hear anything suspect in what I said. Sweet Marie. Obviously nothing happened in the sex department. That's good, though. She's so fragile emotionally that she could be easily hurt.

I hear the man called David say he's going to get the paper out on the front lawn, then that same squeak of a screen door opening and closing.

"That's good. Myrtle and I were concerned about you."

"I'm fine, really, Cate. I was just overwhelmed yesterday but I'm better now. Every time I get one of those letters, you know,

I relive everything and that makes me feel worn out for a few days. My doctor once said that strong feelings can do that." She sighs deeply. "Please tell Myrtle we're fine."

"I will tell her," I say, making note of her use of the word *we*. "By the way, Marie, who's David?" I ask her quickly so she can give me some details before he comes back in.

"Oh, David." She pauses, still with that sadness that seems so much a part of her. "He's the man I told you about. He was so kind to drive me to your office yesterday. Would you believe that he even made dinner for me last night? I was so wiped out I couldn't do anything. He insisted on cooking the roast I was planning to cook for us tonight. Then, after dinner, he took me out for cupcakes. I had a really nice time. We came back here and stayed out on my front porch just talking until almost twelve. And today, instead of me cooking dinner like I had planned, we're going to picnic on the beach late this afternoon. He came by early to see how I was." Deep ragged sigh. "I still feel guilty for enjoying myself, though, Cate."

"I guess he's the man who picked you up from my office then. Myrtle mentioned someone named David."

"Yes, he's the one. It was just luck that he stopped at my house yesterday to ask me what kind of wine I wanted with dinner on Saturday. Wasn't that thoughtful to come here in person instead of phoning? He said that sometimes talking on the phone is too impersonal."

"A phone call can be pretty personal, too," I tell her, "but, yes, I guess it was thoughtful of him to come see you in person."

"And, of course he had come here right after I found the letter. I was such a mess, crying and telling him that I had to go into the city and couldn't stay with him. He insisted on driving me to your office. I told him who you are and how you're helping me. And Joshua, I told him all about Joshua going missing. David was so kind."

The squeaking door interrupts our conversation. David asks if Marie wants him to put the picnic things and blankets in the car and she says that would be good. She'll be ready in a few minutes.

"I have to go now," she says to me. "Thanks for calling me but don't worry, I'm fine and I'm starting to feel a little better."

"That's good. Enjoy your picnic. I'll call you soon. 'Bye Marie."

As I hang up the phone I think that I should feel happy for Marie. I should be truly glad that she has the possibility of having a relationship with someone; God knows she's been through enough sadness in her twenty-five years of life. I should mind my own business. I should simply do what is, in essence, a job, but for some reason I can't.

Call it instinct, that reactive feeling in my gut that lets me know that something is not quite right—the male voice on the phone made me feel alert and suspicious. Why? I don't know, but the feeling is there.

Suddenly I have the urge to meet him and make a visual judgment about him. Marie is too naive and too vulnerable. Who is this guy David? What are his intentions? She's only known this guy for a few months. Jesus, I sound like my father! But who knows? Maybe a parent's instincts are just as strong as any private detective's.

If I had this guy's last name I could run an in-depth check on him or even ask Will to have someone down at his precinct do it. But, surprising to many people, even the little bit of info I have can be helpful to me. What I do have, a first name and the fact that Marie met him at a community center barbecue, gives me something to go on. Someone may know who he is. I debate going out to Marie's neighborhood and making some inquiries about him, but I've got so much else to do.

My bell rings and I look out the window to see Melissa carrying two couture shopping bags and a small, elegant makeup kit. My two cats, Mouse and Little Guy, turn alert heads toward the door as it opens and Melissa walks in depositing her things on the couch. I watch them slowly relax as she goes over to them. They purr, exposing soft white bellies to her caress. I can imagine them thinking, "No danger here. We're safe."

I hope the same can be said about where Marie is with some-one named David. No danger.

﹌

I observe myself in my bedroom mirror. Melissa has helped me to transform from my everyday jeans-and-sneakers self into a glamorous vision. The dress, shoes, and crystal bag create what I call "the Cate illusion." A tasteful thick gold chain, small dangling earrings, and Melissa's gold Rolex watch complete my look. I've got to admit that I feel beautiful and sexy.

"Are you driving yourself?" asks Melissa.

"I am. I didn't want to have to deal with Will and his mom waiting here in my place while I got ready. That would make me uncomfortable. Besides, Regina Margherita has valet parking. I won't have to hunt for a space."

"Take my BMW," says Melissa. "I'll take a taxi back home."

"You drove your car here? Where in the world did you park it?"

I had assumed she had taken a cab here. I go to the living room windows and see her sea-foam green BMW parked di-rectly across the street from my brownstone. A man is sitting on a folding chair on the sidewalk next to her car. I know him. He's always polite to me, but I've heard Will describe him as a "knuckle-breaker." He supposedly works for some minor mob guys. His aunt lives two doors down from me.

Returning to the bedroom I ask Melissa, "How in the world did you get a space so close to my brownstone? Usually that one where your car is parked is never empty."

"Well, there *was* a car there, but they moved after that nice gentleman watching my car told them I needed the space."

Of course they did. "And he's watching your car out of the goodness of his heart, right?"

"No, I paid him a hundred dollars to make sure it was safe. It's just an incidental."

A hundred dollars! I can't help but wonder what it would be like to have money for certain *incidentals*.

"So, take my car, all right? You'll look fabulous driving it."

"No-o-o-o." I draw out and emphasize the word. "No, no, no. What if something happens to it? I can't, Melissa, I'd be afraid of even the slightest nick. You know how New York streets are, not to mention parking lots, even secure ones."

She observes me from the top of my head to my sparkling crystal heels.

"I just can't see you driving your SUV dressed like that. It ruins the effect."

"Believe me it won't be a problem. I've gone out on cases dressed up and driving my Edge. Besides, I feel comfortable in my own car. The only small problem is getting in and out of the SUV in heels but I've managed that before."

Melissa shakes her head and says that at least she offered. She takes out the new crystal evening bag. "You better get going. It's almost seven-fifteen. What do you want in the bag?"

"Whatever's on my dresser," I say absentmindedly looking in the mirror to adjust my earrings.

Melissa comes out of the bedroom with the things she brought with her, hands me the evening bag, and we go out the door together. She has to go home to get ready for her ten o'clock appointment. Outside she gives me a careful hug, tells me I look fantastic, and we go our separate ways. Both of us, I think, will be dressed to kill tonight for our own personal reasons. Melissa's is strictly for business, and mine? My reason is up for anyone's interpretation.

CHAPTER 16

TRAFFIC ISN'T AS BAD as I'd thought it would be for a Saturday night and I arrive at the restaurant a few minutes before eight. I check myself once more in the driver's side mirror. Good, I look like a woman who is doing well in life and, to quote Myrtle, a first-class lady. "Fine, okay, let's do this," I say to psych myself up.

It's always amazing to me that I've never had any trouble cracking an attacker's ribs with a sharp jab of my elbow or shooting a man who is lunging at me with a knife, but I feel slightly dizzy about having dinner with my ex-mother-in-law. But then her son is a hardened detective who deals with all kinds of horrors on the job and *he* still hyperventilates when he has to see her. Go figure.

The valet waits while I rummage through my new bag for the key fob. It's then that I notice Joshua's key is in my card case. Melissa must have taken everything off my dresser and placed it all into my bag. Generally, when I go out for the evening I leave my card case in a drawer on my night table and only carry one credit card and keys in a small bag. But tonight, because I didn't want to be late, I failed to see what was in the new bag. I place the card case in a zippered section of the bag and hand the fob to the valet.

As I stretch one leg down to the ground the short skirt of my dress goes way up exposing a lot of thigh and my silky blue panties. I see the valet grin as he holds out his hand to assist me the rest of the way out of the car. Steadying myself on my new heels, I smile my thanks and walk toward the restaurant door.

Inside I greet Francesca with a hug and a kiss. She looks gorgeous, and we're genuinely happy to see each other. There is a delicious whiff of lilac. Her perfume is expensive but subtle.

"Cate, you look lovely. How have you been? How are things in the world of private investigation?"

"I've been well, thank you Francesca. Business is good; I can't complain. And you? Everything going well with you?"

"Oh yes, I'm in town for a short while mixing business with pleasure. The museum is looking at a new exhibition and I'm on the committee to approve it. That's the business." She smiles and looks at Will. "The pleasure is spending a little time with my son and having dinner with you both. Of course I don't know how much time Will has to spend with me. That awful murder case! It's all over the media, television, Internet, papers. And I understand that there was another one last month, correct?"

Will has on his professional face, the one he uses with reporters when he won't give any details on a case no matter how much they press for answers. "I can't discuss any of it. Let me just say we're working it."

"Of course, Will. I understand," she says smoothly and, turning to me asks, "How's your friend Melissa? Is she still in public relations?"

Will looks at me and lowers his eyes. He knows what Melissa does, accepts it, and lets it go. He's a detective but not, as he tells me, vice. His attitude is live and let live and mind your own business unless it directly concerns you.

"Um, yes, she is. I'll tell her you said hello," I say too brightly. She's met Melissa a few times and thinks she's wonderful. When she asked Melissa what line of work she was in, Melissa, without missing a beat, told her she was in public relations. And that's not exactly a lie.

"Oh please do. Such a lovely young woman. You know, I wonder if she might be interested in doing a marketing plan for the museum. We need a fresh, modern campaign."

"She's incredibly busy right now," I answer. "*Lots* of work."

"I can imagine! She's bright, articulate, and very personable. I'm sure that she's in demand a great deal. Oh well, it was a thought." I see Will muffle a laugh.

She turns to other topics and regales us with stories about the museum while we look through the menus that have been placed in front of us. I begin to relax. Will tells us a funny story relating to a suspect and I talk about the incident with the parking ticket. Maybe we can get through the night being pleasantly cordial. I hope so.

But then I see the look in her eyes as she glances from Will and then to me, as if she's sizing up our feelings for each other. She pointedly looks at my hands, noticing that I'm not wearing any rings. Her smile is sweet but her eyes look determined and my hands begin to sweat.

Between the main course and dessert, and after we've killed two bottles of Merlot, she steers the conversation toward couples who have reconciled. Will tries to introduce other topics but Francesca is as ruthless in her personal interests as her son is in his police work. She may look delicate but inside she's all steel. I can see where Will gets his determination and toughness.

"Love is funny, you know?" she smiles. "People make mistakes, it happens, but when you realize you love someone, well that's what's really important, don't you think?"

She goes on to tell us about people who got back together after their divorces. After fifteen minutes of this I have to say something. Her idea of *true love conquers all* is just too Disney-princess for me.

"What if love isn't enough?" The false calm of the wine makes me ask the question, which I regret the second it is out of my mouth. I've fallen into her trap.

"But love is always enough!" Francesca declares. "If you love someone, truly love someone, anything, and I mean any problems, Cate, can be resolved. You," she looks at me and then at Will, "just have to consciously work at it."

"Mom, maybe there are some things that are harder to re-solve," says Will coming to my rescue. "People can love each other but that might not be enough to sustain a marriage. It's complicated for a lot of couples. Marriages break apart because of a lot of different reasons. Constant fighting is one of them."

Francesca sighs, then smiles. "Seriously, Will, do you really believe what you just said? Your grandfather, my beloved father, was fond of saying, 'Marriages are made in heaven but so are thunder and lightning.' I believe that's true but I also believe that love is the glue that keeps it all together during, and after, the storms. Don't you agree, Cate?"

"I don't think so, Francesca," I say firmly. "I think Will's right about some things being harder to resolve in a marriage. There's so much more to a relationship than love."

Francesca takes what I've said and turns it to her advantage. "So ... you and Will do agree on something!"

The server comes by just then to ask about desserts and after dinner drinks and I see my opportunity. I take a deep breath, excuse myself, and seek out that time-honored bastion of female sanctuary, the restroom.

Ten minutes later I'm adjusting my bustier top in the mirror when the door of the ladies room opens and Will walks in.

"Excuse me, didn't you see the sign on the door? Ladies?"

"My bad, wrong room," he says but makes no attempt to leave.

"Get out now, or I swear, damn it, Will, I swear I'll ... tell Francesca!" I say stupidly, the wine blurring my thoughts and making me unable to think of anything else.

"She'd say go for it. It might help us to, what did she say, *reconcile*? Anyway she sent me to get you. She thought we needed some alone time to talk."

"Someone might come in," I warn.

"Not with the out-of-order sign on the door."

"What out-of-order sign? I didn't see any sign." I turn, annoyed, and face him.

"The one I borrowed from the server. I gave him a twenty. Restaurants always have that type of sign available just in case of an emergency." He takes my hand. "By the way, you look beautiful, really, really beautiful."

"Thank you," I say trying to pull my hand away. "This doesn't qualify as an emergency. I think I'll just end the evening now. I'll tell Francesca that I have files to read and need time to work on a case."

Will pulls me close to him and kisses me. "You're tense, baby, relax," he breathes into my ear. "We *can* get through this dinner without mishap, I promise you. Shhhh, baby. Let go. I was always able to get you to relax, remember? Just breathe."

He's right; his hands know just what stress-relief buttons to push.

"This isn't fair to Giles," I protest.

"Giles isn't here. I am," he says before kissing me again. "By the way," he whispers in my ear as his hand slides up the skirt of my dress, "How's your tailbone? Still sore?"

After a few minutes and some close encounters of the erogenous kind, my stress is significantly lower and I feel more relaxed. I also feel like shit because of my relationship with Giles.

Will convinces me that we should walk back to the table together. "Look if we give Francesca some type of hope, even the smallest bit, maybe we can end the evening on a positive note."

"But we're giving her false hope."

"That may be but, haven't we done that in our work? Thrown someone off by lying a little, let the perp feel comfortable, so we can get what we want?"

He's right. I know I've done it myself when I needed information. Make my suspect feel at ease. It's kind of like good cop, bad cop except the good/bad cop is only one person. You let them see you as tough and then change your demeanor to let them see you as a person they can trust. It works very well.

I agree with him and we go back to our table together. Will even pulls my chair out for me and places my napkin on my lap.

Francesca smiles warmly at the sight of the two of us.

"Everything all right?" she asks brightly. "You were gone quite a while."

"Yes, everything is fine," says Will before I can answer. "We were just talking."

I hate to admit it but Will is right. Give a little false hope to someone and you are able to get what you want. He winks at me, Francesca takes it as a good sign, and the rest of the evening goes a little more smoothly.

The delicious hazelnut chocolate tart coupled with the cappuccino and shot of Benedictine has left me pleasantly full. A little too full I think, feeling my stomach press tightly against the bodice of my dress. I check Melissa's watch and see that it is almost twelve-thirty. We've been sitting, eating, and talking, for over four hours. There are only two other tables still filled with diners. The staff doesn't seem to mind even though the server brought our check a half hour ago. No one rushes you at Regina Margherita.

As the evening is winding down, I tell Francesca about my cold case and even take Joshua's key out of my bag to show her. She examines it and hands it to Will.

"This is a key to a type of strongbox," he says. "It looks like one that I had when I was in my teens."

"You had a strongbox?" Both Francesca and I look amused by this admittance of personal boyhood information.

"Oh, yeah," he laughs. "I had to hide my Playboy pictures from Francesca. So, remembering the skills I learned in woodshop, I made an opening and a hinge in the wooden shingles right outside my bathroom window, hollowing out a nice little niche. Inside that I put a small, locked, metal box. The shingles closed right over it. That's where I kept all my treasures, money, baseball cards, *porn*."

Francesca shakes her head and raises an eyebrow but she's smiling.

"You had easy access to them when you needed them. It was practically in your room."

"Easy access and no one was the wiser."

"So it could be in the house; I just haven't found it yet." I say mostly to myself.

Will looks at me. "You're talking about the McElroy place, aren't you? But you looked all over that house. You were pretty sure there was no hiding place that you could see."

Francesca looks at me questioningly. Will fills her in on what I've told him about the McElroy cold case. She acknowledges the sadness of the case with a small nod.

"But you know, about that key? Children are pretty good at hiding things from their parents," says Francesca. "The fact that Will had his own hiding place doesn't surprise me at all. Some things need to be hidden because the child feels that they are personal and private."

I know she means Will hiding his porn but her words are true for other reasons. I think that Joshua McElroy had something he felt needed to be hidden and he hid it near where he could get at it when he needed it. Just like Will with his treasures, it had to be accessible. I look at Will and I know what he's thinking. If I'm able to find the locked box, the *key* I hold in my hand will lead me to the reason Joshua McElroy went missing.

My mind goes back over the house and the yard. It can't be the yard because it's too open. If Joshua came back to get something it would have had to been *in* the house or *on* the house itself. I think of shutters, windowsills, shingles. Suddenly I'm wide awake and the relaxed feeling from wine and Benedictine have disappeared from my head. I have to go back to the McElroy house as soon as possible.

A small argument erupts as Will places his credit card on the bill. Francesca insists on paying for dinner for all of us and I hand Will three twenties.

"No, Mom, *I* am paying for this. Let me do it. How often do I get to take you to dinner? Cate, take this money back."

Francesca continues to refuse to let him pay for a few more minutes, then gives in. I think she realizes that it's a male ego thing. As for me, I'm happy to get my money back.

With the bill paid, we go outside and walk Francesca to Will's car. Because he's a detective he always parks his own car in case he gets a call, off-duty or not, to a crime scene. He doesn't need other cars blocking him. I hug Francesca and she tells me that she hopes she'll see me soon, really soon. I let the implications slide and just say that I enjoyed having dinner with her.

"I'll be right back. I'm just going to talk to Cate for a second," Will says as the valet brings my car up.

"Take your time, Will," says his mother happily and ever hopeful.

At my car he thanks me for coming tonight. "I couldn't have done it alone. She makes me a little crazy sometimes. Anyway, thanks, Cate."

"That's okay. Dinner was good and your deception played out well. Thanks for thinking of that, otherwise I would have had to leave early."

He opens the door and helps me in looking obviously at my legs and the way my dress rides up.

"Blue ones to match the dress, huh? Nice touch. I didn't notice them during our encounter earlier. Blue bra too?"

Oh he is exasperating! "I'm not wearing a bra," I say a little too loudly. The valet glances our way and muffles a laugh with a discreet cough. "*Good night,* Will. Pleasant dreams."

"You too."

⚬

No pleasant dreams for me. Once I have a possible lead on a case, it gnaws at me until I can act on it. On my way home I leave a message on Marie's phone telling her I need to search Joshua's bedroom again and to leave a key to the house with Mr. O'Leary.

Now I lie awake looking around my bedroom. My dress is draped over a chair and the silky blue panties that Will admired were removed by Giles a half hour after I came home. No questions asked about my night, no talking at all—just hot passion coupled with guilt on my part.

Giles sleeps easily. He once told me that the trick to sleeping well is to love the day you had. To do that, you had to create a life filled with satisfaction. Giles has a job with meaning, makes good money, and enjoys his life. But for me, some of my days are not so lovable. Maybe in my line of work with so many ifs and unknown dangers, loving my days is not so easy.

The key that is still in my crystal purse is on my mind. Mentally I go over the rooms in Marie McElroy's family house. I dismiss the downstairs ones and concentrate on the upstairs. Josh's bedroom, Marie's bedroom, the one that had belonged to their parents, and the tiny bathroom situated next to it. *Where* would Joshua McElroy be most likely to hide something?

Will had said that he had hidden his treasures behind a set of shingles. The McElroy house has no shingles, just flat pieces of siding. I didn't think there was a hiding place behind those. I need to see the house again otherwise I can't make a correct decision. Giles mumbles something in his sleep and turns over toward the window. I close my eyes, drift into a restless sleep, and dream of Peter Pan holding a key. His face looks remarkably like Joshua McElroy with his haunted eyes.

〜

"Where are we going, Joey?"
"Someplace special, Father, a very special place."

CHAPTER 17

EARLY THE NEXT MORNING Giles and I leave the brownstone together. As we're about to go in separate directions, he surprises me by saying he'll see me later in the week. "You're busy with this cold case. I know what it's like to get caught up in your work, Catherine. It's all-consuming. The last thing you need is a distraction. Work on what you need to do and I'll call you in a couple of days." Seriously, he is way too nice a person for me but he's right; I need my time completely undivided right now.

My office smells musty after a weekend with no open windows or air movement. Even though the place has what passes for central air, each office has its own controls. Air-conditioning doesn't do it for me and I am lucky that the old building still has windows that can be manually opened. Even the smell of the streets is better than the funky odor that is a staple of old buildings. Sometimes Myrtle is here before I roll in and she has turned on the air and sprayed air-freshener all over the place. Me, I prefer the smells of the city to canned fragrance. I also feel too closed in when the windows aren't open.

I check my voice mail messages. There's a request for donations to the state police fund—something Will once told me they never do by phone so I know that's a scam, a woman calling to tell me a credit card I don't even have is overdrawn, and a man who is interested in retaining me to check on the activities of his teenage daughter and her boyfriend. Except for the one from the father of the teen girl, I delete them one by one and wait to listen to the last message. It clicks on and a slightly familiar voice comes from the machine.

"Hi, this is a message for Ms. Cate Harlow. We briefly spoke by phone a short while ago when you called the Paterson Diocese office. I don't know if you remember me. My name is Father Richard Boyd. I'd prefer that you, uh, that you ... do not call the diocese office and ask for me. This is confidential. I'll call back during the week. Thank you. Goodbye." His voice sounds urgent and disappointed that he hadn't been able to speak with me.

The call came in at 4:12, Friday afternoon. On Fridays Myrtle leaves at four.

Every other day she's here well past five but Friday is her hair and nails day and she has an unbreakable, standing appointment for four-thirty.

Richard Boyd. I remember the name; he was the priest who had the boyish voice, the one who referred me to the older priest whose whole jocular demeanor changed when I mentioned the name of the murdered clergyman.

Father Richard Boyd doesn't want me to call the diocese office. That in itself is interesting, as is the fact that he said he would call back. It has to be important. He must have remembered my name and gotten my number online. It's too bad that I can't speak with him now. Damn! I debate whether I should call him anyway, but decide against it. Sometimes you have to wait for information to come your way.

I sit at my desk and pull out my laptop. Keying in *murdered priests* and the words "New York area", a whole bunch of news sites come up immediately. I click on the most reliable one and read what their updates are. There aren't any; the original news is just being repeated, sensationalized *ad nauseam*. Then I click a news video that shows the spot in Central Park where the body was found. A reporter talks about the fact that there are no leads and that this is the second body found within a few weeks. She doesn't know about the one found last year in upstate New York—no one in the media does. That's good; there's enough of a feeding frenzy as it is with two priests mutilated and murdered, and no suspects.

The names of the victims have not been disclosed. There is a tacit agreement between the media and the police on all murder cases not to reveal names until family members have been notified. Though their respective dioceses have been informed of the murders, it has been difficult to locate any family members for the priests. It isn't surprising. This is usually the case when an elderly, unmarried person dies or is the victim of murder. Most only have nieces and nephews who truthfully don't want to be bothered. This is especially true if there's no inheritance. No one wants to put themselves out for funeral arrangements and expenses. So far no relative, or even friends, have come forward to claim the bodies. The burials will have to be handled by their respective dioceses after the bodies are released.

"Well, look who is here before me," says Myrtle as she's walking in the door carrying a Timothy's bag that I know is filled with coffee, and another bag with Harry's pastries.

"I thought I saw your car two blocks down when Harry was driving me here. That's why I made a stop at Timothy's." She puts her bag down. "Did you check the messages?"

"Yes, I did, and listen, Myrtle, there's something I want you to do for me. It is really important."

"All right. Tell me what it is and I'll make sure it gets done."

"I'm going out to Marie's house early this afternoon and I doubt that I will make it back here before five. I'm expecting a very important phone call this week. It will be from a Father Richard Boyd. I don't know if he'll call today, but he will call sometime this week. Whenever the call comes in you need to send it to my cell phone immediately. Just tell him to hang on and patch it through to me. Tell him that I do remember him and that I am anxious to speak with him. Oh, and Myrtle? Change the outgoing message to let clients know the office closes at four on Fridays, okay?"

Myrtle is writing all this down and nodding her head. She rarely asks questions about my cases knowing full well she'll get all the details eventually.

"What's up at Marie's?" she asks. "Everything okay with her?" She hands me a large coffee and a pastry concoction called a bow tie.

"Yes, I guess it is," I answer, sipping the coffee and biting into the sugared icing of the bow tie. "This is simply a routine visit, just need to check something there."

Myrtle gets up to put on tea for herself and asks me when she can turn on the air. The unexpected spring humidity is frizzing her hair.

"In a few minutes, Myrtle," I say standing near the windows looking out at nothing in particular, just the traffic on the street. A soft sound gets my attention and I glance down at the nest of doves. The babies are getting bigger and they can be left alone for short periods. I don't see the parents.

"Myrtle? Can you bring me the bag of bird seed with the scooper that's by the coffee-maker?"

She brings everything over and smiles at the baby birds.

As I scoop out a small portion and place it in a feeder on the fire escape step, I heard a distant cooing sound.

"Feeding the birds; it's supposed to be good luck, you know," muses Myrtle. "Look Cate! There are the parents, across the street on that other building. Probably were searching for food, bugs and such. The place under the overhanging roof is a great place for termites to hide. Those birds fly back and forth across the street quite often during the day. You're not here a lot so you don't always see them. Those babies need food. Can you see the adult birds on that building?"

"Where?" I say looking to where she's pointing. "I can't see them."

"There, honey. You can just spot their tails under the roof's edge. See?"

"Oh, right, now I see them." As I look, I see the birds emerge from under the edge of the roof of the building across the street. The edge …

I put my coffee down and stare. The edge of the roof, also known in architectural terms as eaves. The eaves! Of course they're a great hiding place for termites and … anything else. I grab my phone and bag and run out of the office.

Hello, Peter Pan.

⋙

Ringing Mr. O'Leary's bell, I have time to look around at the houses and check out the architecture. I especially look at the eaves on several houses, the McElroy house included. I've always loved old homes and had at one time actually dreamed about becoming an architect. There's such beauty and grace in old buildings. Even modern ones have their own beauty in their energy and fluid lines. But I was so much better at solving problems, following elusive clues, and finding something that others disregarded; even as a child I could figure out who-done-it in a movie or story before other people had any hint of a clue. As frustrating as it can sometimes be, I love what I do; I'm in the right profession.

Mr. O'Leary opens his door and I can tell he's happy to see me standing there. My appearance is a break in an otherwise mostly solitary day for him.

"Well, lady detective! How are you? Just got back from the store a half hour ago. I bought you that nice fresh-baked raisin bread. Been waitin' for you since."

He hands me a small envelope. I open it and there's the house key as well as a note from Marie.

"*Hi Cate,*

Here's the key. I'm sorry about not returning your call but I didn't get home until late. David took me to a movie and then we had dinner out. He seems nice and understanding of my feelings. I know you'll like him when you meet him. He might be painting the porch railings today if he can get out of work early so you might see him later. I think he said he's working until one; he's a vet's assistant. ~ Marie"

"She givin' you the details on that young man she's seein'?" says Mr. O'Leary. "Took her out a few times and came over for dinner two days ago she told me. Hope he's a good one. Don't know if I like him; only met him once. Still, Marie never did have a steady fella after her brother went missin'. She took care of her mother and then the dad. Tried real hard to hold things together. Doin' that, well ... that leaves no time for a steady beau."

I agree with him. Marie hasn't had it easy at all and made no time for herself. Mr. O'Leary tells me that when I'm done he'll have his coffee-with-a-kick waiting for me along with that delicious bread. I tell him to give me a couple of hours and he has a date.

"A date? Ha! I'm flattered. But you're too pretty for an old geezer like me, lady detective. You need a young fella like my great-nephew Hal."

I laugh at the thought that another *young fella* is what I need. It's enough for me to juggle the two I have now. I smile and ask Mr. O'Leary if he has a ladder I could borrow. Joshua McElroy may have been good at climbing in and out of windows to reach the eaves but I definitely need a ladder.

"Sure, lady detective. I've got one, friend of mine made it for me years ago. Not goin' to ask why you need it, just goin' to remind you of your tree-climbin' episode."

Yup, lost dignity and bruised tailbone. No reminder needed.

I follow him to a shed at the back of his house and haul out an old wooden ladder. It looks as old as Mr. O'Leary and I hope it's still okay to climb. It's just a plain ladder that doesn't close, made in a straight up and down line. It looks and feels as if it were made a hundred years ago.

"Goin' to finish up my laundry now. See you later, Cate," says Mr. O'Leary as he ambles slowly toward his back door.

The McElroy house looks quiet and peaceful. There are eaves up near the bedrooms. A twittering from the trees tells me there are birds nearby. Trying to judge from the outside where Josh's bedroom is I put the ladder up against the left side of the house near the eaves. Josh's bedroom was on the left and toward the back. Taking a breath, I test the first few steps and they hold my weight. It feels a little rickety but I climb up slow and steady.

"Do you know why swallows build in the eaves of houses?" Peter asks Wendy Darling.

I think about the words of *Peter Pan* as I steady myself on the third highest rung of the ladder.

I am directly under Josh's bedroom window and gripping the thick windowsill. Balancing and rising up on tiptoe, I try to see inside his room. As far as I can see, everything looks the same as the day I went in and investigated: a veritable shrine to the missing.

Looking up at the eaves, I realize that to reach them I will have to stand with one foot on the top rung of this old ladder and the other balancing on the windowsill. It's a shame Mr. O'Leary didn't have a longer ladder. The window frame is old wood but it feels solid as I grip the sides. I might be able to grab the top of the frame with one hand and use the small penlight I carry to look up under the eaves. Even though there doesn't seem to be any openings inside them, I have to check it out.

Heights don't bother me and I take the penlight out of my pocket to help me see if there's anything there. I close my eyes and take a deep breath, preparing myself to make the climb.

"Hello. Need any help?" A man's face appears in the window startling me so much that I almost lose my footing.

"Whoa, hold on. You okay? I didn't mean to scare you." He grabs hold of my hands on the windowsill. "Maybe you'd better climb down. Hold on tightly until I come outside and I'll steady the ladder for you."

I grip the sill and look at a man who appears to be in his late twenties. He's dressed in jeans, an old shirt, a knit cap that comes down to his ears, and wearing aviator sunglasses.

"Who are you?" I finally say, steadying myself.

"I'm David. You must be Cate, I guess. Either that or you're someone about to break into Marie's house."

So this is David. What's he doing in Marie's house while she's at work? Maybe there's more to this relationship than I thought. Either that or Marie is a little too free with handing out house keys. David didn't get his from Mr. O'Leary; that protective elderly man would have told me about it.

"David, how about coming outside to meet me? It's better if we're both on solid ground, agreed?"

He laughs and says, "Sure. Want me to hold the ladder until you get down?"

I don't answer, begin my descent quickly, and am standing beside the ladder before David makes it downstairs. Mr. O'Leary is sitting on his porch, watching us.

The human mind, with all its so-called higher intelligence, likes to blame things on imagination. If we feel uncomfortable when we first meet someone, the mind says it's only our imagination. Humans are very good at pretending that everything is fine, we're only imagining danger. In that respect, animals have it all over us in the area of intelligence; they trust their feelings. If it doesn't seem right to them, they don't debate it. It doesn't feel right, so it's wrong. Done. Over. Out of here.

David holds out his hand to me and I look directly at him as I shift the penlight from my right hand to my left to shake hands. In that moment, I know that there's something off about him, something I don't like. As I've always said, I go with that gut animal instinct because it has never failed me. Maybe Mr. O has it too; he said he didn't know if he liked David.

The man standing in front of me, the one of whom Marie said in her note "*I know you'll like him when you meet him,*" tells me he's here to do some painting for Marie and that she came by on her break to let him in so he could change his clothes. Obviously Mr. O'Leary was still at the store when this occurred. David says he's sorry if he scared me.

"You didn't," I say. "Just surprised me that's all. I don't scare easily."

"I've never met a private detective before. That must be pretty interesting work."

His pandering concerning what I do for a living doesn't work on me. I ignore his phony interest in what I do and ask him when he's going to start painting.

"Oh, as soon as I do some sanding on the old railings, I guess." He pauses. "Marie says you're looking into her brother's disappearance. Reopening a cold case, right?"

"Yes, I'm working the case but I prefer not to talk about it. It is confidential, I'm sure Marie has told you that."

"She's told me a lot about it—the letters she has received, and how you're going over every detail from ten years ago." He looks at me as if he thinks I'm going to share info on my case. I don't blink.

"If she has, David, that's her decision, but I am not going to talk about anything involving it."

"But do you think he's alive? I mean, after all these years? Where do you think he is?"

"I already said that I can't discuss this."

"Right, I understand. Ethics and all." He changes tactics. "There are so many things in the news that are horrible. Missing children, assaults on the streets, and that story about a murdered priest—I try not to even listen to the news much. But I guess in your line of work you have to listen."

"Part of the job. And speaking of that, I have to do my job now so if you don't mind, I'm going to go into the house for a while. It's necessary for me to be alone to do my work. Is there anything you need to get in there before I start?"

David looks a little put out by my abruptness but says, "No, I got everything I need. Of course I understand that you need professional privacy."

He tells me it was nice to meet me and as we shake hands again, the penlight in my left hand falls to the ground and lands next to David's sneaker. Before he reacts, I squat to pick it up and notice a dark reddish stain on the top of the sneaker. He sees me looking at it and says, "I guess you know blood when you see it, being a detective and all."

Not necessarily. It looks like a lot of things that are red. The stain could be catsup, tomato sauce, or paint for all I know, but I just nod. Let him think I can spot blood a mile away. It adds to the mystique of the private detective.

"I'm a vet technician and I was assisting with a surgery at the animal hospital. The blood must've soaked through my scrub booties. I'll have to bleach it out tonight."

"Yeah, bleach will do the trick." I stand up. "I use it all the time. Works wonders."

I've never used bleach to get rid of a bloodstain in my life. Usually I either send the item to the cleaners or throw it out. Luckily for me, very little blood has ended up on my clothes.

As I'm walking away toward the front door, David calls out that the door is open.

"Oh? Okay, David, thanks for telling me. I'll be sure to lock it when I'm done here."

Inside the house I make a quick run-through. Nothing looks as if anyone else is living here besides Marie. Even her fridge seems to still only have food for one. So David has not yet charmed himself into her house or her pants. Marie is too innocent to see anything wrong with him. Glancing out the front window I watch David sanding the old railings on the front steps. He seems intent on what he's doing. I quickly lock the front door and run around to the back one to make sure it's locked as well. I want privacy and not nosiness.

Upstairs in Josh's room I lean out the window as far as I can and shine a light on the eaves. As far as I can see there aren't any openings. The wood looks as if it is starting to rot, though. Some chips of wood are breaking away from the eaves. Other than that I don't see any openings.

After I'm done I snoop through Marie's room again and find it spotless. Not one thing out of place. Near her dresser is a small bookcase just like the one in Josh's bedroom. As I noticed on my first visit, her book collection is eclectic; there are self-help books, romance novels, and classics sharing shelf space together. I see an old copy of *Peter Pan and Other Works* by J.M. Barrie next to a new book titled *And Then I'll Be Happy! Stop*

Sabotaging Your Happiness and Put Your Own Life First.

I take the book by Barrie and notice that it is dog-eared and well-worn, as if the reader had thoroughly enjoyed it and wanted to re-read favorite parts. One page has a bookmark in it as well as having been turned over to mark it. Joshua's and Marie's code.

"Do you know why swallows build in the eaves of houses? It is to listen to the stories."

The light is better at the window and I walk over to read a little of Peter Pan. It's a great children's book and more. What adult hasn't wanted to fly away to Never Never Land to get away from things every once in a while?

The sun is shining through the window in Marie's bedroom and I feel its warmth on my face. I look outside and see Mr. O'Leary pruning his hedges. David is probably still sanding or has finished that job and gotten around to painting the railings. Leaning my elbows on the sill, I look around, debating what I should do. I put the book back in its place and decide that I really need Mr. O'Leary's coffee with a kick.

⟿

Spend enough time with Mr. Albert O'Leary and you will come to know about every single thing that happened in his neighborhood over the last fifty years. He's a great local historian. He tells me stories about neighbors, local stores, whose kids are walking on the wild side and whose marriages are shams. The spiked coffee puts me in a mellow mood and I am careful to sip slowly.

"Got a sort of treat today, miss. Picked up some cream-cheese spread to put on that raisin bread. I'm gonna fix it up for us right now. You just sit there."

The sun is shining, making rainbow sparkles on the houses. Marie's house is directly in the path of the sun's rays and they hit above the bedroom windows. It's a peaceful house that is hiding a secret, Josh's secret.

I look at the eaves above Josh's room again but I know there's nothing there. This really is a very peaceful neighborhood. My gaze travels over the dormers and eaves of the McElroy house.

The corner of my eye is caught by a sliver of a glint above and to the right of Marie's room. The sun playing tricks, maybe the rays are hitting a stone or chip of paint up there. I get up to take a closer look. Inside the overhang of the eaves there is a glint of something that looks shiny and metallic. If I move I don't see it but standing still it is very visible. Just a chink in the wooden eaves.

"Do you know why swallows build in the eaves of houses? It is to listen to the stories." What had Marie said about that line? That Wendy told her brothers bedtime stories so they'd fall asleep. *"I did the same for Joshua; I was good at making up stories to help him relax."*

"Do you know why swallows build in the eaves?" Because they want to hide something, Peter? The Peter Pan eaves Josh mentions in his letters have to be the ones where he heard the stories; in Marie's room. That glint tells me there may be something there in the eaves near Marie's room, high up by the roof's edge, far outside her window. Easy for a tall teenage boy to access , and Mr. O'Leary had said that Joshua was a nimble boy, climbing in and out of the upstairs windows and climbing the drain pipes.

I put my coffee down and head toward my car just as Mr. O'Leary comes outside carrying a tray filled with goodies.

"Hey, Cate! Where you goin'?"

"To get a bigger ladder," I call over my shoulder.

⮜

"Where have you been all these years my son? I have prayed for God to bring you back to me and He has! It's a miracle that we're together here now. Do you believe that?"

"Yes, I do believe it."

CHAPTER 18

GETTING TO THE BOX hidden there was made a whole lot easier for me when I remembered that, while we were having dinner with his mother on Saturday, Will mentioned that he was taking Monday off this week. I call him from my car on the way to the hardware store.

"Will? Hi, sorry to bother you. What are you doing?"

"I just got back from the gym and I'm going to take a shower. Want to come take it with me?"

Give the man credit: he never gives up trying to get me naked.

"Nope, I already showered. But I need your help. Are you going to be busy?"

"Why? What's going on? I can tell this isn't a social call."

"I need a ladder, a really long metal one. Your cousin, the one who does roofing lent you one a few months ago. Do you still have it?"

"Boy, you get right to the point, don't you? Yeah, I still have it. *Why* do you need a ladder?"

"If I tell you, you'll think I'm crazy and you won't bring it here."

"I already think you're crazy, and where's 'here'?"

"Marie McElroy's house in Queens. The cold case file."

"Queens? You want me to come to Queens? Now? This is my day off! I had plans."

"Please? It's really important. I may have found something big concerning the case."

He says absolutely nothing for a couple of minutes, then, "Can I take a shower first? Believe me you'll appreciate it if I do."

"A quick one then, okay? I'll send the address to your cell phone and you can key it into your GPS. Thank you, Will. Seriously, I owe you."

"You sure do." And he hangs up.

At the hardware store I get a sharp hand pick tool and a bottle of lubricant guaranteed to dissolve rust. I'm betting that if there is a metal box, it will be rusted shut after ten years of sitting in a moist wood opening.

On the way back to the McElroy house, I call Marie and tell her I need her permission to do something at her house that might damage some of the wood on the outside just a bit. I don't tell her exactly what I'll be doing and don't mention the eaves or what I suspect. No good getting her hopes up. I just promise her that I'll be careful not to do much damage.

"Oh, Cate, don't worry about damage. If there's a possibility of a clue about Josh I don't care if you wreck the house! I'll come home. I can be there in a half hour."

"I don't think that's necessary," I say and tell her I'll call her if I find something. I use all my charm to convince her to stay at work. Truthfully I want to check out anything I find alone. I don't want anyone else touching evidence.

It takes Will about an hour to get to Queens and he arrives not in the best of moods. While he's untying the ladder from the roof of his truck, I quickly fill him in on why I need it, the problem of David, and my need for privacy with what I'm doing. I introduce him to Mr. O'Leary, who has been not so discreetly watching me walk around the house, go back inside, and look out second floor windows.

"Mr. O'Leary, this is Will Benigni; Will, Mr. Albert O'Leary."

They shake hands and talk for a few minutes. I'm sure that Mr. O'Leary thinks that Will works for me and I have to smile at that thought.

With Mr. O'Leary supervising and Will holding the ladder steady for me, I climb to the top and am easily able to reach the eaves. At first it looks as if there isn't anything there but weather-scarred broken wood; maybe the sun *was* only glinting off a chip of paint that looked shiny in the glare. Looking closer, though, I can see there is definitely something that does look like a piece of metal. I carefully chip away the larger rotted pieces with the pick. My hands are sweating and the rotting wood flakes stick to my fingers. Larger pieces fall to the windowsill.

Suddenly the plinking sound of metal hitting metal makes me aware that I have hit something that might be the jackpot and I am right. I hurriedly break the old wood with my hands making an opening large enough to insert my fingers. Looking into the opening, I see it. Hidden deep within the wooden eaves is a narrow metal box. It had been wedged into an opening that looked to be about a foot deep and six inches wide. Using the pick and my fingers, I wrestle it slowly out of the wooden opening. Splinters jab into my palm.

Once the box is free, I hold it against my chest with one hand and fish Joshua's key out of my back pocket with the other. The key certainly looks as if it will fit but, as I suspected, the lock is rusted shut.

"Does the key...?" Mr. O'Leary begins to yell up the ladder. Will turns and says something to him and Mr. O'Leary is quiet. I see David and a few neighbors standing a short distance away from them watching me. Will calls my name and nods at me as a signal to come down.

"Well?" says Mr. O'Leary in a stage whisper when I'm on solid ground and cradling the box inside my sweatshirt. I don't answer him.

"Did you find something important?" David asks quietly, coming to stand in front of me. I'm about to tell him what I told him before about privacy when Will takes over, pulling out his

NYPD detective's ID and his badge.

"I'm Detective Will Benigni, NYPD." I see Mr. O'Leary's mouth drop open with that statement. "This is a cold-case private investigation by Cate Harlow. It can only be discussed with the person who hired Ms. Harlow. I'd appreciate it if everyone would just go back to whatever they were doing and not ask any questions. There's nothing to see anyway. Everything's over."

Turning to me he suggests we walk back to my car. I glance at Mr. O'Leary who nods and gives me a brief smile. He knows that Will had to talk the way he did to get rid of David. David walks quickly around toward the front of the house, pulling his phone out as he goes. Probably calling Marie but I can handle that later.

I turn toward Mr. O'Leary and call out that I'll be back for the coffee kick soon.

"Make it real soon. 'Bye, lady detective."

I am sitting in my office with only the desk light illuminating the papers I found in the metal box. Will followed me back to my office where we used the rust dissolvent to clear the lock. Myrtle insisted on putting paper towels on my blotter so I wouldn't have a mess from the rust and solvent on my desk. I didn't care; I just wanted the box opened. After cleaning away the rust from the lock I took the key and, after a few tries, it turned in the lock and the box opened. It was after five.

"Cate, this is your case. Check out what's inside. I'm here and if you want to share what's in there, that's fine." Will sits in Myrtle's chair and puts his feet up on her desk. Myrtle doesn't seem to mind and she busies herself by the copier.

Inside the box is a brown canvas bag that contains rolled up papers. They are dated and in order. Sifting through them quickly, I am stunned by what I read and say quietly, "Will? You have to look at this." Then I add, "You too, Myrtle."

There are newspaper and magazine clippings about the sex scandals that have been rocking the Catholic Church for years.

They are a veritable timeline of sexual abuse and the extraordinary efforts the church took to keep these horrendous crimes hidden.

While most of the clippings and copies from books are dated no more than fifty years ago, there are some going back to the fourteen hundreds. I see copies of historical documentation of atrocities committed with the official approval of the Church. One of these was the authorization of procuring young boys for the castrati choir. There are explicit legal testimonies from some of the castrati detailing the sexual abuse they endured at the hands of the priests all during their boyhood.

I find handwritten papers, obviously copied from old files and books, on what happened to Dutch boys in the 1950's who were abused by diocesan priests.

"Dutch boys who accused priests of sexual abuse, including sodomy, were surgically castrated to rid them of (what the Church declared was) their homosexuality, but also as a means of punishing those who dared accused clergy of this abuse," wrote one Dutch investigative journalist named Joep Dohmen. He discovered that the castrations were done by Catholic doctors recruited by the Roman Catholic Church while the young boys were students or altar boys living on church grounds. Performed in psychiatric wards, without any type of anesthesia, the surgical castrations were authorized by the Church hierarchy, official seal and all.

Will gives a low whistle and mutters, "Christ." Myrtle closes her eyes and shakes her head.

We read about one of the victims, a young man named Henrik Heithuis, who was castrated at the age of twenty in 1956 after accusing several clergymen of years of rape, which began when he was ten years old.

After the castration, Heithuis spent the rest of his life in a mental hospital, a psychiatrist who examined him stated officially, "This man has been totally maimed: physically, emotionally, and mentally."

There is a clipping about Church-authorized payouts to sexually abusive priests after they left their dioceses and of these pedophiles being provided with room and board, courtesy of the Church. I find a newspaper copy of a letter written by SNAP to a Catholic archdiocese asking, *"In what other occupation, especially one working with families and operating schools and youth programs, is an employee given a cash bonus for raping and sexually assaulting children?"*

There are hand-drawn pictures of the hideous yellow-eyed hyena and the innocent animal victims. The pictures have the same themes that were found in Joshua's backpack.

And there's something else—something that explains the sadness in Joshua's eyes in those pictures at the McElroy house. Written in a boyish hand is a detailed account of Joshua's sexual abuse at the hands of a parish priest. A journal of papers, folded and tied together with string, begins with the account of his first abuse at the age of nine to his rape at the age of ten and continuing until a few months before Joshua McElroy went missing. The priest called the rapes penance for the boy's sins. Joshua had decided he had only one desperate course to take. *"I have to run away because no matter how much pain it causes my family, no matter how I hurt Marie, I have to do this to survive. They are all so unaware of what has been happening. I can never tell them just as I can't let him ever, EVER, hurt me again. He has destroyed my spirit. And Joey, the one everyone called a sweet kid, a good boy—Joey is now dead."*

Who is Joey? Was he abused also and did it cause him to take his life?

There's a bottle of Kentucky bourbon in my desk drawer. A client had given it to me as a present after I helped her discover that her husband, who had filed for divorce, had a girlfriend and a significant amount of money hidden away in a Cayman Island account.

I pour two stiff drinks into plastic cups for Will and for me. Even Myrtle takes a shot but adds water to it.

Now I know why Joshua drew predators and innocent victims and why he had a fascination with reading about people who were able to escape their captors. There's a possibility that he may have run away with that boy named Joey. I ask Will to do a check on missing children named Joey from that area. He keys the specifics into his phone and sends it to The Center for Missing Children and local authorities.

"My God, Cate. We're looking at details of a crime that was ongoing for over seven years. You need to find out if that priest he mentioned is still around. This is convictable evidence here. You might want to take it to our sex crimes unit to see what they have to say." Will pours himself another drink and hands me the bottle to do the same.

"I will do that, but first I have to decide how to tell Marie or if I even *should* tell her anything until I can locate this priest. I'm assuming he's from St. Matthew's."

"Yeah, you'd better do that first. Once sex crimes get hold of it, it's out of your hands. They won't want a private investigator involved in what they're doing."

Myrtle is sitting there looking out of the window. It's well past the time she usually leaves and she's already called Harry to say that she'd be late. Without taking her eyes away from where she is looking she says, "Do you think that Marie had any idea of what was happening to her brother?"

I look at Will and he shakes his head.

"No, Myrtle," I say firmly, "Even if she suspected that something wasn't quite right, I truly believe she didn't know what was going on. Most family members and close friends never know or even suspect what's happening. And we have to remember that Marie's family was very deep into their religion. You have to see the house—religious objects and pictures are everywhere. It would be hard for Joshua to tell them what was happening and just as hard for them to believe it. Even though they loved him, they would find it incomprehensible that it was happening. Plus, he was led to believe that this was his penance for whatever sins the priest told him he had committed.

"You know, Melissa said to me a few days ago that religion is a subtle form of brainwashing. Subtle because it begins in childhood when you're so young and your mind is malleable. Subtle or not, it's still brainwashing and the effects of it are powerful."

"'Give me the child until the age of seven and I will show you the man,'" quotes Will. "That's attributed to Ignatius Loyola, a man who had a strict military background until he decided to form the Jesuit order. The members of the order are also known as God's Marines and that alone says a great deal. Get a child in his formative years, tell him what he should believe, and he will grow to manhood believing all you have told him is true. Goes for girls too." I nod in agreement.

"And because of the brainwashing the child never tells anyone about the sexual abuse. He or she feels ashamed, almost as if they were to blame. Look at the recent comment made by a priest-psychiatrist who counsels pedophile priests! He said that youngsters were often to blame when priests sexually abused them because the child was the seducer." I stand and stretch.

"A vulnerable kid can be led by the abuser to believe that bullshit. Brainwashed to believe the victim is the bad one."

"Maybe all religions are brainwashing," says Myrtle who goes to her synagogue only on high holy days. "I don't feel especially brainwashed, but then I'm pragmatic."

"What about you, Will? Do you feel brainwashed?"

"No, but then Francesca had no problem changing religions when she was dissatisfied with the one in which she was raised. That led me to believe that no religion is infallible. You?"

"Me? I didn't grow up in a particularly religious family. My parents were loving and kind but I was exposed to different beliefs and ideas. I know as much about Buddhism as I do Christianity. I'm more spiritual than religious. Add to that that I have a hard time with those who I think abuse authority."

We grow silent then and just sit and sip our bourbon. I know alcohol is supposed to blur your senses but sometimes I think it clears them. So much about Joshua and his disappearance made sense now. Even the utter neatness of his room. Now I no longer thought that Marie had put it in perfect order after her brother went missing. It was more than likely left like that by

Joshua. Sexually abused children need to be in control of the simple things in their lives, and having everything in its place is a way of being able to control their environment.

I am going to wait a few days to tell Marie what I found. She needs to be prepared first. She has called my cell phone and the office leaving messages on both for me to call her back. I will, but not yet. There's more to this story than just Joshua running away. I just have to find out what it is and that will take a few days.

With bourbon glasses in hand, the three of us go back to the papers to see if there is a clue that may have been missed. Myrtle makes copies of everything in the box, Will and I read through the articles and Joshua's notes. It's going to be a long night.

⟡

"I remember the first time you served Mass as my altar boy. Do you remember that?"

"I remember everything, Father."

CHAPTER 19

WE DIDN'T LEAVE MY office until almost midnight. Even Myrtle stayed and, instead of having her wake up Harry to come pick her up, Will drove her home. I waved to them as they drove away. Long day for all of us but at least I had found out why Joshua went missing. Now I had to decide how to use the information to find him alive – or not.

I am sitting in my car with my eyes closed for just a second when I feel someone try the driver's side door handle. A mugger, a rapist is my first thought. I react by opening the door quickly and slamming it into a man who is trying to get into my car. He wobbles backward, yells "No!" and falls unsteadily forward into me as I quickly get out of the car. His weight knocks into me hard. He tries to punch my face but I duck sideways. There's a heavy smell of cheap wine on his breath when he is up against my body. Balling my fists, I clock him with a right to his face follow up by two kicks to his body and another punch to his jaw. He goes down in a crash next to the open door of my car. I give him a solid kick in the ribs and then place my foot on his throat.

"Stop it! Don't hurt me anymore. Stop it. He said you wouldn't hurt me. I was supposed to talk to you! Get the hell away from me!"

With my foot still firmly planted on his throat, I reach back into the open car and grab my gun off the seat. "Who are you?" I shout, pointing it at him. "Sit up and let me see who you are."

He keeps his hands over his face and scrunches into a fetal position. He is sobbing and saying, "No, no more, please don't hurt me."

I keep the gun on him but lower my voice. "I won't hurt you. I just want to know who you are and why you're trying to get into my car."

After a few minutes he tries to sit up but stays hunched in a protective position, shoulders down and arms folded over his chest. He looks up at me through a mess of dirty hair half covering his face. "Are you gonna shoot me, lady?"

I have to determine if he has a knife or a gun on him. "Show me your hands."

He unfolds his arms and shows me that his hands are empty.

"Stand up. Tell me who you are."

He has difficulty standing but finally gets up crying and wiping his nose on his sleeve. There isn't enough light to determine his age but, from his clothes and the body odor coming from him, he appears to be an inhabitant of the streets. There is a dark puddle forming by his feet and I see that he has wet himself. I lower the gun.

"I'm not going to shoot you. Just tell me who you are, okay?"

"I'm Bo's friend."

~⋙~

Bo's friend—no name, no anything, just Bo's friend. Bo the homeless man to whom I give money every week, the man I bought lunch for recently, the Bo who told me he had a friend who didn't like priests.

I put my gun away; I don't want to scare him. It's bad enough that I see swelling under his eye and on his chin when I look closer at him. Maybe I should take him to an emergency room. Probably not though, if he's like Bo, he shies away from doctors and hospitals, afraid that they'll make him go to a shelter or psych ward. Most street people fear authority.

"Let's go sit over there on the curb, Bo's friend," I say quietly. "Do your ribs hurt?"

"Huh?"

"Your side, this side. Does it hurt?" I touch him gently and he winces. Shit. I probably broke a rib or two. He needs to be checked by a doctor. "I'm going to call a friend of mine to check you out," I say, pulling out my cell phone to call Giles.

"I'm not goin' to no hospital." Even through his alcoholic haze, he looks scared. I lay a hand gently on his shoulder and say, "Don't be afraid, he'll come here to you. He's a good guy."

Within twenty minutes of my call a sleepy Giles pulls up next to my car. He has a bag with him that is not technically a doctor's bag but has the necessary medical supplies needed for emergencies. I introduce him to the man I kick-boxed into submission.

"Hi Giles; thanks for coming. This is Bo's friend. I think his ribs might be broken."

Giles lifts an eyebrow but says nothing except hello to my victim. "My name is Giles and I'm going to make sure you're all right. Can you walk?"

When my victim nods yes, Giles suggests to me that we all go into my office for privacy. Bo's friend is hesitant about going into my building but Giles convinces him that it's better to be examined inside my office since the police might show at any time. Nice lie well told. Bo's friend understands that. Besides hospitals, he probably avoids police too.

It's interesting to note that in the thirty minutes or so since the incident occurred, there has been no sign of a squad car or an ambulance. Nobody on the block has called the police or EMTs, which speaks volumes about the inhabitants of the area. People see things but no one wants to get involved.

Upstairs in my office, Giles checks out Bo's friend and asks me, "Your handiwork?"

I shrug my shoulders and nod yes. "I thought I was being attacked."

"Pity the guy who attacks *you*."

It turns out that one of his ribs is more than likely cracked, but not broken. Giles can't be 100 percent sure unless an X-ray is taken. But since Bo's friend won't allow us to take him to a hospital he has to go on feel and experience. He tapes it up and tells my victim he'll check in on him tomorrow, late afternoon. Then he cleans the wounds on his face, gives him some common over-the-counter meds for inflammation and pain, and tells him to sleep flat on his back. He makes Bo's friend lie down on my couch.

"Do you have a place to sleep?" he asks.

"I sleep at Bo's place."

Giles looks at me to confirm that Bo indeed *has* a place but I shake my head. I really don't know.

"Where is that?"

Bo's friend looks at me defiantly for a minute then back to Giles. "The warehouse, down the block. He has a room down the stairs in the back. Bo's got a warm place. He's lucky."

"Keep lying there and just rest for a few minutes."

He does as he's told. I sit next to him. "Why were you trying to get into my car?"

He looks at me as if I should know why.

"Bo *told* me to talk to you. He said you'd buy me pizza if I talked to you."

"Talk to me about what?" I tiredly wonder if Bo tells all his friends on the street that I'll buy pizza for them if they only come and say hi.

"Nothing. I forget. But he said you would buy me pizza if I talked to you. He said it's important for me to talk to you."

"Are you hungry?" I ask. He nods. "I don't have pizza but I do have doughnuts from this morning. Let me get them for you."

I get the leftover box of pastries Myrtle brought in earlier today. There are four big gooey ones left. With that open box and a bottle of water, I walk back to Bo's friend and set it all on a cart that has nothing on it but computer paper.

He devours two before he even opens the bottle of water. Then looking at Giles he says, "I like doughnuts. They fill me up."

"Come back tomorrow afternoon after five thirty and I'll have pizza," I say encouragingly.

"That's a promise, she will," Giles tells him. "Finish up and we'll walk you down the block." To me he says, "Let's get him over to where your friend Bo has his place and then we can leave. It's going on one thirty and I can see that you're beat."

He checks my right hand, which swelled significantly from its collision with the jawbone of Bo's friend. "Ice it when you get home and take some aspirin."

We let our guest devour the last two doughnuts and the water. I give him two more bottles of water to take back for him and Bo and we all troop downstairs to the street.

"Remember to come back tomorrow around five thirty. I'll have pizza for you. You can bring Bo too." I smile winningly but Bo's friend isn't about to become friendly with the woman who cracked his ribs and gave him a swollen jaw. Giles repeats what I said and tells him that he has to check his ribs tomorrow.

"It's really important that I check you. If you're injured too badly someone might have to call an ambulance. I know that you don't want that. It's better to come here."

He nods his head yes to Giles and then looks at me.

"Can we go *out* for pizza? Like you did with Bo?"

"Only if Dr. Barrett says that your ribs are all right." I play my card like a pro. With a promise of going out for pizza I can make sure that he'll show up to let Giles examine him.

"Can I tell Bo we're going for pizza?"

"Yes, absolutely. Tell him we're going out for pizza and whatever else you want," I say expansively. I feel horrible for having done what I did to him even though I thought he was a mugger or worse.

Giles and I walk Bo's Friend down the block to the old warehouse where he disappears into a dark stairway. On the walk back to where I always park, I fill Giles in on what I found out about Joshua and his abuse. Giles stops in the middle of the sidewalk, lets out a low whistle, and puts his arm around me. He doesn't say a word, just holds me for a few minutes.

Back at my car I thank Giles again and he pulls me close for a hug. "Go home, get some sleep. I'll be here tomorrow around six." He sniffs the bourbon on my breath. "You okay to drive?"

"Yes. That little episode with Bo's friend woke me up. I'm fine."

"Does he have a name other than Bo's Friend?"

"Not that he would tell me."

He watches me get into my car and buckle up. "Good night, Cate. Be careful driving."

"You too, Giles. See you tomorrow."

And I drive home with my thoughts running the gamut, from Joshua McElroy who was sexually abused by a parish priest and had no recourse but to escape and disappear, to a homeless man named Bo's friend who wants to talk to me.

CHAPTER 20

AFTER FALLING INTO BED and sleeping a restless five whole hours, I found myself, at six in the morning, wide-awake and filled with rage over what I had read in Joshua's journal. Grabbing my tennis bag, I set out to hit some balls against the volley wall at the park.

My swollen right hand is wrapped with an Ace bandage because I was too tired to ice it when I got home last night even though I did take ibuprofen for the pain and inflammation. I feel the ache every time the ball hits the racket but that's good because I need focus. I'm pretending that the ball is the pedophile who ruined not only Joshua's life but, through his acts, shattered Marie and her whole family. Thwack! Forehand, backhand, thwack! I play this mind game for an hour and then go home to shower.

Despite a minimum amount of sleep, I feel energized. My plan, after a quick stop at my office, is to go to the rectory of St. Matthew's and find out what I can about any priests and their relationship to Joshua. But first and foremost, I need coffee.

⤙

Myrtle is not in her usual place when I come in; she's standing by the window cradling a mug of tea. There's the smell of fresh coffee and a small carton of half-and-half next to the pot.

Without turning around, Myrtle tells me that she didn't have time to stop at Timothy's but the coffee I smell brewing is the next best thing.

"Sure, okay, Myrtle. That's good. You all right?"

She turns toward me and I can see she had less sleep than I had.

"Last night Harry woke up when I came in. He's a light sleeper. He could see that I was upset and I told him about Joshua McElroy. Oh, I didn't tell him anyone's name, just mentioned what had happened. It's in the news; you see it all the time about clergy abusing children. He didn't ask any personal questions, just sat and talked with me until I felt better.

"I know that these things happen, Cate, I know that the courts are handing down judgments and convictions both to the individual abusers and to the churches. But this cruel crime has never entered into my own little world. Now with Marie and your case, it has. It isn't truly personal, I know, but it bothers me to come this close to it. I was a grade-school teacher; I taught children the same *age* Joshua was when he was abused. They are so innocent and vulnerable at that age. This is a horror."

I grab my mug and fix my coffee the way I like it then check the fridge for yogurt. Myrtle has stocked it with pomegranate and blueberry. I choose the pomegranate and settle at my desk.

"Myrtle, most of my cases are simple; the cheating spouses ones are nothing that you can lose sleep over. Only a few of my clients can be called tragic. I agree with you, this is a horror, but I'm going to bring this horror to a close and hopefully get justice for Marie. I'm starting to believe that Joshua may very well be alive. If he is, I want to find him."

She turns back to the window. "I hope to God you do, Catherine. I hope you do and soon."

≈

The call from Father Richard Boyd from the Paterson Diocese comes in as I'm driving out to St. Matthew's in Queens and Myrtle forwards it to my cell, which is synched to my car phone. Pressing the answer button on the steering wheel, I say, "This is Cate Harlow."

"Ms. Harlow, this is Father Richard Boyd. I called you a few days ago."

"Yes, I got your message. It sounded important. "

"I think it is. The priest, the one you called about a few weeks ago, a Francis Xavier Murphy? Well, the name came up in the accounting audit when our new system was finally up and running. I came across some records with his name next to a code that I hadn't seen before. I was curious so I checked the code against a list we have. Francis Xavier Murphy *was* a priest in the diocese for thirty-seven years."

"Was?"

There's a long pause.

"I'm going out on a limb here, Ms. Harlow. I only called you because of what the code states and it bothers me."

"What does it say?" I signal right and pull over to the side of the road as quickly as I can. I need to concentrate on what he's telling me.

"He's a legal dependent."

"You mean he is taken care of by the church for life. That's nothing new Father, that's par for the course for all religions. Almost all major ones provide those benefits to clergy."

"If you mean that the Church will take care of all those who go into religious life, yes, that is true, but this is something different."

"How so?"

"Francis Xavier Murphy went through a process called laicization."

"And what is that?"

"Basically, an agreement to leave the priesthood but it is stipulated that you will still be taken care of. Sometimes there's room and board supplied by the church for a period of time and you get to keep your small pension and health benefits. And that's fine; men have requested laicization for various reasons, one of which is to marry. Naturally the benefits stop if a former priest marries. Some request the process because they feel they can't keep the vow of celibacy even if they don't want to get married."

"But something didn't seem right about this one so I dug a little deeper to find out why he left. What I found, in a hidden file, was that this Francis Xavier Murphy was also paid $20,000 as '*incitamentum relinquere*.'"

"If my Latin serves me correctly, that phrase means an incentive to relinquish."

"You're absolutely correct. That's *an incentive* to leave the priesthood and that alone explains everything." He pauses again. "Ms. Harlow, this man you called about? Records indicate sexual misconduct with a minor. In blunt terms, it means he was paid to leave because he is a child molester."

We speak for another fifteen minutes and I thank him for coming forward with this information. But I have to ask why he would go against the hierarchy of the church.

"Why do it, Father? It's been kept secret for a reason and I'm certain that your superiors at the diocese would make sure there were unpleasant consequences for anyone leaking this out."

"Ms. Harlow, I became a priest not just because I wanted to serve God but because I wanted to *help* people. People who were unhappy, or lost or just plain needed someone to talk to. Heaven, Hell, pro-life, sins—none of that matters to me. It's helping people deal with all the crap life throws at them that's important to me. Truthfully, I am disgusted with what has been allowed to happen within the confines of the Church. The cover-ups, the male-dominated bullshit; even here most of it is nothing more than an old boys' club that hides the evil done and protects those who have committed the molestation by promoting them and moving them to other parishes. And now this—paying them off and taking care of them for life.

"What has happened in the priesthood fills me with intense anger and, God forgive me, but sometimes when I hear about a crime committed against these monsters, I think that, just maybe, the men who call themselves priests, the ones you found mutilated, deserved the awful punishment. Almost as if it is God's revenge. I want the younger generation of priests like me to make positive changes and to help those who have been damaged by the sexual abuse allowed to run rampant."

I sigh deeply. "I have to agree with you there. Listen, I won't give you as my source but I've got to call the lead detective on this particular case and let him know."

"If it helps him to make his case, the use of my name is fine with me."

"Thanks, Father, but that's not necessary. It can be done so no one knows who leaked what. By the way, can I just call you Richard? You can call me Cate."

"Sure. Not a Catholic?"

"No, I'm not, but that's not the reason. I'm guessing that I'm older than you."

"Well, I'm twenty-six."

"Oh, yeah, definitely older, Richard. An older sister," I say hurriedly.

After our conversation, I call Will at headquarters and give him the new information. Will tells me he'll take a trip out to the diocese again later today and he thanks me for my info.

"Just remember, Will, don't use that young priest's name. He says he won't mind but I'd prefer that you didn't. It was enough that he came forward with this information."

"No source revealed on my end. I'll call you later."

The Roman Catholic Church of St. Matthew encompasses an entire block that includes the church itself, a rectory, a convent, and a small elementary school. Except for the school, the buildings look gothic and dreary. There's a sign on the rectory door that reads, *Please ring bell only once. If this is an emergency please call 212.555.7043 and a priest will assist you. Thank you.*

I make a note of the number in my mind.

Ringing the bell on the side of the entrance, I wait and finally hear footsteps hurrying to the door. A sturdy, elderly woman wiping her hands on an apron appears, standing in the open doorway. "May I help you?"

"I'm Cate Harlow and I would like to see the pastor if he's available."

"Do you have an appointment with Father Morgan?"

"No, I don't but if he's in I would like to speak with him. It's confidential but—I can assure you—very important."

"Well ... I don't know. Father is very busy."

"It's an important matter that concerns one of the parishioners. I can't say more than that." I hand her my card.

"You're an investigator?"

"A private detective." The word "detective" seems to carry more weight with people, private or not.

She looks skeptical but waves me inside to sit and wait on a wooden deacon's bench. I decide that being charming may be my best bet. "Whatever it is that you're cooking smells wonderful," I say smiling at her. Praise the cook, possible information there through a bit of gossip.

"Oh it's only a turkey potpie," she says, obviously pleased. "Do you like potpies?"

I smile sweetly. "My grandmother used to make them for me all the time. She made them from scratch." Actually Nonna Rita never made a potpie in her life but she was a whiz at whipping up a great white clam sauce with linguine and tons of clams and shrimp.

"Oh I do too; the homemade ones are the best." She smiles kindly at me. "Please, have a seat. If Father can see you, I'll bring in some refreshments." Her footsteps click down the polished hardwood floor in the hallway and disappear.

The outer room where she has left me leads into what looks like a small office area. There's one three-drawer file cabinet, a roll-top desk, and a rather large laptop computer. I hear voices down the hall, but no one is nearby so I step inside. The cabinet isn't locked and I quietly pull open the top drawer. A glance at the neatly arranged files inside show me that the information contained in them has to do with budgets and bills. The second drawer seems to be stuck and I don't want to chance making a noise to open it. I try the third and it slides open. There are voices drifting down the hall.

"...Cate Harlow, she said, Father. Here's her business card. Shall I tell her to wait?"

"A private investigator? I have no idea what she can want with me but this is not a good time. I'm the only one in today. If it were an emergency with one of the parishioners then ... but I don't think this is an emergency. I may not be able to see her today at all. I have no way of knowing how long this will take and believe me this is an important meeting for us. I really am sorry. Ask if she can come back tomorrow. I'll be available then."

Her shoes make the same clicking sound as before only this time she's coming back to where I'm supposed to be. I push the drawer closed gently without getting a chance to see what is inside. When she returns, she finds me seated on the bench, legs crossed and hands folded.

"Father Morgan is in the middle of a meeting and won't be able to see you today but perhaps you could come back tomorrow? No? I'm sorry. Can I get you something to drink then, before you go? Father usually has herbal tea around this time and I'll be bringing some into his meeting. I can get you a cup."

The smell of freshly brewed coffee gives me an idea. I have learned that people who work alone can be a great source of information. They are usually unobtrusive to their employers and observe a lot of what's going on.

"No, thank you so much. I'm more of a coffee drinker. I love the smell of coffee coming from your kitchen."

"I'm a coffee drinker too! It's my one vice. Listen," she comes to stand next to me, "I'm still working in the kitchen, but if you'd like to come back there with me we can have some coffee. It's fresh-made."

"Thank you so much, I'd like that."

Walking back to the kitchen I make note of the layout of

rooms off the hallway: a TV room with a couch and two reclining chairs to the right of the hall, followed by a small dining room. Another office, with floor to ceiling bookcases, and a bathroom on the left—too open for any secretive activity.

I assume the bedrooms are upstairs but again it would be difficult to take a child up there without being noticed. Molesters like to work in secret. Joshua's torment had to have been done elsewhere, somewhere that was hidden from everyday view.

The woman taking me to the kitchen is named Bette and she is the housekeeper at the rectory. She gives me coffee that is hot and strong but I decline the apple turnover she offers. The room is warm and has that homey feeling of a well-used kitchen. Putting a tray of pastries and tea things together, she takes them to where the pastor is having the meeting.

When she returns she begins to chop up vegetables and puts them neatly in a casserole dish before she pours her coffee and takes a pastry. Sitting across from me, Bette tells me that she has worked here for over forty years.

"That's quite an accomplishment, staying in one job for that long," I say admiringly. "You must have seen some changes over the years. Demographics, new parishioners."

"We're still pretty much of an Irish American community. But we do have a new priest, Father Miguel Ruiz, who does the Mass in Spanish."

"So, you've seen changes here at the rectory too. You know, with priests coming here and leaving for other parishes."

"We don't seem to have much of that. Father Ruiz is the only new one here in quite some time. Of course, we have had our share of priests who have been elevated to higher offices, but only one left. That was Father Moore. He was made a monsignor, God bless him, and well deserved, too. He was here for about fourteen years and he even stayed here for a while *after* he became monsignor, stayed for four more years. Then he suddenly left."

Remembering my conversation with Father Richard earlier this morning about priests being made an offer to leave the church, I ask as casually as I can, "Oh? Why did he leave? Where did he go?"

With obvious pride, she tells me that he's now working in the office of the archbishop.

"The whole parish is so proud. He's a brilliant man, did wonders for the parish, and so kind. We miss him here."

"Do all the priests have different duties? I mean you said that he did wonders for the parish. I guess they all have their own unique talents." Then I add, "God-given talents."

"Oh yes. Some are very good at the business end—you know, making the money we receive from the diocese stretch as far as it can. They make sure that all the programs we run are funded, not only through the quota we receive but also through fundraisers. Father Morgan is very good at that and he's really good at talking to business leaders for contributions. He's talking to a group of business people right now, trying to get their help in repairing the roof of the school. Father Hogan helps him too on that end but he's so much better at doing things like Pre-Cana counseling, you know, talking to couples about to be married. He has a great rapport with young adults.

"Now Father Moore, he was excellent with the children. He organized sports activities, got the new gym built for our traveling basketball team. Was in charge of the altar boys and then, when the Church allowed girls to assist at Mass, the altar girls. The children all loved him."

"I guess he began his priesthood here then, right?"

"Oh, no. He had been at two other parishes before he came here. Didn't stay long at the other ones though, two maybe three years each. He went wherever His Excellency the archbishop sent him. A true man of God. His service at St. Matthew's was the longest and we're lucky we got to have him here. Everyone loved him, especially the children."

I have to be careful to phrase my questions so they don't sound like an interrogation.

"I would assume he misses being with the kids then. What are his duties at the archbishop's?"

"Oh, he's still involved in programs for the children of the archdiocese. He oversees new programs and mentors boys who are interested in the priesthood. Some of them are as young as ten, yet they seem to have that calling to serve God and he recognizes that in them. He always spent a lot of time mentoring the boys here."

"He sounds like a wonderful person," I say politely. "How long ago did you say he left?"

"Nine years ago, yes, going on ten now. And," she leans forward, lowering her voice, "I never thought that it was just that the archbishop had an opening in his office that made him want to leave. He loved it here, told me that he could have just as easily stayed here and commuted to the archdiocese every day. It's only twenty minutes. No, it was more than that. He told me his heart was broken and that's why he had to leave. *Bette,* he said to me, *I have a broken heart because I have lost someone dear to me.* Poor man!"

I make my face look concerned and sad. "What happened, Bette?"

She bites into the pastry and shakes her head. "It was so sad. A young teenage boy went missing. He was one of monsignor's altar boys; starting at the age of eight he served all monsignor's Masses. Such a nice family he came from! Every Sunday at eleven o'clock Mass you'd see the McElroy family there, the mother, the father, and his sister; that was the Mass *Joshua* McElroy served with monsignor back when monsignor was still Father Moore. They were together a lot, those two. Father took a special interest in him; Joshua was a quiet, timid boy.

"No one knows what happened to him. He just disappeared one spring afternoon when he was, oh, about fifteen, yes, fifteen years old. Monsignor was so distraught over it that he simply had to leave here. He took it very hard, that disappearance."

"I'm not from around here so I never heard the story. Does the family still live in the area?"

"The sister does, lives in the same house where she grew up. The parents, oh, that was so sad! First the mother died three years after the tragedy, then the father followed about a year later. That poor girl! The Lord has given her so much to bear. I see her at the nine o'clock Mass almost every Sunday. Very pretty, always lighting candles at the Virgin's altar."

"Do you think that this Joshua was kidnapped?" I ask.

"You know something? That's funny that you should ask that." She shakes her head. "Most people *did* assume that that was what happened to him. The police never found a body so murder was ruled out I guess. But ... I don't think he was kidnapped and neither did the monsignor."

"No? What did he think happened?" I lean forward toward her.

"It was the only time I ever saw him angry. He said he thought that Joshua ran away and *then* he said that what that young boy did was one of the most selfish things anyone can do."

"Why selfish?" I ask.

"Monsignor said that the boy was selfish because he was hurting someone who cared about him very much. Monsignor Moore loved that boy like a son." Or like a pedophile "loves" his victim. Bingo, Bette.

"Where are we going, my son? Is the restaurant far?"
"We'll be there soon, Father."

CHAPTER 21

WALKING TO MY CAR, my cell rings and it is Will. He's returning from Paterson after a "friendly little talk" with a Father Mulcahy and associates.

"Nice work, Private Investigator Cate Harlow," he says with a grim laugh. "This Mulcahy was very cooperative after I told him that he could either talk with me of his own accord and show me any and all files on the dead priest, or I could get a subpoena that would allow my people and me to make a holy-shit mess of his filing system which would include confiscating all the computers in the place. Funny how he was more than willing to talk to us."

"You're the man," I say.

"And he *asked,* but I didn't tell, how I got the info. I keep my promises, Cate; no source revealed."

"Thanks, Will. Much appreciated."

"Where are you?"

"Queens, at St. Matthew's Rectory. And speaking about people willing to talk, I got a great deal of information from the housekeeper about the priests who live there and about a certain Monsignor Moore who seemed to have had a close and personal relationship with Joshua McElroy. She said that the monsignor was very distraught over Joshua's disappearance, loved him, and I quote, *like a son*."

"The sick reasoning of the child molester," I hear Will sigh and curse.

"Yes, and get this: it seems that he was at two other parishes, very briefly, before coming to St. Matthew's."

"Could be he was moved for a reason. The Church hierarchy has been known to do that if they receive a complaint of sexual abuse."

"True. Listen, I'm heading back to the city soon. Keep me updated on your case, okay?"

"Yeah, I'll keep you in the loop. What are you going to do with the information you received today?"

"Well, this Monsignor Moore, who I am pretty certain is the abuser Joshua documented in his journal, is now ensconced in the archbishop's office directing youth activities there and mentoring young boys who think they want to be priests. Great opportunity for a pedophile. I'd like to talk to him about Joshua McElroy; who knows what info he might be hiding that could lead me to Joshua. But I have to figure a way in without him becoming suspicious of my reason to see him. I'll work it out while I'm driving back. It's a long drive and that's good for thinking."

"All right. If I can help in any way, just ask."

"You know I will. Thanks, Will."

After the conversation I lean on the fence surrounding the church proper and watch the kids running around the play area. I know what Myrtle means about that age being so innocent and vulnerable. I see smiling faces, hear goofy laughter, and watch innocence at play. Damn all people who harm children! Destroying innocence and trust.

"Ms. Harlow? Cate!" I hear my name called and see Bette waving at me. She comes walking over to where I am, a bit out of breath. "You had a phone call. I think it was your office trying to contact you. They asked if you were still here and I said that you'd just left. Then I came outside and saw you standing here. You should probably call them."

No one knew I was coming to St. Matthew's except Myrtle,

and she would have called my cell. Someone is checking up on my whereabouts; the question is who. I smile at Bette and say, "I'll call my office. Thank you for telling me."

"No problem," she says, "It was a pleasure talking with you. I'm glad I met you."

She goes back into the rectory and I walk toward my car conscious of every person I pass and of any cars parked near mine. Who would call looking for me at St. Matthew's rectory and, more importantly, who would know that I came here? Myrtle is scrupulous about never letting anyone, with the exception of Will or Giles, know where I am when it involves a case. Am I being followed? By whom and for what reason?

I scout the area. The cars in the surrounding lots look like they are parked for the day. There's no one near where I'm parked, but to be on the safe side I remove my gun from my bag and stick it into the front of my jeans as I approach my car.

I check my car carefully keeping my hand on the gun. Nothing. I open the car door quickly pointing my gun into the back seat. No one hiding there. I walk around to the front of my car and pop the hood. Nothing suspicious. Then, just to be absolutely certain that there's no danger, I get down on the ground and look under the car for an explosive triggering device. With the work I do, you never know what nutcase might crack and want revenge. The underside of the Edge is clean and I get in, starting the motor with just a bit of trepidation. Dialing my office the phone rings three times before I hear, "Catherine Harlow, Private Investigations. May I help you?"

"Hi Myrtle. Just checking in to see if there are any calls. Anyone looking for me?"

I don't want to alarm her so I don't mention the call at the rectory.

"Let's see, the call I forwarded to you earlier from Father Boyd, and Giles called and said something about pizza and Bo's friend—that's a mystery to me but he said you'd know and he'll call you back later. Marie McElroy left a message while I was out of the office getting a carton of half-and-half, saying she'd call later. Then a credit card company called saying that they want your business back, seems they don't like you getting out of debt, and Harry called to tell me he's making peach strudel. That's it, honey."

"Anyone come to the office for me?"

"No, I would have told you. Oh, by the way, the couch smelled rather funny, sort of sour, when I walked in this morning so I called a cleaning service to come in to clean it."

"Thank you Myrtle. Must be mildew from the humidity or something," I say thinking about Bo's friend and his urine-wet pants.

"Possibly. You never want the air conditioner on so it *could* very well be mildew. Anyway, are you coming back soon? I can get us lunch if you're back within an hour or so."

"Sure thing. Something light, maybe a grilled chicken salad from Enzo's? They do deliver."

"You got it, honey. See you in a bit."

⮑

My mother once told me that, "A secret is only a secret as long as you don't tell anyone." Good advice when you're a child and pretty handy when you're a private investigator.

When you're dealing with a cold case that involves a missing person who might very well still be alive, you have to tread very carefully. Any knowledge that you have in hand needs to be used with discretion. That means that even though the client who hired you has the absolute right to know everything that is happening in the case, it isn't always in their best interest to know it immediately. Sometimes their knowing crucial information can actually impede your work and put an end to the resolution of the case.

Then, too, if a missing person is alive, you don't want to tip your hand. If they've been kidnapped, which was more than likely *not* the case with Joshua McElroy, the person holding them can move their victim out of your reach. This was shown in the case of a Utah girl whose captor knew the police were on to him and moved his hiding place and the girl several times.

But if a person has chosen to leave and hide like Joshua, you also don't want him to know that he is about to be found. To prevent any of this from happening, you keep what you know a secret. If you have to share information and details, you do it sparingly and only with someone you trust implicitly. For me that person is Will Benigni. He takes law enforcement seriously and holds anything said in confidence as sacred.

These are my thoughts as I sit in my office and have lunch with Myrtle. The grilled chicken salad from Enzo's is delicious and as I eat I think about what I've learned. I know that Marie can know absolutely nothing right now about what I've found in the box hidden in the eaves or about my visit to St. Matthew's. I'll give her the box with only the few drawings that were in there. The rest—the journal, the newspaper clippings, and historical copies of atrocities—I'll keep for a later date.

"You're certainly quiet today, Cate. How did it go at the church office?"

I know Myrtle can keep a confidence, but I feel it's probably better not to tell her too much. There's a lot riding on the bit of info given to me by the church housekeeper and I need to work it for all it's worth if I want to find Joshua and also bring a pedophile to justice.

"I did find out a few things but I need to work on it by myself for a while. A lot is at stake right now. And Myrtle, while we're on this topic, I'm not telling Marie what I found in the box her brother hid. I think it's traumatic to tell her before I am able to act on what the contents reveal. The time will come when she has to be told but not right now."

Myrtle gives me her favorite stern teacher look then smiles. "Have you *ever* once known me to reveal anything about a case unless you okayed it? Look up the word discretion in the dictionary and you'll find my picture."

"I know; I'm just edgy about how this will all play out. Still love me?"

"You're hard not to love."

"Tell that to the men I know."

She just shakes her head and mutters, "Hmm."

***

For the rest of the day I work at my desk. On the archdiocese website I find phone numbers and email addresses from the archbishop's office and scroll the listing. There he is, a Monsignor Bernard Moore complete with picture, phone number, and extension, followed by his email address. I look at his smiling face for a long few minutes. Dressed in the majesty of his office, the monsignor looks at the camera with a smug smile. His eyes have a staring, hungry look. A look that is eerily similar to the stalking yellow-eyed hyena in Joshua's drawings. I try hard not to think about what he has done to Joshua McElroy. Monsignor Moore looks as if he thinks he's untouchable and as if he is unstoppable in what he is doing. Let him think that all he wants; he hasn't met me yet.

I call Marie back knowing that I have to lie, which is difficult for me. It isn't that I feel guilty about lying; for me, that's easy if it gets me what I need. But Marie is the one who sat in my office and asked me to be completely honest with her about what I found out. *"Promise you won't hold anything back. No matter how bad the information is, I have to know everything."*

She believes the lie I tell her about the contents in the box. "The box only contains a few drawings; I can drop off the box when I get a chance." Marie sighs. "Imagine, Joshua hiding something in the eaves! That line from Peter Pan must have given him the idea." Then she hesitantly asks me if she can come to get the box at my office.

"I'd rather drop it off, Marie. Right now I've got someone checking it for prints to make sure that it is indeed your brother's so it's not in my office anyway. I'll get it back to you as soon as I can."

"Thank you, Cate. I ... I trust you."

Trust me. Thank God.

***

At ten of five Myrtle calls Harry for her ride home. She can drive but she's told me more than a few times that having Harry bring her to work and pick her up after work gets him out of his little world. Harry's a retired accountant who only works during tax season. The rest of the year he occasionally golfs, but mostly he experiments with baking recipes he finds on the Internet or on cooking shows.

"The cleaners are coming tomorrow around eleven, Cate, but I don't think they will disturb you. I'll be in at nine with coffee and Harry's strudel."

"I'll see you then but I'll get the coffee at Timothy's. It's my turn anyway and it's right near the place where I'm picking up my new smartphone. You just bring the strudel."

"All right. Have a good night and don't forget to lock up."

⌒≈⌒

After Myrtle leaves, I put everything away and power-down my PC to sleep mode. Then I open a window about five inches just to get the stale smell out of the room. The nest with the doves is still active. The babies are snuggled in and I see the parents across the street on a telephone wire. The dim light I leave on gives off a nice glow and I sit and stand by the window and watch the rush-hour traffic. There's something irrationally calming about city noise. It allows me to think. Bo's friend, maybe he is the one Bo said hates priests. Who knows? If he is then, with luck, tonight I'll find out why.

At five thirty on the dot, I hear a timid knocking on the front door downstairs and run down to open it. Pizza time is coming up. Bo is there with his friend who won't make eye contact with me.

"Why'd you hit him?" Bo begins as soon as he sees me. "I told him you wouldn't hurt him. I said you would give him pizza. Why'd you hit him, huh?"

Bo hasn't said this much to me so fast in all the time I've known him. Usually he parcels out what he says in simple sentences very sparingly.

I explain that I thought his friend was a mugger or a rapist. "It was late Bo. He grabbed the door handle of my car and tried to open it. How would I know he was your friend? I'm sorry I hurt him." Turning to his friend, I emphasize my words with, *"Really* sorry."

Bo still looks upset as we climb the stairs and I tell him that as soon as my friend Giles gets here, we're walking the few blocks to get pizza. Then I ask him what his friend's name is. "I can't keep calling him Bo's friend, can I? He has a name."

He looks at his friend who is staring intently at the wooden doorframe outside my office. "He don't have a name."

"What do *you* call him?"

"Nothin'. I just say 'Hey.'"

"Do you have a name?" I ask Bo's friend.

He looks at me for a minute before going back to examining the door frame again and nods his head yes but says nothing. His jaw is bruised and swollen where I punched him and I don't want to think about his ribs. I decide not to push it; maybe Giles can get a name out of him.

Thankfully Giles arrives fifteen minutes later carrying his medical bag so I only have to sit in silence with Bo and his friend for a short period of time. My few attempts at getting the conversational ball rolling fall flat so I haul out the pastries we always seem to have in our office, courtesy of Myrtle's Harry, and let them eat.

"Hi, Cate. How're we doing here?" Giles walks in the door of my office and takes in the scene of the two men and me sitting there. He walks over to Bo's friend and asks him how he's feeling. "You need to take off your shirt so I can check you before we go for pizza. How did you sleep?"

Bo's friend takes his shirt off a bit unwillingly. I turn away so he won't be embarrassed. Giles gently unwraps the binding he put on him last night. Taking a quick glance back at Bo's friend, I wince when I see his side.

"Sleepin' okay. It was warm. On my back like you said." He looks at Giles with trust and something bordering on idol worship as Giles gently touches the rib area.

"How is your breathing? Any pain when you breathe?"

"No, I can breathe. It don't hurt too much now."

"Well, I'm going to re-tape your rib area. You can remove it in two days and I'll come back here to check on you next week. I think you'll be fine."

Giles takes some sterile pads out of his bag, saturates them with a liquid disinfectant, and gently swabs the bruised area. I know he does pretty much the same procedure on the bodies at the morgue. He finishes up by putting Bacitracin on the healing cuts.

Giles is kind, compassionate, and confident. This is a man with whom my parents would have encouraged me to have a solid relationship. A man most people would say I was lucky to have with me. And truthfully, I care a great deal about him. He's as different from my ex-husband as can be—not that Will isn't kind, but Giles is more open in his compassion and shows his genuine concern for Bo's friend. Maybe it is the doctor in him.

When everyone is ready to go I call Enzo's and ask for an outside table for four people. Then it's down the stairs and out into the evening for pizza.

~≈~

"Where are we? I don't believe I know this area."

"Come out of the car with me, Father. I have a surprise for you."

CHAPTER 22

FOR A WEEKNIGHT ENZO'S is crowded. Honoring my request the owner has put a *Reserved* sign on a table away from the sidewalk and near the side of his trattoria. When the server comes over to take drink orders, Giles tells him to also bring two large antipasto salads and an order of mozzarella sticks to start off the meal. Bo and his friend look happy and settle on one pepperoni pizza and one covered with chicken parmigiana.

There's not a lot of talking when the food arrives except for Giles and me. The others quickly begin eating in that same way I saw Bo devour the pizza last week: heads down, food held close to their bodies, afraid of having someone steal it. I notice that Bo seems to be the one who is in charge, making sure that his friend gets a big portion and pushing a can of soda over to him.

Giles grabs my hand under the table and shakes his head slightly acknowledging the survival skills of life on the streets. There are a few curious people who glance at our table but most of the crowd there is involved in their own end of the day meal. The city may be indifferent to our problems but it is accepting of all its inhabitants.

I hear Bo whisper something to his friend, who looks from me to Giles and back again. He shakes his head *no* but Bo seems trying to convince him to talk to me. I hear, "You didn't want to come see Father Pat for doughnuts. You told me you hate priests but Father Pat is a good guy. Maybe a priest smashed you once, huh? Why don't you like priests? Tell her why. Come on, she's a good lady even though she smashed you. I said you would talk to her if she bought you pizza."

Giles leans over the table and says to Bo's friend, "You know you can tell me anything, right? Well, you can tell Cate anything, too. Believe me I wouldn't lie to you. I made sure you didn't have to go to the hospital, didn't I? So, I think you can trust me. And I trust her."

Looking at Giles he says simply, "I don't like priests. They're bad people."

"Why are they bad?" I ask. I keep my voice calm and low. I don't want him to be afraid to answer. "Has any priest ever hurt you?"

"They're bad people. They do ... bad things."

Here it is. Pushing him to list what *they* do will not elicit details. All he's willing to share is that bad things have been done.

"They do bad things? That's why you hate them?" asks Bo looking at his friend all hunched up over his food. "No they don't! They're good, they help people, they ..."

Bo's friend shakes his head no and hunches farther down in his seat.

"I like priests. I was an altar boy," says Bo with a hint of pride. "Remember the priest you met who gave us coffee and something to eat? He was dressed like him," he points to Giles, "so you didn't know he was a priest. He's a good man, that priest. I think all priests are good."

Another headshake and a whispered *No*. Bo, however, is insistent.

"You got to tell me why though. What bad thing did they do? Why don't you like priests? You're a Catholic, you said so. Why don't you like priests? You got smacked hard or somethin'?"

Bo's friend looks like he wants to cry. Giles leans toward Bo and cautions him to stop asking his friend about priests but Bo is relentless in a childlike way.

"*Why* don't you like priests? I like priests, they're good to me Father Pat, he ..."

Suddenly Bo's friend says a little too loudly, "A priest touched my body in a private place when I was a little kid, and he made me touch him! I hope he dies! Another priest at school did bad things to me, too. He did it after school when nobody was around. I want him dead too."

Our fellow diners at the next table turn to look and Bo's friend hunches deeper into the chair. He's silent for a few minutes and they turn away and continue with their meals.

The foggy-minded necessity that allows Bo's friend to survive on the street lifts and his next words, though low, are strong. He looks at Bo with clarity and says, "The man who was in the van? The man who gave me the coat? He said that priests should die. A lot of people think they should die. He was with some group that had a van. One guy would talk to the street people like me. He asked us if the priests ever come by. I told him I hated priests and he stopped to talk to me. He said that it was okay to hate priests; he hated them too. I said I wanted to kill the priests who did things to me and he said they deserved to be killed. He said that we had to punish them because God wouldn't do it."

Bo looks at his friend completely stunned and says, "Don't tell me that!"

"It's true, Bo, they should all die. I hate priests. You don't know about what they do."

The written images described by Joshua McElroy's journal come back to me in a flash. The man sitting in front of me, the one who is Bo's friend, is older than Joshua by at least twenty years yet they share that common horror of sexual abuse. Centuries of it going on and no one stopped it.

Then I think, *Is it possible that Bo's friend might have met someone who is in one of the vigilante groups that may have been involved in the priests' murders?* If he has then I have to proceed slowly. The clarity that came over Bo's friend can easily fade and he can revert back to the person who stays hidden within himself. Victims of abuse sometimes bury the horror deep inside their minds in order to survive. I quietly ask him, "Are you sure that you heard this person say that priests *deserved* to be killed?"

So low that I can hardly hear him, he mumbles, "Yeah. It's a group who brings us clothes and stuff, but they hate priests too."

"Where are they?" I lean closer so I can hear him. "Can you find them again?"

"I don't know. Downtown somewhere is where I got a coat and a blanket from a man. But I don't see him ever now."

"What did the van look like?" I ask. "Any signs or any words on it would be helpful."

"White, it was white and dirty, really dirty. I didn't see words. And it was real old."

Giles interjects, "Did this group have a name? They must have called themselves something."

Bo's friend looks up and I see his eyes look clear and cold. "I think that the other guy, the one driving the van, said the group was called memory, only it *wasn't* memory, it sounded *like* that word but it was *different*. Like in a church, like some prayer, a memory, you know—a *mem*ory. I forgot the real word because it isn't English. A church word … I hate church."

"Memory," I say the word aloud.

A prayer, a group named after a word said in church, maybe a prayer. A prayer not said in English so it has to be in Latin, the original language of the Church. Instinctively, I run Latin words for memory through my mind: *memoria, memento, memoriis.*

"A novena," says Bo suddenly. "Church words. I don't understand them. My mama took me every Monday night to a novena. I know the memory prayer, a prayer you say to God's mother to remember you."

"To remember!" I say. "In Latin that would be *memorare*. Is it *memorare*?"

"Maybe." Bo's friend has begun to withdraw again.

"The memory prayer everyone says at the novena," Bo says smiling triumphantly.

Memorare.

A group named after a prayer that is a plea for help.

"When was the last time you saw this man?"

"Maybe last month, maybe, I don't know."

"At the same place?"

"Yeah, maybe. I go to different places. Downtown though."

"You better call Will," Giles tells me. "He can start having the police canvas the downtown areas right away."

I'm way ahead of him. I already hit speed dial for Will's cell number.

Will has taken down all the info I have given him and lets me know that he's getting it to the detectives who deal with the crimes against the homeless downtown. I also tell him about the incident that occurred last night between Bo's friend and me, as well as Giles's part in helping me out.

"Catc, I need to talk directly with the guy who told you about the group, Memorare. Maybe he can give a description of the man who gave him the coat to one of our sketch artists. I can show him pictures of vans that might help us also. Can you get him to the station tonight?"

"I can *try* but I don't think so. He's leery of cops."

"Call me back in thirty minutes. If he won't budge, I'll have to come get him."

"Is there any chance you can talk to him at my office and *not* bring him to a station? You can bring one of the sketch artists here too. Believe me you'd be better off doing this. You'll get more out of him in a familiar place. I already told you he knows my office."

"Right, the ME's makeshift emergency room for Harlow crime victims."

"Very funny. I knew he wouldn't go to the hospital and I had to call Giles to check him out. I thought I broke his ribs. We had to take him somewhere indoors and my office was the logical place."

"All right." Big sigh. "I'll call one of the sketchers to meet me at your office. I'm leaving now so I'll see you in a few." He adds,

"Look, if this guy trusts Giles, tell the ME to stay put for me. Your victim might feel more comfortable with someone who he knows has already helped him."

"He'll stay; no problem there."

⟨⟨⟩⟩

Detective Will Benigni has the foresight to change to jeans and a sweater so as to not appear too official looking and he doesn't even flash his badge when he comes to my office. He uses his considerable charm on Bo and his friend, and even though Bo knows Will's a cop, he seems to relax when Will engages him in a conversation about pepperoni vs sausage pizza. Good call there. The detective does know how to relax people when he wants to do so; I should know.

Arriving a few minutes after him is a young woman who is one of the best sketch artists around. I don't know her, but Will has told me about her. She has a nose ring and several tats and Bo immediately takes a liking to her. To get Bo's friend to relax, she starts out sketching me, then Giles, and finally Bo. Even though he has gone back into his shell for a while, between Giles, Will, the sketch artist, and me, we're able to get a considerable amount of info about *the man* from him. He looks through pictures of vans that Will has had sent from the precinct to my office PC, but none of them seem to be the one he saw.

After a couple of hours we're done. The sketch artist has the picture of a pleasant-looking man whose sole distinguishing feature is a zigzagged scar high up on the left side of his forehead near the hairline, an average height white male in his early thirties with black hair. Except for the scar there's not much to go on; it could be anyone. The face does look vaguely familiar to me but I don't remember seeing anybody with that distinctive scar.

Bo and his friend leave after the artist is finished; Bo has to catch the crowd of cars taking people home late from work. Once they stop at a light, Bo goes to work cleaning or trying to clean their windshields. Will has as much information as he's likely to get and he wants to stop off at his precinct office to talk with his team. He waves a quick goodbye and heads down the stairs.

The sketch artist is packing up her things, and watching her I get an idea. Going to my file cabinet, I pull out the picture of Joshua that Marie gave me and walk over to her just as she's snapping close her portfolio.

"Can you age this face about ten years?" I ask her. "I used old computer software to do it myself but I know you can do a much better job."

"Sure. That's simple enough. When do you need it?"

"Tonight? I'll pay you for your time."

"No, this is easy to do on a computer. Got a scanner? Good."

She takes out a small laptop called a notebook from its case and puts in near my scanner. "I need to scan the picture into my notebook and make a few adjustments with the computer-generated aging program. This program I use is top-of-the-line brand new. It's amazing what it can do. You said ten years, right? That's not hard at all."

Within thirty minutes she shows me the original picture alongside the computer-aged one. Joshua has progressed from a fifteen-year-old boy to a twenty-five-year-old man. They look the same as pictures you might have of yourself at different ages; you're the same person but with a face that has lived a little more. From her notebook she emails the face to my PC and I color print it. I hand her a twenty, which she refuses graciously.

"Take it. You're doing me a huge favor, you don't even know."

"Give it to that guy who was here, the one who gave me the details for the picture of that man he met. He needs it more. That'll be payment enough for me."

She and Giles wait in the hall while I lock up and then the three of us go down the stairs together and walk her to her car. We wave to her as she drives off.

"Buy you a drink?" I say, turning to Giles who smiles tiredly and nods yes.

"It has been one hell of a night, Catherine. We could both use a drink."

"Good, let's walk the three blocks to The Rose. I need the

exercise."

And in the unseasonably warm April evening with the smell of the city mingling with the scent of the early arrival of lilac bushes somewhere nearby, that's exactly what we do.

CHAPTER 23

THE DISTINCTIVE SMELL OF Timothy's coffee wakes me up. There's an extra-large cup sitting on my night table alongside a bag containing Taylor ham and egg on a bagel. Next to the bag is a note: *"You look too sweet to disturb when you're sleeping. I went for a run and stopped at a Timothy's for coffee and bagels. Early call. Talk to you later. Enjoy! Giles."*

I look at my disheveled bed along with the clothes on the floor and smile. Then I reach for the coffee. After a couple of sips I get up, grab the bag with the food in it, and head to the kitchen to eat. The wall clock tells me that it's six-thirty and I hear the usual morning sounds coming from the street below. Looking out the window I see that my street has come to life.

My day is planned. I'm going to look up good old Monsignor Moore. To do that I need to look professional and respectable so after my shower I go through my closet to find the right outfit to wear. I settle on a soft deep yellow summer sweater and pair it with the crème-colored slacks I wore for my lunch with Marie. Yellow pumps complete my look. I pull my hair into a low full bun at the nape of my neck and apply minimal make-up.

On my way to my car I make two calls; one is case related. The second is to Myrtle at home to tell her I won't be in until the afternoon.

"Okay honey. See you later. I'll save two of Harry's cannoli for you."

⊱

The office of the archbishop is easy to find. It's in a sprawling complex of buildings, which includes the archdiocese cathedral. Parking is a bitch though and I find myself several long blocks away from where I have to go. I'm not used to wearing pumps and wish I had on sneakers instead.

Inside the outer office I encounter a receptionist in a glass-enclosed area who asks me why I'm here and who I want to see.

"I'm here to see Monsignor Bernard Moore, if I can. I want to set up a service group for my church, for boys between the ages of eight and twelve," I lie smoothly. "Bette, the housekeeper, from St. Matthew's Church in Queens? She told me the monsignor would be able to help me." I smile in the prim and proper way I've seen Myrtle smile when she is requesting something from a stranger.

"Oh, I'm … so sorry, the monsignor isn't … isn't here." I watch her facial expression and she seems tense. She won't make eye contact with me and her right hand clenches and unclenches a pen. Something's not right. "I'm quite sure he would love to help you but he's been called away on … urgent church business. We don't know when he'll be back. It could be … quite … a while, I'm afraid. Would you like to leave a number or e-mail where you can be reached?"

"Yes," I say and give her my home number. My voicemail there has a generic message. She looks at it and says, "And your name as well, please."

"Cate, spelled with a *C*, last name Harlow. Thank you so much. I'm sorry I missed him and I really hope I get to meet him soon."

"I'll give him the message upon his return. You have a good day."

"You too."

⊱

"Hello, is Father Richard Boyd available? This is Cate Harlow. Tell him it's important."

Every good PI has sources. Most of them come from what is known as the criminal fringes—petty thieves, druggies, hookers, and those who know enough about crimes committed on their home turf to be able to give solid leads and details. They're like lawyers in that they get paid a retainer to keep their eyes and ears open for your purposes and when they do bring in information they get paid a bonus. Everything is completely confidential between us. I have a few very good sources from the criminal fringe on my payroll but not as many as some investigators I know.

Then there are the other sources you pick up unexpectedly. These are generally people who give you information willingly out of a sense of moral code. They're reliable and honest the same way a person who witnesses a car accident is ready and willing to give an unbiased, accurate account of what they saw to law enforcement. Father Richard Boyd is one of my honest sources and I'm not above using his help to find out what happened to Monsignor Moore, if anything.

A few minutes pass, then I hear, "Hello? Ms. Harlow?"

"Call me Cate, please, Richard ... Listen, I need your help with something relating to another priest, a monsignor. Is your computer system only able to access your own diocese or can you link into other ones?"

"This one here only accesses our files at this diocese. Why?"

"Shit! Sorry, Richard, that just slipped out."

"That's all right. You should hear me curse when the Yankees are losing. What do you need?"

I tell him the Monsignor Moore story and explain why I want to see if he went through a process of laicization. "He could be a lead on my cold case. I just thought the systems could link up from one area to another."

"Sorry, *that* they can't do but there may be another way."

"How?" Someone honks his horn at me to see if he can get my parking space. I roll down the window and tell him I have car trouble and am waiting for AAA. He flips me the finger and drives away disgruntled.

"If this monsignor did go through laicization I *can* still find out. There's a national list of every priest who either retires from active service or leaves the church. It's a bookkeeping system really. Even if he was *asked* to leave, his name would still be on that list. I have to get into the main system, but that's shouldn't be too hard to do."

"This is short notice, but is it too much to ask you to find that out today?"

"How about a couple of hours? Let's see, it's almost ten now; I'm pretty sure I can get back to you with what you need by early afternoon. Will that work for you?"

"That works really well. Thanks Richard."

That's one of the best things about moral code sources. They're willing to get you what you need as soon as possible. I tell Richard I'll be back at my office by noon and I'll wait for his call.

While I'm in the parking lot I key in an address to my car's GPS and open my bag to take out the computer-aged picture of Joshua. Then I start the Edge and follow the audio GPS directions.

The building I'm looking for is just outside of the city, a faded red brick one that looks as if it was built in the 1920s for immigrants who came from Ellis Island and needed a place to live. It has a defeated air about it as if it still holds the sadness and homesickness of its former inhabitants.

I park my Edge across the street from the building, grab the large manila envelope on the passenger's side seat, and walk over to take a look. A sign inside the foyer listing the office tenants shows me that the place I want is located on the second floor. I walk up the two flights rather than take the elevator that sounds like metal crunching on metal. Getting stuck in that old box could become a life and death situation if no one knows a person is in there.

The second floor is less gloomy than the entry on the first floor and I find the office easily. A sign on the door reads, *The Survivors Network of Those Abused by Priests. All are welcome.*

I open the door to find a neat little office inside with several desks. A man is talking on the phone and two women seem to be discussing what looks like a flyer that has just been printed out. One of the women notices me and asks if she can help me.

"Yes, I'm looking for a man named Carl. I called early this morning. My name is Cate Harlow."

"Oh yes, Cate, I'm the one who took your call. I hope you don't mind me calling you Cate. We use first names here so it feels less formal and restrictive."

She tells me Carl is in the back room and that she'll take me to him. Her smile is gentle and I can see people feeling comfortable talking to her. "He's putting together a flyer and e-mail for our members. He'll only be a minute."

The back room is a combination office-lunch area. Carl is sitting at a small desk with a laptop. A screened-off corner section reveals a refrigerator, microwave, Keurig coffee maker, and a table with a couple of chairs.

"Carl, this is Cate Harlow. She called you this morning."

Hunched over his computer in concentration, he offers a wave and a "Hi." After he keys in a few more words he sits back and exhales like a man who has completed a much-needed task and is at last satisfied with his work.

"Hello, Cate. Glad to meet you," he says pushing his chair back and getting up. "Let me grab a chair for you and then see how we can help. You said on the phone that you were looking for someone?"

"I'm looking for a young man about twenty-five years old who may have come here."

"Do you know if he was abused?" asks Carl, "Or is this someone from some religious group trying to infiltrate our organization to stop what we do."

"This young man was abused by a priest from the age of nine until he was fifteen. He left home at fifteen; murder was ruled out because a body was never found and unofficially it's believed that he was a runaway. The police file on him has become a cold case. He would be twenty-five years old now and there's good reason to believe that he's in this area. If he's been here within the last year or so at any of your meetings, then I'll know for sure he's still close by. I'm acting on behalf of his sister who has retained me to find out what has happened to him."

Carl looks at me levelly and says kindly. "Have you tried any of the many homeless shelters in the city? Have you checked with substance abuse clinics? Many of the adults who were sexually abused become alcoholics or drug users. A lot of abuse victims make it to the cities where no one knows them so they can hide what they erroneously consider to be their shame."

"Those places were thoroughly checked right after I took the case. I found nothing."

"I'm sorry Cate, I didn't mean you *hadn't* checked them as part of your job; I know you did. My God, sexual abuse and rape are terrible, unforgiveable crimes when they happen to adults. Imagine how much more traumatic it is when it happens to a child! The memories are rooted so deeply it's hard if not impossible to be able to live a normal life. Even normal sexual relationships that most people take for granted can trigger the horror of what happened in childhood. Living in a drugged or alcoholic haze helps to dull some of the pain for a while.

"We try hard to bring solace to the victims by demanding justice from the legal authorities. It's only in the past decade that priests were prosecuted at all." He sighs, "I am a survivor, Cate. I make it my business to make sure the courts don't forget us."

"What about revenge? Are there any survivors coming here who want justice no matter how they have to get it? Take justice into their own hands, so to speak? There has to be a tremendous rage at having been sexually abused and having been unable to stop it."

Carl stands and asks me if I want anything to drink. He has iced tea in the fridge he says. When I say yes, he stands up, walks over to the refrigerator, and gets two bottles. He comes back to sit opposite me again, taking a long sip before continuing.

"Revenge? Sure. There have been people who come to meetings who we discover want nothing more than to get back at the person who damaged them and they want to do them physical harm. They're angry and filled with pain. They don't stay long because they soon find out that that is not what SNAP is all about. We do what we do legally. You can't allow visions of vengeance to cloud your mind. The lawyers who work with us are incredibly good at getting the judges to understand what this terrible crime has done to countless lives. Each successful prosecution is a victory for the survivors."

"Have you ever seen *this* young man here? His name is Joshua McElroy," I ask taking the new computer-aged picture of Joshua out of the envelope.

He takes it out of my hands and looks hard at it for a few minutes shaking his head.

"Yes, yes I've seen him. He used to come here with another young man, a—wait, I remember the other man had a lot of anger at what had happened to him. He felt our organization wasn't doing enough. What was his name, what was …? I'm sorry I can't remember the other man's name; I only remember him because he had a deep scar high on his forehead. They came here about two years ago. The one man with the scar was very open in his anger; he made some of us feel uncomfortable with his rage. But this man … Joshua you said? He was very withdrawn and quiet. He just sat here and sometimes drew pictures on a pad." He snaps his fingers. "You know what? I have a picture he left here one night. I intended to show it to one of our health volunteers who's a clinical psychiatrist, but I get so busy that I completely forgot I had it. The artwork is worthy of a Stephen King novel."

He goes to his desk and rummages around in a drawer. "Here it is. *You* tell *me* what you think of this."

The picture has the same theme as all of Joshua's drawings; a baby animal whose parents are unaware that he is being stalked by a yellow-eyed, sharp-fanged hyena.

I look at it and hand it back. "When did Joshua and his friend stop coming?"

"Oh, I think the two of them came sporadically for about six months and then they just stopped showing up. It happens; some people want and need to talk about the sexual abuse, others simply can't. It's too raw, too upsetting to recall. We lose too many members that way. They can't see themselves as survivors, only as victims. And of course the vengeance-driven ones see our organization as weak."

I give him my card and ask him to call me if he does see Joshua again.

"You can call either of the numbers on the card but if you're calling after five, call my cell phone. It doesn't matter what time you call me. This is information that I need to know."

"I will call if I do see him here. Good luck with your search. I hope you find him," he says without much conviction.

As I drive away I get a feeling that someone is watching me.

⚞

"It's dark, Joey. Where are we? Please put on a light. Where are you? Joey? Do you hear me?"

The only answer is a door quietly closing, then complete darkness.

CHAPTER 24

FATHER RICHARD BOYD GETS back to me at one thirty in the afternoon at my office with the information I need. Monsignor Bernard Moore was indeed going through the process of laicization at the request of the archbishop himself.

"He fought it Cate," says Richard Boyd over the phone. "From what I can gather, there was a formal paper filed by Monsignor Moore requesting to be transferred to Italy for six months. He wanted to be placed in a specific monastery there for what he said were health reasons. That would delay the process of laicization for a while. His request was denied. I think the archbishop was pressured to make Moore leave."

"You say specific monastery as if this is a place that's known to priests who want to have a place to hide."

"There are places where any clergy who are ill, physically or mentally, can go to recover. These places have existed for centuries. Usually these monasteries, and there are a few scattered around the world, are for those whose spirits are sick, those men who need to live quietly and contemplatively for a period of months. The therapeutic approach is intense prayer and penance. It used to be for young priests who had fallen in love and wanted to leave holy orders to get married. It was a mandated time-out for them if you will. I don't know if that's true anymore though. Now, well, I *have* heard rumors that some men accused of sexual abuse have been sent to these places over the years."

"But basically it's a place where a pedophile could go to hide with the consent of the hierarchy," I say. "It keeps them from being prosecuted by the law."

"It sure seems that way, but many in the Church are cooperating with the legal system now, so I can't be sure. However, and this you didn't hear from me, I know that there are archbishops who have moved priests accused of sexual misconduct from parish to parish. The older priests here speak about it sometimes. Moore may have been one of them."

"Where is this Monsignor Moore now then?"

"That's the thing; no one knows *where* he is. He seems to have disappeared. I did some snooping around and found out that he was supposed to attend a very important meeting with the archbishop in the late afternoon about two weeks ago. That day he went for his usual mid-day walk and never returned to the residence. When he didn't show up for the meeting, his room was checked, but he wasn't there and nothing was taken. All his clothes and even the special silver chalice he was given when he became a monsignor were still there."

"Are you sure the church isn't hiding him, Richard? Maybe sent him to another diocese? That's been documented in the past." I know I sound cynical but pedophile priests have been hidden before.

"That's always a possibility, but I don't think that's the case here. There's nothing to indicate that and there would be what I like to refer to as 'cryptic monetary footnotes'—a sentence about a possible change of residence or a domicile review. I don't see that here. I think he's really missing."

"Okay Richard, I'll have to take your word for it." I pause. "This must really be bothering you; I mean you *are* a priest after all."

"Yes, but I'm one of the good ones, remember? I do have to tell you though that this is certainly testing my faith, but I can handle it. I pray a lot and then go for a run."

"All right then I guess I can ask you for one more favor. I need you to look up the name of a murdered priest from upstate New York. I was the investigator who found his body last year, same method of murder and mutilation as the others, but no one ever knew much about him." I give him the name of the first murder victim. "Can you find out if he went through that process of laicization?"

"I'll try to get back to you either late today or tomorrow. I don't want anyone here knowing what I'm doing and I've got other duties waiting for me."

I tell him there's no rush, just a personal need to know. I hang up thinking about how this one particular priest is one of the good guys and how hard it must be for him to do what he's doing. God bless him.

I need to talk to someone in charge at the archdiocese office. Remembering what Will had told me about his meeting with the archbishop in New York City, I pretty much know what to expect. Outrage, denial, hidden threats, and anger—I'm prepared for all of them. Before I leave for the archdiocese, I think about just how I'm going to gain access to a top-ranking cleric there and get him to talk to me. I make a decision; I'm going in as the private detective. No lies about why I want info, no illusions. I need to go home and change into my jeans and sneakers. No frills, no lady-like image. I need to look tough.

"Myrtle, put my cannoli in the fridge; I won't be back until late."

She just nods and says she'll see me later or tomorrow.

≈

The archbishop totally loses whatever cool he had when I was first ushered in. The fact that he had received me as calmly as he did is to his credit. I had shown my ID and pretty much intimidated the receptionist by making my voice loud enough so that people waiting in the outer office looked at us. Lucky for me there were several important-looking people there.

The priest who was called by the receptionist didn't want

to make a scene, which I assured him I was perfectly capable of doing if I didn't get to see the archbishop.

Admonishing me to *please lower your voice* he brought me directly to a waiting area outside the archbishop's office. I sat for exactly thirty-eight minutes before the door opened and a voice told me to enter.

The archbishop's haughtiness and look of disdain doesn't intimidate me one bit. He looks at my private investigator's license, tosses it on his desk toward me and says, "You have fifteen minutes Cate Harlow. Make the most of them."

I explain why I am here and what information I want from him.

"There is ample evidence to suggest that a Monsignor Bernard Moore who resides here is a pedophile. That's a crime for the police, not for me, but his past actions directly relate to a cold case I am investigating. I need to speak with him on this matter, but my sources tell me he has somehow vanished. And that has happened only after he was asked to undergo the process of laicization."

The bishop quickly hides his look of surprise at my bluntness. Looking sternly at me he says, "I have no idea what you are talking about and I have no more time for this nonsense." He waves a hand at me in dismissal. I'm not deterred.

"If the monsignor is being hidden somewhere at your orders, you are harboring a pedophile, and, as such, are an accessory to a crime."

His Excellency looks up and narrows his eyes at me.

"You people come here to my archdiocese, in the very place where I live, my sacred home, and not only demand, but *expect,* that I will give you information about one of my monsignors? You treat a man of God like a *common criminal?* You track him down as if you are a hunter. It is unjust that you act in this manner, Ms. Harlow. I am outraged and so, I am sure, is God. This is sinful."

I am pretty ticked off by what the archbishop is saying and am having a hard time keeping my own anger under control. I manage to take a breath before I speak.

"Playing the God card won't work with me, sir. With all due respect your Excellency, the monsignor *is* a criminal; he's a *pedophile*."

"Stop using that word, Ms. Harlow!"

"Why would I do that? That's what we call a man who has sex with a child, a *pedophile*. There is solid written evidence that he raped a boy as young as ten. I'm quite sure that child wasn't the only one. And to be blunt, sir, no one would have to track him down if the Church had dealt severely with him and other pedophile priests and made sure they were voluntarily brought to justice, instead of hiding their heinous crimes. All you did was move these criminals, these predators, from one hunting ground to another every time you sent them to another parish. Do you even *realize* what you've condoned by your inaction? Don't speak to me of injustice, sir; the horrible injustice is what you and others in the church's hierarchy have willingly allowed to be done to millions of innocent children. The real sin here is that you *knew* what was happening and you *did nothing* about it, nothing."

"How do you *dare* have the audacity to speak to me in this manner?"

I refuse to defend what he terms my audacity and continue.

"You know about laicization, Your Excellency, and so do I. Some pedophile priests are actually *paid* money to leave the clergy, which means that they're protected and helped to transit out of the priesthood. Instead of bringing this hideous crime to the authorities, you choose to give them the means to start a new life. What about the lives of their victims? Are you aware that the sexually abused child grows into adulthood damaged and filled with horrible memories? Alcoholism, drug addiction, even suicides are rampant for those victims."

The archbishop leans back in his chair still fixing me with a cold stare.

"I'm not easily intimidated either, Ms. Harlow, and certainly not by the likes of you. I refuse to give you one bit of information about any of my clergy. You have no legal proof, there are no police with you, no one is handing me a warrant. You're just some hack private investigator who wrongly assumes that you can muddy the reputation of a highly religious and respected man with lies and falsehoods."

"Lies and falsehoods? Excellent sermon, Your Excellency, but save it for your congregation. I'll write a statement for the prosecutor's office that I suspect you of having harbored a pedophile. That makes you a criminal also. The police will be visiting you really soon."

"Get out!"

"How many other pedophile priests have you hidden and helped to continue their vile activities?"

"Get *out!*"

The priest who showed me into the waiting room appears from another room. The bishop coldly tells him to escort me out.

"Show this person out of my office, out of the residence, and off of the property."

The priest comes close to me and reaches for my arm. I glare at him to keep his distance from me as I walk out into the hallway.

"You know, his Excellency is a good and holy man," says the priest, opening the outer door for me. "Do you know Latin?" I nod and he says, "His Excellency is truly *qui vivit in sanctitate.*"

"'A man who lives in holiness'? Really, Father? That's not the impression I got. *Diabolus hic vivit,*" I say to him as I step outside. "The devil lives here."

CHAPTER 25

MYRTLE MOTIONS TO ME as I hurry through the door. It's sweltering outside and, for once, I'm grateful for the air-conditioned confines of my office. She grabs me over to the side of her desk that is hidden from my own by a decorative screen.

"That young man is here. David? Says he's a good friend of Marie McElroy. I'm guessing that he's the David who picked her up here a few weeks ago. He didn't give me his last name." Myrtle's antennae are up. She doesn't trust people who don't give their full names.

I see him sitting in the chair close to the window away from me. He's got on the same knit cap and aviator shades as the first time we met. David gets up from his chair and looks over at Myrtle's desk. He can't see me but I'm sure he hears Myrtle whispering.

"It's okay Myrtle, I've met him." Then turning to walk toward him I say tersely, "David, what an unexpected surprise. You should have called. I wasn't expected back until late. You might have waited all day in vain." I watch his face for any reaction to my cold professional greeting. There's nothing. "How's Marie?"

"That's what I'd like to talk to you about if you have a minute."

I sit at my desk facing David, which forces him to sit across from me.

"Sure, but a minute may be all I have. I'm working a case. Have a seat. What's up? Is anything wrong?"

David looks at me and makes his face fill with concern.

"I haven't seen Marie for a couple of days; I've been very busy with work, you see. But I do know that the last time we spoke she was upset. I know that she's very concerned with what you found in the eaves of her house. It belongs to Joshua so it's very precious to her. It's a shame she wasn't home the day you found it."

I keep a professional neutral look on my face.

"Actually it was probably better that she stayed at work. There was no guarantee that I would find anything, so she might have come home for nothing and lost money from her paying customers. What's the real reason you came to see me, David?"

He's taken aback by my bluntness but recovers enough to give me a plausible reason for being in my area.

"I was in the city visiting a friend and decided to stop by here to see if I would be able to bring the box you found to her house. You do have it here, I assume. Really it's no bother for me to bring it to her. I know she'd really like to have it."

"Did Marie ask you to get the box?"

"Well, no, but, since I was in the city ..."

I try to make a quick judgment of the situation. The fact is that Marie *wasn't* concerned when I had spoken with her concerning the box I found. She easily bought the lie I told about it only containing her brother's drawings and seemed to be okay with my telling her that the box had to be checked for prints before I could release it to her. If she was that concerned about getting it, I know she would have called me directly. David may be good at faking emotion but his eyes tell me he's lying about Marie. And quite frankly, what does he want with the box anyway? Is it the fact that he thinks he'll make a good impression on Marie by bringing it to her or is he one of those men who only feel masculine if they see themselves *in charge* of a situation? I can't get a good read on him. "That's very nice of you David, but I'm afraid that I don't have the box in the office."

His head rears back slightly when I say that and too quickly he says, "Is it at your home? I can go with you to get it."

"Uh, no, actually the box is at the forensics lab. I wanted to make sure that it is indeed Joshua's so they're checking it for his fingerprints."

David's mouth becomes a hard line and I see sweat on his upper lip.

"But *Marie* can identify the box as her brother's. Why did you send it to a lab?"

He sounds irritated. He knows he's overstepping his bounds because he quickly says ingratiatingly, "I mean, I don't think it was necessary but I guess you know better than I do. You're the professional. I'm just worried about Marie, you know. I don't like to see her upset."

He smiles at me in a placating manner. I smile back, watching his demeanor.

"I wouldn't be able to give the box to you anyway, David. Only Marie can claim it when forensics is done with it."

That comment hits him; he doesn't seem to like the fact that I wouldn't give him the box even if I had it.

"Listen, David, as I said I'm working a case and I really have to get back to it. If Marie is concerned or needs to ask me any questions, tell her to call me anytime. I'll always get back to her, I promise."

I begin ushering him toward the door but he turns and asks when I think the box will be released. I pretend to check the calendar on my smartphone.

"Since this is a cold case and not a priority, the forensics lab will put it last on their list. They should be done with it, oh, maybe next week? I'll call Marie and let her know. Take care now, David."

Closing the door firmly on a frustrated and annoyed David, I glance at Myrtle who simply says, "I don't care for that young man at all, not at all. Too pushy if you ask me." I agree with her. "By the way, Catherine, Dr. Barrett called and said that the bodies of those two priests have been released to Church authorities. He thought you'd want to know."

I nod but my mind is on the man who was just here. David's visit nudges me to bring Marie her brother's journal. It's going to be difficult for me, and emotionally draining for her. I'll call her to set up a time for tomorrow when she'll be alone. It has to be done.

⁂

"Hi Cate, c'mon in," says Marie, holding the screen door wide. Before she closes the door we both wave to Mr. O'Leary, who is sitting on his front porch. I told Marie that the information I had was for her eyes and ears alone. I was very blunt in telling her that I didn't want anyone else at our meeting. She was surprised but told me that she would be alone on Saturday all day, so that was the best time to come over.

Usually when I have to give my clients information I have them come to my office. With Marie, I thought it would be better for her to receive the news at her home. I didn't want her driving after I told her about her brother's abuse. I figured that I could stay with her for a while, and then there's the presence of Mr. O'Leary, who's right next door. Entering the McElroy home I feel a little sick to my stomach. What I'm about to do is going to impact the world Marie has known since she was a child. It is one thing to be aware of the sexual abuse rampant in the Catholic Church but it's a whole other ballgame to know that someone you love has been one of the victims. Having thought it over during a very sleepless night, I made the decision that I wouldn't show her the journal right away. I'd only feed her some of the information and see where it led. I was especially interested to know about her own relationship with Monsignor Moore when he was at her parish even though I was certain that that she knew nothing about what had happened to her brother. She might also be able to shed some light on the boy named Joey in her brother's journal. So far Will's contacts in The Center for Missing Children have turned up no one named Joey who went missing from Marie's area ten to twenty years ago.

In the living room I notice she has a plate of cookies and what looks like a pitcher of lemonade on a tray. Right now I'd like to add some of Mr. O'Leary's Irish whiskey to the pitcher. She sits across from me as she did the first time I came to her house. I wave away the cookies and the lemonade. Marie looks at me expectantly.

"Marie, I do have some news about the box I found in the eaves. Besides the drawings that were inside, there were some papers in there, a sort of journal that Joshua wrote. I have them in my car but, before you read them, I want to prepare you for what is in them. Your brother may have been with someone named Joey. I believe they were together so at least he wasn't alone."

She looks confused. "Joey? I don't understand."

"Did you ever know a boy named Joey?"

"Well, of course I do." Marie laughs a little nervously. "But I don't ..."

"There was a boy named Joey whom your brother mentions. If you know him or of him can you tell me who he is?" I need to just say it and so I do. "Your brother's journal says that Joey is dead."

"Joey? But Joey ... Oh my God! Joshua mentioned Joey and said he was *dead*?"

"Yes, he did. I'm so sorry, Marie. How well did you know Joey? "

She shakes her head in disbelief and looks baffled.

Seeing the look on her face I ask, "What's wrong? What do you remember about Joey?"

"Joey's not dead, he *can't* be dead."

"Marie, I know that this is difficult for you, to find out that a friend has died is upsetting, I know that, believe me I do. But I have to tell you that Joshua wrote in his journal that Joey was dead. Unfortunately there's more; I got the impression that this boy Joey may have committed suicide. I'm sorry to have to tell you this."

"No, Cate, you don't understand at all." She laughs again and stands up looking at the mantle over the fireplace. I'm afraid she's going to start getting hysterical as she did in my office a few weeks ago. Maybe I should have brought Myrtle. Marie looks at me smiling sadly and says, "Joey's not dead. His letters prove that he's not."

"Letters? Marie, what are you telling me? That this boy Joey also has left letters for you over the years, the same as Joshua? Why didn't you mention that to me?"

"No, no, Cate, you don't ... Joey, my God, I haven't heard him called that name in years. He didn't ... he said that he didn't want... oh my God..." She sits down and puts her head in her hands.

"Marie, *who* is this Joey? Knowing that could help me find Joshua."

"It's him."

"Who? Who is him?"

"Joshua. Joey is *Joshua.*"

I'm taken aback for a minute thinking that maybe Marie doesn't understand what I'm telling her. "I don't understand, your brother's name is Joshua."

She gives a little laugh and looks at the pictures on the mantle.

"His name *is* Joshua, that's his legal name, but my folks, you see, my folks called him *Little Joey* because he looked so much like our dad, whose name was Joseph. Here, see?"

She walks over to the mantle and brings back two framed black-and-white photos. "These are pictures of them when they were both six years old. My mother had my brother's picture done in black and white to match the one of our father. That's my dad in the picture on the right. See how much my brother looks like Dad?"

It is remarkable. I examine the pictures I had seen on my first visit to Marie's house and it's as if I am looking at identical twins separated by twenty-six years. Josh McElroy is the spitting image of his father, Joe McElroy. The black-and-white picture I thought had been made to only look dated is actually an older one taken of Joe McElroy years before his son was born.

"When Josh was fourteen he told everyone that he didn't want to be called Joey anymore," she said putting the pictures back on the mantle. "I guess he wanted his own name, his own identity. Remember I told you that when we started high school he insisted that he be called Joshua?"

"Yes, I do." I'm thinking fast. Joey is Joshua so ... "Tell me, did anyone else ever call your brother by the name Joey? Teachers, other kids, family members?"

"Oh sure, my grandparents did, my father's sister and brother, sometimes close friends. The teachers, no, never—we went to a Catholic school and the nuns were real strict about what they called our 'baptismal names.' They didn't like nicknames. That's kind of funny because ..." she stops suddenly, remembering.

"Because why, Marie?"

"Well, because even Monsignor Moore called my brother Joey."

She sighs. I hold my breath then let it out slowly. A small spark of a memory about her brother had been lit. She remembers something about that priest, something she has suppressed.

"He was Father Moore when we were little children. I remember he was elevated to monsignor four years before, before ... before Joshua went missing." She shakes her head as if to clear it. "There was a big celebration with the archbishop coming down and all. We all went, well, all of us except my brother. He said that he had a bad stomachache that night so we left him home alone. He was eleven and Dad said it was okay 'cause we had this big dog, Wolf, who wouldn't let anyone he didn't know come in the house. He was so protective of us. If he knew you, he was fine. Times were different then; kids did stay in the house alone."

She looks at me as if she wants me to tell her that, yes, times were different and that an eleven-year-old being allowed to stay home by himself back then was okay. I don't tell her that my own parents didn't let me stay home alone until I was seventeen. Being an older couple, they were super-cautious. I smile slightly, nod, and let her continue talking.

"Anyway, I remember that the monsignor was really upset that my brother didn't come. Said he hadn't seen Josh for over three weeks. He even left the celebration for about an hour to go check in to see how my brother was feeling. My mom thought that was so kind of him. Dad even gave him his key to the front door so Joshua wouldn't have to get out of bed to answer the door. Monsignor always told my parents that Joshua was his best altar boy. They spent a lot of time together, you know. He ... you know, he's a priest."

Marie's face changed, as she seemed to be seeing her brother alone at home that long ago night, feeling sick to his stomach. At home with a faithful dog who wouldn't let a stranger come in the house.

No, no stranger was safe with Wolf, only family, friends, and people he knew.

People who were welcomed into the house by family members.

Wolf may have been there but she knew her brother was really alone.

"Did this Father Moore help your parents cope when Joshua went missing?"

"Oh, yes, yes he did. He was so distraught for them. I remember he had tears in his eyes when he came over here after my dad called him with the news. He joined in the search for Joshua and was here almost every day. It was almost like he was desperate to find my brother. Father Moore wanted to know if Joshua had left any note or said anything to us. He said that he loved Joshua so much, he said, it was almost as if Joshua was his own child. He ..."

"Go on, Marie."

"He ... loved Joshua."

My gut instinct is telling me everything now. Gently taking

Marie's hand in my own, I look her full in the face.

"Marie? Can you answer one question for me?"

She nods, a little surprised by my intentness.

"I don't want you to think about your answer, understand? Don't hesitate, just say yes or no, I don't want an explanation. Just a simple yes or no. Okay?"

She nods again and I took a deep breath, never letting go of her hand and still looking directly in her eyes. "Did you trust Monsignor Moore?"

Her lips curled faintly with disgust and her eyes looked hard. "No."

I went to my car and got the box. Back inside the house I showed Marie Joshua's journal and for the next half hour she reads every word as tears run down her face.

❧

"Do you know what religion means in an Irish Catholic family, Cate? The Church is infallible, the priests are above reproach."

It's been two hours since Marie finished reading Joshua's journal. She's stopped crying and the first signs of outrage at what happened to her brother are beginning to take hold. The small box is in her hands.

"If you're a kid you just take it for granted that the nuns can hit you and you won't tell your parents. You understand that the priests are second only to Jesus himself; their authority is unquestioned. And, oh my God, how can you even *begin* to tell your parents that a priest touched you in a sexual way? Imagine how horrible that would be for a kid? And if your parents did believe that horror, what do you think they could, or even would, do? You *don't* accuse a priest of molesting or raping your son or daughter. Oh my God, I should have known! That priest always made me feel … uncomfortable. Why didn't Joshua tell me? Why didn't I realize what was happening to him? Maybe I could have done something."

I get up and put my arm around her shoulder. Maybe this

isn't a strictly professional thing to do for a client but this woman has just been dealt a heavy blow; she needs a little comfort.

"It doesn't work that way Marie. We don't always know what's going on with someone we love. Chances are very good that Joshua would have denied it if you questioned him about what you thought was happening. Pedophiles are very good at threatening their victims and making the abuse seem as if the victim somehow wanted it or, worse, deserved it. Don't beat yourself up about this Marie. You aren't to blame for not knowing."

Marie takes a deep breath and is silent for a few minutes, then, staring at the box in her hands she says, "The Church ruled people's lives when I was a kid. You aren't Catholic; you don't know what it was like. As much as I love my faith, I will tell you that the Church back then could dole out punishments if its authority was questioned. A very good friend of my mother was divorced. When she died and a funeral mass was scheduled by her son, Monsignor Moore stopped her casket from being carried into the church because, according to church law, divorce is a mortal sin. She was denied a Catholic mass because of her sin. A friend of the family did a quick prayer service at the gravesite. Believe me, when I was a child the priests were feared more than the cops. We believed that they had the power to send you to Hell."

She cradles the box as if she is holding her brother. I touch her hand.

"I wanted to give this to you personally Marie. David came to my office yesterday asking for it, but I told him that I could only give this to a family member. He said you were upset that I hadn't given it to you."

She looks surprised. "I don't why he thought that. I never really discussed the box with him except to say that you still had it. . I figured you would give it to me when you were finished with it, just as you said you would. I would never ask him to get it from you."

"Marie, this might not be the best time to ask you, but what exactly do you know about David? I mean you let him into your house when you weren't home. You haven't known him for that long."

She shakes her head. "No, I haven't known him that long, you're right. It's only been a few months since I met him. But he's very polite and he's never tried anything with me, you know what I mean. All he ever did was kiss me on the cheek and hold my hand. I guess he's shy. He's sympathetic and understanding about Joshua. Actually besides you, David is the first person I've really talked to about my brother. Why are you asking me?"

"Myrtle and I just feel protective of you, Marie, that's all. David, well, I don't know him at all. I'm naturally suspicious I guess." I sigh. "And I really wish the box hadn't contained such misery for you. Are you going to be all right? I hate to leave you alone but I need to talk with the police about this ... monsignor."

Her eyes become hard when I say the title of the man who caused so much pain for her brother and whose actions destroyed her parents.

"Are the police going to arrest that disgusting man? Please tell me he will be punished. I have to know he can't get away with what he's done to Joshua."

"Yes, he will be arrested, I can assure you of that." *When they find him*, I say to myself.

"I'll be okay, Cate, but I don't want to stay in the house. I think that maybe I'll go over to Mr. O'Leary's, sit with him for a while. I have to talk to someone and he's always been good to me. Just sitting with him is what I need right now. I can't be here."

We walk outside together and Marie, holding the box tightly against her chest, goes toward the O'Leary house.

"Tell Mr. O'Leary I'll come and visit soon," I say, walking toward my car.

⁓

"Joey? Joey? Are you there? I can't see anyone. It's too dark here. I'm cold and I can't move. Where are my ... Oh God! Joey?"

CHAPTER 26

THE PRECINCT MY EX calls his home for as many as ten hours a day is noisy and filled with the sound of phones and talking. There are suspects being processed for crimes, and several in handcuffs. The desk sergeant knows me and ushers me through to Will's desk. He's on the phone as I come in, talking in that calm, serious tone that somehow is both placating and intimidating. I hear, "Yes, that's right. It *is* being covered. That's all I'm allowed to say. Yes, I sure will, you too." As he slams down the phone I hear, "God damn, fucking idiot."

"Bad day, Will? And it's still early."

He gestures me over to a chair near his desk. "Some hotshot young reporter and I are having a pissing contest. His online paper gave him the backburner Central Park story and he's trying to make a name for himself. The bastard makes a practice of calling the precinct every week for updates on how we're handling the murdered priest case. Generally I'd just hang up on him but his father is some minor politician and just happens to be a golfing buddy of the police commissioner, so he had him call here." He looks at me. "So what kind of a day are *you* having?"

I tell him that I just came from giving Joshua's journal to

Marie. He shakes his head and asks, "How's she doing?"

"Handling the news as best she can—outrage, sadness, guilt at not realizing what was happening to her brother. I left her over at Mr. O'Leary's. I hope to God he gives her some of that Irish whiskey! After what she read today she deserves to get a little drunk."

I go on to tell him about Marie's recollection of Monsignor Moore and how it was the nail in the coffin that confirmed that he is a pedophile.

"Well the bastard has to be found. Hand your info over to the sex crimes unit in Queens and let them handle that part. All you have to do is find Joshua McElroy—if he's still alive and if he wants to be found, that is."

"Yes, there is that. Finding someone who doesn't want to be found is becoming my specialty. I'll let you know how that's going. I hope your day gets better."

"Highly unlikely, but thanks for the thought. See you around."

There's a message from Giles on my cell. Instead of returning the call, I decide to take a run over to the morgue to see what he wants before I go back to my office. On the way I call Queens sex crimes and tell them I'll be faxing them info on a pedophile case I've discovered.

Giles is in autopsy when I get there so I wait in his office. On his desk there's a picture of us outside a Broadway theater. I remember that night; it was the first night he came back to the brownstone and that we slept together. I hadn't had sex in quite some time back then and I remember Giles making love to me with an intensity and sweetness that had me completely undone. He wasn't Will, but the sex was good.

"Hey!" says a voice behind me and I jump a mile. Giles is standing at the door.

"You okay?" He comes over to me to give me a kiss and a hug.

"I'm fine. You just startled me, that's all. There *is* a morgue right across from your office, you know. "

"I think you saw too many horror movies when you were a child," laughs Giles, smacking my butt lovingly. "My patients, if you will, pretty much stay put." He gestures to the morgue. "Be that as it may, to what do I owe the pleasure of your very lovely company?"

"You called me."

"Well, it's always nice to see you but you could have just returned the call. You didn't have to drive down here. I know you're busy working a case."

"I needed a short break since I'll be working late today. What's up?"

"It's a little strange. Someone called my office around nine o'clock today asking about a box that you supposedly sent to be checked for fingerprints and other evidence. The problem is that my staff checked the in-files and can't find anything sent from you. But this man, who says he's from your office, has actually been down here twice this morning to pick it up for you. I was in autopsy all morning so I didn't get to meet him but members of my staff said he was very aggressive in his demands. Now I know the only people in your office are you and Myrtle Goldberg Tuttle, so what's going on? Has Harry Tuttle given up baking goodies and joined *Catherine Harlow, Private Investigations?* Know anything about this?"

"Actually no, this is the first time that I'm hearing this. I never sent anyone here and if I ever was to do that, you know that I'd call here first. But I think I have a good idea of who may have come here."

"Want to share his name?"

"Not right now. I want to deal with this in my own way. Thanks Giles, I'm going back to my office." I lean in for his kiss and he asks me if I want a late dinner tonight at a new Mediterranean place that has just opened up near my brownstone.

"Sounds good. Make it for around nine and I'll meet you there."

Driving back to my office I think about what Giles has told me. Who else knows the story that I told Marie about having that metal box checked for proof that it really is her brother's? Only one other person knows; the same person who came to see me about bringing the box to Marie. Now the question I need an answer to is why that box is so important to him. Why does he want it so badly?

⚮

Taking the steps two at a time I rush into my office. I need to add today's notes to the McElroy file. The door is ajar and Myrtle is not in her usual place when I come in. She probably just stepped out to get something, I think, closing the door and looking over toward my desk. Except__ Myrtle is so safety conscious that if she steps out even for a few minutes she makes it a point to *lock* the door and it isn't locked now. Something's not right.

My gun is in my bag and I slowly reach for it. "Myrtle? Myrtle, are you here?"

I hear a muffled banging sound coming from the tiny bathroom. I go over to the door, gun pointed, and slowly open it to find a gagged and tied-up Myrtle wedged between the sink and the toilet. Putting my finger to my lips, I slowly look out the bathroom door and survey my office. No one is in sight. Holding my gun ready I make a cautious round of the office, looking under the desks, out on the fire escape, and carefully opening the closet door. The safe looks as if someone went at it with a hammer but it is unopened. Nothing. Papers from my desk are strewn on the floor and the drawers are open and empty.

I hurry back to the bathroom pulling my cell phone out as I go and hitting the speed dial for 911.

"Oh God, Myrtle! What happened? Are you all right? Are you hurt?"

She vigorously shakes her head as I put my gun on the sink and bend toward her to remove the tape from her mouth. "Cate! He knows, he knows about ..." I shush her as I listen to a dispatcher say,

"911, what's your emergency?"

I give my name, address, and ask to have an ambulance

come ASAP. Then I call Will.

"Benigni, leave a message."

As I begin to record my message, Myrtle screams, "He's still here! The one who ..." but I never hear the rest. The last thing I remember are her eyes going wide as she looks over my shoulder and says, "Him! That's him!" Then something heavy hits me on the side of my head and I collapse into blackness.

~⁂~

My hands are duct-taped behind my back and I try hard to focus. My vision is slightly blurry. I'm in the junk-filled backseat of a van of some type, which is traveling pretty fast down a street I don't recognize. But I do recognize the voice of the person driving. It's Marie's David who is looking at me in the rear-view mirror. He turns briefly to make sure that I'm conscious.

"You should have locked the door after you closed it, Cate. Some detective you are! I was hiding down the hall." He half turns to me again and says, "You look a mess. When I hit you, you went down and smashed your mouth pretty hard on the sink. Sorry about that but it couldn't be helped. By the way, that paperweight on your desk was just heavy enough to knock you out."

Maneuvering to look at myself in the rearview mirror I see dried blood caked on the left side of my face along with a swollen split lip. I curse myself for not having been more alert and professional. I was so concerned about Myrtle that I forgot to secure the area; by not doing that I left myself and Myrtle vulnerable. My head is throbbing and I have to concentrate on what David is saying to me. My Smith & Wesson and cell phone are on the front passenger seat. David smells of liquor. This is a volatile situation.

"David," I say, my mouth dry and numb, "This is kidnapping. It's a federal offense. That carries a prison term. Don't do this; don't ruin your life."

"Ruin? Ha! Too late. My life was ruined when I was *gently raped* at the age of nine."

I lick my lips to be able to speak. "There's nothing gentle about rape, David. I'm so sorry that it happened to you."

"Oh, my rapist, the son-of-a-bitch priest who did it to me cried after it was over. He told me he loved me and said he was as gentle as he could be. That is what I meant by a *gentle* rape." He laughs bitterly. "The bastard did that for four years, at least once a month, sodomized me and then cried. Four fucking years!"

My mind is trying to think but I feel dizzy. It's possible I have a concussion. I struggle to stay alert. *Keep him talking, engage him in conversation. Make him see me as a person. Stay awake, God damn it!*

"What happened to you is the most horrible thing that can happen to a child. I can't tell you how sorry I am that you had to suffer like that. But, seriously, David, kidnapping me isn't what you want to do. You need help to deal with your childhood trauma. You need to talk to someone and I can help you find the right person."

"I *have* talked to therapists, no help there. I even went to a support group that was supposed to help. They're nothing more than a bunch of weaklings, victims, they have no strength."

"You're a smart man David. You certainly sound educated and you know what you're doing. You know this is wrong."

David laughs again. "Educated! I was a freak in college; all I did was study and go to class. I couldn't date. Thanks to my holy rapist, I see sex as disgusting. That makes me a mental eunuch; I can feel nothing sexual without feeling disgust."

I keep looking out the window, trying to figure out where we are. We seem to be out of the city but I can't be absolutely sure. Think, Cate, what the hell can you do? You're an animal trapped in a steel soundproof box on wheels with a predator. This is a crazy man you're dealing with.

Duct tape is the choice most kidnappers use on their victims because it renders a person nearly immobile. I hate duct tape. It is impossible to get free of the tape without something sharp to slice through it. I feel woozy and, stupidly, I remember my one encounter with duct tape and Will. It was during one of our lusty encounters a year after our divorce. It's amazing what memories will come unbidden into your mind at inopportune moments.

I shift position and feel the small pocketknife I carry in my right back jeans pocket pressing against me. It's attached to a pocket flashlight—both necessities of the PI trade. My jeans are tight, probably because I'm eating too many of Harry's goodies, I think, and I can't maneuver myself into the right position to pull the knife out of my pocket.

A loud, angry honk from a passing driver and a sharp swing of the van jolts me forward and into the reality of my situation. I lick my lips again and concentrate. David is speaking to me again.

"You had to find it before I could get at it, didn't you? That goddamned box that held all the information we need to help our cause. I met Joshua two years ago when he came to work cleaning cages at the vet's office where I worked in upstate New York. I could see that he was holding in all this guilt and anger and I knew, just knew that he had to have been abused like me. One abuse victim can spot another, I guess.

"After we became friends, Joshua was still so embarrassed and ashamed of what had happened to him that he wouldn't reveal who his abuser was, even to me. It took me quite some time to find out the name of the priest who raped him. Learning that Joshua had kept a journal, documenting dates and details of every single instance of abuse, and hidden it, was a real gift. I introduced him to the survivor's group I formed, the Memorare. We remember everything that was done to us and we exact severe vengeance on our rapists. With his documentation of what he endured, he can be the shining light, the brave poster boy for our cause. His testimony alone can drive us." He looks at me in the rearview mirror and says, "Are you paying attention, Cate? I have a lot to tell you."

I struggle with nausea and try to focus on what he's saying.

"It was months before I was finally able to convince Joshua that we needed the information in that box. I knew he put letters in Marie's mailbox a few times. He just had to be careful of that old coot next door. That bastard nonagenarian watches everything that goes on in this neighborhood. I'm surprised that he didn't know that Joshua put something in the eaves a few nights before he left." He laughs with a strong bitterness. "But Joshua was afraid that someone would see him if he came back to get the box for us. So if he wouldn't come and get it, I decided that I would. I had to find a way to get it when no one was around. I made it my business to meet his sister Marie so that I could get at that damned box. That was the only reason I started seeing her. These pedophiles, these sick bastards, need to be punished by their survivors. Last year I was able to begin our true work.

"Make no mistake; I am a survivor not a victim. Those priests who were found dead deserved their punishments. I am proud to have been able to punish them for their crimes. You know all about that, right, Cate? The priests who were found dead? Meet the man behind the murders."

"The priest murders. You're involved in that."

Whatever alcohol he drank is making him reckless; he's bragging. That's a bad sign because it means he intends to kill me. No murderer tells you what he's done and allows you to live.

"You'd never guess it, would you? I certainly don't look like a killer. People always said that I looked like a choir boy!" He laughs again, mirthlessly. "But then guess *what*! I *was* a choir boy and my rapist was the choirmaster!"

My left eye is blurry but that may be because of the blood that dripped into it. I blink my eyes rapidly to clear them both.

"You, Cate, you should have been nicer to me. Actually, you were the one who was involved in my very first murder. Small world, huh? Remember the one in upstate New York? That was my debut. I wanted the world to know. But that murder story was buried; no one knew about it. The goddamn cops hid it. I had to do something more dramatic so I decided to use Latin, the language of the church, to leave messages. Then I dumped the bodies in more public places. I'm the one who sent the detailed ME report to the archbishop. It's just like writing one up on the animals at the vet's which I do all the time." He's on a roll and bragging about his crimes.

"The last one was pretty damn good, don't you think? Sending the information and a picture to the archbishop *and* the New York cops! Sent right from the laptop in the trunk of my car. A member of the Memorare knows how to make tracing our IP address almost impossible."

He takes a swig from a bottle. "Why were you so unfriendly when I met you at Marie's house? Why didn't you like me? Did you think that I might hurt Marie? No, never. She's as fragile as a flower. Pretty Marie, she has nothing to fear from someone like me."

David sighs deeply and the smell of alcohol rises with his breath. "I could have had you work for the Memorare to help us track down these pedophiles, these miserable priests, and bring them to justice, our justice."

"I could never do that, David. I'm a licensed PI. If I can bring a criminal to justice, I do it legally. What you're doing isn't justice."

"That's really too bad. I think you would have been an asset to our cause. And who's to say what justice really is? What was it Genghis Khan said to his enemies? 'I am the punishment of God. If you had not committed great sins, God would not have sent a punishment like me upon you.' I still want you to see how we enact justice though. I'm taking you there now. It's a shame but after you witness our brand of punishment, you will never be seen or heard from again. You're a liability."

"I've already sent your name to Detective Benigni and the police. They'll find me."

He laughs, shaking his head, "No, you haven't. You didn't know I was the one who tied up that nosy bitch in your office. You didn't have enough time to send anything important before I knocked you flat and took your phone."

I'm not about to plead for my life, but it's not because of pride. No matter what I say to him, David is not about to let me go. I have to stay alert and wait for him to make a mistake. Maybe I'll get lucky and some alert cop will pull him over for impaired driving. The one advantage that I have is that he *has* been drinking. Alcohol may make a person reckless but it also does one other thing: it dulls the reflexes. My eyes go to my gun on the front seat; I need to be able to get that gun.

The back seat of the van is a mess of old clothes and fast food bags from the Bar-B-Cue Chicken Barn. David swerves around a corner and I fall against several crumpled bags that smell of oily chicken and stale fries. Trying to get into a sitting position again, my wrist pushes against a half open bag and I feel something hard. Pushing into the bag, my index finger feels the serrated edge of a plastic knife. I almost laugh. Can that cut through duct tape? I curse under my breath.

But then I remember something that Melissa once told me. One of the many classes she is always taking was about plastic products used by the American consumer. The utensils used at any given place, she had said, depended on the type of food sold. Most fast-food places sell burgers and salads and so it makes sense that they would have flimsy white plastic knives because they don't need to cut through anything thick. But places like Bar-b-Cue Chicken Barn use knives made of clear, thicker plastic to cut through the overcooked micro-nuked meat.

David's driving is bouncing me back and forth but, after some bungled attempts, I manage to shove the fingers of my right hand into the open bag and feel around for the knife. My kidnapper's erratic driving makes it difficult but I finally grasp it. I feel a sharp cramp as I bend my wrist to slide it under the tape.

As David continues talking I work the knife back and forth, rustling my foot over a paper bag on the floor to cover the sound of the knife scraping against the tape. My fingers are tingling and getting numb from my hands being in one position. I scrap the edge against my wrists as much as against the tape. The tiny scratches I'm making feel like annoying paper-cuts. Where the hell is he taking me?

CHAPTER 27

MY CELL PHONE LIGHTS up and buzzes, doing a little shimmy on the front seat.

It's Will. "Cate, where the hell are you? If you're able to answer, do it now." Will's voice is frustrated as well it should be. Even with all the tech help available, he can't find my exact location. He's calling my phone in the hopes of pinging my whereabouts off of one of the many mobile towers even though he knows he won't get my exact location. The towers can only identify a large general area.

Startled by Will's voice, David opens a window, takes my brand-new phone and throws it out onto the street, easily eliminating any chance of police help in finding me. The knife cutting through the tape is a slow-go but it is working. My fingers are numb.

"You okay? You're awfully quiet back there," says David. I'm almost through the tape. Maybe if I play the victim card he'll fall for it. Getting out of the car is what I need to do.

"I'm so dizzy, David. I feel like I'm going to throw up!"

"Sorry," he says with little concern. "We're almost there. You'll be fine."

My wrists are free. I can try to grab my gun.

"No, you don't understand. I'm, oh God, stop the car!" I

make retching sounds hoping that I don't really vomit. The truth is that I *am* feeling very nauseated.

"Look," he says, "We're almost there. It's only a block away from here. You can hold it."

"No, I can't, now, please! I'm going to throw up right here!"

Cursing loudly, David pulls quickly to the side of the road. As he breaks to a screeching stop I act. With one quick swinging motion I reach over the seat, grab my gun, and jam it into the back of his head.

"Give me the keys and then get the hell out of the van! Now!"

David does as he's told, stumbling out and falling to the street. His cap falls off and I see a zigzag scar on the left side of his head near the hairline. Recognition hits me. David is the man in the sketch artist's drawing; the one Bo's friend met who said priests deserved to be killed. And I can assume that the van is the same van Bo's friend described; it is dirty and it is white and old. I get out slowly, feeling a wave of dizziness.

"It's you. You're the one looking for priests aren't you? You go scavenge where the homeless are."

"A lot of the homeless have been victimized by priests; they become drunks and drug addicts because of what was done to them. Someone stronger like me has to find those child molesters and punish them. They deserve to die."

"Get up and empty your pockets," I say, still pointing the gun at him. "Make no mistake, David, if you try anything I *will* shoot you."

He does as he's told. There's no cell phone in his pocket but he does have a roll of duct tape, which I grab.

"Where's the place you were taking me?"

"Down the block."

"Where? Which building?"

"The one on the left side, downstairs."

I look down the street and see a building flanked on either side by vacant lots with demolished parts of what look like factories. There is no street sign. It's unfamiliar to me; it could be any one of many once thriving areas hit by socioeconomic problems and a higher rate of crime on the outskirts of the city. People leave and it becomes suburban blight.

"How many are in your group, the Memorare?" He doesn't answer. I nudge him hard with my Smith & Wesson. "How many?"

Staring at me defiantly he says, "Five as of now, but there are going to be a lot more."

"How many are in the building now?"

He shakes his head, laughing. "Bitch!"

"How many? Answer me!" I smack his jaw with my gun and draw blood. "How many?"

Stunned, David answers me. "Just one person. He's bringing justice to his abuser. That's what I wanted *you* to see."

"Where are the others?"

"Out canvassing for survivors," he says angrily. "Fuck you!"

A wave of dizziness hits me and I step crookedly to the side. David suddenly lunges at me, knocking me sideways, but I regain my balance. He's disoriented from the booze and before he can come at me again I swing my gun hard against his temple. He goes down in a dead slump. I check his pulse; he's still alive. Then, putting the gun in my jeans I quickly wrap his hands tightly behind his back with the duct tape and tape his legs and ankles together before taping his mouth shut. I shove his body as far under his van as I can. With any luck, the combination of alcohol and the blow to his head will keep him out for a while.

My exertions have upped my adrenaline level and that's good. I try to do a few running steps in place to get my blood circulating, close my eyes tightly and open them, then head down the street to where someone is carrying out the justice of the Memorare.

⁓

The building that David pointed out is a deserted one that has no sign of life except a few rats that don't bother to move at my approach. They're New York rats and fearless. Taking out my penlight and holding my gun, I move around them and head toward the back of the building looking for a basement door. Down a dark flight of stairs behind the building I find it. Cautiously I try the handle and find it unlocked.

The basement is dark and dank-smelling with a dirt floor. There are shelves stacked to the ceiling. It might have been a wine cellar at one time or an old community pantry, decades ago. There's a faint smell of stale urine and emptied bowels coupled with a stronger odor of old bleach as if someone had tried to clean the area at some point. The bodily smells, however, seem to float above the bleach as if they are more potent. I also smell the distinct, coppery odor of blood.

I let my eyes adjust to the dark, which is illuminated by a small crooked-necked lamp on an old desk. Holding my penlight and gun in front of me I squint, canvassing the room, checking corners, and shining the light along the wall. On the far side of the room there's another door with a thin strip of light coming from underneath it.

I walk slowly over to the desk. By the dim low-watt bulb I see what look like strips of paper. Getting closer I can see that they're not paper at all; they're clerical collars. Neatly printed letters inside the collars are words in Latin: *peccatum vestrum*: your sin; *iustitia nostra*: our justice; *Dei poena*: God's punishment. There are also what appear to be some types of surgical tools. Someone is getting ready to commit a murder and mutilation and leave the body behind with a message.

I hear a moan coming from behind the second battered old door, and the sound of sobbing. As quietly as possible I move toward the sound and gently slide the door open a crack. The overhead light is bright and I blink my eyes against the glare. A man is standing with his back to me but I can see he's holding what looks like a surgical scalpel in one hand as he leans over a body on a table in front of him.

"Joey, Joey, don't do this, Joey!" pleads the man lying naked and restrained on the table.

There's that heavy coppery smell and I see a lot blood on the towels under the man.

"They hurt me so much, Joey, those men with you, they hurt me. Why did you let them hurt me? I'm bleeding. Help me. I need a doctor, Joey."

"I'm *not* Joey! Joey's dead. I'm not the weak boy who obeyed you, you sick fuck!"

"Joey, please help me. I love you like a son. Joey, help me, I hurt so much."

"Shut up! Don't call me that name! Don't say that name. You deserve the pain, you deserve more!"

Cautiously I inch the door open and move forward and squint in the light. I quietly suck in my breath. From the arch-diocese picture I saw of him online, even bloodied and battered, there is no mistake that the person restrained on the table is Monsignor Bernard Moore. I have to act fast.

Standing in the doorway I point the gun at the man with the scalpel and demand that he drop the weapon. When he turns to look at me, I find myself looking into familiar hazel eyes sprinkled with brown flecks. Eyes I had seen sad and crying, and just once, laughing; Marie McElroy's eyes. But this time I am looking into the eyes of her brother. Joshua McElroy is standing in front of me, a male version of sweet Marie. The scalpel in his hand is held expertly. I have a strong feeling that he knows exactly how to use it.

I take one step sideways so that I can have full view of what Josh is doing.

"Joshua, drop the weapon," I say calmly, holding the Smith & Wesson level.

"No! *You* drop your gun."

"You know I can't do that, Joshua. You know I won't."

"Who are you?" he asks with a touching simplicity, the question of a lost child.

"My name is Cate Harlow. I'm a private investigator hired by your sister Marie to find you. You need to drop your weapon."

"Marie?" He looks at me with so much sadness and pain that I feel heartsick.

"She wants to see you, Joshua. Marie misses you so much.

Put the scalpel down. You don't need to do this."

"I don't want to commit murder, that's not who I am. I want justice."

"Then let me call the police, Joshua, and they'll put this criminal in prison."

"No! I'm not taking the chance that he'll get away with what he's done. There is no justice for people like me. David says we have to make our own justice."

"Not true, Josh. David's wrong. The system isn't perfect, but I promise you that this bastard will get what he deserves and you and all his victims will get justice."

I ease forward slowly so as not to startle him. "You know what happens to child molesters, pedophiles, in prison, Josh? They're on the bottom of the food chain in there."

I nod toward the man on the table keeping my eyes on Joshua. "He'll spend the rest of his life rotting in a jail cell somewhere being raped repeatedly by sadistic prisoners who hate child molesters and rapists, and the guards will turn a blind eye to what's happening. Josh, they'll turn away from his screams and his pleas to stop, just as this monster turned a deaf ear to your pleas."

"God will punish you if you don't help me, Joey. He will send you to Hell!" screamed the man on the table in terrified desperation. "You will burn in Hell forever!"

Josh gasps and tears roll down his cheek. When he says that to Josh I want to smash my gun against the monsignor's mouth. That disgusting monster! Still using the name of God to try to instill fear. Slowly I edge closer toward Joshua.

"Monsignor Moore," says Josh quietly, "I *know* what it is like to be in Hell. You brought me there, remember? Don't talk to me about God. *Your* God is the one who abandoned me to a hell of *your* making. I stopped believing in God a long time ago, you child-sodomizing bastard." He takes a deep breath and continues. "Do you even comprehend what you have done to me? How you stole my innocence and destroyed my life? I will never be a whole man. You made me see life as perverted, dirty, and sick. How many other children's lives did you destroy after me? How many?

"You know," Joshua laughs, "David slits the throat of the priests he punishes and watches them die. It's rather quick if you cut the carotid artery just right. Not a whole lot of suffering. Then, after they're dead, he cuts off their dirty, ancient pricks." Joshua wipes away his tears.

"But me, see, I've been thinking about this day for a long time, ever since I joined this group really. When I found out that the church was going to pay you off to disappear, I thought we'd never catch you. Oh yes, David found out that information about you through one of his contacts. You were so protected! But David, he was patient, he told me to just keep waiting and that the day would come when you were caught off guard and brought to justice. My justice." He laughs again. "You came to me so willingly! So happy to see me! Did you think we were going to resume our … relationship? This place should remind you of that old school basement where you brought me to do my special penance, what you called the *bad-boy* penance." He closes his eyes and takes a deep ragged breath. "Anyway, I'm not going to do what David has done to those child molesting priests."

"I knew you couldn't hurt me, Joey. I knew you still loved me," babbled the old priest with relief. Looking at Joshua's face, I know Monsignor Moore didn't understand that Joshua had a different torture in mind.

"My justice, do you want to know what my justice will be?"

"You want me to say I'm sorry if I hurt you and that I'll make it up to you? I have money, Joey, I'll help you. I know that's what you want from me. You help me and I'll take care of you."

"You sick, sick bastard!" Joshua's voice rose in anger. "*Sorry*? You think that's what I want? Having you say you're *sorry* and giving me money? No!" His voice lowers and he says softly, "No, no, you don't get to say you're sorry and have that mortal sin absolved, oh no. I don't want you to say you're sorry." He takes a step to the side and stares at the wall, sighing. "Don't worry though; I'm not going to slit your throat."

The man on the table was blubbering hysterically and watching Joshua with hopeful eyes.

"Thank you, thank God," the priest mutters.

Joshua smiles almost sweetly, boyishly, as he walks closer to the table.

"No, I'm not going to do that. I already told you, my justice is different from David's. I would never cut your throat." His voice is as soft as if he were speaking to a frightened child. "That would be too quick a death. I ... want ... you ... to fucking suffer."

"Don't curse, Joey. That's a sin."

"A sin? Well, one more won't matter now will it, Monsignor, because I'm about to commit a mortal sin. You see, you miserable pedophile, what I'm going to do is this: I'm going to castrate you slowly so that you feel every single cut of this scalpel, I'm going to slice off that part of you that you used to punish me. I remember your *bad-boy* penance all too well—do you? You should; you enjoyed it so much. Well, *I* will enjoy castrating you. Then, I'm going to watch you bleed out slowly and die in agony. I want to hear you beg me to stop the way I begged you. That's my justice. Where's your God now?"

Monsignor Moore screams a high-pitched scream of terror. I'm standing a few feet away from them and I say his name softly. "Joshua."

"I have to do this. I have to do it alone! He is mine to punish, don't you see?"

"All I see, Joshua, is a young man who has suffered the most horrible abuse a child can suffer. I also see a disgusting pedophile who isn't worth your being sent to prison for murder. Let *him* be the one who goes to jail." I edge closer. "You're not a murderer, Josh, you're a good, decent person."

"No, I'm not. I ... I know what terrible things have been done here and I never tried to stop them from being done. I have hatred in my heart. I want him to pay for what he did to me."

"He *will* pay, Joshua. I promise you, I do, that I will make sure this bastard goes to prison and gets exactly what he deserves. You have no idea how horribly he will be treated by other prisoners. They'll make him suffer agony. Please, for Marie's sake, drop the weapon and let the police and prosecutors go after him. You deserve better, Joshua. You deserve a chance to begin the normal life that was denied you. Let the man who did this to you rot in jail."

"Whore!" screams the monsignor. "Don't listen to her. She doesn't know what she's saying. Help me. I need a doctor, a hospital. I'm bleeding."

Joshua looks at the monsignor but lowers the scalpel. He turns toward me.

"I love you like a son, Joey," babbles Monsignor Moore. "You know deep in your heart that I love you."

If he hadn't said those words the tense situation might have turned out differently. But those cruel words, the words of a true pedophile, squashed any chance of Joshua dropping the weapon and letting me call the police. He turns and, with a cry of rage, slashes a gash in the right leg of Monsignor Moore close to the pubic area. Angry tears blind Joshua and his aim is off. Still, the blood from the leg wound begins to pool. He raises the scalpel once more.

"Joshua, stop now or I will be forced to shoot you." My voice and my hands are steady but I feel sick to my stomach. He ignores me and is about to slice again when I fire, making sure to only nick his arm but causing him to finally drop the scalpel.

I move forward and kick the scalpel away. Josh is bleeding but a quick look tells me my aim was true—just a flesh wound. I put my gun in my pocket and grab a cloth from a nearby shelf to bind his arm.

"Don't move Joshua. I'm sorry but I had to do that. I don't want you going to prison for murder. Just don't move."

Moving over to the table I feel myself gag. The leg wound looks deep. For a minute I think of letting this monster bleed to death but that would be too good for him. I want to see him tried and convicted. I look around for something to stop the bleeding and press the extra towels I find on the table to the wound.

"Joshua, do you have a cell phone?" He nods, dazed. "Give

it to me and tell me exactly where we are, street name and loca-tion."

It's an old phone and the signal bars are low but I'm able to call 911. After I give our location and situation, the dispatcher assures me they'll arrive within ten minutes. I also tell her where the cops can find David and the van.

Until the EMTs arrive I hold the towel to the monsignor's wound, saving the life of a brutal pedophile and watching his innocent victim, Joshua McElroy, sobbing on the dirt floor.

CHAPTER 28

THE SCENE UNFOLDING IN front of my eyes is surreal. The EMTs have stabilized Monsignor Moore and are loading him into an ambulance. I hear him praising God and blessing the EMTs. Then I watch Joshua being led away in handcuffs and know that what's happening here isn't right or even fair. This young man was destroyed when he was only eight years old by that vicious pedophile who is now being taken to a hospital where he'll have expert and gentle care. Joshua is the real victim, and he is headed to a precinct holding cell. The EMTs released him to police custody after having cleaned and bandaged the flesh wound. Where's the justice in this scenario?

Of course the law doesn't see it that way. Having translated legal documents for ten years I know that. The letter of the law says that Joshua is a kidnapper and a possible accessory to several murders and mutilations. My only hope in all this is that the monsignor will survive and be charged with, and convicted of, the continuous rape of a minor, and other sex crimes. In child sexual abuse cases there is no statute of limitations for prosecuting first-degree sexual misconduct.

There are lawyers who specialize in helping adult survivors of sexual abuse and there will be someone who will defend Joshua when he is charged. He was looking to punish the man who

damaged his life and that trauma alone should count for something. "Do you know how Myrtle is?" I ask Will as he walks over
to me. The dispatcher call came through his police scanner.

"Good, she's good. She was checked out and released; just
bruises and she jammed her shoulder on the sink when she tried
to get up from the floor. The emergency room doctor said she'll
be fine with a good night's sleep. Harry was a nervous wreck but
she calmed him down." He's writing something in a small notebook. "By the way, our tech guy, Max, was finally able to trace
the IP address to a computer in the trunk of your kidnapper's
car, which was parked in a high-rise garage. And we found *him*
where you left him, stuffed halfway under the van." He looks at
me before adding, "Nice work with the duct tape."

I sway forward a little and Will puts his arm around my
waist. "How are *you*? You've got quite a bump on the side of
your head, babe."

One of the EMTs approaches us. "Detective Benigni? The
patient is stabilized and we're leaving for the hospital now. That
young man you arrested will be referred to the prison infirmary
later today so we're done here." He points to me. "Are you taking
your colleague to the emergency room to get her checked out?
I know you said she doesn't want to ride along with us but she
does need to be seen by a doctor."

Will assures him that he will take me to be checked out and
I let him lead me to his car. I'm taken away to the ER with police
lights flashing and siren howling and my ex-husband reaching
over to hold my hand as we race away.

⚓

"How are you feeling, honey?"

I open my eyes to see a concerned Myrtle standing next to
my bed, her arm in a sling. I don't even remember coming home.

"I'm okay. Are *you* all right?" I struggle to a sitting position,
groggy as hell. There are male voices coming from the living
room and I hear Giles and Will talking in low tones. "Whoa,
Myrtle, whatever they gave me made me zone out for a few min-

utes."

"More like two hours," says Will, who has appeared in the doorway with Giles.

"You *have* been out for a while," smiles Giles, coming over to the bed. "It isn't so much what they gave you, Cate; it's what you've been through. Your body needs to rest. I wrote down what drug you received along with any possible side effects. All the information is on your kitchen counter. Since you wouldn't stay at the hospital for observation, Will and I decided that I should monitor you and make sure that you're okay. Now lay back down like a good girl, okay?"

"I'm going to the precinct to check on Joshua McElroy," says Will. "We'll talk later."

"I think I need to come with you. Marie might need me."

"Jesus! Can you *never* do what you're supposed to do? You were conked on the side of your head and needed stitches and you're damned lucky you only have a slight concussion. So stay put, got it?"

Myrtle shushes Will and takes my hand. "I spoke with Marie; she's dealing with all this very well. And she's so happy that Joshua is alive. You can talk to her later. Just rest honey; I'll be here." Looking at Will and Giles, she adds, "You both should go now. I'll take care of her." Myrtle's word is law, it seems, and like a good girl I lay back and try to do as she says.

***

Getting roughed up has made me grateful for my friends. Melissa has called three times to see how I am and sent flowers and enough gourmet food for a week. Giles came by later that night to check on me and said he'd be back in the morning. Marie called to tell me how grateful she was that I found her brother alive.

"I know you're supposed to rest, but I wanted to thank you, Cate," she says crying into the phone. "You gave me back Joshua and that's all I wanted. Thank you, thank you!"

"Marie, are you alone? I don't want you to be alone tonight."

"No, no I'm not alone. Detective Benigni was here and he was so kind to me. And Mr. O'Leary is here with me too. He even came to the, you know, the … place where they're … holding Joshua." She can't seem to bring herself to say the word jail. "I'm okay. Did you know Mr. O'Leary's great-nephew is a law professor? Mr. O is asking him to look into how we can best help Joshua."

Good old Mr. O'Leary. We talk a bit more but I feel weary and my stitches hurt so I tell her I'll talk to her tomorrow. I fall in and out of sleep.

Harry brought some double-stuffed cupcakes with him when he came to pick up Myrtle. She insisted, however, on staying at my place in case I needed her. I later found out that she and Harry were in the middle of watching a *Law and Order* marathon when Will unlocked my front door sometime around twelve thirty and sent them home.

I half-wake in the night to find warm, strong arms around me. "Giles?" I whisper sleepily. Someone shushes me and brushes my hair back from my face, rocking me to sleep again. The next morning on my way to the bathroom I find Detective Will Benigni asleep on my couch.

⁓

Within a week I'm back at my office with a large bandage covering my stitches. I feel good, not good enough to whack some balls out at the court, but good enough to return to work and to walk over to Enzo's for a hot sub. It's a nice warm spring day.

Later back in my office as I'm idly watching the baby birds begin to take their first flight, I think of what has happened in a week's time. I gave my statement and my report to the authorities and the sex crimes unit. Two days after he was pronounced out of danger, Monsignor Moore was arrested in the acute care center of the hospital. After his arraignment at the same hospital, he was confined to his room there and handcuffed to his bed. No bail was set and he was remanded to custody.

David was arrested for the brutal murders and mutilations of the three priests. He's being examined by a slew of psychiatrists, and who knows when he'll come to trial. Will and his team confirmed that David's victims were indeed pedophiles and that the hierarchy in the Catholic Church, through their respective parishes, had aided and abetted their sex crimes by transferring them from parish to parish and through the process of laicization. Charges are being brought against all who hid the heinous pedophilia so rampant in the church. The first victim, the retired theology professor whose body I had found in upstate New York was found to have been David's choirmaster, sixth-grade teacher, and his rapist.

A call from Father Richard Boyd confirmed that the first murdered priest had also been financially supported by the Church. Father Richard told me he's praying for us all. He also told me he's thinking of entering a half-marathon; prayer and running seem to be his saving graces.

Joshua was arraigned in front of Judge Antonia Veccarelli who kindly set his bail at $500,000. She could have set a much higher one or denied him bail altogether. The bail money was put up by Mr. O'Leary. It seems my ninety-something moonshiner is a wealthy man. He's been saving his money in high yield CDs and bonds for years. As he said to me when he came by my office with Marie and Joshua, "What the hell am I going to do with my money anyway? It's just sittin' in the damn bank. Might as well do some good for good people."

Marie was right when she said that she sometimes felt as if Joshua was watching over her for the past ten years. He was. He never left New York State. Joshua McElroy had planned his escape for over two years and saved birthday money, his allowance, and cash from neighborhood jobs. He knew exactly where he was going when he left: an isolated old railway depot upstate. Joshua planned well. He had blankets, clothes, a can opener, and lots of canned goods in his gym bag to sustain him.

After a few months he found a small farm where he worked odd jobs for room and board. The woman who hired him was old and nearly blind; Joshua told her he was nineteen. She probably had no idea Joshua was a fifteen-year-old runaway. A few years later, he found a job in a veterinarian's office cleaning cages and caring for injured animals. He is a survivor the same as those survivors he read about.

He feels tremendous guilt over not being there for Marie when their parents died. The horrible fear of seeing Monsignor Moore again kept him away and he cannot forgive himself for giving into that fear, even though Marie says she understands.

I gave Marie the name of the head of the legal team at SNAP. I had called their office three days after I found Joshua. They charge a sliding fee and I think that maybe along with Mr. O'Leary's nephew, they can help Joshua's case. They're the experts in cases of priest molestation. They also recommended a therapist well versed in cases of child sex abuse.

As for Joshua, after his release on bail, he sat on the couch in my office while I spoke with Marie and Mr. O'Leary. Myrtle kept a conversation going with him and fed him Harry's cherry tarts and iced tea. At one point I heard a soft boyish laugh and was surprised that it came from Joshua.

Marie hugged me goodbye and I told her I'd be there for the trial. She wants me to keep in touch and I'd like to do that, but not for a while. She and Joshua need to get through a lot together and come out with new lives. Joshua came over to me and thanked me for, as he put it, saving him.

"You saved yourself, Joshua, because you're a good and decent person. Never forget that." He just shook his head sadly.

When they were leaving Mr. O'Leary gave me two quart bottles of his aged whiskey and told me not to be a stranger. "How many years you think I got left, lady detective? Come see me while I'm still alive." I said I would.

My social life has been put on hold for a while; I've been pretty busy. Work has picked up for *Catherine Harlow, Private Investigations* in the way of corporate security, long-lost relatives, and the always lucrative wayward spouse cases. I think Giles understands. Since he's been named president of the New

York State Association of County Coroners and Medical Examiners, he's been busy, too. Professionally we're swamped.

Giles and I have had dinner several times and he's stayed over at my brownstone twice, but that's about it. He has mentioned moving in together but I'm still not ready. We do speak on the phone almost every other day and it's always nice to hear his voice.

⤲

Two months later in the sweet month of June, I had sex with my ex, the charming Detective Benigni. He came over to my office one night while I was working late. I can't prove it but my private investigator's gut instinct, the one that rarely fails me, thinks Myrtle may have told him I was there alone and needed company. He came on the pretext of bringing me a super large Timothy's hazelnut coffee and to keep me company while I worked. We knocked back the coffee with some of Mr. O'Leary's whiskey, which I had left in the office.

Maybe it was the way he smelled, that nice clean just–showered male fragrance and the way he looked in his jeans and NYPD polo shirt. Will always did have a good body. Or maybe it was the way he winked and smiled at me when relating a funny story about something that happened at the precinct. Or maybe, just maybe, it was some colossal cosmic event where the stars seem to be aligned and you're not in absolute control of what you do. It's also possible that I was horny and knew that Will could scratch my sexual itch.

Whatever it was, I let him seduce me and O'Leary's potent brew did a good job of dulling any twinges of guilt I felt about Giles. Will knows exactly what erotic buttons to press and pretty soon he had me completely undressed and damn ready for action on my newly cleaned couch.

"You got a landing strip?" says Will eyeing me appreciatively as he takes off his clothes.

I close my eyes and sigh. The landing strip. I had gone with Melissa for a waxing and had gotten talked into the strip. I kind of liked it.

"Yup, I do. Let me put it into aeronautical terms. There's a strip of land that a pilot follows when the plane is coming in for a landing. It guides the pilot to the exact right spot."

Lying down next to me, he pulls me closer to him. The body next to me is comfortingly bare and I snuggle into his chest. His fingers gently raise my head to look up at his face.

"Baby, let me tell you that a good and experienced pilot can guide his own plane in for a landing without *any* help where it will settle nicely into a warm berth."

And he's so right.

Sometime during the night, my cell phone buzzes and voice-mail picks up the message.

"Hello, this message is for Cate Harlow. Please, I need to meet with you as soon as possible. My name is Jennifer Brooks Warren and someone has been hired to kill me!"

AUTHOR'S NOTE

Although *For I Have Sinned* is a complete work of fiction, there are issues within the book that are based on fact. The following notes have been thoroughly researched and documented by investigative reporters and media.

The Church sanctioned surgical castrations of Dutch boys who reported sexual abuse by priests in the 1950s. This proven fact was brought to public attention by journalist Joep Dohmen.

In 2012, Father Benedict Groeschel, CFR, a psychologist, and director of the Office for Spiritual Development for the Catholic Archdiocese of New York, made this statement concerning the sexual abuse of children by priests: "In a lot of the cases, the youngster ... is the seducer."

The process of laicization allows a priest accused of pedophilia to be removed from the priesthood. The action may be voluntarily requested by the priest or it may be involuntarily applied by the Church. In many cases this process has helped sexual predators to avoid criminal prosecution.

News media confirmed that under the leadership of certain US archbishops, dioceses paid individual sums of $20,000 to priests accused of molesting children to "help them transit to a new life."

In 2013, priests accused of pedophilia have been found to be living in a New Jersey retirement home, paid for by the Newark archdiocese. The home is located near several schools.

In 2014, St. Louis Archbishop Robert Carlson, testified in court that he didn't know it was illegal in the 1980s for priests to have sex with children. Though he was in charge of investigating claims of sexual abuse and pedophilia in his diocese, he admitted that he never went to the police, even when a clergy member admitted to him that he had engaged in "inappropriate behavior" with a child.

SNAP, the Survivors Network of those Abused by Priests, is a real organization that has helped bring attention to the sexual abuse of minors committed by the clergy in the Catholic Church. The organization has successfully pursued justice for the survivors of sexual abuse.

It is to be duly noted that there are many compassionate priests within the Roman Catholic Church who, like the two fictional priest characters Father Richard Boyd and Father Pat in the book, abhor what has been allowed to happen within the church they love and who devote themselves to helping the survivors of these sexual crimes.

ACKNOWLEDGEMENTS

Thank you to editors Joe Coccaro, and Courtney Davison for your positive support, incredible insight, and for helping to make this book the very best it can be.

And of course, many thanks to the readers who chose *Sins of the Father*. I hope you enjoyed the adventure!

Forgive Us Our Trespasses

Prequel to *Sins of the Fathers*

Coming Summer 2018

A Cate Harlow Private Investigation

PROLOGUE

"CATHERINE HARLOW PRIVATE INVESTIGATIONS."
I answer the phone on the fifth ring after having located the handset under a pile of folders. Keeping a neat and tidy desk is not one of my skills.

"Yes, good morning. I'd like to speak with Catherine Harlow if she's available."

It's a man's voice with a proper, well-modulated tone. I can hear prep school in the intonation of every word. "This is Dewitt Arthur Benedict calling from Hollow Hills Valley Residences."

It doesn't ring a bell, but it may be a client and God knows the coffers of *Catherine Harlow, Private Investigations*, not to mention my personal checking account, are practically empty. It's been a slow couple of months. That happens occasionally.

"I'm Cate Harlow. How can I help you Mr. Benedict?"

"I'd like to meet with you on a very confidential matter. I'll be in the city today and, I realize that *it is short notice*, but the matter is of major importance and it is necessary that I retain you as soon as possible."

"Today? I don't know if there's an opening today. Can you hold for a minute while I check my daybook? My secretary is on break right now. Thank you.”

I let him hold for about three minutes while I stare out the window and hum *Yellow Submarine,* which is a song just under three-minutes. I read somewhere that three minutes is an acceptable amount of time to keep someone on hold. Make them wait longer than three minutes and the person on the other end is annoyed and ready to hang up.

I have nothing on for today but it doesn’t pay to have a client think I have no other cases. One, they’ll think I’m not as good as my website says I am and so business is slow and, two, if they think *that* then they’ll try to get me to lower my fees.

“Mr. Benedict? Sorry to keep you waiting. I am booked pretty solid but, let me see what I can do for you.” I take a professional pause. “Yes, I can switch my two o’clock appointment for today to tomorrow. It’s a simple follow-up to one of my cases so that should be easy enough to change. Is the two o’clock time good for you?”

There’s a long silence followed by an exasperated sigh. “*Nothing* this morning?” Exasperated sigh and short pause. “Well, I guess it will have to do. I *assumed* you’d be busy.” Another few seconds of silence, then, “I cannot *stress* the importance of meeting alone with you, no secretary need be present. This is a *very* private matter that needs absolute discretion, and confidentiality is a premium.”

“Of course Mr. Benedict. Discretion is a high priority for my investigative firm. I pride myself on my confidentiality.”

“That is what I am counting on. No leaks to the press, *definitely no police*, no one else must know. Let me add that I am willing to pay very handsomely for your services and discretion.”

I sigh. His words ‘pay very handsomely’ seem as if my client will pay me well to hide a criminal activity. There is one thing I do have to tell him, well-paying client or not.

"Mr. Benedict, I am obliged to tell you that if a crime has already been committed, or if you are privy to one, I am required by law to inform police authorities."

"No crime committed here, I can assure you of that, Ms. Harlow. It is simply a private matter that requires a confirmed confidentiality. There is no crime of which I am aware."

"All right, that shouldn't present a problem then. May I ask how you heard about my agency?"

"Quite frankly I found your site on the internet. The testimonials from clients attest to your prowess as an investigator. I felt that your agency would be more than acceptable for what I need. As your site says, your clients seem to feel that you are very good at what you do and confidentiality is a top priority with your agency. That impressed me."

I smile. A month ago I spent four thousand dollars to have a professional website created and was starting to worry when it would begin to produce solid results. Maybe this is just the beginning to a lucrative period at *Catherine Harlow Private Investigations*.

"Well, I'm glad the website led you to us," I say in a professional tone. "Before we meet perhaps you can give me some particulars about this case, Mr. Benedict."

There's a pause on his end of the line, then, "No, no, Ms. Harlow, I would prefer not to discuss this matter over the phone. Definitely not over the phone, no. I will divulge what information you need when I see you this afternoon at two o'clock. I have your address and directions to your office here. Thank you for your time. Good-bye, Ms. Harlow."

"I'll be here, Mr. Benedict. Good-bye."

And, with that settled, the office of *Catherine Harlow, Private Investigations* has a potential paying client.

———◦◦∝◦◦———

At nine-forty-five on the dot my part-time secretary Myrtle Goldberg Tuttle comes bustling in carrying a large container of my favorite Timothy's Coffee Emporium blend and a bag containing yogurt, bagels, and half-and-half.

"Catherine, the door was unlocked again. You really should lock the door when you're alone. *I* always have it locked even when we're here together. And, *you're* here all by yourself. It's not safe for a woman alone."

She clucks her tongue at me. Myrtle was a junior high teacher until about six years ago. She says she's part-time but she's usually here from her on-the-dot nine-forty-five arrival until after five PM. Maybe she considers herself part-time because she takes an hour lunch and because on Fridays she leaves promptly at four o'clock for her unbreakable hair and nails appointment. She knew, and was close to, my parents who were also both teachers. She and her husband Harry are a kind of second mother and father to me. I love her to pieces but I think she worries too much.

"I do have a gun here you know. I feel pretty safe with that."

Myrtle rolls her eyes and mutters, "That gun!"

I go over to give her a hug and get my coffee. "Myrtle I'm a private detective. There are times I *need* a gun. I'm licensed for it and know how to use it very well. Stop worrying about me, at least until there's a real reason."

She looks at me and says, "May there never be a *real* reason I should worry."

To change the topic of conversation I tell her we have a paying client coming in at two o'clock this afternoon. "He says he's willing to pay handsomely, Myrtle. Sounds good, huh?"

"Sure, now *I* can get paid."

She smiles at me as she says this. Harry's a semi-retired accountant who only works during tax season but, along with what he makes, her teacher's pension, and her "part-time" job they seem to be doing just fine. Truthfully, I'm usually the one who is in need of instant cash and on occasion have been sustained by the generosity of Myrtle and Harry.

"So who is this well-paying client?"

"Dewitt Arthur Benedict. I've already looked him up on the internet, and through an acquaintance of mine who works with IAFIS at the FBI. Anyone who works in a health care system has to be fingerprinted so his prints are in the system. No hits on any criminal activity."

"What did you find? Big money? Secret organization?" Myrtle plugs in a pot to heat water for her tea.

"Well, his education seems to have been garden variety prep school, nothing especially striking. He did graduate NYU with honors and now he's the director of Hollow Hills Valley Residences, a posh adult living center and nursing home in upstate New York. Personal record says married, no kids and his only brush with the law is a contested parking ticket. He sounded polite enough during our brief early morning conversation but he was adamantly insistent about confidentiality and wants to meet me alone."

"Hmmmm," is all Myrtle says.

I sigh. Truthfully Myrtle should stay. Look up the word confidentiality in any dictionary and you'll see Myrtle's face next to the definition—she's that good at keeping professional or personal confidences.

"I'll insist that you have to stay, Myrtle."

"Don't lose a client because of me! He's wants privacy, he'll have privacy. I just hope he's not some crazy with designs on a woman trapped alone on the second floor of an office building."

"Myrtle! For God's sake, I can take care of myself. But the hell with what he wants. I've decided that I will insist that you stay. I will tell him I need you here for, whatever, phones, email. Oh hell! I don't need an excuse. This is my office after all. I decide who stays here."

"All right, Catherine. You do what you think is best. If I stay, you won't even know I'm here."

For the rest of the morning we work quietly together—me reviewing previous cases and updating my website, and Myrtle fending off telemarketers and making an appointment for me to meet with the CEO of a limo service. She puts the company's owner on speaker so I can hear him say that he wants to hire, "A female dick, you know, one of those woman private detectives to surveille our drivers. Ya got one who can look like a hooker so the guys don't get suspicious?"

Myrtle assures him that something can be arranged and takes down his information. She looks over at me and says, "Still got those hooker heels from that pole dancing case last year?"

"Back of my closet just waiting for a chance to emerge."

We have a quiet lunch delivered from Enzo's my favorite Italian trattoria and at one-fifteen I go outside to walk a bit and get the kinks out of my legs from sitting so much. I need to be active and lately, as I learned in Miss Farron's physics class in high school, I've been "a body at rest likely to stay at rest" unless some more cases that get me out of the office come my way.

∝

I love what I do and this was not always the case. Being a private investigator is a far cry from my previous form of employment. I used to be a law linguist for the state of New York. That's a fancy term for someone who translates the Latin of legal terminology into the English of layperson's terms. I was very good at it too because languages have always fascinated me and most times I worked alone.

My ex-husband, Detective Will Benigni, used to jokingly call me *Cate, the Cunning Linguist*. Funny, ha-ha—I was in love and lust and I liked that, too.

But, finally, my marriage with the charming Will Benigni was coming to an end—even the great sex wasn't enough glue to hold us together any more—and I felt that a real change was needed.

My fantasy dream of becoming a private detective began to seem more like a possible reality. I found a cheap but clean office in an old building and opened my agency.

For a few years, it was just me, a phone, and a laptop. My pride made me refuse alimony, and money was really tight. I took any case that I could find. Tailing people such as cheating spouses or kids whose parents wanted to know where they were, and who they were hanging around with, became my specialty. And then I accidentally hit gold.

Through a paralegal for whom I had done some free surveillance work, I was given the cold case of a baby who had been stolen from a hospital nursery, over twenty years ago, when she was just three days old. The biological mother had recently had a stroke and the father wanted to give it one more try to find their baby.

That was the Reynolds case and it had garnered some real media attention. I had been able to locate the baby, now a twenty-two-year-old young woman, living in another state. No one had been able to find her and the paralegal had thought fresh eyes might help the case. It had taken me eight months of intense research and following obscure leads to find her but my success in reuniting her with her birth parents had made me a mini-celebrity and I was interviewed on several morning news shows.

As positive word of mouth about my investigative abilities spread and more clients were hiring me, I found that I needed someone to help out with the files, computer as well as paper. Myrtle Goldberg Tuttle was a perfect choice.

Because she had been a friend of my parents, I had been invited to her 'retirement-from-teaching' party. I casually mentioned that I was looking for someone to help out at my office. The next day Myrtle showed up at nine-forty-five, told me she could only work part-time, and has been with me for three years, improving my work environment and my life. Take what she did to my office.

The original layout of my office was pretty simple when Myrtle first saw it. It was really just a large room with two desks in it—mine by the window and a smaller, empty one a few feet from the door. Myrtle took one look at the room, and decided that I needed a private office area.

"We need a wall," she'd said.

When I protested that I had no extra cash for any major renovation and that besides, I didn't own the building so major upgrades were out of the question, she argued there were ways to simulate a wall.

"Simulate? A wall?"

"Yes, I said simulate," said Myrtle. "You'll see and I promise it will cost you very little."

We argued back and forth for about five minutes concerning cost versus a client's visual impression of my place. Winning this type of argument with Myrtle was almost impossible so I gave in.

"Whatever Myrtle, as long as it doesn't involve too much money," I said as I threw my hands up in surrender.

The result of Myrtle's simulation is a beautiful, heavy, scrolled wooden screen, bought at an antique shop for three hundred and fifty dollars that literally divides two-thirds of the room, hides my desk from the door, and gives me a private little office. Coupled with a small couch and comfortable leather chairs that she bought from an estate sale, the office of *Catherine Harlow Private Investigations* looks professional and fairly upscale. Mrs. Myrtle Goldberg Tuttle is a gem.

ONE

I SEE A TAXI PULL UP to my building and a distinguished looking man in his fifties, holding a leather portfolio, step out of the back door. He looks at a slip of paper and then up and down the block for an address. The neighborhood isn't very upscale and his distaste is evident. If this is my client, he is twenty minutes early. As he's leaning in to say something to the driver I walk quickly back to my doorway, race up the stairs to my office, trip over my own feet and fall onto the landing, slamming my left knee hard. Shit!

Opening the door to the office, I hobble to my desk, taking deep breaths to appear calm and in control of all situations. Myrtle looks at me questioningly and starts to say something but a shake of my head, and a warning look at the door, stops her. When Mr. Dewitt Arthur Benedict opens the door to my office, Myrtle is busy on her computer and I am "pretend-talking" on my cell with what I hope is an air of professional concentration.

"May I help you?" I hear the prim and proper voice of Myrtle speaking to the man who has just entered.

"I have an appointment with Catherine Harlow. I am Dewitt Arthur Benedict and I had requested that we meet alone."

"Yes, good afternoon Mr. Benedict. I'm Myrtle Goldberg Tuttle, Ms. Harlow's secretary. Please have a seat and I'll tell her you're here. She's on a business call with a client at the moment. I see that your appointment is for *two o'clock*."

Myrtle deftly puts Mr. Benedict in his place by reminding him that he is early for his appointment and that I'm a busy woman with other clients.

"Can I get you some tea or coffee, Mr. Benedict?"

"No nothing, thank you. I, uh, I do realize that I'm a bit early. Just let Ms. Harlow know I'm here please and remind her of our agreement for discretion."

"I'm sure no reminder is necessary."

Myrtle's face appears around the side of the screen. "Your two o'clock is here," is all she says then turns and walks back to her desk.

At two on the dot I leave my inner 'office', and walk over to where Mr. Benedict is seated, my hand extended.

"Mr. Benedict? Hello, I'm Cate Harlow. Please come into my office."

He shakes my hand and repeats what he said on the phone about being alone. "I did request that we be alone, Ms. Harlow. You do remember my request certainly."

"Yes, I understand, sir, but my secretary regards discretion and confidentiality in the same manner I do. Mrs. Tuttle has been with me for a number of years now and is highly regarded by me. I see no reason to make her stop the crucial work she is doing for me and leave. Believe me your case will be completely confidential."

He looks at Myrtle who is sitting at her desk, head bent over a file of papers seemingly completely absorbed in what she's doing. Benedict looks as if he's about to insist on our being alone then shakes his head slightly and follows me to my desk.

Sitting across from me he says, "Very well, Ms. Harlow. I'm here and the situation is rather urgent. Truthfully, I don't have the time to find another qualified investigator and contacting the police is out of the question. However, time really is of the essence." He pauses and gives a piercing look. "I assume I have a client privilege here, yes?"

I nod my head affirmatively.

"Fine, then let's begin. I am the director of Hollow Hills Valley Residences. You've heard of it?" Benedict says this with a certain pride.

"Yes. In upstate New York." I don't tell him I checked him, and Hollow Hills, out online and through various sources. His phone number alone on my caller ID was enough to get me started. But let him think I've heard of the place because of its ritzy reputation.

"We're what I like to refer to as a boutique care center. We're small for a reason; the care is better and we get to know all of our residents. We have three areas at Hollow Hills. The senior suites and assisted living housing are both very upscale and state-of-the-art. Then we have the nursing home, same type of environment and accommodations. This is also upscale and provides the very best health care available.

"The residents all have personal monetary accounts for their own needs. To say that we have a certain reputation to maintain is rather unnecessary. Our residents come to us for the excellent care and privacy. Many wish to remain anonymous. We have well-known names living there."

I nod and take notes, careful to observe Mr. Benedict as he is speaking. I watch his mannerisms and body language. He's got something he wants covered up is my professional guess. He'll continue to extol the virtues of where he works to impress me with his importance as director. It's a subtle form of intimidation; he's saying, *'I'm important so you'd better be impressed.'*

I'm not.

What he doesn't realize is that by talking exclusively about Hollow Hills and his exalted position, he is giving me the real reason why he is here—he's out to save himself. Whatever has happened at Hollow Hills could adversely impact his career and position. A position he doesn't want to lose. The fact that he's here in person tells me that the insistence on discretion is his only major concern. I let him talk for a few more minutes, and when he pauses, I interrupt him.

"You are retaining my services because of an incident that recently happened at Hollow Hills and not for your own self, correct? Because you're only telling me about yourself and not what happened. Please tell me about the incident."

Dewitt Arthur Benedict's head rears back in surprise at what I have said but he recovers quickly and half-smiles at me. "I see that you *are* good at what you do, Ms. Harlow. You are quite correct. I am retaining your services on behalf of Hollow Hills. That is true. But, again, discretion is needed and all expenses you incur, plus the bill for your professional services will be paid by me. All bills must come only to me, are we clear on that?"

I nod assent and ask him to tell me what has happened.

"One of our residents has gone—missing."

"And you don't want the police involved. Is this person someone with a well-known name, is that it?"

"No, no, not at all. No one famous. An elderly man, diagnosed with slight dementia, although speaking with him, you'd never know that. A bit of memory loss is all. Very intelligent and astute. He's a retired philosophy professor. Money seems to be no problem—all his Hollow Hills bills are paid on time every month from his own money market account similar to a trust fund set-up. Before we can even consider someone as a Hollow Hills resident we have to know that all expenses will be paid, present as well as future. We are not a charity. That may sound harsh, I understand, but that has always been our policy.

"Professor Hendricks' combined checking/savings account is quite substantial and he can withdraw from it for anything he wants at any time, which he did. We have twice-weekly trips into town for anyone who cares to go. There's shopping, a small children's zoo, a park, and some cafes. The residents are always supervised I may add."

"A retired college professor with a substantial savings account? Except for deans and others in administration, most people in academia don't make a great deal of money. Any idea as to the source of the prof's largesse?"

"No, I assume he may have inherited money or gotten monetary awards. Truthfully, Ms. Harlow, we at Hollow Hills don't pry into the business of our residents. We just need to be satisfied that all expenses will be paid without any problems."

I ask him to tell me what happened.

"Yesterday afternoon most of our residents were outside after lunch. We have a violinist or a flautist who play in a small gazebo as the residents sit in the garden and listen to the music. Our residents walk around the gardens and some go into the greenhouse where we grow herbs. Of course, some patients have visitors whom they can certainly bring into the garden. We want them to feel as if Hollow Hills is their home, which, of course, it is. All in all, the afternoons are very pleasant this time of year.

"Around four o'clock the staff begins to help patients who aren't ambulatory back to their suites and usually by four-thirty everyone has left the garden. Some family members extend their visits by going back to the patients' rooms to spend more time together."

"Are the rooms checked to see if everyone has returned?"

Dewitt Arthur Benedict looks a little disconcerted. "Actually, no. Dependent patients have an aide with them at all times during the day. As for the others, the staff are only required to check on patients who require afternoon medication. Mr. Hendricks only received his meds, for arthritis, in the morning and was independent. As I mentioned the dementia is slight, no meds for that needed at this time, and of course he is evaluated monthly."

"Give me Mr. Hendricks full name, his age, and his suite number."

"Robert Hendricks, professor emeritus. He lives in suite 2431. Our records indicate that he's seventy-five years old. Professor Hendricks first lived in our senior housing for a few years then transferred himself into our assisted care area about a year ago. He had had a doctor's consultation concerning his dementia and, even though it was still very slight, he was being proactive, you see."

"You mentioned that family members visit in the afternoons.

What about the professor; any family members come to see *him*? Non-family visitors?"

My client shakes his head no and says that as far as he knows there is no family and he doesn't remember seeing him with any visitors.

"Phone calls or letters?"

"Not really. He does receive a monthly statement from the bank but that, and the usual junk mail we all get, is about all." He pauses then says, "It is sad Ms. Harlow, but we do have some residents whose only family seems to be other patients and our staff. It happens. I assume the professor is one of them."

"So he's never, to your knowledge, had a visitor at Hollow Hills."

Mr. Benedict shakes his head no.

"Who first noticed that the professor was missing and what time was it?"

"I left at three o'clock yesterday afternoon for a dental appointment and I received a call at home around seven-thirty in the evening from my administrative assistant, Mrs. Angela Coletti. Part of her duties include greeting the residents in the dining hall every evening. Professor Hendricks is usually at his table in the dining room near the south window a few minutes before six o'clock dinner. When she didn't see him there, she was a little concerned, but not overly so. However, at six-forty-five, when he still hadn't shown up or answered his phone, someone was sent to check on him to see if he had decided to dine in his room. It isn't unusual. Some patients do that occasionally and he did it once or twice. Mrs. Coletti thought that perhaps he had forgotten to call the dining service. But, when she was told that the professor didn't answer the knock on his door, Mrs. Coletti went over to his suite and opened it with a master key."

I wait for him to continue, keeping my face impassive but he looks at me a bit defensively, obviously feeling he needs to explain why his assistant would use her key to enter a private suite.

"We *only* enter a residence in what we perceive to be emergency circumstances, such as a possible health crisis. Our residents' privacy is sacrosanct, you understand."

"I do, Mr. Benedict. Please go on."

He continues with a shake of his head. "But Professor Hendricks wasn't in his suite. Mrs. Coletti, along with the staff, immediately searched the surrounding area before calling me. She even sent several of our staff to canvass the area outside Hollow Hills and go into the town. I returned to Hollow Hills immediately and she and I questioned the staff and residents. Ms. Harlow, the truth is that no one remembers having seen him after lunch, not the staff nor the residents. He wasn't anywhere that was familiar to him—not the small chapel where he attends services, nor any cafes in the town. We searched well into the night, and this morning as well, before I called you."

"And who made the decision not to call the police? This is an elderly man with some dementia who may be in some type of danger after wandering away."

He stares out the window for a few minutes before answering me. "*I* made the decision. Frankly, Ms. Harlow, I cannot even imagine what would happen to Hollow Hills if word got out that a resident had disappeared from our facility. We are a private care facility and pride ourselves on having a safe and well-ordered haven. People trust us with their lives, and families trust us with their elderly mothers and fathers. If the news got around that we 'lost' a resident, well, that trust would no longer be applicable. Not to mention the chaos of having the police all over the grounds frightening our residents and having that get back to family members. Hollow Hills would, well, it would *cease* to be."

I write all this down in my small notebook. I find it easier and faster to scribble it all down by hand than keying the info into an iPad.

"You mentioned that the staff takes residents on shopping excursions. Is Professor Hendricks one of the patients who go on the twice weekly trips to town?"

"Yes, he will go into town most weeks. He likes shopping and then having lunch in one of the cafes there. Of course," he adds hastily, "the patients are *always* supervised. Yes, always supervised."

Right. Sure they are. If that were the case, DeWitt Arthur Benedict wouldn't have had to state it twice.

"Mr. Benedict, is your staff paid well?" My question takes him off guard.

"Paid well? I don't quite understand what you mean. They're paid what the state requires."

"And that would be what?"

"Nineteen dollars an hour. What does that have to do with this case, Ms. Harlow?"

I tell him that any info, no matter how seemingly unimportant it may be, is crucial to all missing person's cases. What I don't tell him is that when you hire people to do a job that is boring, doesn't take a lot of energy, and only pays minimum wage, you will not get high quality staff. Mistakes will happen.

We talk a bit more about Professor Hendricks and I ask a few questions about the set-up of the grounds and the buildings, and all exit areas. It seems there are gates surrounding Hollow Hills but the gateways only have minimal security and are intermittently watched by regular staff members.

"You don't have a security system, cameras and such, or a security company monitoring the grounds then, Mr. Benedict. That's dangerous."

He shakes his head, annoyed at my blunt statement.

"Have you ever thought about hiring professional security guards or having a high-intensity camera system installed?"

"Not necessary, Ms. Harlow. The staff does their job and I assume they do it well," he answers sharply.

I back off. No need to push his buttons. I need this job right now. It should be simple enough. Ninety-five percent of these cases end well—the person is found, confused and a little scared, and returned back to where he lives. I have every confidence that this is going to be one of those cases.

"All right, Mr. Benedict. I'll be up at Hollow Hills this afternoon around four-thirty. I'll be talking to any staff members who were the last to see Professor Hendricks and I'd like a quiet, secure office for those talks."

"Yes, of course, Ms. Harlow. I'll have Mrs. Coletti's office made available. She is indispensable to Hollow Hills and to me. Again, however, I caution, please be discreet."

And, on that note, he stands, shakes my hand, and walks out the door with a curt nod of his head to Myrtle.

"Pompous little man," says Myrtle with a grimace.

TWO

UPSTATE NEW YORK IS A pretty place to be in early spring. Manicured lawns, beautiful mansions. I'm admiring the view as I'm on my way to Katonah, an unincorporated hamlet within the town of Bedford, Westchester County. According to the New York Times online, Westchester County is home to seven billionaires; I believe it. A former client of mine who is a psychiatrist told me that the hamlet of Katonah is where doctors and lawyers, who have a drinking or drug problem, go to get clean and sober. "It's quiet and hidden and classy," she had said. "A perfect place to disappear for a while."

She's right. Truthfully, it is a hidden gem and when the pleasant robotic voice of my GPS tells me that my destination is one hundred yards on the right, I barely notice the driveway of Hollow Hills. It's hidden by thick, high, flowering bushes and would be easy to miss by someone not knowing the area or not having an insistent GPS repeating, "You have now arrived at your destination. You have now arrived at your destination."

There's an open gate and a young man wearing a shirt with a Hollow Hills logo nods at me as I glide my car through the entrance way and up a winding, flower-lined road past well-kept two story buildings. If I didn't know better, I would think this was a gated community of fashionable townhouses. I don't see much in the way of security—as Mr. Benedict told me, there are no guards or cameras, just staff members. It seems that Hollow Hills may spend lavishly on appearances, but cut costs in other ways.

I see a parking area a short distance from the sign reading Hollow Hills and head over. In the lot, I park my Ford Edge carefully next to a silver BMW and take notice of the other cars. Lexus, BMW, a Mercedes—obviously those visiting here have money.

I'm glad I went home to change clothes and dress professionally for the meeting in a navy blue linen sheath dress and three-inch heels. It was a wise choice. Walking into a place like this you need to look as if you fit in.

As I'm walking over to what looks like the main building I observe the people coming and going about their day. There are some well-dressed older people walking with younger men and women in more casual attire. The younger ones have to be staff— they seem to be overly professional in their stance and their demeanor towards the older people. They're definitely not family members.

Mr. Benedict has someone waiting for me on the veranda of the building. Even though she appears elegant in a dark skirt and white long-sleeved blouse, she looks harried and stressed.

"You must be Catherine Harlow," she smiles mechanically. "You're right on time. I'm Angela Coletti. Please call me Angela. Would you join me in having some coffee in my office?"

All of this is said in a smooth well-practiced way as if she's used to interacting politely but distantly with people in her work. I tell her coffee will be fine and that she can call me Cate.

Her office is elegant and well appointed with leather chairs, a bookcase, and a large, desk complete with computer. The coffee is poured from a silver pot and served in pretty little cups. There are petit fours, which I decline.

"Crème and sugar, Cate?"

"Just crème, thank you."

"Mr. Benedict has asked me to lend you my office while you conduct interviews with the staff. How else can I be of service to you, Cate?"

I ask her to tell me about last night when she first suspected that Professor Hendricks had gone missing and she pretty much tells me what Dewitt Arthur Benedict had said. The professor was missing from his usual place, she sent someone to check on him, she found that he wasn't there and a search was begun. Then she called Benedict.

"I'll need the names of everyone who interacted with Professor Hendricks on a daily basis. And a recent photo of Professor Hendricks if you have one."

"Yes, I can give you those names. He didn't have an appointed caregiver, you know. He was free to come and go as he pleased and, by that, I mean that he did take advantage of the shuttles that went into town. His dementia is mild so there was no reason to restrict his activities. And of course, our residents are never alone when off the premises."

I smile. What she says parrots what Mr. Benedict said about supervision of residents at all times.

She opens a desk drawer and looks at a list before she hands it to me. "These are the people Professor Hendricks sees almost every day. I even have his doctor's appointments listed. Dr. Laura Genesee isn't in today, but I'll give you her number. When we've finished our coffee, I'll call the staff members in here and I'll go look for his photo."

Angela Coletti sits back, crosses her legs, and fixes me with a calm, pleasant look. I know that this relaxed position and look are meant to convey a confident person who is in charge of the situation—I've done it myself when talking to clients and police. We talk about Professor Hendricks, her position at Hollow Hills, and finally edge around to what she thinks may have happened to the professor. She politely tells me that she has no idea and I tend to believe her. It isn't her job to keep track of the comings and goings of the patients. Her job is to be pleasant and polite.

It takes me two hours and fifty minutes to interview those who have daily contact with Professor Hendricks. From all accounts, he was a pleasant man who liked listening to opera and was a regular at Sunday morning services and Tuesday evening Novenas at the small Catholic chapel a mile from Hollow Hills. He was driven to and from the chapel each time. No one knows anything much about him but all say basically the same things— quiet, nice, and never had a visitor.

"Yeah, the professor," says one male staffer, "Nice man, very polite, always asking me about my kids and all. I hope he's okay. Truth be told, I don't know why he might wander off, but who knows, huh? Sometimes the dementia just suddenly gets worse.

That happens. It's a sad disease, you know."

Another staff member, the aide who gave Hendricks his arthritis medicine in the morning, says that she saw him the morning he went missing and there was no indication that anything was wrong.

"Such a nice man," the aide sighs.

"Professor Hendricks, yes, always polite. Quiet though. Poor man, never had any visitors here." This statement was from the shuttle driver. She smiles.

"He loved going to town. Went on little shopping trips, buying small trinkets or maybe a shirt or sweater. And he was so happy the last couple of months every time we went into town. Just so happy like he'd found the town a wonderful place to be."

I ask her how long the excursions to town lasted and she tells me they leave Hollow Hills at ten-thirty in the morning and return no later two o'clock, "The residents need to rest in the afternoon, miss."

"Who usually went with him to town?" I ask the shuttle driver. "Was he friends with anyone in particular on the trips, any person who went shopping with him or had lunch with him?"

"Oh, the professor was friendly with everyone here. He liked Mr. Rowlings—played chess with him and all."

"So he sort of hung around with Mr. Rowlings. They were together on the excursions into town then."

"Oh, no. Mr. Rowlings never went to town. He's, well, he's incontinent, can't control his bowels, and he doesn't like—well, that's just how it is."

"I understand. Was there anyone else who maybe was close to the professor when you took him to town?"

She shakes her head. "Sorry, miss. We'd get to town and the professor would go off to a store or the small children's zoo there. He was on his own but Larry, the other aide who comes along on the trips—uh—you know, he always watches out for the residents. He lets them go off on their own but he's supposed to always know where they are. He waits for them."

She looks down at her watch. "Sorry, miss, I got to go now. We're going to town tomorrow and I have to make sure the shuttle is clean and ready."

I look on the list of names. Larry. There's only one person with that name. Larry Palter, the first person I interviewed, the one who said, 'Sometimes the dementia gets worse.' I think I need to visit the town tomorrow and observe exactly how carefully Larry watches the residents away from Hollow Hills.

Angela waits five minutes after the shuttle driver has left the office before coming in to see if I need anything else.

"Cate?" She looks at me gathering my things. "Have you finished? You're more than welcome to dine with me later in the staff dining room if you wish. The food is quite good."

I thank her but decline. "I have everything that I need for now. Thank you for giving me your office today."

"Oh, my pleasure, of course," she says with practiced politeness. "Can I do anything else for you?"

"Yes, I need to see Professor Hendricks's room and possibly walk around the grounds. I need to check the area for myself. Don't worry; the other residents will simply assume that I'm a visitor."

"Of course, Cate. I'll go open suite 2431 now. Just pull the door closed when you've finished. It will lock automatically. Stay as long as you need to stay."

The suite Angela Coletti unlocks is pleasant and spotless. It certainly looks like an upscale place to live. There's a living room, dining area, kitchen, a bedroom, and a smaller den-like room with a large new flat-screen TV and a Bose unit. Nice. The furniture appears to be high-end and not the type of items most people on a fixed income would have.

I walk slowly through the suite noting that the only pictures in the living room are two framed ones. One shows the professor in what looks like a lecture hall and the other is one of him posing with faculty members in academic robes. In his bedroom, I search through his drawers, which contain only clean, neatly folded clothes.

There's a church bulletin on a night table along with a bottle of prescription pills labeled Tramadol. The label states that Tramadol *"alleviates pain caused by osteoarthritis without causing gastrointestinal bleeding or ulcers."*

In the top drawer of his night table, I find eyeglass cases, a remote for the smaller flat screen TV in the bedroom, and a few old Polaroid snapshots. There are several pictures of a young Hendricks—standing alone in front of a church, one of him shaking hands with an older man in front of the same church, and another of him standing with a group of boys. I take pictures of the snapshots with my phone.

Then I check the entire suite carefully, even lifting the area rugs to look underneath, but there is nothing that gives a clue to Hendricks's disappearing act. Perhaps I muse, as I close the door of suite 2431, he *did* get confused and simply wander off.

But, something in my gut tells me there has to be more to it than that simple explanation. It was still daylight when he went missing, there are nothing but roads around here, and no places to hide. He's an elderly man—how far could he have gotten? Why hadn't the staff been able to find him? If he had been picked up by a Good Samaritan who happened to be driving by, surely the driver would have alerted the police and the professor would have been returned safe and sound. It doesn't make sense that he went off on his own.

After changing my pretty but uncomfortable heels for the sneakers I always keep in my car, I walk the perimeter of the vast Hollow Hills property. There are four gated driveways on the property and three of them are open wide. I see only one staff member near the gate by which I entered, there's no one by the other ones. Truthfully, anyone could come into Hollow Hills. No one stopped me or asked why I was here. Professor Robert Hendricks could have walked out without anyone noticing him.

It seems as if the professor has simply vanished without a trace.

Angela Coletti is waiting in the parking lot when I finish my surveillance of the property. I shake my head no to her question, "No trace at all?"

She sighs and say, "If you need anything else from me, Cate, don't hesitate to call."

"Sure, thanks, I will," I answer

"Here's the picture of Professor Hendricks you wanted. It was taken this past April at Easter time."

I look at the photo of an older man who is sitting in a chair smiling at the camera, someone who looks at peace with the world.

THREE

A T TEN O'CLOCK THE NEXT morning, I am sitting in the Hollow Hills parking lot, waiting for the shuttle to leave. I've got my coffee, a half-eaten bagel, and a bottle of cranberry ginger ale. I'm ready for a few hours of surveillance work.

Eight people are laughing and talking as they get on the bus for the excursion into town. Most of the residents are able to get on without assistance except for one woman with a cane and a man with a surgical boot on his foot. Larry helps them get settle and then goes to sit across from the driver. As the shuttle goes towards the same gate by which I entered, I start my car and follow at a short distance.

The trip to town takes about twenty minutes and on the way, I make a mental note of the small Catholic chapel that must be the one Professor Hendricks attended. I'll stop there on my way back from town.

The driver of the shuttle pulls into one of the wide angled spaces on the street that small towns seem to favor over a regular parking lot. I park a few spaces away and watch the residents exit the bus. Larry stands ready to help those who might need his aid. There is a flurry of talk and laughter as the residents of Hollow Hills walk to wherever they have chosen to go. Larry walks behind them then stops at a bench to sit. I hear one woman ask him a question.

"What time do we have to be back here, Larry?"

"One-forty-five, Mrs. Perry," he smiles at her. "I won't let anyone leave without you, you know that."

Mrs. Perry giggles. Larry seems to have a nice rapport with the residents. He was patient and kind, helping them get on and off the bus, and he seems very respectful.

The shuttle leaves and I watch him sit alone on the bench and pull out his phone to text, play games, or whatever. The cell phone and all its bells and whistles is a sanity-saver for bored people.

For the next half-hour, I stay in my car and observe him sitting there. No one comes over to him and I can feel his boredom. As a private investigator, I'm fairly used to sitting and waiting—the pay-off for me is solving a case and a healthy payday. But Larry looks bored and miserable—low pay, no mental stimulation. And I will bet that he doesn't give a damn where the residents have gone in town.

My phone buzzes and I see a text from the man I'm currently dating. Giles Barrett, the NYC medical examiner. We met about nine months ago and he was a sure cure for my post-divorce lonely love life.

"Dinner later, 'round 8:30 okay? Working late. G."

I text back yes and continue watching my target as I sip a bottle of cranberry ginger ale and wait. As it happens, I don't wait long.

Larry suddenly gets up, looks around quickly, and moves off towards the road. I watch from my car and notice a dark green Dodge waiting a short distance away. Larry waves at a woman who's in the driver's seat. I watch him get into the car, kiss the woman, and see the two drive away as I start my engine and prepare to trail them.

Following a car is easier than anyone knows. Most people don't pay any attention to the traffic behind them not really. It's not like in the movies or a TV crime show where the person being followed suddenly seems to realize a car is trailing after him. In my experience, drivers are oblivious to what's behind them. The average person is too caught up in his or her own life to do more than obey traffic rules and get from point A to point B. If I'm not on a case, I tend to act the same way.

The car makes a right turn and goes down a shady side street where it stops in front of a small white house. I drive past and, in my rearview mirror, I watch Larry and the driver get out and embrace, then hurry into the house. It's eleven-fifteen. So much for "constant supervision of the residents of Hollow Hills."

⁚

"You gonna make my life hell and tell my wife? Or are you just going to report me to Coletti?"

Larry is pissed and puffing angrily on a cigarette as we sit on a bench waiting for the shuttle to return to pick up the residents.

"Neither," I say. "Your wife and Coletti don't need to know anything."

I see his shoulders relax and hear him exhale a deep breath.

"But," I continue, "the price for my silence in this matter, Larry, is that you tell me exactly what you know about the professor and his little sojourns here."

He throws his cigarette on the ground and snuffs it out with his shoe. "I don't know a whole lot. I know he liked coming here, especially lately. I thought maybe the ol' guy had found a townie, you know, some elderly woman he was seeing here. That's happened before. These old people? They still got a little urge for some time under the sheets, you know?" He smiles and shrugs.

"I mean, he was always so excited to come here and there aren't a whole lot of things to do really. He was always in a fantastic mood when we were going back to Hollow Hills. But where he went when he was here? Damned if I know." He pauses."But, you know what I really think? I think the dementia was getting worse. I saw it happen with my aunt. They start making things up. Once Hendricks told me something weird. He said he was a priest and everyone called him Father Bob. Then he made the sign of the cross on my forehead. I remember thinking, 'Here we go. Just like Aunt Lydia. Looney-land.'"

I shake my head at that comment. "Okay, Larry, if you remember anything else, call me. I'm going to check out some of the areas outside of the town."

It's been three hours of walking through the pastoral area of Katonah. I'm tired and about to go back to my car when I spot a hidden drainage ditch near a stream. It might be worth examining. As I begin to circle it, someone calls to me.

"Miss, miss, lady! Whatcha looking for?"

A boy of about twelve is watching me. He's straddling his bike on the other side of the vast ditch.

"Want some help?"

"No, I'm good." I yell out and continue following the drainage ditch around a sharp bend.

"Hey, lady! Watch out there's a lot of drunks come down here. I think maybe there's one of them over there. Must've really tied one on, ya know?"

He points over towards the other side of the drainage basin and I see it. A nude body, lying on its side, covered slightly by the sludge churned up by last night's heavy rain. As I approach it, a smell of feces and urine carries over to me in the slight June breeze.

"Stay back!" I yell to the boy who's begun to bike over. This looks like a dumpsite and I don't want the area disturbed, plus, I don't want the kid to see it up close.

"You really don't want to come any closer, trust me on this okay? You don't want to see this." He hesitates then stops, feet planted on each side of his bike.

A dead body. This is a fresh dump—the body hasn't begun to decay yet. There are some flies buzzing near what has to be congealed blood and I see a line of ants crawling on a leg. What appears to be some sort of narrow black fabric is wrapped around his neck. Fighting the gagging sensation in my throat, I squat down by the body to inspect it. The black fabric is a priest's collar.

From the picture given to me by Angela Coletti, I recognize the face as that of Robert Hendricks, professor emeritus, late resident of suite 2431 of Hollow Hills. But, where the picture shows the professor smiling and peaceful, the expression on his face now is one that is twisted with pain and fear. I look closer—it looks as if something has been jammed inside his mouth. A bird or rat? What? Mob guys, the goodfellas stuff dead rats or canaries in the mouths of snitches. Was the professor in with a mob? And what's with the collar?

Gingerly I turn the body over on its back, look at the front of it, and feel hot bile fill my mouth. His body has been mutilated. There's a blood-encrusted area where part of his genitalia has been removed. The object stuffed inside his mouth isn't another creature; it's his own severed penis. I turn aside and vomit.

I retch and retch until there are only dry heaves and I sit back hard on the ground. I want to scream or run or both, but I won't. All right, okay, I have to do this. Steadying myself with one hand on the ground, I get to my feet, shaky but okay. The young boy is still watching me.

I pull my phone out of the pocket of my jeans and begin to take pictures of the front of the body. Snap! Snap! My iPhone clicks away taking clear pictures of the grisly scene.

Forcing myself to do so, I shove the body over on its stomach. There's more horror. My hands are shaking as I see that the man has been viciously sodomized with some type of metal bar. I snap pictures of this cruelty and then move away from the body. I have to call the police. This is obviously a murder.

"Katonah police department. Sergeant Billings speaking."

"Sergeant, this is Cate Harlow. I'm a licensed private investigator from New York City. My license number is 420731-6632."

I can hear him keying the number into a computer system that will verify who I am.

"I believe a murder has been committed. I'm at the crime scene now where I discovered the body. It's by the drainage basin on," I squint over at a county sign, "East Zone 4538-A. This place looks like the dump site, not the scene of a murder."

"Did you touch anything? The body or any objects lying around the scene?"

"No," I lie. "The deceased looks to be a man in his late seventies."

"Okay Ms. Harlow. I'm sending a car and contacting the CSI unit. Can you stay there until they arrive? We need to take your statement. What were you doing in the area?"

"I was on another case." I hold the phone away from me. "I'm losing you, sergeant. The connection is fading. Sorry. I'll be here waiting."

After we hang up, I call Dewitt Arthur Benedict at Hollow Hills. He's stunned and for a few minutes is unable to speak.

"The police? You called the police?"

"Mr. Benedict, a man has been murdered. It is my responsibility to call the authorities. I'm calling you to prepare you for any investigation."

There's a long pause, then, "All right, I will be able to deal with them when they come here. Have you told them anything?"

"No, and I won't. I gave you my word. But, speaking of telling anyone anything, did Mr. Hendricks ever tell you that he was once a priest?"

"A *what*? A priest? No, no he didn't. Why would you think that?"

"When I found him, he was wearing a collar worn by Catholic priests," I say and hang up.

In the distance, I hear the sound of sirens. The kid on the bike hears them too and silently waits for the police excitement he hopes will come.

The police search for a motive and a suspect turned up nothing and the murder of Professor Robert Hendricks, aka Father Bob, was eventually relegated to a cold case file. No one was ever charged in the murder and there were no solid leads.

Still being discreet, I tried for several months to find any leads into the murder—anything, no matter how small, that might point the way to a suspect. I came up as empty-handed as the cops had.

To this day, it baffles me that there was nothing at all to connect anyone to the murder. There simply *were* no suspects or leads. A dead trail with just a dead body. There was very little to go on and I finally placed the case in my own 'cold case' files. There were other clients and other cases that needed my attention.

But, it's still there in the back of my mind. Eventually I need to resolve it. I hate unfinished business.

Mr. Benedict's check, a very hefty one, came to my office three weeks after the body was found. By his very generous payment, Dewitt Arthur Benedict let me know how grateful he was that I was able to keep the story contained and out of the news. His job was secure and the residents of Hollow Hills were led to believe that one of their own had simply passed on of natural causes. Life goes on.

I didn't know it at the time but the body I found in Katonah was only the first of what came to be known as the 'priest murders'.

A year after discovering the body of the professor, I received an early morning phone call from my ex-husband, Detective Will Benigni, one of NYC's finest. He called to tell me that a nude, mutilated male body, wearing the unmistakable collar of a Roman Catholic priest, had just been found off of Interstate 95.

"Sounds very similar to the case you worked last year. You interested in taking a look and offering your opinion?"

www.ingramcontent.com/pod-product-compliance
Lightning Source LLC
Chambersburg PA
CBHW032208190626
46810CB00019B/2183